THE ATLAS

THE GAME AT CAROUSEL

BOOK 3 — THE ATLAS

ROB M. LASTREL

Podium

Cover design by Andrew Clark

ISBN: 978-1-0394-5511-5

Published in 2024 by Podium Publishing
www.podiumentertainment.com

THE ATLAS

CHAPTER ONE

THE LETTERS

*I*t was there on a grassy hill that we decided our fate.

The dirt road leading to Berryman's Dive remained unused for over an hour. It felt like Carousel didn't want to disturb us as we contemplated what had just happened and planned our next move. We took a rest under a shade tree and discussed our own little conspiracy.

We had come to the town of Carousel believing it would be fun. There would be a centennial celebration and an endless lake party at Antoine's brother's lake house. My biggest worries were whether I would do well at horror movie bar trivia and whether I would make friends.

We had been tricked. Carousel was not a good time. Though, to be fair, we did spend a lot of time at the lake.

This place was a horror world, a cinema-flavored hell built for no purpose other than to create pain. We ran around pretending to be characters from the silver screen. There was no way out. We were just starting to believe that. The veteran players certainly believed it. Some of them had been here for decades.

But maybe that was all wrong.

Dina Cano, who always wore her ripped jeans and brown leather jacket and never talked to anyone unless she had to, had been invited to Carousel in a series of letters that I read over and over again.

My first impression of her had been when she destroyed a pumpkin display just after we first arrived and then dared the haunted scarecrow, Benny, to kill her for it. He had happily obliged. I thought she was either crazy or so severely skeptical that she just couldn't believe what Carousel really was.

But that had not been true at all. Dina knew what this place was. She had been warned up front. She was just testing it.

I remembered her smiling as she was revived from her beheading. This was why.

She was here on a mission to conquer death and she had just been shown it was possible.

She believed her son could be saved from his cancerous fate, that somewhere in this literal hell there might be a miracle just for her.

And we were here to help her.

She really did live up to her Outsider Archetype.

Antoine Stone lay on the grass, satisfied that in some way we had found progress, that we had found a way forward even if we didn't know what was going on. The terror he hid behind his gaze loosened its grip when he found out Dina's secret. Carousel had given him the Athlete Archetype because the Student Body President Archetype wasn't a thing. He had been on track to rule the world someday, but instead, he ended up in Carousel.

"I knew something was happening. I knew we weren't just stuck here with no way out," he said gently, his eyes watching the blue sky above. "Couldn't just be here for nothing."

"I know you did," Kimberly Madison, his recently official girlfriend, whispered back to him. What he couldn't see from his position on the ground was the hesitation in her eyes. Not everyone was as ready to accept what was ahead of us.

Kimberly had been a small-time influencer back in the real world, but she was the biggest thing our college campus had to offer. Carousel had not been kind to her or anyone else. Her glow had faded, but she wouldn't admit to something like that. She was the Eye Candy Archetype, which was only partially as vapid as it sounded.

She didn't lie in the grass with Antoine. She stood, arms folded like she had a stomachache, staring ahead, lost in thought. Tears would not have been out of place on her cheeks, but they never came.

"You know," Camden Tran said as he paced back and forth with one of Dina's letters in hand, "this might explain why so many players are trapped here. Think about it: what if they all had 'quests' and they just failed?"

This thought excited him. I could relate. If the players back at Dyer's Lodge had been stuck here for so long because they failed some inane test, that would mean there was hope for the rest of us.

"I always wondered why Carousel would keep around players who weren't accomplishing anything. Maybe they were just here to teach us how to play!" Camden added. He didn't smile, but I could tell he wanted to.

Our time at Carousel had only changed Camden in the way he dressed. He looked perpetually ready to lie back and drink a mai tai. His shirt wasn't even buttoned up all the way, and he had picked up a pair of white sunglasses that he never actually wore.

His greatest fear was that his siblings might be lured to Carousel, just as Antoine had been lured in pursuit of his older brother, Christian. To avoid this dread, he alternated between being overly analytical and chilled out.

At that moment, he was all analytical.

"We need more information," he said. "If others have received a similar mission as Dina, that would confirm it. We need to ask around. Of course, the vets don't like talking about dead players, so that will be an obstacle . . ." He continued murmuring to himself.

He was the Scholar Archetype. He was also my oldest friend. It had been a while and Carousel wasn't the best way to reunite, but I was glad to not be alone.

I sat down at the base of the shade tree, tearing through letter after letter. They explained what Carousel had in store for Dina when she got here. They explained storylines, death, tropes—they explained everything a new player would want to know.

Dina had been prepared in a way the rest of us could only dream of.

Anna Reed, another of the people I had known before we came to Carousel, sat down next to me and whispered, "So, what do you think?"

"I think Carousel, or whoever it was that sent the letters, did a terrible job of gaining my trust," I said.

Anna furrowed her brow. "Why do you say that?"

I set the letters down on my lap and said, "They keep saying what a danger Carousel is and told Dina she can get her son back, but they don't ever explain why this is happening. I mean, why would they help Dina? It doesn't say what this place is or anything."

Anna nodded her head and tightened her ponytail. She was trying to stay calm, trying to keep the rest of us calm. It must have been difficult when she didn't know what was going on either.

Dina overheard my comment. "I didn't trust the letters either," she said. "I ignored them one after another. I didn't come here because I trusted whoever sent them. I came because I had no other choice."

"I understand that," I said. "I just wish they had told you something deeper, you know? It's a horror-movie world. Reviving the dead seems appropriate, but I don't see a happy ending is all."

Suddenly, images of *Pet Sematary* started flashing in my head. I almost told Dina, "Sometimes dead is better," but I didn't. Referencing movies was a different kind of Film Buff. I had an Aspect now. I was a Filmmaker, not a Fanatic. Whatever that meant.

"Don't you think I know that? Don't you think I lie awake at night fearing the same thing?" Dina asked.

Oh boy. Confrontation was not my strong suit.

Luckily, Anna was there to say, "Dina, you've had a long time to wrap your head around this. We need some time too. This is big."

Dina walked away but didn't stray too far. She didn't want to find an Omen waiting for her.

Anna was our Final Girl. She had been my next-door neighbor growing up, and if I didn't know better, I would say she was taking this place better than any of us. Truthfully, I don't think she would ever show weakness in front of anyone. She was steady like it was her job.

"Is that what you're thinking, Riley?" Camden asked. "This is a trap of some kind?"

"Of course," I said. "That's not to say we shouldn't pursue it. I don't want to spend the next twenty years here. I'm game for a little disappointment."

"What's one more trap?" Camden added with a laugh. "Sure would hate for something *bad* to happen."

We laughed in the face of death because we had died already. That was yesterday's fear. Today's fear was being stuck in Carousel forever.

Even before Dina's letters had been revealed, Carousel had given me a code spelled out in the names of horror movie tropes delivered to me at the end of an ill-fated storyline I had not survived:

Friends in High Places
Watching Over You . . .
Stick to the Plan
A Glitch in the Matrix
Accidentally Captured on Film
Back to Where It All Started . . .
A Story within a Story
Who You Truly Are . . .
This Is Going to Sting a Bit . . .
The Intrepid Guide Who Knows the Way

I had tried rearranging them to make the titles spell out a coherent message. That seemed like the way to go. *Friends in high places, / Watching over you . . .*

I was certain that this was correct. Someone had the power to manipulate Silas the Mechanical Showman, who was interacting with us for better or for worse. The NPC employee at the pawn shop had been clear that this was a pairing.

A glitch in the matrix, / Accidentally captured on film.

That had been the other pair that he had shown me. The only glitch we had seen was a result of finding Secret Lore and a Lovecraftian monster whose powers appeared to be strong enough to disrupt the red wallpaper. It was difficult to separate what was a glitch and what was actually a feature of Secret Lore, but there was definitely something like a glitch in that storyline.

Some of these trope titles had been featured inside of Dina's letters. It was all connected.

I was certain that Dina's way was the way forward. That wasn't the sticking point. We all agreed on that.

The thing we disagreed on was how to move forward.

"If this has happened before, the first person to talk to is Christian," Antoine said. "I know the vets can be tight-lipped, but he'll talk to me."

Dina, who was watching us from far away, said, "No!" She walked back to us and added, "This is supposed to be a secret. I don't even know if I was supposed to tell you."

Antoine sat up. "A secret? Why would we keep secrets?"

I noticed his eyes flicked in my direction as he said it.

"The letters told me to keep it secret, to pick my allies carefully," Dina said.

"My brother has been stuck here for eight years," Antoine said. "I'm telling him as soon as I get back. He's high level. We need his help."

Dina was not amused. "This is exactly why I didn't tell you all anything. I knew I shouldn't have asked for help."

"Hold on now," Camden said. "We can't just go telling everyone. If we tell Antoine, he's definitely telling his teammates, and they have their own friends that they'll tell. The letters were clear that it should be a secret."

Antoine shook his head. "Why would this need to be a secret? What positive outcome could that possibly lead to?"

"The friends in high places not abandoning us, for one," Camden said.

"If they don't want us to tell just because, then they are clearly not our allies," Antoine said.

It was true. If our "friends" wanted to help, then letting us ask other players for help would make sense—if this place wasn't Carousel.

"Are you not getting what kind of place this is?" Camden said. "If this is a quest, it was assigned to us. Getting help invalidates that. Tell him, Riley."

They all looked at me.

I took a deep breath. "Camden's right. This place is based on horror movies. Asking your brother for help is the smart choice in the real world, but that's explicitly what we are not supposed to do. If characters in horror movies were allowed to do the smart thing, there wouldn't be horror movies."

It was always my job to remind them that the rules that governed this world were not about logic. They were about narrative BS designed to make low art. Limiting how much help we could get made sense for Carousel.

"Also," Dina said, "you were there when the vets told us about that Psychic who sent players to their deaths. He was clearly working for the enemy. How can you say that there isn't another player getting folks killed? Hmm? Do any of you even know what happened to the group that got here before us? Because I don't. No one will talk about it."

Winston Ashwood was his name, though not his real one. He had given people psychic guidance that resulted in them being postered. No one knew how long he had been at it before he was found out.

"You think someone at the lodge is a traitor?" Antoine asked with a crack in his voice. "You think my brother might be a traitor?"

Dina didn't answer at first. She swayed from side to side, her dark hair billowing in the wind. "I think you all might be traitors," she said. "Doesn't the existence of NPCs make you question if anything here is real? We'd be fools not to expect something like that."

Antoine was . . . not angry, but he was certainly aghast at the implication.

Anna got up from her seat next to me.

"Whoa," she said with an intentional calmness, "I don't think anyone is accusing anyone of anything. We're just talking."

"Christian is not some kind of . . . I don't know what you're suggesting. He would never," Antoine said.

"Who says he's even your brother?" Dina said. "I mean, he did talk to you with video messages, right? Who says your brother is even really alive?"

Antoine took a breath. "You think I haven't considered that? You think I haven't realized that the greatest trick Carousel could pull is to make me think my brother is alive? I have no choice but to trust him. If I'm going to trust you, there's no way I'm not going to trust him."

Dina shrugged her shoulders.

"Look," I said, "there is a possibility that everything is a trick. If that's true, then we can't win anyway."

Sure, horror movies sometimes did the fake out where everything was an illusion, a nightmare, a false reality. If that was the case, we were helpless.

"Exactly," Camden said. "We have to assume that everything we see with our eyes and the rules of this universe are real, or else there is no point in planning at all. I'm okay with making that assumption."

There was silence for a moment, then Dina said, "I'm not accusing anyone. I just think we should keep it a secret. The letters haven't lied so far."

Antoine just repeated, "He's been here eight years. Maybe just a clue that something is happening. We don't have to talk about the letters. How about just telling him what the demon said?"

The demon Dina had just won a wager against had told us that there was a man in violet lights who had tricked him and that he was who we had to look for.

Dina pursed her lips.

"Antoine," Kimberly said softly, "do you really want to risk . . . This might be our only chance. I . . ."

He looked at her. I didn't know if I was seeing betrayal or what, but after a moment, his expression softened, and he put his arm around her.

"Look," Camden said, "we are having this discussion prematurely. We need to talk to the vets and see if something like this has happened before. If people getting invitations to Carousel has precedent, then we need to research those cases. I don't know how we're going to get the vets to talk about it, but still."

The vets were superstitious or at least very touchy when it came to dead players or any attempts to leave. It soured the apocalyptic lake-party vibes they all worked so hard to cultivate.

"I say that's the plan," Anna said. "Let's ask around, but try not to let on what we know. If this has happened before, we could learn from it. If it hasn't . . . We'll decide what to do then. I think we all need to agree to trust each other. There's no sense in bickering. We aren't the enemy."

Camden nodded. "We all need to agree. And research the letters. Also, we need to know if anyone else was brought to Carousel at a different time than they thought. That has to mean something."

Dina had left for Carousel eleven years before she arrived without noticing. Had the letters not captured our attention, that might have been huge news.

"I'm in," I said. "I don't know if the vets will talk to me, but I'll definitely try."

Anna, Camden, and Dina all agreed.

Kimberly nodded her assent. Antoine cursed, but then said, "The moment we can tell Christian, I am. He deserves to know."

That was our decision. On that dirt road in the middle of nowhere, we decided to move forward. We had no idea what would happen because of that decision.

When we first got here, the distance from town to Camp Dyer had been a common topic of complaint. As time wore on, the distance did nothing but heighten anticipation. As we marched down the backroads to get to the lakeside summer camp, there were fewer and fewer Omens.

It was hard not to get excited about that.

The woods got thicker and the air hotter. The eastern shores of Lake Dyer were in perpetual summertime.

After a few miles of dirt roads, we found the sign for Camp Dyer and knew we were home free.

The sun was starting to set, and the stars were coming out as we arrived. I could see smoke from the night's bonfire rising over the trees.

My happiness at seeing the peaceful setting was buffeted by another secret I had to keep.

Dina looked back at us one more time as we approached the front door of Dyer's Lodge as if she was making sure that we were going to keep her secret.

We were. No one wanted to smother the spark of hope her letters and "quest" to save her son had lent us. If the person or entity who had written those letters was telling the truth, Dina's journey was a big piece of the puzzle.

Dina was through the door, and the rest of us were right behind her.

As soon as we walked in, we were greeted with a loud "Hey!" from a familiar voice.

It was Todd Corrigan, one of the higher-level vets. He was a tall man with a perpetual smirk, like he was laughing at a joke that no one else could hear. Todd Corrigan, the Comedian—one of the few people who embodied their Archetype perfectly.

Todd got a look at us and immediately ducked his head out the back door and yelled, "They're alive!"

A loud cheer erupted from those out back at the bonfire. Through the giant westward window I could see dozens of smiling faces cheering our arrival. There was a smell of barbeque in the air, which reminded me I was hungry.

A quick glance around the lodge's common area told me that things had changed since we left. There had been a mad dash as the vets worked on their strategies to find more Secret Lore.

Ever since my friends and I had been taken on the eldritch tour by a demented storyteller and found out about the Secret Lore collectibles that were hidden throughout storylines here in Carousel, the vets had had a renewed energy to find more.

The chalkboards with all of the Secret Lore information had been filled out with tons of new stuff, but they had all been moved away from the main area, and new boards were being set up where they had been. At the top of one of the new boards, the words "Western Excursion" were written.

The Western Excursion was the big run that the highest-level vets had been prepping ever since Valerie had earned an Excursion Train ticket after the

Grotesque storyline I had been selected for. They were nearly ready to depart, apparently.

Soon after Todd announced our return, we were waved out onto the back deck, where most of the players were congregating, eating ribs that Grace had made in a large smoker that hadn't been there before. The vets were always scavenging goodies from storylines back in Carousel, but a smoker was a big haul.

As soon as we got out there, Antoine's brother Chris found him and, after a quick evaluation to see his mental state, put his arm around his shoulders and said with a laugh, "A five-day storyline! After that nasty business, you go out and disappear for five days?"

He put Antoine into a playful headlock.

Christian Stone once had a lock on a professional football career. Unfortunately, eight years ago he disappeared off the face of the planet. Turned out, the place he had gone was Carousel. Antoine didn't hear from him again until "Chris" reached out to him with an invite to Carousel. It turned out that the invitation was just a cruel trick by Carousel to rope Antoine and the rest of us into getting trapped here.

I could tell he felt guilty about that. Heck, Anna had told me that Antoine felt guilty for getting tricked too. Anna and Camden felt guilty for inviting me.

I didn't feel guilty about anything—not until the axe murderer had showed up, at least.

Antoine's mood picked up as he wrestled with his brother.

"Five days?" Camden asked as he picked up a plate. "We were gone three days."

Todd, who was nearby, said, "Nope. Five days. Chris here was about to call the NPC police to go out and look for you. He wanted to round up a posse."

Chris rolled his eyes. "You must have got done early," he said. "Storylines always take how long they take. There's no use trying to understand it. Now, if you don't mind, I need to know what you've been up to!"

That was a fun fact. Where had we been for the extra two days? How did we not notice them passing?

I soon found myself loading a plate with a variety of meats. Sleep would have to wait.

"So, where did you go?" Chris asked as he released Antoine from the headlock. "Lara used her clairvoyance and said you were underground but that something was blocking her. We were worried."

"We *were* underground," Antoine said. "We got locked up in a facility for a psychic experiment by a bunch of scientists working for a corporation."

"KRSL?" Todd asked.

Antoine nodded. He pulled out his enemy ticket, showing that he had killed a KRSL Agent.

"They're all over the place. They sell contaminated pharmaceuticals, do shady cover-ups, engineer zombie viruses, the works," Chris said.

We sat and talked about *Subject of Inquiry* for thirty minutes or so, detailing everything we had been up to, from Dina being locked in a cell for a couple of days to me watching the facility from the cameras.

We didn't talk about the nearly botched Finale. Kimberly was still upset over it, and it would have ruined the mood. She sat with Anna and picked at a salad.

They were whispering with each other.

Maybe they were unsure how to discuss Dina's letters or the fact that she was apparently kept on ice for ten years before arriving at Carousel at the same time as my friends and me.

I didn't know how much help I could be. I hadn't formed too many friendships since I arrived. It was pretty much just Camden and Anna, the two people I knew before I got here. Even Antoine and Kimberly felt like acquaintances sometimes.

The conversation didn't move in the direction we had planned.

As we talked, Sam, an Adventurer Archetype I had met a few times, glanced at me and stared for a moment. He was looking at me on the red wallpaper. After a while, I had learned to pick up on when someone was doing that.

"You got your Aspect," Sam said.

I nodded. As I did, I realized that I could see his Aspect too. That information had been invisible to me before. I could always guess it, of course. A Bruiser Archetype with a bunch of Bully tropes was a Bully-Bruiser. Now that I had my own Aspect, I saw them listed on a plaque under everyone's movie poster.

Sam's poster was of him climbing in a cave with a headlamp. Behind him, the glint of an axe was visible, being held by an unseen assailant. "Samuel Wheeler is The Adventurer."

Despite that, he still had his original base archetype, Athlete, though the poster for that was not visible. His aspect? Health Nut.

Not the best name, but it wasn't any worse than Fanatic or Hysteric. It made sense he would be a Health Nut, I supposed. The guy had not let Carousel keep him from his exercise regimen.

I started looking around at the vets to see what Aspects they had chosen. Before I made much progress, I was interrupted.

"You did get your Aspect!" Lukas yelled from across the deck. He must have been eavesdropping. He got up and walked over to me. I observed that he had a trope called They're Talking about Me, Aren't They? that allowed him to read lips. He was a twitchy kind of guy with wild hair and a little too much enthusiasm for sacrificing himself in storylines.

"What was the feat you had to do to trigger the Aspect choice?" Todd asked. "It's been a while since we've had a Film Buff around. I don't remember it."

"I had to die in a storyline after leveling up to twenty-one Plot Armor," I said.

"Me too!" Lukas said. He raised his hand for a high five.

I reluctantly raised my hand to his, and he slapped it hard.

Lukas was a Frantic-Hysteric. That made sense.

Todd was a Joker-Comedian.

Chris was a Sport-Athlete.

Whoever named those things must have had really weird taste.

I let myself get distracted as I read each of their Aspects. I felt like I was learning a lot about the vets that I hadn't known before. They were assigned their Archetype, but they chose their Aspect. I found it interesting. The higher-level players could be hard to guess, as they slowly unlocked their other Aspects in addition to their chosen Aspect.

"My Plot Armor is twenty-one," Anna said. She had just gotten the two stat tickets she needed to get there. "What do I have to do to choose my Aspect?"

It was a good question. She couldn't exactly die in a storyline to get hers.

Valerie was quick to tell her the bad news. If she wanted to get her Aspect, she needed to be the Last One Alive in a storyline.

Valerie was a Team Leader-Final Girl.

She would know.

"Why don't the Soldiers have their Aspects yet?" I asked. There were three Soldiers that I could see. I had only really gotten to know one of them, Garrett. None of them had Aspects.

I looked around for someone who might know the answer.

"Soldiers have to clear a rescue mission to get their Aspect," Todd said. "Kind of hard for them to do that."

It certainly was. Carousel had gotten rid of rescue tropes long ago after players abused them to power-level. Without rescue tropes, there were no rescue storylines.

After some more discussion, we learned all of the required feats each of my team would need to do to get our Aspects.

Antoine would have to best a strong or fast monster in a contest of physicality during the final battle. Camden would similarly have to outwit a Savvy-based enemy in the Finale. Kimberly would need to give a five-star performance in a storyline that was at or above her level. Dina would have to complete a storyline Unscathed, while also helping resolve the main plotline.

Those sounded more like actual feats than simply dying in a storyline. But still, they didn't have to die.

The conversation was lively. Becoming experts at the Game at Carousel was a beloved pastime for the vets. It helped them survive. Heck, maybe that was the reason they *had* survived. They talked about it enthusiastically and were always happy to give their insights. They weren't as happy to talk about other subjects.

Specifically, everyone's lives back in the real world and all of their fallen comrades.

"So," Antoine asked loudly for all around to hear, "does everyone get lured to Carousel the same way? Did everyone know someone who was here?"

"This conversation again," Todd said. "Newbies, newbies, newbies. Always know how to kill a party."

Antoine laughed. "I just want to understand. I mean, it's not possible that everyone was lured in like I was, is it?"

Christian shook his head. "No, plenty of people came here looking for time-shares, will readings, new job listings. Carousel gets creative. There's no shame in it."

Antoine looked at his brother for a moment. "How did you get lured here? You said it was a party of some kind?"

Chris glanced at Todd and said, "Basically. A friend of ours thought she was taking us to a mountain town for some fun. I had an argument with my girl-friend, so I was up for anything. That's all there is to it."

At this point, even Antoine could see a general evasiveness, but who knew what that was caused by. Even with the scant information we were given, it sounded like they were invited by someone who was now deceased.

"Anyone ever get invited through letters?" Antoine asked. "I mean, video messaging is a neat trick, but I'm sure in Carousel it's a recent thing."

Chris took a swig of his beer and nodded. "Sure," he said. "Letters from loved ones, coupons in the mail, brochures, that sort of thing. All the time. Phone calls mostly, though."

If people were being invited by Carousel itself, surely that would have been the moment to mention it.

Antoine, sensing the conversation was bringing everyone down, left to go get drinks for the table while one of the vets changed the subject quickly.

My friends and I quietly looked around at each other. No luck.

From there on in, the conversation continued in much the same way it normally did, with the vets reminiscing about their time in storylines. Carousel was a weird place, where the death game we were forced to play was considered a light subject.

As things moved forward, I started to grow tired—if not physically, then spiritually. Nothing a magic sleeping trope couldn't fix.

I left the back deck and made my way inside with an eye for my bunk. As I entered the lodge, though, I saw Arthur and Adeline over near the Western Excursion board. They were arguing.

"Why does it have to be you?" Adeline asked. "Is this because you don't think they can handle it, or is it because you think they will do something stupid?"

"Yes," Arthur answered.

"They are high enough in level, and they have been working as a team for as long as they have been here," Adeline said. She was whisper-yelling.

"I have to go," Arthur said. "I need to be there."

"Why?" Adeline asked. "There are plenty of storylines where having a Monster Hunter around would actually make things worse. You know that, right? Sending in a team with a variety of flexible Archetypes is more logical. You like logic, right? There was a time when being a tough guy wasn't your biggest concern."

"I can be a Scholar if need be," Arthur said. "And what they are planning to do has nothing to do with logic. They think I'm a fool. The moment they get over there, the mountain will be a day's hike out . . . They won't be able to resist jogging over and checking it out. They pretend they just want to go to scout things out, but I know what's going on. I remember back when you were less trusting."

"You haven't been a Scholar in a storyline in a decade," Adeline said. "You're out of practice. And they earned my trust. Honestly, it's not even about trust. If they want to make a break for it, there is no reason to stop them. We can't expect them to just grow old here with us."

"I need to be there to make sure that they are safe and smart," Arthur said.

Adeline paused and stared at Arthur.

"To make sure they don't *disappear?*"

He didn't answer. I knew why.

I could hear the axe murderer breathing just from her mentioning the disappearances. Adeline had lived in Carousel for nearly twenty years and still didn't know the secret of the axe murderer, but that didn't mean she didn't know anything at all. She knew that a little knowledge could be a liability.

"I don't know what you're talking about," Arthur eventually said. He was breathing heavily. He heard the footsteps too.

Adeline pursed her lips and turned away from him. "I've given you a lot of leeway . . . Sending you out there risks all of our lives."

"I'm no good here," Arthur said. "I can't rescue anyone. I can't just sit around and wait, hoping they come back. If it really is the way to the other side of the mountain, I need to be there. If it isn't, I need to be there even more."

The mountain on the other side of the lake was the goal of all of the vets' planning. We knew it was important. We knew that when lightning struck over there, we could see the flash against the red wallpaper, which bewildered the mind. We knew that on cloudy nights, purple lights could be seen reflected on the clouds from something on the other side of the mountain.

There wasn't a person here who didn't yearn for a way over.

I noticed Adeline's eyes lift toward the door where I was standing. I started walking toward my room, hoping not to make things awkward.

"Filmmaker, huh?" Adeline asked. "Instead of . . . Critic or—"

"Fanatic," I said. "Filmmaker was the best fit."

"Good to hear," she said. "You all are making some real progress."

I nodded and said, "Thanks. Ready to sleep for a week."

"Try to be awake for the brief tomorrow at noon," she said, pointing at the Western Excursion chalkboard.

"I'll be there."

As I left the main hall and found my way to Camden's and my room, I made eye contact with Arthur.

I could guess the real reason that Arthur needed to go on the Western Excursion. What they were about to do could very easily cross the line into cheating. Their plan was to try to reach the lights on the other side of the mountain from the west.

Someone who had seen the axe murderer needed to be there so that they could tell if they were going too far.

At first it surprised me to hear that none of the high-level vets had seen the Rulekeeper. But the more I thought about it, the more it made sense. Most people who had seen the Rulekeeper had done so when their team-mates got chopped to bits. Then, separated from their original teams, level-ing up became pretty difficult unless they got lucky and found a new team to take them.

More than that, knowing that there was a mysterious entity enforcing the rules probably prevented players from leaving their comfort zones enough to level up.

As I fell into my bunk, I stared out the window. I could see the NPC campers playing hopscotch and daring each other to go explore the forbidden cabin.

I felt that I would lay there contemplating everything that had happened the last few days for hours as had become my habit, but I greatly underestimated how easy it was to trigger my Out like a Light trope. I had never had the chance to try it out before. Ten seconds after my head hit the pillow, I closed my eyes and didn't open them again until morning.

*　*　*

And it was glorious.

I rose with the sun, rested and ready to take on a new day. A day that wouldn't have any invisible monsters or security duty.

I actually woke up smiling.

A peek at the top bunk told me Camden was still asleep. He hadn't woken me when he had come in the night before.

I made my way out of the room and into the main hall of the lodge. Other players were up doing their morning routines.

Several were reading a newspaper that was delivered to the front door. They had split it up and were each reading different parts. It listed scheduled Omens, sales at various shops, and stuff like that; all kinds of useful information was available if you knew how to read between the lines. At face value, it was just a normal small-town newspaper.

Lukas the Hysteric was filling his jug with coffee.

As he saw me, he sheepishly asked if I wanted any. I waved him off. I was plenty awake.

I took a seat on a couch that faced the corner where the chalkboards for the Secret Lore had been relocated and tried to see how much information they had found.

They had not actually done any new runs yet but had spent time gathering information at each known location. It was all very well and good. I still had a bad feeling in the pit of my stomach about it, but I would be happy to be proven wrong.

Knowledge of Secret Lore had fallen into our laps without us working for it. That felt off for me. I couldn't say why. Someone with a huge pull in the upper echelon of Carousel's workings had ensured we would get our first piece of Secret Lore and had trapped Antoine in a nightmarish situation to accomplish it. I thought caution was in order.

My morning contemplations would not last, as I was interrupted by a screaming Outsider.

It was Travis Haley. I hadn't seen much of him since after the Grotesque storyline, when he was being an ass. He was a jerk with a bright smile that let him get away with a lot.

Travis. Criminal-Outsider. I wasn't surprised at his Aspect choice, though I was pretty confused at being able to see him on the red wallpaper. Normally, Outsiders could block that. He must not have equipped that trope. Of course, I could have simply leveled up enough to get past it, or he may have whitelisted me.

"You goddamn idiot," he was yelling.

"Travis, I'm sorry. I said I was sorry already," Bobby Gill stammered as he walked in the door with his tail between his legs. Bobby and his wife Janet had arrived in Carousel at the same time I had. She had "disappeared" when the axe murderer had come around and cut her in half. He still didn't know that.

"We know you're sorry! You don't have to tell us that," Travis's brother Vernon yelled, walking in the door behind them. "Sorriest bastard I ever seen!"

No one ever accused the Haley brothers of being original.

On the red wallpaper, I saw that Vernon was a Bruiser with a Bully Aspect. So, they both lived up to their Aspects.

"What are you screaming about this early in the morning?" one of the vets yelled down from upstairs.

"We aren't going to be babysitting anymore," Travis yelled.

Travis normally had a way of sounding angry without looking angry on his face. He was boisterous, for sure, but he also looked like he was having a good time.

Today, he looked wounded, maybe even scared.

I took a deep breath and hoped that he wouldn't see me. It occurred to me that I could go to sleep to avoid him. I could lie down right there on the couch and be out like a light. The thought of it put a smile on my face.

I regretted it immediately.

"You think it's funny?" Travis asked, having locked eyes with me. "Well, Bobby here just nearly got us all killed. You want to know how?"

I did, but I didn't want to help him humiliate Bobby.

Travis didn't wait for an answer. "He spent so long talking to some nobody NPC off-screen that he was Written Off permanently. Disappeared when we actually needed him for once."

"Travis," Bobby said, "I didn't know I would be Written Off that soon. I thought I had more time."

"You wanted to go on this storyline. We told you it was dangerous. We told you we needed everyone to play their part," Travis said. "We can't take you with us anymore."

Bobby was very upset. He hadn't exactly been doing well since his wife . . . disappeared. Now he was getting really emotional.

"There are six more houses on Toother Street," Bobby said. His voice was cracking as he spoke. "I just need your help for a little longer."

Travis didn't give in. It looked like he was biting his tongue.

He took a deep breath.

"I'm sorry, Bobby. You're a good guy, but this isn't going to work out. If Tori hadn't made it out of there, we would have all died. Permanently. Even you."

Travis almost looked ashamed. Whatever storyline they had been on had not gone well for them. From the sound of it, they must have made it out narrowly.

After a moment of looking conflicted, Travis bounced back to his ornery self.

"So," he said, fixing his gaze back toward me, "you got your Aspect. All grown up, aren't you?"

"Yep."

"Well, everybody finds their way eventually," he said.

He walked past me and turned down a hallway toward his room.

I looked back at the entrance where the rest of his team were still stumbling in. They looked tired and stressed.

A dozen or so onlookers had dragged themselves out of bed to see what the commotion was about. Most of them went back to their bedrooms.

Bobby sat himself down in a chair on the other side of the room from me and stared in my direction. He looked pensive. I had some idea of what he was thinking about. I thought it involved me.

He was investigating Toother Street. That was the same street we had gone to when running the Grotesque storyline. The same one where his wife died permanently.

CHAPTER TWO

SNOWBLIND

I got tired of Bobby staring in my general direction and decided to take a cup of coffee outside onto the porch. There was a table there that I could use. I needed to examine my tropes and decide which ones I would be taking into the next storyline. I finally had enough of them that I couldn't just take them all without exceeding my limit.

We had been told that background tropes would affect the storylines we were in. I understood that, but I never really grasped how significant the impact could be until our most recent storyline. I questioned whether I even needed that background trope, given that I only had one trope that could be equipped with it. The background trope didn't count against my limit of eight. The first background trope was free.

Maybe it just rubbed me the wrong way that Carousel had incorporated my actual grandmother into its story.

It was true that the scouting trope it allowed me to equip was useful, allowing me to gain tons of valuable insight into any storyline we might encounter, but ultimately, I usually just unequipped it in storylines anyway.

My Director's Monitor trope gave me the Deathwatch ability. It had been pretty stressful and, ultimately, not very useful in the last storyline, but if I used it a lot, I could probably get more tropes to go along with it that might actually make it so I could help my friends. Flashback Revelation could be a game changer, but it would take some major prep work to get working. Being able to send a message from beyond death, even if it was just an echo of something I had said earlier, might make the difference between winning and losing.

I knew for a fact that Lara had a trope that gave her Deathwatch. I needed to find her and discuss it. I hated the idea of dying in every storyline, but I hated the idea of being useless more than that.

I sat at the table, and I took out my tropes. As usual, my growing stack of tickets was far larger outside of my pocket than it seemed to be when it was inside of it. The tickets' magic was perplexing even when you were aware of it. In fact, it was like the tickets weren't even in my pocket to begin with.

Unfortunately, a huge percentage of my tropes were those that I had gotten after the Grotesque storyline. They were the ones that I couldn't even use because they were for the wrong Archetype.

Hidden message or not, they were a hassle to sort through.

As I contemplated this, Dina came out on the deck to join me. She didn't say anything, but she made eye contact and gave me one of those forced half-smiles that I had come to know as her greeting. She must have seen that I was looking at these tropes again.

"The glitch can't be the unknowable host," Dina said. "That was your theory, right?"

We had taken some time to review my secret message tropes after her quest revelation. We had already gone over them half a dozen times, each time leaving us less certain of what the clues were actually pointing to.

"Still my theory," I said.

"Have you watched it yet?" she asked, referring to my new ability to rewatch old storylines thanks to Director's Monitor. That had occupied much of my morning.

"Yep. It's a short anthology. Most of it doesn't even make sense, because entire scenes were missing. Not just the stuff that was off-screen but a lot of the on-screen stuff got cut. All of our scenes after I picked you up on that wagon were cut from the storyline with the cloven women. All I can see is Anna's storyline."

"Are you sure there's not anything else?"

There were a few things but nothing notable. Watching through the Straggler storyline was pretty normal. I had been able to do it in fifteen minutes that morning. Carousel managed to piece together a nice, tense *Are You Afraid of the Dark?* style short from the footage, culminating in Antoine being left behind.

"There's nothing," I said. "I spent the last two hours watching it, and I'll probably watch it again half a dozen times. Anything that even hints at the existence of the unknowable host is completely cut. Honest. That entire final thing with the storyteller was gone too."

If I was being honest, the freakiest thing about that entire film, other than the fact that I was watching it in my head, was the complete lack of context for much of what was happening. If I hadn't been there, I wouldn't even know what the plots of some of those stories were.

"What else could a glitch in the matrix accidentally captured on film mean?" Dina asked. "We should go find Carousel Family Video and watch the actual tape."

I shrugged. She might have been right.

Carousel Family Video. My Director's Monitor trope mentioned it.

"Just one more thing we need to ask the veterans about," I said.

"Don't tell them why you're asking," she said.

"I won't."

Truthfully, I was glad that I hadn't seen anything noteworthy when rewatching the campfire anthology. That entire ordeal left me sick to my stomach and not just because of the effects of the unknowable host's aura . . .

It was time to go inside for the brief on the Western Excursion. A lot of the players who had been there awhile were excited about this particular endeavor. I tried to force myself to be optimistic about it too. I would have to wait to decide which tropes I was going to bring into the next storyline. I had let myself get distracted.

Arthur stood in front of everyone and waited for us to get quiet. This was the first time since I had gotten to Dyer's Lodge that every single player was there all at once. Over a dozen teams worth of people gathered to hear about the Hail Mary plan Arthur and the other high-level vets had prepared.

"We used to do these briefs because if a team didn't come back, we wanted others to follow in their footsteps and rescue them," he said. "Now we do them for the opposite reason. We're going to show you what the plan is. If we don't come back, that means our idea is bad and you shouldn't do it."

With that, he took a seat.

Valerie was up next to actually explain what was going to happen.

"We've spent all of our time since obtaining the excursion ticket scouting out any destinations west of Carousel. The *Carousel Atlas* actually has a lot of information, so players from before went out west a lot. We knew of The Hanging U Ranch, but after doing some thorough digging at the travel agency and city hall, we were able to determine that there is another destination that is physically closer to the mountain. The atlas writers apparently didn't think that was useful information. I guess if you can only get to a place by train, its position isn't important. Unfortunately, the map at the train station doesn't actually show the destinations in their actual physical locations relative to Carousel; it only shows that they exist.

"Malison's Last Resort and Spa, in a mountain town called Snowblind, is the closest. It's only a few dozen miles west of town. From what we can tell, there are at least two dozen different storylines in the Snowblind area. There are six that we could find in Malison's. Of course, we're not actually sure how accurate our intelligence is given the distance, but we have a lot of experience working off of partial information, as you well know.

"Arthur was able to determine that there are a variety of monsters in the area, including a yeti and a wendigo, so we will be surrounded by nature. Sam tells us that there is an abundance of buried treasure on the mountain range and that the skiing there is top-notch."

She was trying to inject humor into her brief. People laughed, but there was an uneasiness in the room. Whatever this place was, it was part of the unknown. If there was one thing that I was beginning to learn from Carousel, it was to fear the unknown.

She told us which team members would be making the trip, but we already knew for the most part.

Arthur the Monster Hunter.

Valerie the Final Girl.

Chris the Athlete.

Todd the Comedian.

Jordan the Doctor (Coroner Aspect).

Sam the Adventurer.

The first four were around sixty Plot Armor, but Jordan and Sam were in their forties. Valerie explained this. The fact was that Doctors and Adventurers were particularly useful. A Doctor for obvious reasons and an Adventurer because a lot of their tropes dealt with things like climbing mountains and surviving in the wilderness. They would be fools not to take one with them. Using background tropes to try and replace them would mean that they wouldn't be able to equip other more important tropes. Because of this, they made the cut when several other higher-level vets didn't. The unknown did not reward redundancy. It rewarded preparation.

They had actually found a map of Snowblind. Funny enough, it was labeled as "Snowblind, Carousel." As if Carousel was both a neighboring city and the state or country that Snowblind existed in.

"We found this in city hall," Todd said. "I had to make this poor lady behind the desk laugh for ten minutes as a distraction while they searched for it."

"It was more like three minutes," Chris said.

The map they showed was old and incomplete, but it was pretty interesting, though there wasn't much to it. I could imagine a few of the storylines that could be found in Snowblind. I'd bet any amount of money that there was at least one evil snowman there.

All laid bare, their plan was simple. They pointed to a place on the map that they said *should* have a road. The map was old and not complete, so it was possible that there was a road there. They wouldn't know until they made the trip.

Based on their understanding of the physical location of both Snowblind and Carousel, any path between the two should lead directly to the mountain with the lights.

It was apparent how badly the veterans wanted to know what was on the other side of that mountain. They had allowed themselves to rest all of their hopes and dreams on the exit being there. Players in Carousel had been trying to get to the other side of that mountain for over a decade. It was just this impossible goal that represented everything to them.

I wasn't even sure that they knew the full history of how many players had gone missing trying to sneak over to the mountain on the other side of the lake.

But the veterans were not the only people who got excited. Dina was also sold on the mountain with the lights because of what the poker-playing demon had said about needing a man and some violet lights. She had his whole frantic speech memorized.

The brief went on for a while as they reviewed every piece of information they had found. It was amazing what scouting tropes could do if you collected enough of them and used them wisely. Valerie carried the *Carousel Atlas* around and showed its pages like it was a storybook being shown to a kindergarten class. As she did, Camden looked at me funny and then back at the atlas. I could see the wheels turning in his mind.

The atlas might have the clues we needed. The question was, how could we get a hold of it? It wasn't under lock and key, but it was restricted. I'd have to think about that.

I listened intently because even if they didn't succeed, there was still a lot to learn.

Of course, even if they made it over to the part of Snowblind they were trying to get to, and even if there was a road that led back toward Carousel, there was no way that Carousel would make it that easy.

I knew that.

Arthur knew that.

Everyone in the room knew that.

And yet, when the presentation was over, we all clapped and cheered and talked about home just as they had when Secret Lore became viable again.

Even false hope had its place in keeping spirits high.

I felt the tropes in my pocket. If our friend in high places was really there and really trying to help us, then we would soon have a real chance of escape.

I hoped.

CHAPTER THREE

THE CAROUSEL ATLAS

Back in our room, Camden pounced on me.

"We need the atlas," he said. "Every attempt we have made has been a bust. We need to look in the atlas."

"Yeah," I said. "Let me just go ask for it real quick."

He laughed. "They are protective, but this isn't Fort Knox. Just grab it, and we'll put it back later."

I shrugged. "Good thing we have you here to plan the capers."

"What would you do without me?" he said. "And there's the other thing." The way he said "the other thing," I knew I was not going to want to hear it. "Is it possible that Dina's letters are related to the disappearances?"

My heartbeat increased. I heard footsteps and breathing like the axe murderer was behind me. I even turned to look.

"I have no idea," I said. The mere thought alone of acknowledging that I knew something about the axe murderer was enough to cover my back in hives.

"Right," Camden said, his eyes glazed over. "Just talk to your people about it."

He knew I couldn't talk about it.

I really hated the way he said "your people" as if I was in some exclusive cabal.

I didn't nod or anything. I just left the room. I wasn't being rude. I just couldn't stick around there.

As it grew later into the night, the common room started to clear out until it was just me. Finally.

The other groups had been using the *Carousel Atlas*, also known as the survivors' Bible, for their research. The higher-level veterans used it to plan the

Western Excursion, and when they weren't using it, Grace and the others needed it to plan their Secret Lore runs.

It was finally available. It wasn't exactly off-limits, but we hadn't "earned" the right to use it whenever we wanted. Veterans put new players on a sort of information diet to keep them from doing anything stupid.

They were also protective over the book itself. It held a lot of precious information.

I grabbed it off the table where it had been left. It was surprisingly heavy. I walked back to my room with it and opened the door to find Camden lying in his bunk.

"I've got it," I said.

He nodded.

The book was so large that it would take me hours and hours just to learn how to navigate it, but Camden didn't have that problem. His Eureka! trope would make our search as easy as Googling for the answers.

"I knew you could do it," Camden said. "Let's get it out of here before the cops show up."

"Here," I said, hefting it into his arms. "I'll go get the others."

Soon my friends and I were gathered in a gazebo outside with a lantern, far from anyone who might hear what we were there to discuss.

"I can already tell you that there are pages missing," Camden said. His Peer Review trope told him that the book had been altered. That made sense. It was designed to research monsters and magic, but the *Carousel Atlas* had much more precious information. Arthur had probably altered it to prevent people from trying things that had later been determined to be against the rules.

"Carousel Family Video," I said.

Camden stretched his fingers and started flipping through the pages of the large book. The atlas had been written and edited so many times that it looked like a scrapbook. Many of the pages were covered in sticky notes, Polaroids, and various random literature, like flyers and other documents.

The first page Camden showed us was a map. It was folded into the book and had to be unfolded so that we could see its entirety. It was of Carousel. "Property of City Hall" it said in the corner. Lots of handmade notes had been written around the map.

The map listed everything from Patcher's Family Farm in the east, where we had met Benny the Haunted Scarecrow, to the western side of the lake. It did not include the mountain or the building on the other side.

"Here," Camden said, pointing to a small strip mall near the University of Carousel. In small letters, the words "Carousel Family Video" were written.

"What's that little symbol next to it?" Dina asked.

"Gravestone," I said. Rounded edges on the top. Square edges on the bottom. A small cross in the center. It was a gravestone.

"That must mean that it's dangerous," Kimberly said. "Or that somebody died there."

Camden nodded. "Might have happened a long time ago." He pointed to the corner of the map where someone had written "RW, 1996."

"Are those initials someone's name, or does that signify something else?" Anna asked.

Camden flipped through the pages. "I'm guessing it's someone's initials. There are lots of initials throughout the book. I don't recognize them all."

"That was before Arthur and Adeline got here," I said.

Camden continued to flip through the book until he found another entry for Carousel Family Video.

"'Carousel Family Video: rewatch old storylines for a low price. No Omens,'" Camden read.

"That's great," Dina said. "We need to go there as soon as we can."

Camden shook his head. "There's another entry. 'Manuel went missing at Carousel Family Video. No leads. No storyline. What now?' It was written by someone named Jessica."

"Is there a Jessica here?" I asked. I wasn't the one who would know everyone's name.

Kimberly shook her head. She would know. She knew everybody.

"Look," Camden said. "There used to be a register of every player in the back of the book. But it looks like it was restarted about six years ago. It even has us in it. The original got torn out. You have no idea how much is missing from this book. The red wallpaper is filled with alerts."

His ability could show him that a document was tampered with, but it couldn't show him what had been there before.

Why would the register get torn out? Was Arthur trying to disguise how many people had gone missing without winding up on a missing poster? No. That couldn't be it. People knew about those who went missing. They just didn't know what happened to them. There would be no reason to get rid of the register for that.

"Anything about letters from Carousel like Dina's?" Antoine asked.

This was the big question.

Camden flipped to a few different areas in the book. "There was something related to that," Camden said, "but it's gone now. I don't know exactly wha—wait a second."

He flipped a few pages and started looking over a page that talked about the mall.

"This is strange," he said. "Eureka! is telling me there is information on this page, but . . . I don't . . . It's not here."

I craned my neck so that I could look at the page properly. It contained a flyer about a store opening in the mall, a small hand-drawn map of the mall, and lots of little notes about each store. Most of the notes were written on a piece of yellow legal-sized notebook paper that was taped to the page and folded so that it would fit.

Camden lifted up the yellow page and folded it over out of the way.

"There," Dina said, pointing to small grooves in the paper.

"Where?" he asked.

Looking closer, I saw that someone had written something on a piece of paper above the page we were looking at. They had written hard enough that their words were carved into the page below. The original page was gone, but the imprint remained.

Camden's ability told him there was relevant information on that page, but it couldn't help him read something that was all but invisible any better than a normal person could.

Camden lifted the book up at an angle so that the light from the lantern would shine on it differently and subtle shadows would reveal the words accidentally etched into the page.

"Just a second," Camden said. "There are letters that didn't imprint fully. I have to fill in the blanks real quick."

He stared at the page intently and then began to read slowly, interpreting the etched marks like hieroglyphics.

He started to read.

"The fortune teller told Zoe her quest went wrong and it was our fault. I don't know what any of that means. Zoe was really upset. Her missing poster said she was killed at the mall. I wish she had trusted me enough to tell me what was going on. I'll never forgive myself. TC."

"Quest," Dina said.

That was the same word that the fortune teller had used to describe Dina's mission to revive her son.

"Oh my god," I said. "This *has* happened before."

"When? Is there anything else about it?" Kimberly asked.

Camden shook his head. "Nothing."

There was a short silence as we all thought about what we had just learned.

"It might have happened eight years ago," Anna said.

"What makes you say that?" I asked. It was a very specific guess.

"TC," Anna said. "Todd Corrigan. He came here with Chris and Valerie, right? Eight years ago."

"Chris . . . ," Antoine said. Pieces were clicking together in his mind. "He must not have known. He would have told me. No wonder he was acting weird."

"There are members missing from their original team," I said. "Maybe this Zoe was one of them."

"Exactly," Antoine said.

"We can check the missing board," Camden suggested.

It was a good idea.

We were out late discussing everything we could learn from the book. I even saw several references to Deathwatch, but we didn't have time for much. There were little clues like, "Wallflower use Deathwatch here," or, "Vision of Death works well in this storyline." But nothing about the Film Buffs' version of Deathwatch that Camden could find. There was a section that explained what Deathwatch was, but it didn't go into much detail. Film Buffs were rare. Not as much was known about them. We needed more time to sort through all of the little details, but it was getting late. We would have to get a hold of it again later.

Before we went in for the night, I had one last request.

"What about rescue tropes?" I asked. We hadn't taken the book to look for that, but I couldn't resist.

Camden looked through the book. He found a section written by Adeline.

"'There were once tropes called rescue tickets that could be won from certain storylines around Carousel. They would allow you to bring your fallen friends back to life by completing the storylines they failed. Every Archetype had its own rescue tropes. They disappeared in fall 2010. I cannot understand why Carousel would do this. I thought it wanted us to get to the end. Research has failed to find the reason. Scouting tropes have failed. We do not know why they disappeared or how to get them back. What will we do?'"

The *Carousel Atlas* had the "official" version of what happened. That wasn't surprising. The truth was a secret only a few knew.

"Whoa," Camden said. "There used to be a lot of stuff about them in here. There are easily thirty pages missing or more."

"Why would they tear that stuff out?" Antoine asked. "Just because they couldn't figure out how to get them back doesn't mean no one could."

I stayed silent. It was a good question. All someone really needed to remove was the stuff that talked about abusing them. Removing all knowledge didn't seem productive.

In fact, the bulk of the atlas's information was about specific storylines. Information about the players or a dozen other things was missing.

Strange.

We talked about it as we headed back to the lodge. I tried to stay as quiet as possible. Soon we had the book back where it belonged and were crawling back into bed.

If it wasn't for my sleeping trope, I would not have been able to rest that night. There were too many things to think about.

The next morning, I decided to take a walk around Camp Dyer. It was strange that this place had become my home in the last few weeks, but I hadn't actually explored it.

As long as you didn't venture into the lake, there weren't any Omens other than the one inside of the restricted cabin on the grounds themselves, but still, the place gave an uneasy feeling.

The sound of children's laughter sent shivers up my spine. It was cloyingly sweet. You didn't have to be a Film Buff to know that it was only there to contrast the danger and evil that lurked at Camp Dyer.

As I walked, I got a good look at the restricted cabin. It was locked up, boarded up, and the entire cabin had been encircled in police tape.

Whatever storyline took place at Camp Dyer was so high level that I couldn't even see its name on the red wallpaper. All I saw was "Warning." That was usually what showed up when I looked at an Omen that was just too powerful for my Savvy.

It was incredible that the veterans had decided to make camp at a place with a storyline so strong. But the sentiment that the veterans often repeated was that predictability was more important than anything else when it came to storylines.

How wrong could they be? They had lived when others had died. Dyer's Lodge had been their home for years.

"Can I join you?" a familiar voice asked. It was Roxy.

"Sure," I said.

I expected her to have something to say about the Rulekeeper. We were two of the few people who shared that remarkable secret, but even when we were alone, we didn't talk about it.

"How are you managing?" she asked.

"Better than ever," I lied.

Roxy smirked.

"What are you doing all the way out here?" she asked.

I realized that the reason she had gotten curious was because I was far closer to the restricted cabin than most players ever went. But I had passed it by. That wasn't my destination.

"When I was in the last storyline," I said, "one of the NPCs mentioned having a house out on Lake Dyer. I haven't seen any houses. I was just thinking maybe if I went around the cove, I might be able to see some."

"Oh," she said. "You might. Just remember that NPCs say a lot of things. It only becomes true if you push the story in that direction."

I nodded my head. She was probably right. All of the storylines in Carousel couldn't actually be canonically true. Maybe there were no houses on Lake Dyer. If there were, there's no telling if one of them belonged to some random character just because she said it did.

"So, what do you think of the Western Excursion?" I asked.

Roxy didn't say anything at first. She looked across the lake and gathered her thoughts.

"I hope it works," she said.

"But you don't think it will?"

She shook her head. "I feel like we're missing something," she said. "I doubt we can force our way across the finish line."

I nodded.

We continued walking for as long as we could before additional Omens would start popping up. There was a generic Omen that guarded the woods west of camp. It was a powerful one, just like the one in the cabin. It was there to protect the boundary, I assumed, because it was everywhere I looked along the edge of the forest.

Roxy and I continued talking as we walked back. I asked her how long it took her to be brave enough to use her Looks Don't Last trope, the same one that Kimberly was so afraid of.

"From the beginning," Roxy said. "My team was dead before we even got to Camp Dyer. I was put on another team with Lara. They were already a few levels ahead of me. I did whatever it took to contribute, even if that meant dying."

I wanted to ask her about letters like Dina's, but I didn't know how to bring it up. The more she talked about her original friend group, the clearer it was that one of the other players had been the one lured there. If her group was brought in by letters and a quest, that information likely never reached Roxy. She was here alone.

I didn't know how to broach the subject. I would have to do it a different time.

CHAPTER FOUR

THE INVISIBLE HAND

Another day passed. Another day without running a storyline, without dying. That was a good day in my book.

A thick fog was moving in over the lake. Soon the campgrounds would be blanketed, and the water would be practically invisible under a carpet of haze.

As night had come upon the lodge, several teams had made their way out toward town. They had their favorite storylines to run. They weren't trying to level up or learn anything important. They just wanted to knock out another storyline so that they could live a few more weeks without "disappearing."

My friends were spread out. Anna and Kimberly were talking with a group of ladies about things that induced giggles and excitement. Camden was interrogating another Scholar about something or other. I was sure the conversations would eventually turn toward our real goal: finding out if Carousel normally invited people in the manner it had invited Dina.

Antoine had the best odds of success. He was talking to his brother and Todd. Chris and Antoine had become very close since their reunion. If Antoine could segue the conversation in that direction, he might be able to get us a good lead. We believed Chris and Todd had been team members of a past player with a quest, Zoe.

Antoine was not in any hurry. They were playing a card game. He had told us he didn't want to seem too obvious, that he wanted the truth to come out organically. I suspected he didn't like the idea of pumping his brother for information without telling him what was going on.

I wasn't going to say that, of course.

My job was to talk to the other Secret Keepers—players who knew about the axe murderer. Camden had talked as if we were a club, or as if we were keeping the secret on purpose and not out of fear. I hated feeling like the odd one out.

Still, I wanted to contribute. I went over my list of other Secret Keepers.

Roxy was busy helping Grace clean up. I could talk to her, but I felt I had blown my chance to do so when I had chickened out earlier. Valerie was with Anna and Kimberly. Reggie was in bed, I thought.

The others I didn't know well at all.

Except, of course, for Arthur. That's why I sat and waited for him to arrive. Arthur Clayton. One of the oldest players in Carousel. One of the leaders. If anyone knew something, surely it was him.

It was just a matter of waiting for him to arrive back from the diner, the place where he spent much of his time when not in a storyline. I sat in an overstuffed leather chair and watched and waited for him to stroll up the trail to the lodge.

He did so as the last beam of light disappeared over the horizon, but he didn't come inside. He went around the lodge toward the lake. I had no idea where he was going. I got up out of my chair and went out the back door onto the deck in hopes of intercepting him.

To my dismay, the fog had already hidden much of the area from view.

An overtired Lukas was nodding off on the back deck and halfheartedly warned me to be careful as I walked into the fog bank. He was sleeping on a lawn chair, as was his custom from time to time.

I didn't see where Arthur had gone as I descended into the great sea of wisps. Still, I walked forward. If I could get a line of sight on him, I would be able to see his poster on the red wallpaper, even if I couldn't see him with my eyes.

I walked forward slowly as far as I dared. Nothing was worth stumbling into the lake outside of the designated swim area, and those buoys were two hundred feet down shore from the lodge.

In the distance, I heard water splashing. There was something out there.

I stayed perfectly still. As long as I didn't activate an Omen or wander into a monster's lair, I was fine. I saw swirling fog out in the distance in the area where the splash had come from.

Within a few seconds, the faint outline of a large spiny fin rose above the water and then lowered back down.

Whatever it was, it was so high level that I could not see its name on the red wallpaper, but I could see the poster for its movie. *All Gone Under* was the title. It looked like a generic dinosaur horror. I saw the silhouette of a T-Rex on the poster. A large waterfall led down to an underground oasis in the background while random explorers ran for safety in the foreground.

There was no Omen. That meant the way to activate its story was somewhere else, perhaps in the library or some such place with a litany of Omens.

Whatever the large serpentine creature was, it would still eat me if I made it easy. I had no plans for that.

The splashing continued and there were more swirls, but I didn't see anything else breach the surface of the fog.

Eventually, the creature was gone.

"They like to come out when it's like this," Arthur said loudly out of nowhere.

I almost fell on my butt from surprise.

I swiveled my head. He was out on the docks under the pavilion where we had our lessons with Adeline. I don't know how I had missed him. He sat at a large wooden table with a six-pack of beer.

Trying not to fall in the water with the dinosaur, I slowly walked down the dock toward him.

As I got close, he added, "I don't know what it is about the fog, but the lake comes to life when you can't see it."

He looked out over the moonlit lake and its thick white covering.

There were swirls in the distance. On the other side of the cove, a man in swimming trunks called for help, but his voice didn't carry well with his throat gouged. He was an Omen. He had fallen below the fog before I could see what his story was called. I did notice the hulking humanoid come grab his body and drag it away a few minutes later.

"That's the science camp," Arthur said. "Never run that story. Never been able to get to the other side of the cove."

I nodded. He almost said that like it was a joke, but it might have been a statement of frustration. Arthur had been there twenty years or so, and he had never even seen the camp next door to ours.

I figured this was a sightseeing exercise. That meant I had time to find a way to discuss Dina's letters without discussing them.

"Birds in the distance," I said, nodding to a group of large birds—eagles, perhaps—that were flying over the lake.

Arthur nodded and cracked a smile. "Look what they're carrying."

I stared intently. They were an Omen, sure enough. Activated by . . . investigating the bones they dropped. It was a tough story, too, from the lack of other info I was getting.

"Wow," I said.

Arthur took out a cigar and lit it after cutting it with some cutters he carried. He readjusted his ball cap and watched the eagles fly by.

"Now that's an interesting one," he said. "You can find those bones wherever they drop them. It's always a different place. Big mystery. Vague supernatural quality to it. Part of it takes place in the woods, but not the woods they're flying away from. I once hoped we'd be able to use that story to cross the lake. No such luck. Frustrating."

"I imagine," I said. "Are you just out here watching the Omens?"

Arthur shrugged. "Just waiting to see an old friend."

I wasn't sure what he meant by that.

We waited in silence while a few more Omens revealed themselves to us. A small earthquake revealed a glittering cave in a cliff face west of the science camp. An object of unknown origin fell out of the sky and landed in the lake with a sizzle. It looked like a satellite to me, but it was probably alien in origin. Seductive voices called to us from somewhere out on the shoreline to our left.

Arthur kept an eye on me to see how I was taking it in. The truth was, by the time we heard the sirens, or whatever they were, my nerves were shot. I tried to let my imagination get ahead of me. I thought about how the storyline might play out and how it related to movies I had seen. I didn't want to think about the reality of what waited for us in the fog.

"I thought that one might get you," Arthur said with a rare smile.

"Nope," I said. "That's not how to trap me."

"No?" Arthur said. "How would someone trap Riley Lawrence?"

It occurred to me that this might be a good icebreaker to get him talking about players being invited to Carousel.

"Certain promises," I said. Dina had been promised her son's life. "You think people might come to Carousel for the right reward?"

He shrugged. "People buy into a lot of things when they don't know the true cost," he said.

"No," I said. "Do you think people would come to Carousel if they knew what they were getting into? If they thought they had something to gain?"

Whatever answer he had, I couldn't say, because he had stopped listening to me.

Something was coming.

"Don't say anything. Don't make eye contact. Don't even acknowledge him," Arthur said. He turned in his seat to face me, leaving his right side to face the greater part of the lake.

I turned to him and ignored the vessel approaching the dock.

In my peripheral vision, I saw an Omen approaching in the fog. My Oblivious Bystander strategy required me to pretend not to look at things while I was actually hyper-focused on them, so reading about the Omen on the red wallpaper was practically second nature.

Treble Hooks was the name of the storyline. The poster for the story featured a row of bodies floating a few feet underwater, anchored to the sea floor by fishhooks and fishing lines.

The Omen itself was not clear at first, but then the fog parted, and a large weather-beaten fishing vessel arrived at the dock. I could hear water splashing against its bow, and the wooden boards that comprised its haunted mass creaked. The ship should not have been floating with the damage it had taken to its hull, but float it did.

There was movement aboard.

Watching from the corner of my eye could only reveal so much. At first, I thought they were people—they were people, of course, once upon a time. As the vessel closed in on the dock, I saw that the ship was crewed by spindly wraiths. Ghosts.

"Evenin', folks. Fresh haul from the deep. Plenty of fish to go around," a voice aboard the ship yelled out in a singsong cadence.

Arthur looked me square in the eye as if bidding me to stay silent. I wouldn't have spoken at that moment for anything.

"A fine catch of fish from the dark waters awaits," the voice said. "Any takers?"

I could see the figure that spoke, but it was difficult to isolate them on the red wallpaper. I could see so many aboard the fishing vessel, and many of them out-leveled me and had tropes that obscured what it was I could see.

I heard something poured onto the dock a few dozen feet from the pavilion where we sat. Was it poured? What was it I was hearing? It was liquid, I thought. Then I heard flopping. It was fish flopping on the wooden dock down the way.

"Who has the courage to join me on my boat for a night of fishing?" the figure said. His large decaying vessel swayed in waves too big for the lake, waves like I usually associated with the ocean.

Moments later, another ghastly voice reached out from aboard the boat. "Arthur," the voice said. "I've lost my way. Are you there?"

This shocked me more than the ghostly fishermen.

Arthur, though, didn't move. He didn't speak.

The voice called out to him several more times by name. The more it spoke, the more confused it was.

Then it disappeared. The boat left the docks, taking its whispering voice with it.

The fog remained, and all that was left was the flopping sound of fish on the docks.

I continued staring at Arthur long after the ship had left. It wasn't just fright. It wasn't just that someone on that fishing boat had said his name. It was that I had seen, however briefly, a player poster on the red wallpaper. It was decayed to the point that I couldn't make out what I was looking at. The frame, which would normally be displayed prominently on the red wallpaper for a player, was instead in pieces at the bottom of the red wallpaper.

I had never seen something like that before.

Arthur slapped the table playfully and sucked through his teeth. Then he rose and started walking away from the pavilion and down the dock toward the sound of flopping fish.

I followed, still at a loss for words at first.

Soon, Arthur was picking up the net of fish—ocean fish, from what I could tell. Large deepwater creatures that were so big, Arthur could barely pick up the net and resorted to dragging it.

I found my words quickly after that.

"What are you doing with those?" I asked.

Arthur started to laugh. "I'm bringing them into Grace."

"Grace . . . ," I said. "Don't tell me you want us to eat those fish. They were dropped off by ghosts or . . . something like that."

"Wraiths," he said. "Wraiths are ghosts with bodies, more or less."

I followed him along.

"That doesn't make it better," I said. "Tell me we haven't eaten this fish before. Tell me Grace hasn't been cooking fish hauled up by the undead. Oh god, the lobsters we ate a few weeks ago . . ."

I stared down at the net. Five or six giant lobsters were mixed in with larger specimens from other species.

He laughed and puffed on his cigar. The laugh was all I needed to hear to know the truth. I cursed. Arthur laughed more.

"The food we get from the big box store, Eternal Savers Club, was offered to a devil of some sort. That's part of the plot of the storyline that you have to beat to shop there. Sometimes, it even possesses the food. It's a stoner comedy, kind of. Does that make you not want to eat that food?"

I thought for a moment. Eternal Savers Club was Carousel's answer to Costco or Sam's Club. The fact that it may or may not have been possessed did come as a surprise.

"But that food is still in its packaging," I said. "This . . . feels different."

"Carousel is not a place for people with queasy stomachs," Arthur said. "Look, kid, I thought you knew about the fish. I thought that's why you followed me out here. To help."

He nodded down at the large net of fish.

"Oh," I said. I reached down and helped him drag the fish along.

We made our way back to the pavilion we had been sitting at before, and I asked, "Who was the person calling out to you?"

He puffed at his cigar and readjusted his hat.

"Miles," he said. "Came to Carousel with me. Left one night. Didn't go far."

Even hearing it, I couldn't deal with that information.

"So, he lost a storyline?" I asked. "And now he . . . does that? I thought we just ended up on the missing-poster board."

Arthur let go of the net.

"Yeah," he said. "He's on the board. Can't exactly do much about it, but his poster is there."

That alone wasn't my biggest concern. Players died a lot.

"Why was he the only one there?" I asked. I had seen a lot flash by on the red wallpaper, but only one player.

Arthur took off his ball cap and moved his fingers back through his hair.

"Some players get it in their minds that they have the secret. They think they know how to leave Carousel," Arthur said. "Sent Miles out for fish one night too many. The fisherman's call was just too sweet."

That still didn't compute.

"He entered a storyline all by himself because he thought it was the way out?" I asked. I could never imagine myself believing something like that.

Arthur shrugged. "Some people aren't prepared for the worst-case scenario," he said. "They can't really comprehend that we are stuck here."

Could I believe that? Could I accept that this was it? That this was my eternity?

Arthur continued. "Yes, about your question from earlier. I do believe there are some who would come to Carousel believing they could overcome it. Some people get here and attack it like every other challenge life ever threw at them. They believe that they can get out of here through sheer stubbornness. Unfortunately, Carousel is a place where everything just gets worse. All you can do here is survive. That's the answer. That's the ultimate answer."

I stared down at the fish. If Arthur knew about people getting invited to Carousel in the way Dina had, surely that would have been a time to let me in on it.

"What do you mean, 'everything just gets worse'?" I asked. As far as I could tell, the players had improved their situation greatly over the years.

Arthur didn't answer for a moment. Then he said, "The players that were here when I got here had it better than us. We had it better than you all. We had rescue tropes, after all. Who knows what will be on the chopping block next? The system has fallen down around us, and the people that weren't alive to watch it think it's all some test they can skirt around with a little cleverness."

The system falling down around them? I knew that rescue tropes had been taken offline, but that made it sound like more.

"What was so good about how the people from before had it?" I asked.

Arthur shook his head. "It's not just one thing. It's . . . It used to feel like we had someone looking out for us. Like we were dolls that Carousel was playing with. That may not sound great, but now it feels like Carousel has forgotten about us. 'The invisible hand of Carousel has left us' is what they told me not long after we got to Dyer's Lodge."

"The invisible hand of Carousel?" I asked.

"Yeah," he said, picking the net back up. "It felt like everything we were doing was leading somewhere. We were discovering new things, making progress. Didn't even notice it until it was gone."

"Friends in high places?" I asked.

"I guess," he said. "Not anymore. Come on, help me with this."

I did.

As we made our way through the fog to the lodge, I asked, "If you had the invisible hand back, if you were being guided, would you follow?"

He didn't take a second to think about it. "Yep. In a heartbeat. Now, we're talking the real thing—no half-baked idea that ends with us on a haunted fishing boat. Yeah, in a heartbeat."

I meditated on those words as we hauled the fish inside to cheers from all who were still in the common area.

I got roped into helping Grace break down the fish, which meant holding things while she did all the work.

The next morning, I was late for breakfast. It was being served outside. We were having some kind of fish pancakes, which I didn't quite have the stomach to eat.

As I got there, I found my friends at a picnic table with Chris and a few of the Bowlers—Grace's team, which mostly consisted of Bruiser Archetypes.

"Grace and her team are going to the bowling alley in a few days," Anna said. "They said we could come if we wanted to."

"Oh?" I asked. "Sounds like . . . fun."

Reggie, the Bruiser with a Gentle Giant Aspect whom I had gone on the Grotesque storyline with, was there too.

"We're going to show you how to clear the place in case you ever want to go," he said.

"Thanks," I said, forcing a smile.

Noting my apprehension, Grace said, "You won't have to run any storylines. I know you all are still resting."

That was certainly true. The thought of dying so that I could roll a ball across a wooden floor was not appealing at all. How long would it be until I was willing to die for recreational purposes?

I had not been at Carousel long enough to be ready for a fun night out, but knowing different ways to neutralize Omens would probably be a lifesaver.

I wondered if the bowling alley had an arcade . . .

CHAPTER FIVE

SETTING UP THE PINS

The day the Bowlers planned to go to the alley was a Tuesday. It was important to them that we go on a Tuesday because different NPCs occupied different lanes on different days.

Tuesday was the least crowded day and the only one where the four leftmost lanes were unoccupied. It was also the day with the fewest Omens to contend with.

Sunday night, my friends and I went to the diner for a bite to eat and then headed across the street to find a missing poster with a woman named Zoe on it, hoping it would tell us more about the woman with a quest mentioned in the *Carousel Atlas*.

Camden found it at first glance.

MISSING

Name: Zoe Paulson

Plot Armor: 28

Place last seen: Seasons Party Supply and Costume Shop, East Wing, Jubila-tion Mall

Occupation: Outsider (Newcomer Aspect)

Reward: 480 Dollars

"She was an Outsider too," Dina said. Looking at Antoine, she said, "You really need to talk to Chris about this."

"I will. I don't want to distract him while he's prepping for the Western Excursion," Antoine said. "I'll talk to him at the bowling alley. He said he'd go."

Dina didn't look pleased, but she let it go. She could wait a few more days.

Zoe Paulson had come to Carousel like Dina from what we could tell. And then she had died alone a few months later.

We talked more about what a failed quest from the past could mean and if it really was what we thought it was, but I didn't say much of anything. My mind was numb from theorizing. I wanted to get some answers. I had spent so much time sifting through what little information we had that I was starting to feel a strong sense of dread.

Soon the tension would burst, and I wasn't sure we would be ready.

As I awaited our departure, I had my mind set on finding Lara and discussing the Deathwatch ability. I knew for a fact that Psychics had tropes that granted it, and Lara was one of the more accessible veterans to talk to.

More to the point, of the three Psychics, she was the only Seer and the only one I actually knew. When we had gotten back, she had gone on a run with a higher-level team that lasted two days. It was rare for her to go out on a storyline because she didn't actually have to most of the time.

Luckily, Lara had returned from her trip late Sunday night and was sitting in the common area reading a magazine when I came back from a walk on Monday before lunch.

I quickly made my way to her.

"Lara," I said. "Can I talk to you about something?"

She looked up from her magazine and smiled. "I heard you took my warning to heart," she said. "'Don't suffer in silence.' I was worried that I had been too vague."

"Oh, right. It was very helpful at Second Blood. Thank you," I said.

"You're welcome," she said. "You need another reading?"

I shook my head. "Actually, I died in that last storyline and got this trope," I said, holding out my Director's Monitor trope. "It gives me Deathwatch. I was hoping to ask you some questions about it."

"Deathwatch, huh?" she said with a smile, grabbing my ticket and reading it over. "Carousel Family Video. We don't go there. It's good that you can rewatch storylines on your own. Very interesting."

"Why do we not go there?" I asked. I couldn't let on that we had taken the *Carousel Atlas* and looked it up.

"People have died there," she said. "We don't know how. There are no Omens in the store. Eventually, the older players decided it wasn't worth the risk. Even back when they could rescue people, the players were scared of an Omen that they couldn't find or predict."

I nodded my head.

"As for Deathwatch," she said, "what exactly do you need to know?"

"When you use Deathwatch . . . does anything strange happen?"

She thought for a moment. "I wouldn't say strange. For me, time slows down right before I die, and I have this huge powerful vision of things to come in the story. I can't do anything to change the future without other tropes, so I tend not to use it. For a Psychic, you don't really need to die to find out what happens. I honestly haven't explored that line of tropes."

"Oh," I said. That was disheartening. I considered leaving her be, but I still wanted to know what she had to say about the audience. "I sit in a movie theater with my eyes fixed on the screen."

"That's probably a better experience," she said with a laugh. "Wallflowers with Deathwatch can stay on set if they are permanently Written Off. They watch what happens, but they can't talk to their teammates or intervene without extra tropes. That's probably why they don't use it so often either."

"Oh, that's good to know. The thing is, when I'm in the theater, I'm not alone."

"Not alone?" she said, contemplating what I had told her. "What do you mean by that? There are others in the seats with you?"

I nodded. "I wasn't able to turn my head and look at them, but I could hear them cheering at the end."

"Wow, that's certainly . . . strange. They're probably NPCs."

"Maybe," I said. I wasn't confident about that.

"You don't think so?" she asked. "What are you thinking?"

"Dead players," I said. "Other Film Buffs. The audience."

"The audience? As in *the* audience?" Lara said. "I see. Look, sometimes I have visions that don't make any sense. Things that make me question whether I am seeing a storyline or . . . something else. The way Psychics—and Film Buffs, apparently—work can expose parts of Carousel that aren't as easy to understand. I wouldn't go jumping to conclusions just yet."

I nodded and said, "Thanks."

"Any time," she said.

I went back to my room and shut the door. I lay out on my bunk and immediately started watching *The Astralist* in my mind. There were no claps at the end. I was in an empty theater. The people in the theater, whoever they were, only seemed to stick around to watch live performances. Truthfully, I was a little relieved by that.

Word of our trip to the bowling alley got out and a few other players decided to come along, including Travis and his brother, Vernon, along with their usual team. Bobby did not join them.

Dina went back and forth on whether or not she would come with us. She didn't want to go bowling, but at the same time, she did want to be around to hear Chris talk about Zoe Paulson. It wasn't until Antoine pointed out that he would likely have that conversation in private that she decided to pull out altogether.

On Tuesday at nine in the morning, everyone making the trip met in front of the lodge. Sixteen people in total showed up: my friends, Chris, the five Bowlers, and the five members of Travis's team.

I expected to have to take the lead because of my I Don't Like It Here . . . trope, but it turned out that there were plenty of other scouting tropes that could get us across town safely.

Grace had a trope called The Scary Part of Town that helped detect Omens. Her ex-boyfriend and current teammate Jesse, an Outsider, had a trope called Life on the Streets that also helped. Between them, they could see Omens and avoid them nearly as well as a Hysteric could.

Grace's trope made threats show themselves in some visible way, which was quite the experience. For instance, we passed a community swimming pool with two swimmers, but it had a bunch of people's belongings placed around it on chairs and inside beach bags. Anyone who looked at it would ask the same question: Where are the rest of the people?

My trope told me that you trigger the storyline by swimming or laying out on the chairs. The movie was called *Chlorine*, and its poster showed a snorkel at the bottom of a pool. Its difficulty level was "Something Isn't Right Here," which I took to mean it was of medium difficulty or so.

None of that insight mattered with Grace's trope, because as we walked by, the water in the pool bubbled up and burst like a fountain into the air to signify there was an Omen there.

The drawback to her trope was that some storylines would do more than just show themselves. We found ourselves being followed down the street by a white van, and another time a tree almost fell on us, but we managed to get around it and to safety.

Jesse's trope told him how to avoid Omens but didn't specifically tell him how they were triggered.

"Don't look at it," he said as we passed the pool. That would likely stop you from triggering it, but not in a particularly elegant way.

Between them, we managed to avoid all of the Omens as we made our way through town.

That's where the real education began.

"Listen up!" Grace said. "Here are Grace's Rules for Clearing the Bowling Alley. Rule One: remember what day of the week it is. NPCs and Omens have schedules too. If it's Tuesday, follow the rest of these closely.

"Rule Two: get to the alley before eleven twenty in the morning. Do not make eye contact with the ranting woman's reflection!

"Rule Three: lock the doors and flip over the closed sign at the following times for ten minutes. Don't just leave it that way or the manager will change it when you are not looking and Omens will get in. Lock the back door to avoid The Act of God. It will stay locked on its own.

"Eleven twenty-five: the Quiet Man will arrive and pull on the door. He will leave pretty soon after.

"Twelve forty-five: the coughing scientist will come here for lunch. Don't let him in, but if he finds a way in somehow, don't go near him. He is contagious.

"One thirty: the crying woman with the raspy voice will try to come in and call out a player's name. If they respond to her at all, they have triggered the Omen. Best not to let her in.

"Rule Four: there is a bowling ball bag on a bench on lane four. Do not touch it unless you want to go to hell.

"Rule Five: the birthday party is a bit distracting, but the only Omen is whatever is in the red wrapping paper. While the kids and adults are distracted with bowling, steal the red present and throw it in the trash. If they start opening presents before you do this, leave immediately. If the presents have already been opened, leave immediately.

"Rule Six: do not bowl three strikes in a row. A crowd will start to form behind you to watch, and somehow the Quiet Man will be in it. If you have two strikes, intentionally bowl a gutter and mark it a nine.

"Rule Seven: someone will call asking for a player after one thirty in the afternoon. It is the raspy-voiced woman from before. When the employee calls a player's name, tell her there is no one here by that name.

"Rule Eight: the games in the game corner sometimes play themselves. Do not be alarmed. There is no known Omen related to this.

"Rule Nine: leave by four.

"Rule Ten: no street shoes beyond the carpeted area. This will get the manager angry. He will yell at you and go out back to cool down, leaving the back door unlocked."

Those people must have loved bowling more than I love just about anything. They did all that just so that they could go out and roll a ball down a slick wooden path. Maybe after you had done it a few times you would get used to it, but as Grace listed off her rules, I was second-guessing the trip.

"Are there any questions?" Grace asked as we waited around the corner from the bowling alley.

"Why in the world did you decide to do this?" Antoine asked.

"My brother likes to bowl; I like to solve puzzles. It was great practice learning how to scout out and neutralize Omens. Any other questions?"

Camden raised his hand. "I thought you all ran a storyline when you came here?"

"We normally do," Grace said. "*The Quiet Man*, or sometimes we wait until sundown and do *Red Grease*, which can trap you in any building along this road. We won't today."

She unequipped her scouting trope and led us to the bowling alley.

As soon as we rounded the corner, we saw the ranting woman. She held a large cup and stood in front of the bowling alley staring at herself in the window, which had tinting on it that made it reflective. I avoided looking at her reflection but could not stop myself from hearing her conversation, which was itself quite unnerving.

"Glass and silver, sneaky, sneaky! Ah, the sun's laughter, too bright, too bright! Stolen, it's stolen. Echo of a stolen smile, oh, the twisted waltz. There's always a thread, a thread, holding on . . . Oh, don't cut it, don't dare! I'll unravel, come undone, can't blink, can't. Laughing . . . Are you laughing? Is it you or me? The dark reaches, reaches out, cold as ice, cold as . . . Is that me? Speak, speak up, no voice, just echoes. Trapped, can't move. I should move. No, no, I can't. Spinning, yes, spinning. A stage of silver, the world's a whirl, spinning, spinning. Days go by, night falls, then day again. Still here, still . . . still."

I avoided looking at her altogether once I heard her speaking. Poor woman.

Grace had an alarm that she used to make sure she locked the door and flipped over the sign at the right time. She told us that we had to stop bowling and pay attention for the whole ten minutes that the door was locked.

As we walked in, I was almost shocked by how ordinary the place looked. NPCs bowled and laughed. I could smell nacho cheese bubbling in a crock pot. Hot dogs spun on one of those rolling warmers you might see in a gas station.

I was immediately alerted to the kid's birthday party. I eyed the stack of presents on one of the tables wearily, but the party was just starting, and the red present had not arrived yet.

In lane four, I saw the bowling bag that would send you to hell. The bowling bag was stuffed with clothes in addition to a bowling ball. There were a bunch of lottery tickets ripped in half on the table near the bag, as well as an ashtray full of cigarette butts.

It was a difficult storyline called *Death Toll*. I could not see how to trigger it, but just looking at it sent shivers down my spine thanks to my Hysteric trope.

I could not even think of relaxing or having fun. I got some bowling shoes and sat on a bench near the lanes we were staying at as one of the arcade machines started paying out coins and yelling, "High Score," even though there was no one over there.

Grace quickly walked through the door that led to the area behind the pins so that she could lock the back door.

Shortly after we arrived, an NPC mother and child, who looked scared to death, came in and dropped off the present with the red wrapping paper. Grace's ex, Jesse, went and swiped it off the table and slid it into a trash can before anyone could notice. The mother and child were gone and out the door before any of the kids had even seen them drop off the present.

With everything prepared and death abated temporarily, we started to bowl.

CHAPTER SIX

THE BLACK SNOW

Bowling was one of the many things that I had never been skilled at.

Until I got to Carousel.

I gave myself all those points in Hustle to try to survive using Oblivious Bystander. I had never taken into account how it might help me aim a ball down a wooden lane.

In fact, most of the players were doing really well at bowling. Obviously, Chris was doing the best because he out-leveled us by quite a bit, but I bowled above 130 for the first time in my life in my very first game in Carousel. That was pretty impressive considering we weren't allowed to bowl three strikes in a row.

Antoine was beating me because of his higher Hustle and general athleticism. I wasn't sure how stats worked on things like that outside a storyline, but I could feel it helping me.

Every time Grace's alarm went off, we would all stop what we were doing and watch as she went over and locked the front door and flipped around the open sign.

The first time, a well-groomed man in his early thirties came and attempted to open the door only to leave when he saw that the sign said "Closed." It wasn't an NPC.

It was an enemy.

He must have had a trope that prevented me from seeing much more than that. I assumed he was the Quiet Man Grace talked about. He was forced to go entertain himself elsewhere.

The other unwanted intruders worked the same way. Lock the doors. Flip the sign. Watch until they walked away.

After a long while, a few rounds of bowling, and a few rounds in the arcade, the phone call Grace warned us about came in. Even though we knew it was coming, it still sent a chill down my spine when I heard it. We all waited in anticipation to see which player would be chosen by the woman with the raspy voice.

"Is there a Camden here?" the employee at the desk asked as she placed the phone against her shoulder.

"No one here by that name," Reggie called out.

The employee hung up the phone and everyone cheered and congratulated Camden for being the lucky winner.

We ignored the fact that if he had answered that phone, many of us would likely have died because of it.

We all dispersed into our own little groups. Antoine found an opportunity to get Chris alone by challenging him to Skee-Ball. He was likely preparing to ask questions about Zoe. I could see they were having a difficult conversation. Chris was talking about something, and Antoine stood there, wide-eyed, as if he couldn't believe what he was hearing.

"It looks like Chris just dropped a bombshell on him," Anna said as we spied on them while pretending to pick out new bowling balls.

Was that good news or bad? If it was true that someone else was given a quest to beat the game, that would certainly make me feel more confident in our decision to pursue Dina's quest.

We would have to find out when we got a moment to speak with Antoine.

Travis and Vernon Haley spent almost the whole time alone with their team. It turned out that Travis could be a relatively normal person from time to time. I had half-expected him to harass me because of the comments he had made in the past.

He didn't. It was a pleasant surprise.

As my friends talked and laughed, I found myself forgetting that I was surrounded by danger. I enjoyed being there. At that moment it felt like we were at a real bowling alley hanging out and having a good time.

Maybe the Bowlers were right about taking a minute just to enjoy yourself. I felt at ease in a way that I hadn't been able to since I entered the bowling alley. It almost took me too long to figure out why.

The Hysteric trope that I had been given, I Don't Like It Here . . . , was incredibly useful, but its cost was that it gave you actual anxiety along with the information you received. The fact that I was no longer feeling the same anxiety I had was strange considering that I was in a building with multiple dangerous Omens.

Or was I?

The realization chilled me like a splash of ice water. I looked over at the lane where the bowling bag Omen had been. The bag was still there but I didn't see the Omen anymore. Nothing appeared on the red wallpaper; it was as if I was just looking at a normal bowling bag crammed with clothes.

It was the same with the present that had been thrown away in the trash can. There was no Omen that jumped out to greet me when I looked over there.

Strange.

I turned around and looked out the front window. The entire time we had been there, the ranting woman could be seen talking to her reflection. When I looked again, she was gone.

There were no Omens in the bowling alley anymore.

"Quiet!" I yelled. "Be quiet for a second."

The others heard the panic in my voice and stopped their conversations.

The Omens were gone, but as I focused, I could still feel something. Something distant and growing. Was this normal anxiety or was there another Omen nearby? I couldn't tell.

Then I looked up.

Whatever it was wasn't directly above us, but when I looked out toward the back side of the building and up into the ceiling, I felt an intense burst of fear. Even through the roof, I could tell that there was an Omen outside.

As this realization dawned on me, my anxiety kicked into overdrive, and I walked toward the doors to get a look at what it was.

"The Omens are all gone and there is something outside!" I screamed as I walked toward the door. The others cycled through their own scouting tropes to confirm what I had said and then followed me.

When I walked around the building and looked up in the direction of the pulsing fear that felt like it was pressing against my forehead, I saw it.

The storm.

A single jet-black cloud floated in the distance above a large chemical factory that was pouring smoke into the air. I could see lights flashing around the factory. There was some kind of meltdown.

I saw the Omen.

The Black Snow
Difficulty: Apocalypse. The world is ending.
Trigger: Imperceptible. (Savvy too low)

Whatever this was it was too difficult for me to get much useful information from it. My location scout trope didn't get anything from it. Strangely, my

Hysteric trope told me it was an Apocalypse, but otherwise the Omen looked too powerful for me to be able to see much.

I didn't understand why it was showing me the name and difficulty of such a powerful storyline. Normally the strongest ones didn't tell me anything but that they existed.

"We need to go!" I screamed.

"What is it?" Grace asked.

I told them the name of the storyline. "I've never even seen an Apocalypse level of difficulty," I said.

The veterans looked at each other.

"It can't be an Apocalypse," Travis said. "The next one isn't due until December."

Due?

"I'm telling you that it says Apocalypse on the red wallpaper," I said.

"We need to run," Jesse said. His trope for figuring out how to avoid danger was crude but effective.

"Just a second," Grace said. She pulled out a trope from her pocket. It was called Brain Trust. A quick look at the red wallpaper told me that it allowed a player to copy an ally's insight tropes temporarily. It worked best Off Screen.

Panic overtook Grace's face. I assumed that was the result of my Hysteric trope assaulting her with fear.

"'Any player or NPC who touches the black snow must survive the Apocalypse,'" she read. Her Savvy was much higher than mine, so, naturally, she was able to use my trope more effectively.

I went and talked to my friends about what I saw. Kimberly was terrified. Antoine was trying to look brave. Camden looked emotionally drained like he had back when he had died.

"Well, I'll be," an NPC said from behind us. His voice cracked. He was speaking loudly. "What do you reckon we should do?"

The intrusion of the NPC on our conversation was a little odd, as they usually kept to themselves, but as I glanced back to see who had spoken, I noticed that he was wearing a uniform. A bus driver's uniform. He was just an ordinary NPC.

He had parked a bus right there in the street and gotten out to look at the cloud right where we were. The bus was empty and still running. Was this more help from our friends upstairs?

I backed toward the bus and waved to my friends and the other players.

Travis was far ahead of me and had already loaded onto the bus with his team by the time I got to it.

The rest of us quickly piled into the bus and pulled away.

The NPC bus driver turned and watched but didn't react with anger. He didn't try to get back on the bus. We made eye contact. What I saw on his face was resignation and fear. He stared at us as we left.

As we drove away, black dots could be seen in the sky in the distance as the storm cloud grew. It was snowing.

Travis was driving. Everyone in the back was discussing the issue in a panicked tone.

"Why would Carousel do this?" was a common refrain. This sudden Apocalypse didn't even have the illusion of fairness.

The storm was between us and Dyer's Lodge. We were trying to figure out if we could get around it in time to get back or if it would cut us off as it grew.

And grew.

And grew.

It quadrupled in size in ten minutes and continued growing at an astronomical rate.

"How is there an Apocalypse right now?" Travis yelled from the driver's seat.

The veterans were scared and confused.

All of us were.

When people talked about Apocalypses, I had thought they were just being descriptive of a storyline. I didn't understand they were a separate event.

I couldn't keep track of the entire frantic conversation as it went along but I did learn a lot really quickly as the veterans discussed the plan of what to do.

I learned a few important things.

First, I learned that Apocalypses happened every six to eighteen months. I also learned that players do not ever participate in Apocalypses. Instead, they find their way out of town and stay there until it ends. That was one of the many benefits of Dyer's Lodge: it was out of town—a safe zone for events like this.

There were all sorts of Apocalypses, from zombie Apocalypses to the rise of the machines all the way to alien invasions.

There were numerous signs of upcoming Apocalypses. Usually, this made them very easy to avoid, especially since the Omens were supposed to last for weeks before the Apocalypse actually happened.

The Omen for this Apocalypse had appeared and the snow had started to fall almost simultaneously.

As we went along, I stared out the window and watched as the town reacted to the impending danger.

"Most of the Omens are disappearing," I said. I had to repeat myself because the veterans were so engaged in their planning and conversation. "Most of the Omens are disappearing!" Looking out the window I could see they were being extinguished like candle flames in a hurricane. I knew that when a storyline was triggered, other Omens set in the same location disappeared for a while. The same must happen when an Apocalypse started to spread across town. "But not all of them."

The veterans picked up what I was trying to say.

If we found the right storyline and triggered it, we might just be able to escape the Apocalypse in a completely different way.

"Travis!" Grace yelled. "Change of plans. We're not going to be able to out-run this thing and get around it. We need to go east."

We needed a storyline that could get us away from the black snow.

Travis turned down the next side road and sent us east.

As we drove away, I saw the storm in the distance. From where we were on the road, I could see a long way down the street all the way to where the storm was in the center of the city. The haze of black snow cast a shadow that felt like it covered all of Carousel. In the distance, I could see NPCs walking out of their houses, curious about the storm.

As I stared at the people in the distance, something caught my eye. There was an enemy out amongst the people in the distance. It was too far away for me to distinguish what I was looking at with my eyes alone, but as soon as it was in my line of sight, I could see it on the red wallpaper.

It was too far away for me to see any of its tropes because that ability was proximity based, but other information was still available.

It was called a Lamentation on the red wallpaper. Plot Armor: 76.

The image of the creature on its poster terrified me to the core of my being.

It was a woman. Her limbs were twisted around backward so that she could walk on all fours while her back was to the ground. Her jaw was open, her broken teeth exposed. Tears streamed from her eyes. She was afraid.

Her broken form was not the scariest part.

Jaws emerged from her stomach. They were a dog's jaws; I could tell because its face was there too. Its eye sockets were covered in flesh. Its jaws snarled and drooled. Its tail came out of her thigh, and one of its paws was sticking out of her armpit. A dog leash trailed behind her.

The Lamentation was a mutant amalgam.

I recognized the woman. I recognized the dog.

The first time I had seen them they had been an Omen. The dog snapped and growled at my friends and me as we passed it on the street.

Whatever we did, we could not let the black snow touch us.

CHAPTER SEVEN

UNINTENDED CONSEQUENCES

Y ou know where the airfield is?" Chris asked Travis.

Travis nodded. "I remember the place," he said. "Over by Pit Boulevard."

"You got it."

Chris turned to the bus. "We have a lot of players around or below level thirty. That's dangerous. Omens at the airfield can be leveled higher than that. Grace will divide us into teams to try to make us more balanced and ensure there are higher-level players in each team. No complaints, people. This one is for real."

Grace took out her notebook and pen and started creating team lists.

"Antoine with me," Chris said.

"And Kimberly," Antoine added.

"I can do that."

Grace scanned the bus and started pairing everyone together in an attempt to create well-rounded teams and to distribute lower-level players as well as higher-level ones. After a minute or two, she had the list together and read it all for us.

The plan was to find three separate Omens of the appropriate danger level and create three teams to beat each one. The teams were divided as follows:

Team 1:

Grace: Detective, Plot Armor: 41

Chris: Sport-Athlete, Plot Armor: 58

Antoine: Athlete, Plot Armor: 19

Kimberly: Eye Candy, Plot Armor: 17

Riley: Filmmaker-Film Buff, Plot Armor: 22

Team 2:

Tori: Scream Queen-Final Girl, Plot Armor: 29
Mark: Strategist-Scholar, Plot Armor: 30
Vernon: Bully-Bruiser, Plot Armor: 31
Dirk: Brute-Bruiser, Plot Armor: 38
Jesse: Newcomer-Outsider, Plot Armor: 41
Team 3:
Anna: Final Girl, Plot Armor: 21
Reggie: Gentle Giant-Bruiser, Plot Armor: 40
Camden: Scholar, Plot Armor: 18
Bella: Bully-Bruiser, Plot Armor: 37
Travis: Criminal-Outsider, Plot Armor: 32
José: Soldier, Plot Armor: 30

Anna and Camden looked apprehensive about being separated from the rest of the group. Grace appeared to notice this.

"Reggie is going to make sure that both of you are safe," she said. "Right, Reggie?"

"I'll take care of you," he said.

Everyone moved around to sit near their teams except for Travis, who was driving. We discussed our strategies.

"Which of you is First Blood?" Chris asked.

I was about to volunteer. I would have probably been forced into it anyway because of my artificially low Plot Armor. Before I could, Kimberly raised her hand.

"I can do it, but I left my Looks Don't Last trope at the lodge," she said.

Chris and Grace looked at one another.

"Sweetheart, you can't leave your tropes anywhere. They're always with you. Just reach for it in your pocket, and it'll be there," Grace said.

Kimberly reached down into her pocket. With the shorts she was wearing, her pocket wasn't even large enough to hold one of our tickets, but she pulled out her Looks Don't Last trope. The way she stared at it, you would think she was looking at a ghost.

"How do I . . . use it?"

"Until you get the hang of it, the easiest way to equip it is to take your Archetype ticket in one hand and then place the tropes you want to take with you in that same hand," Grace explained gently.

"I'll split my focus between buffing the weaker players and getting ready for the fight at the end," Chris said to Grace. "I assume you can handle insight and story control?"

Grace nodded and started flicking through her stack of tropes, which she had pulled out of her jacket pocket.

"Antoine, you do whatever we need you to do," Chris said. "Riley, you're Second Blood."

So nice of him to volunteer me. What else could I really expect?

"With Grace as a Detective, the story is going to become a mystery. Be ready for anything until we get a handle on what's going on."

Antoine, Kimberly, and I nodded.

Soon after that, Grace and Chris started traveling up and down the bus helping the other teams figure out their strategies. Usually, whenever veterans went out on runs, they had days or even weeks of planning. This time they only had minutes.

I looked back at Anna and Camden as they were briefed on their team's strategy. I couldn't hear what was being said, but I could tell that they both looked worried.

I didn't have long to think about my teammates. I had to keep my eyes on the road looking for Omens. The further we went, the fewer Omens I could see, and those that I did see were disappearing as soon as I got an eye on them.

I realized that there was a possibility we could get to the airfield and still not see any live Omens. I tried thinking back to the map of Carousel I had seen. I couldn't remember if there were any roads out of town from this direction. Even Patcher's Family Farm, where the corn maze had been, was pretty close to town in the grand scheme of things and would likely not be far enough away to keep us safe.

"The airfield is ahead," Travis yelled.

As we neared it, I was relieved to see that there were several Omens still on the airfield. In fact, those were not the only Omens I saw.

We were coming up on a road with a sign that said "Pit Blvd." It didn't take long to figure out why they called it that. There was a large pit in a lot on the corner of the street. It was fenced off and appeared to have been that way for a long time. I couldn't tell what had happened there.

And then, in the blink of an eye, it was gone. Instead of a pit, there was a parking lot and a large building with a sign that said "Carousel Roller Daze." It was an old-fashioned roller rink. It had been a long time since I'd seen one of those.

The building appearing out of nowhere wasn't the biggest concern. The biggest concern was that the entire building, along with the parking lot, was flickering in and out of existence. Sometimes it would stay there for a few moments and then it would disappear for half a second.

There was an Omen associated with that building.

Post-Traumatic was the title of the storyline. The poster was of a building on fire. The building was the roller rink.

"There's an Omen there," I said loudly for all to hear. It was disappearing off and on, but I wasn't sure if that was because of the Apocalypse or something else. The way it flickered was unlike any of the other Omens I had seen.

"Keep going to the airfield," Chris said. "It's a safer bet."

I couldn't argue with that. We couldn't exactly pull the bus into a disappearing parking lot.

As we passed by the roller rink, I looked inside it through its glass door and saw that the people were wearing eighties fashion getups and dancing cheerfully as if they couldn't see the incoming Apocalypse like other NPCs could.

The bus continued on toward the airfield. The closer we got, the better I could see the available Omens. They were pretty straightforward at the airfield. Load onto the aircraft and fly off toward your destination. It was that simple.

"Can you tell how strong the Omens are?" Grace asked.

The two airplanes were both strong. One of them was called *Preservation,* and its poster featured a metal and glass box against a backdrop of a forest burning. I couldn't see what was in the box . . . something round . . . with . . . hair. The other Omen was too strong for me to even see any details.

There was a helicopter with a slightly easier Omen called *Headhuntress Reborn.*

I told Grace and Chris about what I saw.

"And," I said, "the limousine." I pointed to the parking lot. There was a black limousine outside the small airplane hangar. The driver was standing outside holding a sign that said "Conner Party."

It was called *The Strings Attached.* Its poster featured an ordinary image of a ballroom with dancers wearing masks—a masquerade—except, on closer inspection, it was clear that not all of the dancers were moving under their own power. They were limply being carried around the ballroom in their partners' arms.

Its difficulty level was "Get to the Car Now!"

There was a problem, though. My I Don't Like It Here . . . trope was subjective and gave me ratings based on how strong my team was. But who did the trope count as being on my team at that moment? Was it my original team? Or was it the people physically closest to me?

The difficulty level could be in the twenties or thirties or higher, depending on who it might be. I didn't know how to tell.

As soon as Chris had all of the information I did, he assigned us our stories.

Anna and Camden were going for *Headhuntress Reborn.*

The team with Jesse was going for *Preservation.*

Finally, my team was going for *The Strings Attached.*

As we pulled into the parking lot before we disembarked from the bus, Kimberly hugged Anna.

"See you guys on the other side," Camden said.

"We'll be fine," Antoine said. "We just have to run the story. We've done it before."

Camden nodded.

After pulling away from Kimberly, Anna came toward me with her arms outstretched and hugged me. As soon as the bus was stopped and we had unloaded, she and Camden ran behind their team.

Travis held onto Tori, his girlfriend and teammate, and gave her a kiss as they left for their separate storylines.

"Come on, Riley," Antoine yelled, snapping me out of the weird moment I was having as I realized that many of the players, even the vets, weren't sure whether they were coming back.

I ran toward the limousine.

"Conner party, I presume," the driver said as we began piling into the back of the limo. "As requested, I have fetched your evening wear."

As I took a seat and looked around, I found that the limousine had five available seats. There were clothes hanging from a bar next to the small refrigerator. It was a luxury car, through and through.

As soon as we were all loaded in, the driver quickly took his seat and put the pedal to the metal. Even though he had to play his part as the Omen, it was clear that he was aware of the coming danger.

"How is this thing supposed to get us to safety?" Antoine asked. "If there was a road out of town over here, why didn't we just go there on the bus?"

"If there wasn't a way out, the Omen would have disappeared like all of the others," Chris said. He didn't sound sure.

I started to suspect there were other reasons he put himself and his little brother in the limo instead of the other options available. If you had to choose between getting caught by the storm in a car or an airplane, the choice was pretty simple.

As the limo headed north, I looked behind us toward the airfield, hoping to see a plane taking off from the runway.

What I saw froze my blood in my veins.

Headhuntress Reborn had disappeared from my view. The helicopter was still there, but the Omen was gone. So was the Omen that was so strong I couldn't even read the storyline title.

The only Omen left over there was *Preservation.*

"Turn around!" I screamed.

The others turned and struggled to see what I was looking at. The driver didn't listen to me in the slightest. He was still speeding away.

I beat my fist against the window.

As I watched, Anna and Camden's team ran toward the big blue plane that held the Omen for *Preservation*. They made it to the door just as the other team had loaded in. Travis climbed inside, then Bella and José.

Then the door closed. The storyline must have hit its limit.

The airplane started taxiing away from Anna, Camden, and Reggie.

Everyone in the limo started screaming for the driver to turn around. He ignored us. I could see his face in the rearview mirror. He looked like he understood exactly what was happening. His face was grim.

I tried opening the car door, but it was locked. We were stuck. Our storyline had begun. We had passed from Omen to Choice. It was too late.

Anna, Camden, and Reggie were stranded.

The limousine continued to head north, skirting around the edge of the storm. Eventually, we turned onto a road that I had heard of before. It was called Turn Around Road.

A sign said "Dead End," but the driver continued.

We came upon a bridge. I heard Chris and Antoine begin to talk as we went along. Apparently, the bridge that we crossed was usually out. This road was impassable unless you happened to trigger an Omen for a storyline on the other side.

Kimberly was crying inconsolably.

I leaned my head against the window next to my seat.

I wondered who, if any of us, would survive.

CHAPTER EIGHT

THE BALLROOM

Player Stats:

Player	Plot Armor	Mettle	Moxie	Hustle	Savvy	Grit
Riley	22/2	2	7	4	7	2
Antoine	19	4	4	5	1	5
Kimberly	17	2	5	4	1	5
Grace	41	5	9	7	12	8
Chris	58	14	9	15	5	15

Players' Tropes:
Riley Lawrence is the Film Buff.

Trope Master grants me the ability to perceive enemy tropes, but at the cost of sacrificing half of my Plot Armor.

Cinema Seer buffs the Savvy and Grit of my allies when they hear me predict cinematic and impactful plot elements.

As an **Oblivious Bystander,** I remain untargeted by enemies if I convincingly act oblivious to their presence.

Escape Artist buffs my Hustle to help enact plausible escape plans.

Drawing on my upbringing, **Raised by Television** enhances relevant stats when I take larger-than-life or cinematic action inspired by TV or movies, though it often attracts a downturn in fortune soon afterward.

Director's Monitor allows me to watch the rest of the storyline after my demise via Deathwatch.

Flashback Revelation allows me to communicate with allies while on Deathwatch through flashbacks to my past dialogue.

Location Scout provides a list of primary filming locations within the storyline.

I did not equip **My Grandmother Had the Gift . . .**, **I Don't Like It Here . . .**, **Out like a Light**, or **Casting Director**.

Kimberly Madison is the Eye Candy.

Convenient Backstory allows her to believably change her backstory to assist with the current task, buffing the relevant stat.

Social Awareness allows her to see the Moxie stat of all enemies and NPCs.

Get a Room! boosts the odds of important discoveries when exploring with a love interest during the Party.

A Hopeless Plea forces the captor to explicitly deny her release when she asks to be released.

Pregnancy Reveal buffs her Grit when she pretends that she is pregnant and buffs the father's Mettle if she dies.

That's What I Said! allows her plans and ideas to be "stolen" by higher-Savvy allies, with the success of the plan being determined by their Savvy.

Does Anyone Have a Scrunchie? allows her to shift Moxie points into another stat by putting her hair up.

She will be targeted for First Blood because **Looks Don't Last,** but the longer she survives, the weaker the enemies get.

She did not equip **Carousel Academy Awards** because her last performance had issues.

Antoine Stone is the Athlete.

His **You Were Having a Nightmare . . .** trope allows him to repress or heal mental trauma. He is not strong enough to use its plot-resetting powers yet.

Gym Rat buffs Mettle and Hustle by revealing athletic backstory.

It's Part of the Uniform gives him higher Mettle when attacking with sports equipment.

> **Just Walk It Off** heals the Hobbled status by walking.
>
> **The Playbook** allows him to see the phases of a coordinated plan.
>
> **Time Out!** allows him to go Off Screen during a fight, reducing enemy aggression.
>
> Brandishing a weapon is **Like a Security Blanket,** buffing his Grit and soothing his and his allies' fear, whereas swinging a weapon will temporarily halt an enemy's attack because of **Swing Away.**
>
> He did not equip **Reload After Cut** or **Bad Luck Magnet.**

Chris Stone is the Athlete.

Still a Part of the Team	Buff	Athlete	Sport	Grit/ Moxie	When physically impaired, non-physical endeavors are buffed based on Grit. Through encouragement, allies gain buffs based on the player's injury-related debuffs based on Moxie.
Earned Confi-dence	Buff	Athlete	Stud	Moxie	Gains a small buff with every successful stat check but loses it all with failure. Buffs are fewer and larger as the story progresses. Must maintain a confident persona.
Just off a Win	Buff	Athlete	Sport	N/A	Buffs team's strongest stat based on how many storylines they have won in a row without need-ing to be rescued. Recent rescues result in debuffs instead.

Top of the Food Chain	Buff	Athlete	Health Nut	Grit	Buffs player's Mettle or Hustle when competing with a physically imposing enemy. Non-human enemies give bigger buffs.
Buzzer Beater	Rule	Athlete	Sport	Hustle	The longer the player waits to accomplish a time-sensitive endeavor, the more likely they are to succeed. Activates with 5 seconds remaining. The player perceives a timer.
Pulled Back In	Background	Any	N/A	N/A	Unveil secret background related to a life of crime, intrigue, or espionage. May equip the following tropes: Anything Can Be a Weapon (Commando-Soldier), I'll Just Take Yours (Agent-Soldier), You've Done This Before, Haven't You? (Agent-Soldier), No Body, No Crime (Criminal-Outsider), They Fell Off (Criminal-Outsider), It's About to Go Down (Criminal-Outsider), The Bulletproof Table (GI-Soldier), Surprisingly Well-Connected (Socialite-Eye Candy), Off-Screen Outfit Swap (Recast-Wallflower)

No Body, No Crime	Action Insight	Outsider	Criminal	Hustle	After killing an enemy secretly before the Finale, the player will go Off Screen and be shown ideal places to stash the evidence of their kill. If successful, the enemy will not be alerted to their presence.
I'll Just Take Yours	Rule	Soldier	Agent	Mettle	Ensures that the player will come across a low-level enemy with a desirable weapon if it fits the narrative. Otherwise, such a weapon could be found on an NPC.
You've Done This Before, Haven't You?	Buff	Soldier	Agent	Moxie*	Buffs player's attempts at out-of-character skills or plans, like those a spy or action hero might have, if an ally player is there to watch in surprise at the player's secret competence. Success is based on both players' Moxie and diminishes after skills are revealed to the ally. Must have a realistic explanation for skills ready to go, or else no experience will be gained or there will be possible enemy escalation.
The Bulletproof Table	Rule	Soldier	GI	Moxie	In a Fight Scene, anything the character hides behind will be imbued with the movie magic required to stop projectiles, claws, acid, or similar attacks. Must be at least plausible, and the portrayal must be convincing.

Will-power Is Magic	Rule	Any	Any	Grit	All applicable enemy technology or magic is now resistible through sheer effort. Results vary. Effects vary. This will hurt.
The Sacrifice Play	Action	Athlete	Sport	Grit	Self-sacrifice that leaves the player dead or injured will buff allies' Grit and increase the odds of the current plan succeeding.
Gut Instinct	Insight	Athlete	Health Nut	Grit	The player will be alerted to danger and dangerous people or situations. They will not necessarily know what the danger is or how to prevent it.

Grace is The Detective.

The Ill-Fated Mary Lee Parrish	Rule Insight Buff	Detective	N/A	N/A	The player's old friend, Mary, was a victim of the enemy before the storyline began. Investigating her demise during the Party will bear great insight. Changes to the storyline to fit Mary in will not weaken the enemy and may strengthen it. Avenging Mary's fate will buff the player in the Finale.

Eureka!	Insight	Scholar	Researcher	Savvy	Helps find important information within text.
Get the Truth Out	Rule	Detective	N/A	N/A	The Win Condition is changed to exposing the truth of the mystery underlying the story. The player will be given hints on how to accomplish this. The enemy will too. If successful, the storyline is won even if the players die.
Here's What Happened	Rule	Detective	N/A	N/A	Sends players Off Screen while explaining aspects of the mystery correctly. Players will see flashbacks illustrating the reveal on the red wallpaper. Stronger in Finale.
Cross off the List	Insight	Detective	N/A	Savvy	Player will be informed of whether they have found all important information in a search of a room or an interrogation of a person. Will not know what information remains.

Don't Shoot the Messenger	Insight Buff	Detective	N/A	Savvy	Allies who have found important plot information will get a boost to their Grit as they attempt to return to the player to relay the information.
Human Lie Detector	Insight	Detective	N/A	Higher of Moxie or Savvy	Can see if someone is lying. Will not know the truth.
Hardboiled Detective's Kit	Rule	Detective	N/A	N/A	Allows the player to bring items that a detective might use, such as a camera or gun.
Take Them in Alive	Rule	Detective	N/A	N/A	Greatly improves the chances of inflicting debilitating but non-lethal injuries. Works best on humans.
I Can't Die until I Know	Rule	Detective	N/A	N/A	The player cannot die until they know the truth about the mystery. Of course, there are so many things worse than death. The enemy will reveal the truth shortly before delivering the killing blow.

"Get your tropes equipped before the Party starts," Chris said.

I was not thinking about surviving. Camden and Anna were doomed. I couldn't wrap my head around that. I went numb, barely registering what I was being told.

Chris reached across the limo and slapped me in the face.

"Equip your damn tropes," he said again. "We are all sad. It happens. Now we have to survive. Once the Choice ends, you won't be able to choose."

I started thinking about my tropes. I could hardly focus. I didn't need my Hysteric scouting trope. Now that I had hit my limit, I needed to think about what I was taking into storylines. At level fifteen, the limit became eight tropes and one background trope. It didn't really matter then, because I didn't have that many tickets. The limit would increase by one every ten levels after that.

Eight tropes . . . What would be left behind?

Out like a Light was quick to go. I didn't plan on sleeping. I didn't equip My Grandmother Had the Gift . . . because I didn't need Carousel focusing on me in this storyline, and I didn't have too many uses for it aside from improvisation. Grace and Chris could be the focus. I would do what they said.

I was struggling to cut another trope when Grace did it for me.

"You don't need Casting Director," she said. "You're under-leveled. Anything it would tell you is something we could find out through other means."

That made sense, but at the same time, knowing my role ahead of time was very comforting. It was true what she said. In the Grotesque storyline, another I had been way under-leveled for, all of the information I had learned from Casting Director was revealed soon after by ordinary means.

I ditched it.

That was it.

Everyone was getting dressed in the back of the limousine. It wasn't convenient. I spent a while looking in the other direction while Kimberly and Grace got changed. Teammates in Carousel didn't get much privacy from each other.

Outside, the landscape changed from the flat farmland of northern Carousel to lush wooded terrain with breathtaking vistas and wilderness as far as the eye could see. Occasionally, we would pass a gate with an armed guard posted outside. A sign we passed said "The Carousel Hills."

This was where the richest of the rich lived, their estates guarded by fences and security teams. The road was all cobblestone here, the landscapes designed to be visually pleasing. It looked like the wealthiest NPCs got to miss out on the Apocalypse.

Eventually, the driver pulled us into the largest and grandest of all of the drives. Armed guards in expensive suits stopped him before he got too far. He showed the guard a ticket, not unlike the tickets Silas might award, and the guard let us through.

As we drove onward, we were assaulted by beauty on all sides. We saw elaborate gardens and fountains, magical-looking archways, and topiary animals carved from bushes.

It was paradise.

But the mansion topped it all.

It was huge, like a palace in a fairytale. I could not imagine how many rooms it had or what kind of fortune it had taken to build.

As the driver pulled us up to the entrance of the mansion, the doors finally unlocked, and the needle on the Plot Cycle moved to Party.

I didn't feel ready. I was still numb. On any other day, I would have been theorizing about what sort of horror movie this was, but my heart wasn't in it. Camden and Anna were a loss I wasn't ready for. I never had many friends, and we had drifted apart over the years, but the pain and dread still overwhelmed me.

I kept imagining their faces on a missing poster. How long would I have to be here without them?

There was a knock on the window. I looked up, expecting to see another guard, but instead, I saw a man with red hair and a smirk. His face was mostly hidden behind an ornately designed festive mask.

The man opened the door before the driver could get to it. We all piled out of the limousine, leaving our clothes behind. We didn't really need them. Antoine's baseball bat had already disappeared. It was likely hidden somewhere in the mansion.

As we got out, I noticed that the red-haired man had no information on the red wallpaper besides "Society Member" and the name "Mr. Flamingo," which made sense because his mask resembled a flamingo in an abstract sort of way.

He looked at us like he knew us.

"You made it," he said. "This is going to be marvelous! They said *The Eavesdropper* was just a celebrity gossip magazine. After tonight, we are going to be respected journalists . . . who just happen to write about celebrity gossip."

He looked at us, pulled his mask off, and said, "It's me, Jack. Have you all forgotten why we're here?"

Suddenly his name, "Jack Goforth, *The* Jack Goforth," came into view on the red wallpaper. He was a level fifty NPC. He had tropes I could not see on the red wallpaper, like the Psychic and Detective NPCs.

The masks must block insight into identity.

"I'm sure you'll remind us either way," Grace said.

"We are here to find out what the oligarchs of Carousel do when they are all on their own. There's a story here. I can feel it," Jack said. "Today, we're going to find out how the other half lives. And, Grace, the friend you were worried about is inside. She seems fine. I guess it was a false alarm."

Grace raised an eyebrow. "Mary Lee? She's okay?"

"She's more than okay. Go look for yourself."

Jack turned to the rest of us. "Don't forget, we're undercover here. Don't let anyone know who you really are, or we are all going to jail and getting black-listed, and, worse, we will look like hacks. Let's just hope the real Conner party doesn't show up."

Our masks were included along with our clothing. Mine was an earthy gray with some warm undertones. I couldn't tell the theme. Most of the other masks had themes. Mine just looked like someone made it from dirty clay and dropped it, creating cracks across it. On the bright side, it covered my face more than most of the masks, so it might help me blend in.

As we entered the massive doors, some servants ushered us into the ballroom.

The ballroom was spacious and tastefully adorned. Rich fabrics were draped along the walls and pillars, adding an air of elegance to the room. The dance floor, constructed from an unfamiliar yet inviting dark-colored wood, dripped with a sense of luxury. Glittering chandeliers adorned the lofty ceiling, casting a soft, flattering glow upon the dancers below. Mirrors strategically placed on the walls subtly amplified the grandeur of the space. The room's architecture and careful use of subdued lighting created an enchanting ambiance, making it the perfect setting for opulent gatherings, elegant soirées, or even some sort of sophisticated massacre.

Off Screen.

"Look," Grace said, pointing to one of the walls.

I followed her gaze and saw a woman dancing with a young buff man. She had long blond hair and a shockingly white smile. I could not see any information about her because she was wearing a mask.

"It's Mary Lee Parrish," Grace whispered.

Either she recognized her, or her high Savvy helped her see through the mask's powers. She sounded certain.

"This isn't good," Grace said. "It's better when she's dead."

Mary Lee Parrish was an NPC that Grace could bring into a storyline to get a jump start on solving the mystery at hand.

"She always succumbs to the enemy before the story starts," Grace explained. "If it's a serial killer, she's dead. If it's a monster, she's eaten. You understand. The fact that she is standing there laughing narrows down the ultimate threat of this story."

"So, the bad guys aren't trying to kill us?" Kimberly asked.

"Maybe not," Grace said. "The fact that she's alive points to possession, infection, magic of some sort, or perhaps a fate worse than death."

We all stared at the woman across the room. She looked quite happy.

"I never get to go to parties like this!" Mary Lee exclaimed with a smile.

Grace probably shouldn't have said the phrase "Fate worse than death," because as soon as she did, I saw Antoine's eyes widen. He had already suffered one fate worse than death when he was trapped in the Straggler forest for decades. It took him several seconds to recover his composure, but the fear never really left his eyes.

I looked at Mary Lee Parrish as she laughed, flashing her pearly white teeth. She looked happy. Glowing. She flirted and teased her suitor with an energy and vigor I had rarely ever seen in the victim of a horror movie.

As a waiter came by, she grabbed a fresh glass of champagne and drank it like she had never tasted anything that delicious.

So, which fate worse than death could leave you that happy?

CHAPTER NINE

YOUNG LOVE

The party was in full swing, and I don't just mean the Party phase of the Plot Cycle. People were dancing and laughing. They shared wine, champagne, and conversation.

Everyone I could see was wearing a mask, and because of that, I couldn't tell the enemies from the NPCs; if I didn't try hard enough, I would lose track of my team.

When we entered, Antoine, Kimberly, and I stayed hovering near Grace. It was strange. We were getting used to entering into dangerous situations, but social situations could be the most confusing and intimidating.

One misspoken word could out us as imposters. Would that mean that we just lost? Was it possible to lose before First Blood?

Mary Lee Parrish didn't take long to catch sight of Grace. I thought that was strange, given the fact that Grace was wearing a mask. I wasn't sure what the rules were for the masks, but I had assumed that they would prevent us from being identified.

"Ms. Emerald? Ms. Emerald, is that you?" Mary Lee asked. "These damned masks make it so difficult to recognize anyone. I understand the need for secrecy, but this is just impractical. Come here, darling. It's been so long since I've been up and walking around."

Mary Lee came forward and gave Grace a hug and a quick peck on both cheeks.

When I looked at her on the red wallpaper, all I saw was the name, "Ms. Opaline." Grace could see through that, perhaps because of her high stats, perhaps because Mary Lee Parrish was only brought into the story because of Grace's trope.

Still, the fact that Mary Lee had mentioned the obfuscating nature of the masks, despite the masks not really covering anyone's face all that much, suggested that their power was not meta—that it was not the product of a trope. That would explain why I had not seen anything about the masks' power on the red wallpaper with Trope Master.

It was magic. In-universe magic. How else would an NPC be mentioning it on-screen?

That meant one thing: we were dealing with some kind of sorcery.

"Emerald, do you remember Mr. Chromatic?" Mary Lee asked in a tone that was both hushed and somehow very loud.

"I apologize. Memory doesn't serve. Care to remind me?" Grace asked.

"Mr. Chromatic! You remember him. You hit it off with him at the last society function. Tall man. Dreamy eyes. Wore the mask that looked like a mirror?"

"Mr. Chromatic!" Grace exclaimed. "How could I forget?"

"Well," Mary Lee said, "he got in an accident skiing last month. His body was wrecked. What a waste. He should be around here somewhere. He isn't quite as . . . captivating . . . in his current state."

She started to laugh.

Grace joined in. Apparently, what Mary Lee said was some kind of joke.

Mary Lee and Grace continued to talk. The conversation revolved around things that had happened at previous parties.

Grace—Ms. Emerald—had gotten tipsy and eaten over a dozen shrimp cocktails. ("I had to carry you back to your limousine!"). Mary Lee—Ms. Opaline—had had a wardrobe malfunction. ("Why didn't you tell me sooner? That waiter fell in love, though, didn't he?").

And so on and so forth.

I moved away from the conversation and whispered to Antoine and Kimberly, "You notice none of their old stories take place outside of this building?"

"She hasn't said Grace's name even once," Kimberly added.

"The masks," I said. "Mary Lee knows the person who usually wears that mask. She can't tell that Grace isn't her."

"Magic?" Antoine asked.

I nodded. "That or a head injury."

"Why can we recognize each other?" Kimberly asked.

I shrugged. "I don't know."

There were a few possibilities. We would have to work through them.

As we spoke, Chris came over and said, "My Gut Instinct trope is all over the place. Stay on your toes."

As if we were relaxing.

"You two need to go exploring while we still have time in the Party phase," Chris said to Antoine and Kimberly. "I'm not sure what Film Buffs do but go do that. If you find important information, get it back to Grace."

He had a point. Kimberly's Get a Room trope was exceedingly useful, but they couldn't exactly use it with me around. I was a bit of a third wheel.

Chris found his way across the party, soon chatting up a beautiful woman who showed up on the red wallpaper as Miss Forget-Me-Not. Her mask looked just like the flower.

Deciding to try and be useful, I looked at what Location Scout was telling me about the mansion. The answer was: not much. Location Scout was Savvy based, which meant that our enemy in this storyline must have a high Savvy and was all but canceling out my ability. I could see the ballroom as a filming location. There was an aquarium room, apparently. There was also a myriad of rooms in the basement that were filming locations, but I couldn't see their proper names. I could also tell that over a dozen rooms were simply labeled as guest bedrooms, but they were grouped together on the list, so they must not have been that important.

That was it.

I was going to feel pretty stupid when the only piece of information I could bring back to Grace to help her solve whatever mystery was afoot was that there was an aquarium. Unless a fish was the killer, that probably wasn't going to be very useful.

As I stood there pretending to sip on a glass of champagne, someone across the room called out, "Mr. Gray Amber!"

It was a portly fellow wearing a yellow mask going by the name of Mr. Buttercup. He made a poor choice when he chose his mask. I waved back, and Mr. Buttercup didn't bother coming to talk to me. I breathed a sigh of relief.

As I walked around the party, listening to the classical music played live by a group of masked musicians, more people waved to me, and some greeted me with my fake name.

"Mr. Gray Amber, nice seeing you!" one gentleman said. "I was beginning to think that you had forgotten about us in the hustle and bustle of that merger you're going through."

"Never," I said.

"Mr. Gray Amber," a woman named Ms. Iris said as I passed by. I greeted her in kind.

After I had made another round of the room, I started to regret that I had not received any tropes that were useful in social situations. I didn't have any tropes that could help gain information from the NPCs, but I did have some Moxie, meaning I *could* just talk to them. The thought of it made my head swirl.

Note to self: get an exploration trope so that you don't have to talk to people.

I was much more useful exploring with Oblivious Bystander. I couldn't use my sunglasses and put up my hood because I was wearing a tux, but the mask was bulky, so it might prevent someone to the side from catching my eye line.

I did have my cassette player. I would need to look around and see if it was the right era for that technology to exist. So far, the most technologically advanced thing I had seen since starting the storyline had been the limousine itself, but that wasn't useful. I needed to look in the rooms around the ballroom for a television or a computer or some sign that using my Walkman wouldn't be breaking character.

I eyed the exits. As I did, I saw Kimberly and Antoine sneaking off. I silently wished them luck on their exploration. And then I realized how funny it was out of context to wish them luck as they snuck out of the party for some alone time.

On-screen.

"What has you smiling?" a woman's voice sounded from beside me.

I was not happy to go on-screen. I was counting on being out of sight for most of the movie.

I turned to see a woman called "Mrs. Cloudburst." She was an attractive woman with long brown hair. She wore a dark gray and dark blue mask with an array of raindrop-shaped beads hanging from it.

"Young love," I said honestly.

"It is the best, isn't it?"

"That's what I've heard."

"You know it's not too late now," Mrs. Cloudburst said. "We are as young as the night. Call me Ms. Cloudburst."

"Hello, Mrs. Cloudburst. They call me Mr. Gray Amber."

"It's Ms., not Mrs.," Mrs. Cloudburst said with a coy smile. "Have you ever been to the western tower?"

Western tower? She must have been referring to the spires on top of the mansion.

"Can't say I have," I said. "I was thinking of taking a walk to try and get acquainted with the place. I always like to do a little exploring in places like this."

"Exploring by yourself is no fun," she said with a smile.

I shrugged. "But it's easier to not get caught."

Mrs. Cloudburst let out a hearty laugh. "We'll just have to risk it," she said as she grabbed my arm and started pulling me toward an exit.

At that moment, I realized she had a very different idea of what we were talking about than I did. I noticed another pair of party guests—neither that I recognized—were leaving the ballroom together. *That* was what kind of place this was. No wonder there were so many guest rooms.

Still, with Kimberly using Looks Don't Last, I was unlikely to be in danger. That was another benefit of having a trope like that in play. It freed players up to take risks. I didn't need Oblivious Bystander if I had an NPC with me as a cover story. Once I got my bearings, I could sneak away and do some real investigating.

Mrs. Cloudburst gave me quite the tour of the mansion. The place looked like a Clue board come to life. I was surprised that we needed to take a detective into this story to make it a mystery. There was a conservatory and a gentlemen's parlor, a library with a study, and much, much more. There were trinkets and curios covering every square inch of available space. If we were to loot this place after we finished the storyline, we would make a fortune selling our haul at shops around town.

"Look," Mrs. Cloudburst said, pointing to an open door we passed on the third floor, "they have an old-fashioned sleeping porch. I love houses with sleeping porches."

As we walked, my Location Scout ability started to fill up with new locations. Maybe talking to people wasn't so bad.

Eventually, she took me over to a large bookcase on the first floor and pulled on one of the books, and the cabinet swung open to reveal a winding staircase. As it opened, Mrs. Cloudburst ushered me forward toward the stairs. I started to get nervous. Being out in the open with her was one thing, but in a secluded area, things could get rough.

"Hurry," she said. She pointed to a large wooden door that was reinforced with large strips of iron. "We aren't supposed to use this and the entrance to the wine cellar is right there. Do you want us to get caught?"

"No," I said. The wine cellar must have been pretty high traffic.

She grabbed my hand and dragged me up the staircase, giggling like a schoolgirl. The bookcase closed behind us. We made it to the top to find a small door. She looked over at me and opened it.

Inside, I saw a room with a few pieces of furniture, a small bathroom, and a large bed. There were windows on all four sides of the room, each labeled with one of the cardinal directions.

She pulled me into the room with a smile and shut the door.

Off Screen.

Suddenly, her behavior changed. She let go of my arm and walked over to the window labeled with a large *S*.

She gestured for me to follow.

As I did, I saw what she was looking at. The storm.

In the distance, a large black storm hovered over the area that must have contained Carousel.

The storyline had just managed to make me forget about Anna and Camden.

Mrs. Cloudburst looked concerned. That puzzled me. I thought NPCs knew everything that was going on.

I was Off Screen. No way I could break character.

"The Apocalypse?" I asked.

She looked at me and paused, thinking of the right words.

"Don't worry. It won't make it past the mountains." She said the line like she was telling me, but her facial expressions made it look like she was asking.

"No," I said. "I don't think so."

She nodded her head.

"You've never seen this one before?"

She shook her head and looked back out the window. The expression of worry never left her face.

Some of the veterans insisted that NPCs were not real. I wasn't sure. Here I was in a room with a woman who had, to the best of my understanding, pretended to seduce me so that she could ask me whether she was safe or not. Just like all the NPCs who had been forced by the script to stand and watch as the black snow approached, she was afraid of what the Apocalypse would mean for her.

The funny thing was, I didn't actually know if she was a standard NPC or an enemy. She might try to kill me in a few hours.

There appeared to be limits to what different NPCs were told in their scripts.

"Some people close to me got trapped in it," I said. The words caught in my throat, and I had to keep myself from crying.

Mrs. Cloudburst reached out and gave me a hug.

She started to mess with her hair, and she unbuttoned one of the buttons on her dress. She went back to the bathroom and looked in the mirror to hastily apply a new layer of lipstick. Afterward, she returned to me and loosened my bow tie just a bit so that it wasn't perfectly straight, and she pulled up on my shirt so it wasn't tucked in just right. Then she ruffled my hair.

She was getting us ready for the next scene. We needed to come out of the tower looking like we had just fooled around.

"Cristobal's speech should be soon. You know he would hate for us to miss it, don't you, Mr. Gray Amber?"

I didn't know anything, but the character my character was pretending to be would.

"Of course," I said.

"We had better not miss it," she said and kissed the collar of my white shirt, decorating it with a red lip-shaped stain.

CHAPTER TEN

MR. EVERGREEN IN THE BALLROOM WITH THE KNIFE

Mrs. Cloudburst and I ran through the hallways, laughing and stumbling about like drunk idiots. She was a great actress. If I didn't know better, I would think she was actually enjoying herself. Following her lead, I think I was putting on a pretty good performance.

We were on- and off-screen throughout our time together in that scene. I tried not to focus on it too much so that I didn't get too anxious.

"What year is it?" I asked with a laugh. It was an odd question to ask, but I still wasn't sure. The rooms had electricity, but that was the only piece of technology I could use to narrow things down. I couldn't use my Walkman with Oblivious Bystander until I knew.

I pretended to swig champagne from a bottle that Mrs. Cloudburst had taken from the ballroom.

Mrs. Cloudburst laughed. "I know, it can be difficult to keep track of, can't it? You'll get used to it. It's 1992. It can be strange how time flies."

She got quiet momentarily, and I could see that her mind went elsewhere. But only for a moment.

"I've never been good with dates," I said.

"I don't think you're doing so bad."

I couldn't see her script, but I could see that she had tons of lines that guys wait their whole lives to hear. She made me feel strong, smart, and desirable in a few short scenes.

But I had a job to do.

"Tell me about Cristobal," I said. She had used his name earlier, and it sounded like he was in charge.

She laughed.

"Quite the enigma, isn't he?" she asked. "He hasn't come to Carousel in over a decade. He travels around the world to all of the society's other gatherings. They say he leaves a trail of adoring women and angry husbands everywhere he goes."

She spun around, pulling me down the hallway. All at once, the movement stopped. She put her face close to mine and said quietly, "But that's not what you want to know, is it?"

"I wasn't looking for his travel itinerary, if that's what you mean," I said. "I just want your opinion of him."

"I have the highest opinion of him. I owe everything to him. Like many others, I follow him when he moves to a new place. I've shipped myself across oceans and continents just to be near him. He's the most powerful man in the world. I'm sure most members feel the same. Don't you?"

"Of course," I said.

"We're not together in *that* way," she said, "if that's what you were thinking. He holds no flame for me—at least, not recently."

I got this strange sense that she held one for him.

Perhaps I had pushed too far. Chris had buffed my Moxie with his Just off a Win trope, which boosted my highest stat. Since my Moxie and Savvy were tied, the buff was divided among them. If I pushed too hard, I might not be able to recover. It's not like I had any natural talent for negotiating around human emotion.

I decided to change the subject.

"Now, where is this aquarium I keep hearing about?"

Mrs. Cloudburst flashed a smile.

The aquarium was massive. It contained fish of every variety, but they all had one thing in common: they were beautiful and elegant and swam around that tank like dancers.

"Which one is your favorite?" Mrs. Cloudburst asked.

I looked at the fish. There were dozens, maybe hundreds.

"The blue one with the gray," I said.

She scanned through the aquarium. "Where's that one?"

"Right there," I said, pointing to her mask.

She playfully hit my arm.

"R—Mr. Gray Amber?" someone asked from the door to the aquarium room.

I turned to see Kimberly and Antoine. I was relieved to see that I could still tell who they were despite their masks, though something in my mind was fighting me on it. It was as if the magic of the masks was trying to reassert itself.

"Hey, Ms. Swan Song and Mr. Moonrock," I said. "This is Ms. Cloudburst."

They looked from me to her and seemed very surprised.

"We were just on our way back to the ballroom," I said. "Stopped here for a look at the fish."

Antoine coughed. "We should go. It's getting about that time."

I checked the Plot Cycle. It was nearing First Blood.

"Cristobal's speech!" Mrs. Cloudburst said suddenly. "It's going to be any minute. We need to go!"

She pulled me toward the door and past Antoine and Kimberly. As she did, Antoine gave me a look that said something like, "What have you been doing with her?"

I shrugged my shoulders as we ran back toward the ballroom.

Back in the ballroom, more guests were there than when I left. There must have been at least a hundred members. It was hard to imagine how there were this many elite rich folks in Carousel, but from what Mrs. Cloudburst had said, it sounded like many followed the group's enigmatic leader around, so many of these might not actually have been from Carousel within the story.

It took us a while to find Grace and Chris. Partially because of the masks they were wearing and partially because of how many people there were in that ballroom.

It turned out that we had arrived approximately five minutes before Cristobal was to make an appearance. The crowd was electric. These partygoers were thrilled about the arrival of their leader.

The ballroom didn't have a stage, so I wasn't sure where he was going to show up. It had a strange area in the corner that was closed off by ornate room dividers, but none of the party guests were casting their attention in that direction.

The lights went dark. Smoke started to rise from the center of the room. The party guests quickly backed away from the large circle inscribed into the wood floor. The smoke continued rising until it got so thick that I could not see anything on the other side.

"I love it when he does this!" Mrs. Cloudburst said, giddy with excitement.

As quickly as the smoke rose, it started to fade. The band started to play music announcing the arrival.

Moments later, as the smoke started to settle, a man and a woman could be seen standing in the middle of the ballroom. They hadn't been there before.

Both of them were very striking. The woman was beautiful. The man looked like he was pulled from the cover of a romance novel. He had long, flowing hair and wore his shirt almost completely unbuttoned to expose his chest.

Only the woman wore a mask.

Before me was the man known as Cristobal. The woman he was with was called "Mrs. Midnight" on the red wallpaper.

<table>
<tr><td colspan="2" align="center">CRISTOBAL
THE STRINGS ATTACHED</td></tr>
<tr><td>Plot Armor: 60</td><td></td></tr>
<tr><td colspan="2" align="center">Tropes</td></tr>
<tr><td>QUICK CHANGE ARTIST</td><td>This villain can change into and out of their disguise without being seen or getting caught.</td></tr>
<tr><td>NON-COMBAT-ANT</td><td>This villain cannot be attacked until they attack the player or are otherwise identified as hostile. Attacking them will not be effective, nor will it change the story. It will cause the player to go Off Screen for a time.</td></tr>
<tr><td>BOTTOMLESS BAG OF TRICKS</td><td>The villain has so many different in-universe abilities that they can employ new abilities in the Finale without needing to establish them in the narrative.</td></tr>
<tr><td>FATE WORSE THAN DEATH</td><td>This villain does not want to kill their victims, though, in the end, they will wish they had. Victims are Written Off instead of killed.</td></tr>
<tr><td>WHICH ONE DO I SHOOT?</td><td>Players will not be able to differentiate the villain from other characters through the mere use of observation, insight tropes, or common sense. However, these combined with clever plans and an understanding of lore may suffice.</td></tr>
<tr><td colspan="2" align="center">13 additional tropes not perceptible</td></tr>
</table>

Cristobal received a standing ovation that lasted for eight minutes. That was not an exaggeration. The people in that room loved that man.

Mrs. Cloudburst was no exception. She screamed, cheered, and clapped, and it was everything I could do to match pace so that I didn't look like I was the odd one out.

"My people," Cristobal said whenever there was a gap in the cheering. He had a thick accent that was vaguely European, but I couldn't place it beyond that.

At those two words, the ovation continued for another two minutes.

Finally, the room settled down enough that Cristobal could speak.

"My people," he said. "It brings joy to my heart that I can be here with you today. I am enraptured by the beauty in this room. On any other day, I would stand here and speak about the abundance and happiness that each of us has received as members of the society."

He paused so that people could cheer.

"The decanter vitae overflows with prosperity, beauty, and love, does it not?"

Several people in the crowd started to cheer, "Decanter vitae!" over and over again.

Cristobal held up his hands to silence them.

"I wish I could stand here and share stories of our wonderful lives with you, but as many of you have heard, my dear friend Mr. Midnight has passed. It pains us all that someone who has lived such a beautiful life must leave it behind."

Gasps spread throughout the crowd.

"Oh my god, how could that happen?" Mrs. Cloudburst asked. She sounded truly distraught. "His poor wife."

The woman who had arrived with Cristobal, Mrs. Midnight, looked dreary and sad at the reveal. It didn't take much of a leap to realize that Mr. and Mrs. Midnight were married.

"There has been talk from members of the society who did not love him well enough that I should choose a Third to replace him."

He spat on the ground. This elicited more gasps from the women in the crowd.

"This man was my friend for much of my life," Cristobal declared. "He has only been dead for these three weeks and it is demanded that we already need a new Third? I am disgusted. I retch at the thought of betraying my friend's memory."

People booed in agreement.

Cristobal's speech continued on. He spoke of his many adventures and the many parties he had been to. He walked around the room, giving women—and the occasional man—kisses on their cheeks.

"Cristobal!" a woman with a butterfly mask cried out. "Cristobal!"

She was "Ms. Monarch" on the red wallpaper.

The moment that Cristobal saw her, he walked across the room and embraced her.

"She's so lucky," Mrs. Cloudburst whispered.

"Cristobal," Ms. Monarch said, "I spoke to Mr. Midnight before his death. I've been trying to tell you, but I could not get a hold of you."

Cristobal looked at her curiously. "You have information on his death?"

She nodded her head vigorously. "That's what I've been trying to tell you! I tried to send you messages, but I was unable to find you!"

Cristobal started to fall forward. A dozen hands reached out to catch him.

"This is too much," Cristobal said. "I need to rest. His passing weighs on me so." Cristobal looked pitifully at the ground.

Mrs. Midnight ran to his side.

"Cristobal," Mrs. Midnight said in an accent similar to his, "you must not strain yourself."

She looked up at the partygoers.

"He bears the strain of the current. Without a Third, he is weakened."

Cristobal stood up straight again with great effort. "I must rest, but I cannot stand the thought of being away from you," he said to the guests. "I have asked to have a small bed brought into the room so that I may bask in your presence as I rest. Please send me your strength."

After he said that, the guests lifted their hands upward for a few moments. "Decanter vitae," they said in chorus.

As Cristobal limped away from the center of the ballroom, he said something to Ms. Monarch and held up a hand to her. She nodded.

Mrs. Midnight hauled Cristobal behind the screens I had seen earlier in the corner of the room. The screens were a poor cover. I could see them through the gaps. He lay on the bed. Mrs. Midnight sat next to him and stroked his long hair. She then bent down and kissed him on the lips before leaving to rejoin us on the floor.

As she came back, she gestured to the band, who started playing again.

"That poor man does so much for us," Mrs. Cloudburst said. "No one appreciates his sacrifice for us."

And she seemed so normal before that Cristobal fellow came along.

The night wore on, and eventually, people started dancing again. Mrs. Midnight stood in the center of the ballroom, receiving condolences from the guests.

The needle on the Plot Cycle inched closer to First Blood. It could happen at any minute.

Kimberly was absolutely terrified. She refused to leave Antoine's arms so much that people started noticing.

"Were you close to Mr. Midnight?" one of them asked eagerly.

"Yes," Kimberly managed to squeak out.

Mrs. Cloudburst insisted on dancing eventually. I did my best to follow along with what she was doing but soon noticed that her eyes always shifted toward the screens in front of Cristobal's sleeping body.

It was hard to pay attention to the festivities while we waited for the bomb to go off.

But soon enough, it did.

A scream echoed through the ballroom. The musicians stopped short.

Ms. Monarch, who stood in the exact same place as when she last spoke to Cristobal, was yelling and shrieking in terror.

"No, don't!" she screamed. "Don't, please!"

She didn't move but put up her arms as if defending herself from an assailant.

But there was no assailant.

"It's—" she screamed, pausing as something appeared to strike her in her chest, though no object or wound was visible. "Mr. Evergr—"

She was struck again.

And again.

She screamed bloody murder, but I saw no blood nor weapons of any kind.

"It's Mr. Evergreen!" she screamed out in her dying gasp.

Then, she went limp.

She didn't fall to the ground. No, her arms went limp, and she bent forward, and she stood there emotionless, gurgling.

"She's been murdered!" Mrs. Midnight cried out.

"Who's down there?" Cristobal screamed as he lumbered across the floor toward her. "Someone went down there and killed her!"

Mrs. Cloudburst held me close and asked, "Who would kill one of us? Can you see anything? I'm too far away and I'm nearly blind."

At first, I thought she meant she was too short to see Ms. Monarch, but then I realized she wasn't even looking in that direction. In fact, dozens of people were not looking at Ms. Monarch. They were looking in other directions very intently.

Cristobal sent a man, Mr. Red Rock, to go check on Ms. Monarch somewhere else, ordering everyone else to stay in the ballroom.

People in the crowd were questioning who Mr. Evergreen was. No one seemed to know.

Mr. Red Rock returned some minutes later holding a silver knife covered in blood. He had it wrapped in a handkerchief.

"Someone snuck down there and stabbed her!" Cristobal raged. "Who did this?"

"I didn't find anyone down there, sir," Mr. Red Rock said.

"We will figure out who did this," Cristobal yelled. "Mark my words: we will find who did this!"

Antoine and Kimberly were looking at me like I would know what was happening. My theory was quickly being formed, but we didn't dare discuss it in front of the other guests.

One thing was for sure: Kimberly got lucky. First Blood must have been scripted for Ms. Monarch to be killed. The needle on the Plot Cycle had moved over to Rebirth. Kimberly was passed over and didn't have to die first.

It didn't make a difference to me. I was still next.

CHAPTER ELEVEN

A FAIR PLAY MURDER MYSTERY

The crowd grew into an uproar as party guests began panicking. Many wanted desperately to get downstairs.

"We need to go down there, Cristobal," one man, Mr. Oakheart, yelled over the crowd. "The killer must still be down there! I haven't felt any presence trigger the seal but Mr. Red Rock when he went to check on the body."

"Calm," Cristobal cried out. "Mr. Red Rock, did you see anyone else down there when you went to check on Ms. Monarch?"

"No, sir, I didn't," Mr. Red Rock said. "But I didn't stick around too long. It's possible the killer found a place to hide before I got to the body. There's no way to know."

"How could someone get into the cask room without permission?" a woman cried out.

"That's right," another cried out. "What about the consensus of the living body? How could they get in and out through those protections?"

As they asked questions, the crowd continued to work itself up into an uproar.

"If they're still there, we could all be killed!" one of the women realized aloud.

And just like that, a room of polite, concerned citizens became a mob. The team and I just did our best not to get run over.

Off Screen.

As soon as we went Off Screen, we were pulled aside by Grace and Chris.

"Pay attention to everything the NPCs say," Grace said the moment we had separated from the mob.

Many of the NPCs had run off down the halls. Some stayed behind and watched us. It was like they were waiting for something in the script; Mrs. Cloudburst, Jack Goforth, and Ms. Opaline—AKA Mary Lee Parrish—were among them.

"Anything could be important," she continued. "How many murder mysteries have you all done?"

We looked at each other for a moment.

"Just one," Antoine said.

"Don't tell me you've only done Ranger Danger?"

Antoine nodded.

Grace took a deep breath. "Stay calm and listen. We don't know how long we have between scenes."

Antoine, Kimberly, and I nodded our heads.

"This is a murder mystery first and foremost," Grace said. "There's magic involved with this one, which means that without some constraint, anyone could have killed the victim. Luckily, Carousel only does *fair play* murder mysteries. That means that as time goes by, the rules of the mystery will slowly be revealed, usually through NPC dialogue. Do you understand?"

I nodded.

Kimberly didn't look as certain.

"Everything we learn for the rest of Rebirth and maybe even a little longer than that will be important for figuring out the mystery. We will be given enough information to understand what happened. In fact, collectively, we may already have the information we need, however obscured." She eyed each of us, making sure that we understood. "Now tell me everything that you know."

Kimberly and Antoine started to relay the information they had learned during the party.

"We found this hidden room," Kimberly said. "It was really old; everything was covered in dust. It looked like nobody had been in there in decades. We found this." She reached her hands over to Antoine, who retrieved a small book from his jacket pocket. She took the book from him and handed it to Grace. "It fell off a shelf and opened up right in front of us, so we figured it must be important. It's got some weird pictures in it."

The book turned out to be a photo album, and its pictures told a story.

I did my best to get a good look as Grace flipped through it. The first picture in the album had three people in it. I recognized two of them, one of them for certain. It was Cristobal and Mrs. Midnight. The third man wore a mask identical to Mrs. Midnight. I assumed that he must have been Mr. Midnight. It looked like their bodies were the same, but the masks could have been tricking me. Cristobal, though, didn't have a mask.

"Well, that confirms it," Grace said. "He doesn't look like he's aged a day."

The photograph had a small inscription under it that read, "June 1st, 1906."

"That was almost a hundred years ago," I said. "It's 1992 right now."

Grace flipped the page. The next picture was very similar. It had the same three people in it. The only difference was that they were standing in front of a building under construction—the mansion itself.

And they weren't alone.

Behind them stood twelve other people, both men and women, each wearing masquerade masks similar to the ones guests had that night.

"November 12, 1922," Grace read.

She turned to the next page. The mansion was fully built in this one, and the twelve people behind them had grown to several dozen.

"1938."

She turned the page again.

"1945."

As she turned the pages, it became obvious that the people behind them were changing. Not only were they getting more numerous, growing to the numbers of the present day, but they were getting older. More and more grayheads started to show up in the pictures. Soon, there wasn't a person in the picture under sixty, if you didn't count the three up front.

"1972," Grace read off one of the more recent pictures.

This one had even more people, but something was different. There were no more old people in the background. It was Cristobal, Mr. and Mrs. Midnight, and a collection of young, fit people dressed in tuxedos and dancing gowns.

"Must have been after the time they started doing the body-controlling thing," I said, looking over at the NPC that was still leaning over like a rag doll after the person controlling her had been killed. "The lady I was talking to said something about having to ship herself over oceans and continents. I'm guessing that she was being literal. I assume that the old folks from these pictures are still alive, and most are downstairs."

"I think similarly," Grace said. "Remember, just because this story has magical nonsense in it does not mean it isn't a straightforward murder mystery. If you find NPCs operating under an assumption, then you need to explore that assumption. It won't always be true, but it will always be enlightening."

Turning to me, she asked, "Riley, did you get anything?"

Antoine gave me a weird look that I didn't understand.

"Yeah, I could see some of that guy's tropes, the one without the mask. He's so high level that I couldn't even see half of them, though." I told them all about the tropes I had seen, including the one that worried me the most: Bottomless Bag of Tricks.

"Oh yeah," I added, "there are a lot of guest bedrooms upstairs and a bunch of rooms downstairs that are important, I think, and there's also an aquarium room, but my Location Scout ability didn't get much more than that."

"I was meaning to ask: How are we supposed to beat that guy when his Plot Armor is sixty? Are you going to be able to beat him by yourself?" Antoine asked, looking at Chris.

"I've fought worse," Chris said. "We may have some luck in that department, though. Riley said that this storyline was tough but not the worst. Right, Riley?"

I nodded. "It wasn't the highest difficulty. I don't know how we're up against someone that strong."

"Well, if Riley's right," Chris said, "we may be in luck. Enemies that have a suspiciously high level for the storyline they're in usually don't have to be fought, or else they have some really easily exploitable weakness. In a way, his high level could be a blessing, but I'm not sure how yet."

The conversation went on, and much of it involved Grace reiterating her points about us paying attention to what NPCs were saying.

Apparently, a murder mystery could really go off the rails if it wasn't for the fact that the mystery would continue to be refined further and further as the story went along until eventually, the player would know all the limitations. And hopefully, if they were paying attention, they would know exactly which threads to pull. The problem was that clues often presented themselves for a time and then disappeared forever. Finding them before they did was crucial.

"If we were going for perfection," Grace said, "we might try an escape attempt because our characters would be scared right about now. Of course, it wouldn't work for some convoluted reason. We can't escape this storyline. The attempt would end up getting one of us killed—"

"Or turned into a puppet," Chris added.

"Or, more likely, turned into a puppet," Grace agreed. "I say we just skip that part and focus on solving the mystery. With three under-leveled players, I don't feel like getting fancy. Sound good?"

The three of us nodded.

After a little more coaching and encouragement from Chris and Grace, it was time to move on.

On-screen.

Mr. Flamingo, AKA Jack Goforth, approached us in a hurry.

"What the hell is going on?" he asked. "Is this some freaky murder-mystery rich-person bullshit?" He gestured over at the husk of Ms. Monarch, who still stood limp, like a puppet. "Is this a story for the magazine or my therapist?" His eyes were wide with frenzy.

"Let's not panic yet, Jack," Grace said. "There has to be a logical explanation for this."

"A woman told me I had a nice body earlier, Grace. Then she asked me if I chose it or if it was chosen for me."

"Jack may be right," Chris said. "Did you see these pictures that Antoine and Kimberly found? Weird stuff."

"What pictures?" Grace and Jack asked at the same time.

Of course, Grace knew exactly what pictures he was referring to, but now that we were on-screen, we basically had to go over everything we had just been over from the point of view of the characters we were playing.

That didn't take too long. Luckily, Grace, Jack, and Chris covered most of it. But I did get a few lines in.

"You're not saying what I think you're saying," Jack asked.

"I'm saying everything up here is a puppet and that the real people are downstairs," I said.

"Why did we bring this kid? You're freaking me out," Jack said. "Okay, I snuck into the party in one of the catering vans. I think I could get us back to it and we could find a way out of here. What do you say?"

"Jack, we came here to find a story. We may have just found one. You want to leave now?" Grace asked.

"We work for a celebrity gossip magazine, Grace!" Jack said. "We do not handle things like this!"

"I thought you said we were more than that."

"I was very wrong. We are tabloid journalists. Let's go home."

Grace shook her head. "I need to figure out what's going on here, Jack. Weren't you a serious investigative reporter once?"

"I have a tendency to exaggerate," Jack said. "Even if we did stay, what's the story? Rich people are body-swapping in the Carousel Hills? There is no amount of proof that could substantiate that."

"I need to know," Grace said. "And you are going to help me. You are technically qualified whether you would deny it or not. Now, we need to go over and see what these people are discussing downstairs. Come with me and play it cool. You're Jack Goforth. Pretending to be rich and important is something you've practiced your whole life. You'll be fine."

Grace then walked away from the group and toward the direction the NPCs had traveled.

Truthfully, as Grace had explained, we couldn't escape. We didn't know if escape was a viable win condition. Even if it was, we couldn't do it until the Finale. The only way forward was to solve the mystery and, as per Grace's trope, "expose" the truth, whatever that meant.

As we went forward, the Off Screen light triggered sporadically as the camera captured footage of us and random NPCs making our way through the crowds to get downstairs.

"Do you really think someone is killing us down there?" Mrs. Cloudburst asked in a panic after rejoining me further down the hallway.

"I have no idea," I said. "Don't worry. I'm sure we'll be fine."

The destination all of the NPCs were headed toward turned out to be the door that Mrs. Cloudburst had referred to as the wine cellar. The door had not been opened. Cristobal and Mrs. Midnight stood in front of it.

"Enough!" Cristobal screamed. He lifted his hands, and a bolt of neon blue electricity shot from his fingertips, making a wicked crackle and getting the guests' attention.

Jack gave Grace a wide-eyed stare but stood firm.

"The cask room cannot be entered or exited without our permission. Flooding our way in will serve no purpose. Mr. Red Rock said that he saw no one, and I would like to believe him," Cristobal said. "I understand you are all worried about your bodies. That is reasonable. I tell you the truth: we will find the person who did this even if we have to search every square inch of the mansion to do it."

He continued trying to placate the crowd with mixed levels of success.

"Now he likes Mr. Red Rock," Mary Lee Parrish said under her breath to Grace, but also loud enough for everyone around to hear.

We had stayed toward the back of the crowd.

"What do you mean by that?" Grace asked.

"Oh, nothing," Mary Lee said.

After a few seconds, she continued anyway. "Fifteen years ago, Cristobal tried to exile Red Rock from the society. Red Rock had brought some outsiders in. Cristobal was furious. If Mr. Midnight hadn't stepped in to save his neck, Red Rock wouldn't be here. Now Red Rock's punishment is to be the steward of the Carousel mansion for the next forty years or so. Suddenly Cristobal trusts Red Rock?"

"People change," Mrs. Cloudburst said. "Cristobal is very understanding. He's just protective."

"I never said to the contrary," Mary Lee said. "Guess we wouldn't be surprised if Red Rock makes a move to be the Third. Seeing as they're best friends now."

Mrs. Cloudburst turned to me. "That woman is so obnoxious."

"Yeah, well . . . Maybe she's just stressed from the situation," I said.

"Maybe," Mrs. Cloudburst said. "But the Third must be chosen by the collective. Cristobal knows how important the rules are. For her to suggest someone could sway his judgment . . . It's infuriating."

"I hear you," I said.

"The Third will be a knowledgeable sorcerer from the collective. Not some halfwit who would expose our secrets to the world."

"Maybe you should be the Third," I said.

She smiled and playfully smacked my arm. "I am not a knowledgeable sorcerer. Truthfully, I only joined so that I could keep living, continue the ride, you know. I never really cared for much else."

"Same," I said. I just kept agreeing with her, and she kept telling me things. I wondered if that was how women were in real life.

"Though, it would be nice to be walking around in my own body," she said. "I really was beautiful once, you know."

That was a strange thing to say. Most of the people at the party were, objectively, very good-looking—Mrs. Cloudburst, or at least her host body, included.

"You still a—" I started to say. "Wait. So, the new Third does get to keep their original body?"

This was an obvious extension of the photo book that Kimberly found. The main three didn't need hosts because their bodies didn't age.

Mrs. Cloudburst looked at me like I was an idiot. "Of course. All of the Three do. They don't have to vegetate in casks like we do."

"I've never really thought about it before," I said, hoping I hadn't blown my cover.

Having an NPC friend was quite useful. I would have to try it more often. The more we learned about the strange puppet spell, the better we could solve the murder.

I was certain I would learn a lot more because, as we finished talking, Cristobal started letting people into the wine cellar to check on their bodies.

It was time to meet the society face to face.

CHAPTER TWELVE

THE CASKS AND THE CRIME SCENE

As we stood outside the cellar door, the crowds of masked guests continued to rage and demand to be allowed in to see their bodies.

Some on the periphery of the crowd seemed to be less worried about their fate. They casually stared on and mocked those who panicked. Others stayed away from the main crowd simply so that they could gossip with each other, but they spoke in such hushed whispers that I wasn't able to pick up on the scuttlebutt.

Eventually, a group of people including both Cristobal and Mrs. Midnight left to go search the cellar for any trace of a killer. Many of those closest to the entrance claimed to be able to sense that no one had entered or exited during the time frame of the murder who wasn't accounted for.

"How could someone murder her and leave without being flagged by the seal?" one man, Mr. Oakheart, wondered aloud.

By my estimation, there were all manner of lesser sorcerers among the group. I couldn't see their levels, but by the way they spoke on the matter, I could see that many of them were educated on whatever magical spell protected the cask room below.

I tried to listen intently as Grace had instructed. The things the NPCs were saying were supposed to help narrow the possibilities down. It was difficult when mystery mixed with fantasy. If you didn't know the magic system, how were you supposed to guess the many ways that the murder could have been committed?

Grace was less daunted.

"It appears that until we get confirmation to the contrary," she said, "the murderer did not enter the cask room after the most recent casks were loaded into it, and somehow, they did not leave after the murder. Keep your ears and eyes open for information that could contradict that; otherwise, we must assume that it is true."

Grace seemed to be very confident in her understanding of the nature of Carousel's mysteries.

Naturally, I was more skeptical. In most storylines, it was fully possible for you to miss crucial information, but from the way she spoke about murder mysteries, it sounded as if Carousel would intentionally provide the rules of how the puzzle worked. The way Grace described it, we weren't supposed to spend the story learning how the society's magic worked on a deep level. We only needed the basics.

In this case, we were just supposed to believe that the magical seal had not been broken. As I stood there and waited, I got more and more nervous, and it became more difficult to just trust an assumption like that. This directly clashed with my natural curiosity.

I started thinking that perhaps one of the sorcerers had magically floated a knife to kill the victim, but that wasn't possible, because the victim had seen her attacker and called him Mr. Evergreen.

That left one obvious possibility that I pondered as I walked back to Mrs. Cloudburst.

"Is it possible someone left their cask and murdered Ms. Monarch?" I asked as I approached her.

As soon as she heard me, she started to laugh as if that was the silliest thing she'd ever heard.

Was that my answer?

"I know this can be very frightening, but there's no reason to lose our heads," she said.

Earlier she had been the one freaking out, and now she was talking to me as if I was panicking. Of course, I couldn't know exactly why she had laughed at that suggestion unless I saw the casks that everyone had been talking about for myself.

Eventually, the next scene arrived as Cristobal and Mrs. Midnight proclaimed that the cask room was safe and that there were no unaccounted-for persons within that room.

"Come, my people," Cristobal said. Somehow, in the short duration between when I had first seen him and when he came from the cellar door, I noticed that he was visibly tired and sickly. His hair was greasy and thin, his eyes were dark, and his skin was clammy. "Come see for yourself that your bodies have been kept safe."

As everyone began moving down into the open cellar doors, I was vaguely reminded of being ushered forth into a dark ride at an amusement park. The difference was that I was terrified of what I was about to see. The glitz and the glamour of the storyline so far were not befitting of a true horror movie. I had spent the last few hours waiting for the other shoe to drop.

As we were led down into the cask room, I kept my eyes open for any passages that might lead in or out of the room, but I didn't find any. I knew for a fact that the mansion had hidden doors, but I wasn't sure how I was going to look for them in front of dozens upon dozens of enemies.

The stone steps down into the cask room were large, and as we went down, I noticed that something was missing from the stairway and from the room below: light sources.

There were no torches hanging on the walls to guide our steps. There were no collections of candles left burning to light the way. There were no modern lights of any kind that I could find, and yet, I was able to see. There wasn't much light to see with—the room was lit very dimly—and I couldn't figure out where the light was coming from. This was magic.

Once we reached the bottom, the entire group congregated in an open space where tables filled with strange ingredients and flasks of various sizes and shapes were kept. It reminded me of the Astralist's secret laboratory, except it took a definitive step toward the fantastical and away from the pseudo-science fiction of that story.

These weren't chemicals. These were potions—brews of a magical sort.

But the tables with all of their ingredients could not hold my attention for long. Opposite them was an opening to a large room that must have taken up much of the basement beneath the mansion.

Within it, stacked neatly in rows, were dozens if not hundreds of barrels. Some of the barrels were made of wood, others of shining copper, and still others of glass. The majority of them, however, were made of both wood and clay of some sort and were reinforced with bands of metal.

Other than that, their features were common with each other. They were about the size that I would expect a medium to large wine barrel to be—just big enough for the average human to get into. They had all sorts of copper tubing sticking out of them, which had been connected to a larger plumbing system that ran up and along the ceiling, all leading back to a large bubbling cauldron in the center of the room.

Another feature that the vast majority of these casks had was a glass viewing port like you might find on a ship. Just a round glass window riveted into the cask. Most of the glass windows were completely covered in debris, dust, and a strange green slime.

Because some of the casks were made of green glass, which was mostly see-through, I could roughly make out what was inside. They were bodies, of course.

Naked and contorted to fit their containers, the bodies had apparently been in the liquid for so long that they had lost many of the features that I would associate with the human body.

The skin was puffy and the limbs atrophied. They looked like those sideshow fetuses preserved in formaldehyde. I had seen something like this in a science class, but it had been a fetal pig.

These were grown humans. The glass was foggy, and it was difficult to see through the clouded liquid inside, but I got the distinct impression that these bodies were *very* old. Some of them had been inside their tanks for so long that their hair had grown to such a length that it covered entire portions of the cask.

The entire time I had been walking down the stairs, I had been afraid of one particular thing: the magical seal that was meant to keep people out of the room without consent from the masses.

I was an impostor, so depending on how that magical seal worked, it may or may not have let me inside the room. As I walked through an area at the entrance of the cask room to join the crowd, I felt a strange electrical pulse. I was afraid that I might be triggering some alarm, but, looking around, I saw that others also felt that pulse; they reacted to it like a chill up their spines.

This was meaningful, I thought. It meant that this magical seal did have weaknesses and that as long as the members of the society consented, one could enter. It did not matter if you were the person they thought you were. Informed consent was not needed.

I looked back toward Grace to see her walk through the electrical field, and as I did, she made eye contact with me and nodded. She understood.

That didn't solve the problem, though. Just because an impostor was able to get in and out of the seal, that did not mean that someone could get in and out without being detected. The sorcerers had been very clear that no one had entered or exited unaccounted for.

"Everyone, line up in front of your body so that we can get a good roll call," Mrs. Midnight said.

As soon as I heard that, I started to panic on the inside. I had no idea which of these bodies belonged to the real Mr. Gray Amber. Luckily, before I had a heart attack, I realized that each of the rows had been labeled with a color.

My mask was an orangish-gray color. So, I found the orange line and walked until I found a cask conveniently labeled "Gray Amber."

It just so happened that monarch butterflies, like the one Ms. Monarch's mask had been modeled after, were also orange. In fact, as I walked down the row, I saw that to my left was the green row, and far in front of me was the crime scene.

Mr. Gray Amber, whoever he was, must have been one of the wealthier members because his cask was made of sturdy metal and looked brand new. Of course, that could simply be because he was relatively new and the technology had evolved.

As I stood before him, it dawned on me that the real man I had been impersonating was literally right there in front of me unable to tell anyone that I was an impostor. That had been another fear of entering the cask room: perhaps our real counterparts would be able to open their casks and reveal our identities.

Mrs. Cloudburst had scoffed at my worries that someone could leave their cask, but I still wasn't sure if they were able to communicate. I quickly saw that that was not the case.

Mr. Gray Amber floated crumpled up inside of his cask. He didn't move. All I saw were the strange bubbles that came out of his nose as he breathed. Strange because he wasn't breathing in air. How was he breathing it out?

As I stared into the metal tank through the viewport, I noticed that one of his eyelids was starting to twitch and open just a slight amount. I was quick to turn around and put my back to the viewport. I didn't know if he could see out, but I wasn't going to risk it.

By my estimate, my pickled friend was in his late eighties or early nineties. With any luck, his eyesight in his real body might be poor.

Still, I found myself overcome with nerves.

I decided to study the crime scene a few casks down in order to distract myself. Because green was on the row next to orange, Grace—Ms. Emerald—was directly across from the crime scene. A perfect vantage point for the Detective.

The ground was wet with the liquid that had been inside Ms. Monarch's cask. Much of it had sloshed out as the killer attempted to pull her real body out of the tank in order to kill her. It was hard to look at the poor woman as she lay splayed out over the side of the tank.

Although not all of the casks were made of clay, they were all sealed with it. Inscriptions that I couldn't read had been etched into them before they dried. Ms. Monarch's seal had been destroyed when the killer opened her wooden cask.

After she had been pulled out partially, the killer slit her throat, which had bled down onto the ground and mixed with the liquid from her cask. Blood also flowed from her injured fingers. It appeared that she had tried to defend herself, but the killer's knife was too sharp and her body was too frail.

Her immortality had been cut short.

Ms. Monarch was so old that I could not even guess the age of her body.

After I surveyed the scene, I had to look away. It felt like a great violation to look at a dead body like that.

* * *

Not long after we got there, Mr. Red Rock arrived to cover the body with a sheet.

Cristobal and Mrs. Midnight stood near the crime scene and started asking witnesses if they had seen anything through their real bodies at the time of the murder.

"I didn't even notice at the time," one man said.

A woman nearby agreed. "When the murder was taking place, I don't remember seeing anything. In fact, I didn't see anything until Mr. Red Rock came down to check on the body. You have to understand my eyes haven't been good in fifty years."

The sentiments of the others in the area were similar. A room full of witnesses and no one saw a thing.

We stood there as more witnesses were interviewed. They asked Grace if she had seen anything, and she echoed what the others had said. I did the same a few minutes later.

Cristobal went through the cask room and asked each and every person whether they had seen anything or had any theories. We flickered on- and off-screen as it happened. While we waited, Grace examined the seal on her cask.

I turned and looked at the one on mine.

It was unbroken. I looked around the room and realized that every single cask had that same clay seal, and none that I could see had been broken. I was starting to see why Mrs. Cloudburst had laughed at my guess that someone had left their cask for the murder. If they had, they would surely be unable to reseal it. More than that, I started to wonder if any of these bodies even could leave their tanks willingly. They were so feeble.

This left an even more curious conundrum.

The killer had not left the room, assuming my understanding of the seals was correct. The people in the casks could not have done it without breaking their own seals. Ms. Monarch had seen her attacker but no one else had.

What did that leave? Teleportation? Perhaps the killer was a magical creation or had disguised themselves in the room.

All I could think of were numerous possible explanations, but as I looked at Grace, she was hiding a sly smile.

Had she figured it out?

CHAPTER THIRTEEN

WHO, WHY, AND HOW

As I waited for the interviews to end, I started to survey the bodies in the casks. Trope Master worked on them. As I looked around the room, I found that all of them were enemies. That made sense. It was unlikely that they would be NPCs. Body snatching pretty much ensures an evil alignment.

Unfortunately, they only had two or three tropes. Some were so old they would die with ease, apparently. One of their tropes appeared to block my ability to see anything more than that. Their Plot Armor ranged from standard NPC all the way up to fifty-one.

Oddly enough, I couldn't see any of their names, not even their colorful code names.

SOCIETY MEMBER	
Plot Armor: 3–51	
Tropes	

ON DEATH'S DOOR	This villain is nearly dead and exploiting their weakness will easily procure a victory.
DON'T WAKE THE BEAST	This villain is asleep or in a similar condition. They will not stir without outside intervention. Waking them will transform them into a more dangerous form that plays by different tropes.
DECORATIVE DANGER	This villain's presence is scene dressing. It would be best not to change that before the proper time comes.

Almost all of the Society Members had the On Death's Door trope, and all of them had both Don't Wake the Beast and Decorative Danger.

As I saw it, if I didn't "wake the beast," they would remain feeble test-tube terrors.

I hoped.

After everyone had been interviewed, the party guests started to filter back upstairs. Many chose to walk up and down the hallways in between the casks, double-checking to make sure that they were safe. For a time, I joined them.

I was able to confirm to the best of my ability that none of the seals had been broken. Again, we always ran the risk that some sorcerer might be able to reseal their cask from within it, but I had not run across any information that would confirm that.

Based on the framework that Grace had given us, we could trust that assumption. Carousel didn't want to make things easy, but it also had a movie to make, and watching players stumble around in the wrong direction for hours did not make good cinema. We were not there to dive deep into how the storyline's magic system worked; that was the subject matter of other types of stories. We could rely on certain, uncontested facts. Still, it was difficult for me to give up on the idea.

When I finally made it back to the row with "my" cask, I saw that Grace had struck up a conversation with a gentleman by the name of Mr. Pewter.

I drew close so that I could listen to what they were talking about.

"Of course, I was an engineer by trade before. It was how I made my millions," he said. "Are you familiar with locomotive lubrication? No, of course you don't want to talk about that; why am I asking? When I joined the society, learning how magic worked was a natural curiosity. I am quite the sorcerer in my own right. Well, I am learning the ropes. Say, have you seen the new rooms overlooking the pool?"

"No," Grace said. "Are they nice?"

"They are beautiful, truly beautiful. Not unlike yourself . . . Uh . . . Say"—he cleared his throat—"what would you say if I asked you to go back t—"

"Do you know anything about the magic of these casks? I find it all so confusing," Grace interjected. "I've been meaning to find a *real* sorcerer who could explain these to me. With recent events, I can't stand not knowing."

"Oh, of course. Yes, these casks are something else. Cristobal and Mr. Midnight designed them themselves. You're looking at new magic," he said, slapping the side of the nearest cask. "Oops, sorry," he whispered to the cask, apparently remembering that a person was inside of it.

"In the international world, these are very impressive. Designed off an ancient sorcerer's cogitation. Their special Draught of New Life does the job for you. Puts you in just the right mental state for the magic to work automatically and keeps you alive indefinitely. Genius. Truly."

"That's fascinating," Grace said.

Mr. Pewter smiled and nodded his head enthusiastically. "I've always thought so! For years they just tried to teach new members to do it the old-fashioned way, but it takes decades to learn, so . . . that didn't work." He cleared his throat again and continued. "I still think they should explain this to new members, but they told me that most people don't want to know the details given the . . . uncomfortable nature by which we get our new bodies. But how are we supposed to produce new sorcerers if they don't teach the basics?"

"That's a good question," Grace said. "You know a lot about this."

"Well, like I said, I was an engineer before I came aboard. And all magic really is is engineering. That's what I say. So, I was wondering if you might want to go see one of the rooms by the po—"

"You know what," Grace said. "I just remembered I'm supposed to meet my friends in the ballroom. It's hard to believe how forgetful I can be. Thank you for talking with me! I've really enjoyed it."

Mr. Pewter nodded. "Right, I'll, uh . . . see you on the dance floor."

Grace walked around him and left for the exit. I followed.

Mr. Pewter looked utterly disappointed.

Back in the ballroom, the band had started playing again, and some people had returned to dancing. I felt that was callous, considering someone had just been murdered, but these people had stolen innocent people's bodies and turned them into mind slaves. Cognitive dissonance was probably the only thing holding them together.

We took turns revealing everything that we had learned. In that regard, Grace won first prize.

"I know who did it, and I know how. I could probably guess why," she said. "There are two problems. I cannot reveal what I know until the Finale so that my Here's What Happened trope will function properly. The second problem is that we need evidence. Knowing what happened is only the first battle. We need to prove it. I want you to focus on evidence for motive. That is usually where Carousel likes to throw its curve balls. Without the motive, we can't win, so I want you to devote all of your efforts for the remainder of Rebirth toward figuring it out. It's possible that it's a standard motive—love triangle, power struggle; you understand. I need your help substantiating that."

"Wait," Kimberly asked. "If you can't tell us who did it, how are we supposed to find the motive?"

"If I'm right, we can probably guess *who* did it," Chris said. "We don't have many true suspects. The real mystery is the how and the why, and Grace has that half-finished already."

Grace nodded.

Grace's Here's What Happened trope would take the team Off Screen while she explained who the killer was. That could stop a killer from retaliating. I could understand her reluctance to ruin its potency, but I was frustrated that I wasn't allowed to know what had happened. If Chris was right and it was the obvious person, that meant that it had to involve Cristobal. He was the only named character, and his interaction with the victim was suspicious at face value.

But how had he done it?

The "why" could be simple. Mr. Midnight's mysterious death had been hung out as an obvious clue. It was established that Ms. Monarch knew something about it. Someone had to hide it. We just needed actual proof. In the case of this storyline, proof likely meant rumors and gossip. I felt under-equipped for such a task.

Antoine and Kimberly hadn't come up with any new information since our last group huddle, and Chris had come to pretty much the same conclusion I had about the seals on both the cask room and the casks themselves. Either way, it was old news to Grace.

They knew pretty much everything that I did because of our last conversation about what I had seen with my tropes and discussed with Mrs. Cloudburst. I told them about the tropes I had seen on the vegetative sorcerers downstairs, but that was all I had to offer.

"I want you to go out and find the information we need and bring it back to me. Don't blow your cover to do so. I have contingencies if we don't find the information soon enough, but I don't want to have to use them. You have done a great job so far. Let's finish this thing," Grace said. She was trying to stay positive and keep a strong front, but I could tell she was worried. If not about us, then about her brother, Reggie. I hoped he would be okay.

A few minutes later we had to have that whole conversation again in character for the benefit of the cameras.

With Grace's mandate that we go find the motive for the crime, I finally had the freedom to search the mansion for the information we needed.

I left the ballroom and wound my way through the vast hallways of the estate. I put on my headphones and started walking casually. Up until that moment, my Oblivious Bystander strategy probably wouldn't have been that meaningful, given the fact that I already had a disguise, but as Second Blood approached, I knew that enemies would soon be at the gates, and I would need to be ready.

My strategy was to find people talking and do my best to listen in. I wasn't sure if Carousel would go along with it. Normally, using Oblivious Bystander was a meta-strategy. I was pretending to be an oblivious character. This time I was playing a character who was pretending to be oblivious.

This was a unique situation where my character would, in the context of the story, be acting aloof to the conversations and people he perceived. My character was a reporter of some kind who worked for a celebrity gossip magazine. I was undercover, trying to figure out information about a magical secret society, as tabloid journalists are known to do.

I started to wish that we had attempted an escape earlier. I expected that the doors would be locked and that we wouldn't be able to leave the property. That might give my character more narrative foundation for trying to figure out the truth. It was too late for those types of regrets.

I was going to have to find out if Oblivious Bystander would work when my character wasn't actually oblivious but was just pretending to be. I silently begged Carousel to go along with it.

I made my way through the halls and slowed down at every conversation, listening for important information. For a mansion filled with wicked, rich world travelers, these people sure had some boring conversations. They talked about makeup and their favorite alcohol. They talked about their favorite bands and lamented that they had been dead for decades.

Eventually, I wandered upon a woman who said, verbatim, "I have a secret about Cristobal."

When I listened in, the secret was that she had a huge crush on him. I should have known it wasn't going to be anything meaningful, given the fact that I wasn't on-screen at the time, but I still got my hopes up.

I continued on.

I passed Chris, who was still talking to Miss Forget-Me-Not, but I didn't stick around to listen to their conversation, because it would be a wasted effort. Chris knew what he was doing.

I walked around for what felt like an hour until I finally found something worth my time.

I felt like a fool when I realized that there was a memorial near the entrance of the mansion. I hadn't noticed it when we entered, because I had been concerned with a dozen other things and I hadn't known who these characters were yet. But as I found that area again, I was finally able to lay eyes on a high-resolution color photograph of Mr. Midnight.

I wasn't sure if that would help, but it was nice to match a masked face to a name.

There were some women there standing in front of the memorial, paying their respects. I wondered how long they had been there, going through those same exact motions, waiting for someone to talk to them.

"I would have followed him," one of the women, Mrs. Rosemary, said.

"In a heartbeat," her friend, Ms. Sassafras, agreed.

"This is a nightmare," Mrs. Rosemary said. "I wish he had just done it. Gone through with the plan. I think that lots of people would have left with him and Mrs. Midnight. More than he ever knew."

"We can never be sure now," Ms. Sassafras said. "I need a drink."

I got away from them so that they wouldn't notice me.

My Grit jumped up ten points.

There it was. A power struggle. A small brick that could be used to help construct the motive for why Ms. Monarch had been killed—apparently to cover up the death of Mr. Midnight. Grace's Don't Shoot the Messenger trope had given me a buff to my Grit so that I could bring this information back to her. It was a rumor, but a rumor was better than nothing.

My information would only be a piece of the puzzle, but I was glad to have something to offer.

The needle on the Plot Cycle ticked toward Second Blood. I would need to get the information to her soon. If my estimate was correct, I had less than half an hour. I didn't want to think about what was about to happen to me. I secretly hoped that there would be some plot nonsense to explain why I wouldn't be Second Blood, but I couldn't think of any. I had the lowest effective Plot Armor on the team, so I would be next.

The only question was, where was Grace?

CHAPTER FOURTEEN

CLOSE AND PERSONAL WITH MR. RED ROCK

I searched for Grace for so long that I started to suspect there was a trope interceding in my ability to find her. While Grace did have an ability that buffed my Grit in order to assist me in getting important information back to her, extra Grit wouldn't guarantee that I would be able to *find* her.

As the Plot Cycle ticked closer to Second Blood, the urgency started to increase dramatically. That wasn't the only thing increasing, though. There were sorcerers roaming up and down the halls, looking for some sign of an intruder, a Mr. Evergreen. I felt in my gut that if I slipped up even a bit, they would nab me.

Luckily, I had been pulling off my Oblivious Bystander strategy quite well up to that point, and none of the society members on the lookout had so much as tapped me on the shoulder. I theorized that the mask helped. Oblivious Bystander activated rarely but always helped me escape any awkward questions. I was just glad that it was working given the odd situation.

As I went along one of the familiar hallways on the first floor, I saw two faces that I recognized. Technically, I only saw one face that I knew: Cristobal. But I recognized Mr. Red Rock as well.

They were whispering to each other. I couldn't tell what they were talking about, but it was clearly important, as they were having quite an intense conversation.

They were headed in a direction that I had actually spent some time looking around: the hallway with the aquarium room. Anytime I had a chance to look over there, I took it. I had searched the room when I was with Mrs. Cloudburst but had come out with nothing.

I knew it was significant. It was an important filming location according to my Location Scout trope. Something had to be going on there; I just had to figure out what.

I decided to follow them.

Oblivious Bystander did all of the hard work for me as I pretended to listen to whatever tape was on my Walkman. I had to go slower than them to make the act believable, but it got the job done.

As I expected, when we turned down the hallway with the aquarium room, that was the door they entered. I followed right behind. The room was tinted blue-green because of the aquarium water. Almost everything else was exactly as I remembered it, with vast couches and pillows. This room also had cabinets filled with curiosities.

One thing had changed.

The stone wall on the far side from the entrance had opened up. It was a secret passage. Even from the doorway, I could see that it was a stairway going down. My interest piqued.

The question was whether I dared to look further.

With Second Blood quickly approaching, I realized that caution wasn't going to bear much fruit. I was a goner soon anyway. Might as well learn something.

Besides, I had a plan for Second Blood.

I snuck over across the aquarium room and slowly made my way down the dark stairway to the room below. At first, I thought I had found a secret passage leading into the cask room, which could explain how the murder had been committed, assuming the magical seal did not affect it.

I wasn't exactly right.

As I made my way down the stairs, I started to hear groans and crying. The sound of it put a panic in my chest. Up until that point, I had tried not to think about where all the bodies had come from that the society members had been using as puppets.

Now I knew.

As I got to the edge of the staircase, being careful not to go all the way around so that I couldn't be seen, I ducked my head over and saw the cages. They were filled with people. Most of them were young and attractive, just as the society members desired. Some were comatose, standing limp like a puppet with its strings cut. Others still had some free will and cowered in the corner of the cages, crying but lacking agency otherwise.

No wonder this place was a filming location. That was the most horrifying room in the entire mansion.

I eventually worked up some bravery to try and peek around further to see what Cristobal and Mr. Red Rock were doing, but as I did, I felt a familiar static in the air. The same kind of magic seal that had protected the cask room from unwanted visitors was at work in this room. I knew that if I moved forward anymore, I would find out exactly what those seals did. I doubted Mr. Gray Amber had permission to go in that room.

I realized I had even more information to tell Grace and the others, so I turned and, as quietly and quickly as possible, made my way back up the stairs. I had picked the perfect time, too, because moments after I turned tail, I heard Cristobal and Mr. Red Rock coming back up behind me.

Was it possible for me to leave the secret stairway and get across the room without them seeing me?

I didn't think so. The room was huge.

As soon as I came into the blue light of the aquarium room, another idea struck me as I saw the champagne bottle that Mrs. Cloudburst had brought there when we had been exploring the mansion together. I ran to my left and grabbed the bottle, then fell back onto one of the plush couches, burying myself partially in the large pillows.

I closed my eyes and propped the champagne bottle up next to my hand, pretending to sleep. It was at that moment it dawned on me there might actually be some use to my Out like a Light trope, but I hadn't brought that.

As soon as I was settled onto the couch, pretending to be in a drunken stupor, Cristobal and Mr. Red Rock emerged from the stairway.

I put my best acting chops into that power nap. I couldn't tell whether or not Cristobal and Mr. Red Rock spent time examining me, or if they just strolled out of the room, but I did hear the entrance to the stairway closing.

I waited there for as long as I could bear before opening my eyes, doing my best to maintain the facade of being drunk when I did.

They were nowhere to be seen. Chalk another one up for Oblivious Bystander.

I was running out of time. I needed to get the info I had about the power struggle between the three sorcerers who ran the society to my teammates, and I needed to do it quickly.

The knowledge that Mr. Midnight had considered leaving the society to start his own was not the complete picture, I knew, but we didn't need perfection. We just needed a motive.

As I emerged from the aquarium room, I saw people walking in the direction of the ballroom at a rushed pace. I decided to follow. A large group of people had gathered outside a room that I wasn't familiar with. I couldn't see what they were so interested in.

Fearing that one of my fellow players had succumbed to Second Blood, I checked the Plot Cycle, but that wasn't the case. We were still in Rebirth by a slim margin.

I listened for the news of what had happened to travel to the back of the crowd.

"A body stuffed in a closet," one of the women said. "At least this time it was only one of the hosts. Can you imagine if another one of us had died?"

"Who was it?"

"Their mask was missing. We don't know yet."

It couldn't have been one of my teammates. That would have triggered Second Blood. But why else would someone get murdered?

Chris.

He had a trope for hiding bodies. He could have killed someone who got too close to uncovering our presence.

But where were my teammates?

That question was soon answered. They were inside the room. I wasn't sure what the sequence of events had been. Had they been caught with the body? It was possible they had just gone back in with the crowd. From what I could see on the outside, it didn't look like they were suspects, but I could see them across from the doorway, huddled together. All accounted for.

"This is it," Cristobal cried out from inside the room. "This is the last time that the sanctity of this holy place is mocked. No one here will leave until we have discovered the culprit."

Perhaps I was just imagining things, but Cristobal actually did look confused about what had just happened. If Chris was right and he was the killer, it would be pretty confusing for him when a second body turned up that he had nothing to do with.

The Plot Cycle was a hair's width away from Second Blood. I didn't have time to work my way over to Grace. The temperature was rising, in a manner of speaking. If Second Blood didn't trigger soon, there was no telling what Carousel might do.

I thought about what I needed to do. My character needed to trigger Second Blood.

Ever since I learned the premise of the story after the murder, I had started forming a contingency plan for what I would do at Second Blood. Given all the lore I had learned and my knowledge of the tropes at play, I had a course of action worked out.

It was time to enact it.

I either needed to go to the cask room or the aquarium room. I chose the aquarium room. I then looked around until I found the trigger that would open the secret door. It turned out that it was a rock jutting out from the wall. I pressed it and the door opened.

Next, I did something that I had been dreading ever since I learned the magical power of the masks.

I took mine off and stuffed it into the cushions of one of the couches in the aquarium room. If I was caught wearing that mask, they would identify me as Mr. Gray Amber. They might realize which people had arrived with Mr. Gray Amber, and my team would get caught too.

I needed anonymity. Ironically, the only way to get that was to take off the mask.

I then ran down the stairs until I felt the static of the magic seal.

And I kept moving. My character did not know about the magical seal. I did. He would have acted on the opportunity to check out the lab while everyone else was distracted and then got caught by it.

As anticipated, before I got too far into the room, I was incapacitated and laid to the floor, a drooling mess. It was like I had been tased.

I didn't have to stay there for too long, because a humming sound started to emanate from the location of the seal, and within minutes, Cristobal, Mrs. Midnight, and Mr. Red Rock were bearing down upon me.

Before I could get another villain monologue, I passed out from the pain.

I woke up feeling numb all over my body. I wasn't in the little secret laboratory with the cages of mind slaves. As far as I could tell, I was at the foot of some stairs in the cask room. The problem was that these were not the same stairs that I had walked down earlier.

There *was* a secret path into that room. For a moment, I thought I had solved the murder. A secret path to the cask room would be the perfect way for a killer to get in and out undetected.

But then I felt the familiar static coming from the room. It felt like the same seal that protected the main entrance to the cask room also extended over here. I had gotten excited for nothing.

I was also dismayed to see that Second Blood was not over. The needle rested on it. It had been triggered when I was caught, but there was more to come.

Mr. Red Rock and Mrs. Midnight held my left and right arm, respectively.

"Oh, look who's awake," Cristobal said. "Don't you worry. I intend to find out why it is that you are here, but before that, I have a job for you."

I coughed aggressively. That seal had tested my buffed Grit considerably.

"I'm not a hard worker," I said, trying to sound confident and quippy. Unfortunately, my throat was sore, so I wasn't certain if what I said came across that way.

"Then this is the perfect job for you," Cristobal said. "You see, we are in search of a killer. We thought you might help."

He turned away from me.

"Mr. Red Rock, if you could find someplace comfortable for your host. I will need your services elsewhere," Cristobal said.

Mr. Red Rock did as instructed, giving a nod toward Cristobal. He then turned and headed back up the stairs.

Mrs. Midnight stayed next to me, and though I felt I could overpower her just from the looks of her, I sensed that she was powerful in other ways.

Cristobal walked right through the electrifying seal that closed off the secret passageway from the cask room as if it wasn't even there.

"Wait. How were you able to get through the seal without the consent of the members?" I asked, as much out of curiosity as out of a desire to delay the inevitable.

"Me? I am Cristobal. I am their benevolent leader. I am their beloved savior. I gave them eternal youth." He smiled. "I have this magnificent immortal body. They worship me. Why would they not consent for me to enter the cask room any time I wish?" He started to laugh. Mrs. Midnight joined him.

He turned and continued in the direction he had been traveling. I saw him pull something out of his pocket, but I couldn't tell what it was. He went up one of the rows, the one labeled with the color red, and walked down to one of the casks. I couldn't see which one, but I had a guess.

Then he came back toward me, holding a small glass flask filled with a green liquid similar to the liquid that all of the society members' real bodies were floating in. It was at that moment that I noticed all of the plumbing coming out of each of the casks had little outlet valves, which had meant nothing to me before, but I realized at that moment they were for procuring a small amount of the liquid from inside the cask.

Knowing that Mr. Red Rock was back upstairs and that Mrs. Midnight and Cristobal would stop me if I tried to run in that direction, I did the only thing I could think of that might have some chance of helping. I ran toward Cristobal, right into the seal to the cask room.

A vibration sounded just like from the other seal.

My Incapacitated status started to go off, and I felt myself become powerless to move. My only hope was that society members would be alerted to the seal being tripped and might start barging down the stairs from the main entrance. Perhaps if they saw what Cristobal was up to, it would be helpful in some way. It was a stupid idea, I realized right afterward, as everyone at the party was evil.

Cristobal grabbed my arm and threw me back away from the seal. I landed on the ground hard.

"Come, my love," Mrs. Midnight said. "Let us be done with this."

"At once, my dear," Cristobal said.

He approached me with the vial. We were in Second Blood. I knew that there was no avoiding it. Yet I struggled in vain with every fiber of my being.

Perhaps the only thing that prevented me from panicking was that this was part of the plan, more or less. I just had to hope that I had understood everything correctly.

Cristobal grabbed my jaw. He was very strong. I didn't know if that was because of his magical abilities or simply because of his actual physical strength. It didn't matter. I couldn't fight back.

He brought the vial to my lips and started to pour the contents into my mouth. The liquid felt and tasted like bile.

As soon as it touched my throat, I could feel my natural instinct to vomit being overcome by a tingling sensation. The liquid began to ooze down my throat without me even having to swallow.

By the time the vial was empty, my status on the red wallpaper had changed to Infected and Written Off, in addition to Captured. I kept focusing on the Written Off light, hoping and praying that my theory had been correct.

Finally, after what felt like forever, the light blinked. It only did it every ten seconds or so, but it was enough to tell me that I was on the right track. It sucked that every single bit of action after I had run into the laboratory was off-screen.

My body went numb.

Then it started moving on its own.

"Red Rock," Cristobal said. "Are you there?"

"Yes," my mouth said.

I felt myself fading.

I was a passenger.

The Finale had begun.

IN TIME, PART ONE

"Anna," Camden said as we strapped ourselves into the helicopter, "they're going to be okay."

Was he asking me or telling me?

"I know," I said.

"They will be," Bella reassured me. She must have seen the worry on my face. "Grace is a top Detective. There's no way they lose."

She gave me a sincere smile.

Bella was a stout woman with a loud, confident voice and a take-no-crap-from-anyone attitude. She was a Bruiser on the Bowler team. She had been a parole officer before she came to Carousel. She still was, in some ways, with how she wrangled the men on her team when they started getting rowdy.

I nodded my head and tried to smile.

I felt like I was abandoning members of my team when they needed me most.

I took a deep breath. I needed to focus on the storyline at hand. I couldn't do the others any good if we failed here. I had to survive. That was what Final Girls did, right?

Headhuntress Reborn.

I didn't need Riley to picture what we might be up against with that title. I could almost feel a blade on my neck just thinking about it.

I needed to learn more about the story. I looked around the helicopter for clues. Unlike a certain Film Buff, the rest of us had to actually look for important information. We couldn't just see enemy tropes unless they were displayed somewhere.

The pilot had not arrived yet, but we were not the only people on the helicopter. There were eight passenger seats. Two were filled by a well-dressed woman and an energetic four-year-old—a little girl. They were both NPCs.

As everyone got in and buckled up, she started to speak. We all listened intently.

"Sweetheart, we're going to see Daddy!" She looked into her child's eyes and brushed some thin hair out of her face. "And his twenty-two-year-old 'assistant.' I think he might need a new 'assistant' because he hasn't been answering my calls since he got to Anera Island for his 'business trip.'"

Missing person on Anera Island.

That was the Omen, and, like most, it was not subtle. It was delivered to us through a scripted dialogue from a woman who believed herself to be the victim of infidelity.

"I bet Daddy will be *very* happy to see us!"

The NPC tried to deliver her lines in a happy tone for her child but with enough venom that we knew how angry and hurt she was by the suspected infidelity.

She was failing.

Like all of the NPCs we had seen since the storm began, her fear was evident. It choked out every word she spoke. Knowing of the impending Apocalypse, it must have been difficult for her to play her character.

With the Omen delivered, the pilot was likely to show soon. I hoped.

The little girl didn't understand what was going on. She didn't know the danger of the black snowstorm billowing in the distance. The script would never let her say anything about it even if she did.

She knew that her mother was upset and set herself on fixing that.

She turned in her mother's lap and placed her tiny hands against her mother's face. When a solitary tear fell from the woman's eye, she wiped it with her yellow sleeve.

"Mommy," the little girl said. I could see her moving her lips and trying to find words, but something was stopping her.

"Is Daddy okay?" the little girl asked finally.

Her mother swallowed deeply. "That depends on what we find out when we get to Anera, baby."

Lines.

More lines.

Her voice was soft, and her eyes filled with tears. Her character was a woman scorned. All she could say were lines from her character that would act as an Omen to us.

Lines that signaled, "A man has gone to the island of Anera and not returned. Beware."

How could she comfort her daughter with such restrictions? How could she say words meant to show anger and hurt in such a way that her young daughter's worries about the storm would be quelled?

NPCs had a life even worse than ours. That was my belief. Sure, the veterans talked about them like they were not real or they were not alive, but that was a defense mechanism. Who could look at an exchange like this between a mother and a daughter and deny they were really in there somewhere?

The woman drew her daughter in for a hug. She looked out the window and back toward us.

Finally, a man in a white uniform began running toward the helicopter from the building across the tarmac. He was tall and muscular with an experimental—and not so successful—mustache. It was the kind of facial hair men only wore when they were young or had no one to impress.

"Sorry about my tardiness, folks," the man said as he entered the helicopter. "Traffic was something else today."

After he turned and looked at us, he flashed a pearl-white smile. He wore aviator sunglasses. I got a good look at his face. He was sweating profusely. His cheeks and forehead were flushed. He almost looked drunk. I was not looking forward to how that might play out in the story.

"This is a one-way trip to Anera Island. I have been told that your bungalows are not yet ready, but they have rooms available for you at the retreat next door." He took a deep breath and coughed into his hand. "My apologies. I should warn you: the retreat does have an open bar, so pace yourselves or your memories might check out before you do."

The man strained to smile at his joke.

The storyline was at some kind of tropical hotel, from the sound of it, complete with cheesy jokes. I wondered how the titular Headhuntress would fit into it. I glanced over at Camden. I was glad to have him here. He was usually good in a crisis.

The pilot fumbled around with his controls while we sat in the back seat, still in the Omen phase of the story. He needed to hurry. I wasn't sure how much longer we had before the storm got to us. Our "divine intervention" in finding the bus had gotten us far away from the storm, but it drew closer every time I looked out the window.

I glanced over at Travis. His gaze was focused on the pilot like a hawk. He had a suspicious look that I recognized. I tried to figure out what had him on high alert. Was it simply that the pilot was taking too long?

Travis was an Outsider, and his Outsider's Perspective would clue him into the presence of something strange but not actually tell him what it was. Dina had the same ability. That was where I had seen that look before.

I began looking at the pilot too. I knew he was acting weird, but I assumed it was normal for the storyline. Could it be something else?

Travis started unbuckling rapidly. "We have to go!" he screamed. "Look at the spots on his shirt!"

Spots.

I didn't see spots. Not at first. They were small and difficult to separate from sweat stains, but as I looked closely, I realized what I was supposed to be seeing.

Black stains.

Small round black stains.

Like those you might get if black snow fell on you.

"Everyone out!" Reggie yelled.

I was already out of my restraints and out the door before I even realized what the dots meant. We had not actually activated the Omen. Riley had said that we needed to take off to activate it. The vets' experiences suggested the same.

The black snow on the pilot doomed our run of *Headhuntress Reborn*. We didn't know what the snow did, but we knew that the pilot was part of the Apocalypse since it had touched him. Our escape would certainly fail.

Perhaps sweating and flushed skin were symptoms of the snow. Was the Apocalypse a disease of some kind? We couldn't wait around to find out.

I looked back over my shoulder. The mother and daughter sat still, their fate sealed. The mother had a look of horror on her face. She must have thought she would escape the black snow for a moment. Suddenly, she knew she wouldn't.

I wished I could have done something for them. No one deserved to suffer like that. The NPCs were doomed to sit there until someone came and successfully activated their Omen, as we almost had. They would still be there until the Omen was deactivated. By then, it would be too late for them.

It turned out that I was not the only one who had realized their situation.

After we had all disembarked the helicopter, Bella leaned back in and shouted, "We changed our minds. Get them out of here!"

"You got it," the pilot yelled back. He sounded relieved to get the order.

Bella was a Bruiser with a Bully Aspect. I had never seen that Aspect in action before. I still wasn't able to see Aspects at all, because I had not met the condition required to choose one yet. It was nice to see that the Bully had abilities that could help knock the NPCs out of their scripted prison, if only in limited ways.

The pilot shut the door after us and started to take off.

It was a long shot. The pilot had been touched by the black snow before he arrived. I had no idea what that might cause, but I knew the chances of them surviving were only slightly higher than if Bella had done nothing.

We were out of the helicopter and on our way across the tarmac in a heartbeat.

We ran as fast as our legs would take us. One of the planes had already taken off. It was the one with the hardest storyline, which no one had been assigned to. The Omen must have disappeared before we realized our pilot was infected by the black snow.

The other plane with an Omen was larger and blue. It had already pulled away from the portable stairs the other players had used to climb up. We were going to miss it. I was sure of it.

I was wrong.

The plane stopped suddenly before it had fully turned around toward the runway. The large door flew open.

Tori, a fellow Final Girl and a member of Travis's team, had managed to get the door open. I could see NPCs bustling about, panicked over her actions.

Travis was the first one to the open door. He had to jump up and pull his body up and into the plane.

He turned, grabbed onto a handle inside the plane with one hand, and reached the other one out toward José, his teammate. José grabbed it, and Travis pulled him up into the aircraft.

Next, Travis reached out for Bella, who was nearest. He hoisted her up with an adrenaline-soaked scream. His hand was back out the door in seconds, reaching for mine.

I grabbed for it, but before I reached him, he was pulled back, and the door was shut by an NPC.

"Why?" I screamed. It only took me a second to figure it out. The plane had been larger than the other, but it was still quite small.

There was enough room for the cockpit and eight passengers if the windows told me anything. The plane was full: five original team members who had been assigned to that storyline and three of ours.

We were cut off. Storylines had limits to how many people they took. That was why the Grotesque storyline took so few players when it was activated.

"No!" Reggie screamed.

The plane started taxiing down the runway as the passengers screamed for us. I could hear Bella screaming for them to let us in, but even her abilities had limits.

"We need to find another Omen," Camden said. "Reggie, do you have something you can use for that?"

"Sorry, kid," Reggie said. "That ain't in my bag of tricks."

"Riley!" I yelled. "Riley said there was another Omen when we were almost here. The roller skate building."

We turned around. We had gotten disoriented.

"There!" Camden said.

He pointed westward toward the storm.

Could we make it in time?

The bus had been left in the airfield parking lot on the other side of the tarmac. We would have to run all the way back there and hope that the bus was still working. Surely Travis had left the keys in it. Even then, we were not guaranteed to be able to operate it, because we had no tropes that granted that ability.

Either way, running across the airfield and jumping over a fence at the end was faster.

We ran as fast as we could. It looked impossible.

Every few seconds, the roller rink would flicker away. Every time it did, I worried it might not come back.

We got to the fence. It wasn't very tall, and Reggie threw us over before pulling himself up and over, landing on his back as he rolled.

We were up on our feet in seconds. We still had hundreds of yards to go, and the black haze of falling snow was getting closer and closer. We didn't just have to beat the storm; we had to beat it by enough that not even a snowflake touched us.

"We can't make it," Camden said. "We need to turn back. There might be . . . other Omens somewhere."

He was right. We were running out of time. Soon, the building's parking lot would start getting powdered with black snow.

Reggie was up ahead of me. He was very fast for a larger guy. I could see him shuffling through his tickets. He apparently found what he was looking for because they went back in his pockets.

Then he fell.

I could see his knee hit the pavement hard.

I stopped to try and help him. It was second nature. I couldn't leave a player behind.

"Leave me!" he yelled. "Go!"

He shoved me away, hard. I did as he asked and ran to catch up with Camden.

But it was all for show.

My Hustle rose twenty points. So did Camden's.

I looked over my shoulder and saw the ticket he had equipped on the red wallpaper.

I'm Just Slowing You Down!
Type: Buff/Action
Archetype: Bruiser
Aspect: Gentle Giant
Stat Used: Moxie

It is truly noble when a character acknowledges that they are a liability to their allies and willingly sacrifices themselves to improve their allies' odds of escape.

With this trope equipped, a player can sacrifice themselves in order to help their team escape. To activate the trope, the player must devise a reason that their death or abandonment will help the other players in their escape efforts. If successful, a buff equivalent to the player's Plot Armor will be distributed among present allies' Hustle. However, the player is guaranteed to suffer whatever fate they attempt to flee.

If this trope is used during a chase scene with an enemy assailant, the player will get one chance to inflict injury upon the assailant before death.

If you want to move forward, you have to be willing to leave something behind.

A self-sacrifice trope.

I ran toward the roller rink with every bit of speed I could muster. I wasn't actually moving faster because of my increased Hustle, but the storm . . . I couldn't tell for sure, because of its massive size and the shadow it cast, but I swear it was standing in place.

Our Hustle was so high even the Apocalypse could not outrun us, at least at that moment.

Camden and I ran into the parking lot of the roller rink. With a pull on the metal handle, Camden was inside. Then I was.

I started scanning Camden for snowflakes. I hadn't seen any on the way in, but we needed to be sure. He scanned me for the same.

"I think we made it," Camden said.

"*We* did," I said, looking out the window to Reggie, who was stumbling hopelessly toward the building.

I thought we would have to watch him suffer the consequences of his sacrifice, but Reggie was gone in the blink of an eye. The storm was gone.

Suddenly the sun was shining, and the music of the roller rink was all I could hear.

It was like we had been transported somewhere else, but we hadn't; the airfield was still there. The street had not moved.

We weren't in a different place.

We were in a different time.

CHAPTER FIFTEEN

SELF-INFLICTED INJURIES

I stood in the alcove right at the edge of the magical seal that kept people from entering the area of the cask room where the bodies were kept. I couldn't move. I couldn't speak. I fought the urge to even try. It wasn't time yet.

Cristobal went to the end row behind the casks and started to push them onto the floor. They hit the floor and burst open like black magic eggs. He got half a dozen casks broken on the floor before he decided to stop.

"That should help convince them when they come down," he said quietly as he approached us. "Midnight, you and I will go up the back entrance and then join our followers outside as they clamor to see the destruction. Red Rock, you stay here until the last moment. Make sure that you are seen. Then I want you to get up into the hallways and make sure you get seen there too. We need witnesses. Try not to get that body killed—we still have to question it—but if you do, I will not cry over it."

Mrs. Midnight walked over to me and pulled a small green bit of cloth out of some concealed pocket—a mask. "The masses must find their killer," she said as she placed the mask over my eyes. My name on the red wallpaper changed from "Riley Lawrence" to "Riley Lawrence (Mr. Evergreen)."

They were going to frame me. How did that always happen?

"I won't disappoint you," Red Rock said with my mouth.

"I know you will not. I will be sure to reward your loyalty," Cristobal said. "Pain is a brick in the tower of eternity. Decanter vitae."

"Decanter vitae," I/Red Rock said.

With that, he and Mrs. Midnight went up the hidden stairway before they were seen. They must have had real trust that none of the bodies in the casks would be able to see them. Even those that had just been spilled out onto the floor were not a risk to them, apparently.

Something about the entire event struck me as odd. Why had Cristobal, one of the most powerful sorcerers in the world, not used any magic? He handled me physically. He knocked over the casks with his bare hands. In fact, the only instance I had seen of him using magic was when he used lightning bolts to get the crowd's attention earlier. And, of course, when he had appeared on the ballroom floor in a cloud of smoke.

That's when I had a revelation. Did the cask room prevent people from using magic? Had I heard that earlier? I couldn't remember. Perhaps that was one of the clues Grace had found that had her smiling when she said she knew how the murder was done.

But if Cristobal hadn't used magic, how had the murder been committed?

I would have to wait for Grace to unveil that secret.

I expected that any minute party guests would start piling down the front stairs into the cask room. Then they would get a look at someone they believed to be Mr. Evergreen, and that would be enough to convince them of his guilt.

That wasn't the first thing that happened, though.

The back row where Cristobal had knocked over several casks started to make noises as the bodies in those casks began to move.

Red Rock did not move me any closer, so I didn't get a good view. He did not seem particularly interested.

I watched as one of the figures, a woman whose age was indiscernible due to the prolonged period she had spent in the magical elixir, stood with great effort and started looking around.

"Help!" the old woman cried out. Her voice was cracked and almost unrecognizable as human from how long she had spent in the cask.

"There is no help for you," Red Rock said with my mouth.

The woman turned around immediately. I could see that her eyes were practically white with cataracts. The way these society members had let their bodies deteriorate in their quest for immortality was horrifying.

"Mr. Gray Amber, is that you?"

She had recognized my voice. Her eyes had become nearly useless with old age, but her ears had not.

I looked up at the row she had been in and saw that I was looking at the blue row.

The woman before me was Mrs. Cloudburst. The real Mrs. Cloudburst. Time and disuse had not done her body well. She was both shriveled and bloated. Her wispy white hair nearly reached the floor.

"Mr. Gray Amber," she cried out in a feeble voice, "something has happened. I need your help."

"No Mr. Gray Amber here," Red Rock said. "I'm Mr. Evergreen."

"What? No . . . ," she croaked. "I know your voice. It can't be."

She struggled to see me with her poor eyesight.

It was then that I started to consider the limitations of the masks. When we had arrived, I assumed that the masks were designed to hide the identities of the partygoers. But I slowly realized that the partygoers didn't care about the identities of their hosts nearly as much as they cared about letting other society members know who they were, regardless of what body they were wearing.

Any anonymity the masks provided was just an added benefit meant to prevent the members from recognizing the host bodies and breaking the illusion of their hedonistic paradise.

Mrs. Cloudburst could recognize me by my voice in the same way that my team and I could recognize each other. That would also explain why Grace had been able to recognize her friend, Mary Lee Parrish, despite Mary Lee wearing a mask.

The masks took some getting used to. Even with their powers, it took practice not to look at the body of a person when trying to recognize them instead of their mask.

Mrs. Cloudburst couldn't see the mask, so she had no idea it had been switched.

Red Rock was growing impatient with Mrs. Cloudburst.

"Look, lady, I don't know you, and if you don't stop talking to me, you're going to regret it."

Mrs. Cloudburst started to cry and back away, but the movement was difficult for her atrophied limbs. She fell onto the ground and started attempting to crawl.

Despite knowing that Mrs. Cloudburst was a terrible person who had enslaved a young woman in order to use her as a host, I felt bad for her. Her desperation to just live another day had driven her to this, and now Red Rock was threatening to take away that chance at life.

Of course, he couldn't do it. He would be no more able to pass through the magical seal that protected the cask room than I was able to. Not without consent. Given the fact that he was wearing the Mr. Evergreen mask, I doubted he would get permission.

So, we stood together in my body on the outskirts of the room, waiting to be seen by witnesses.

It didn't take too long for them to arrive. At first they surveyed the damage in the cask room that Cristobal had caused. Then they caught sight of me.

"Is that . . . ?" one of the women shouted out. "That's Mr. Evergreen. He's back!"

As more of the society members started to get a look at me and advance in my direction, Red Rock decided that he had done enough. He turned tail and ran up the secret staircase, flipping a switch on his way up that closed the door behind him. I was along for the ride. But not for much longer if I could help it.

Because this, too, was a part of my plan, more or less.

Step One: Find important plot information for Grace.

This part was simple but time-consuming. The members of the society were very loose lipped, and there were little bits of information to be found in almost every conversation. Most of them were redundant or useless for our purposes, but still, all I needed was the slightest crumb of a clue. I didn't need to know the complete motivation; I just needed something to help Grace make her case.

Finding out there was a power struggle was not surprising, but it was necessary.

If I was able to get that information to Grace, that would be wonderful, but in many ways, it was fortunate that I wasn't able to get it to her.

Yet.

Because by having important information, Grace's Don't Shoot the Messenger trope buffed my Grit by a huge amount. Ten whole points. I would need those for later.

Step Two: Get caught and possessed for Second Blood.

There was no avoiding it. If things were to go to plan, I would have to make the sacrifice. Mary Lee Parrish was a stock character whose entire job was to demonstrate the stakes of the storyline. This storyline was about body snatching. In a way, I was happy to find out that the fate the victims of this storyline suffered wasn't death. Dying was taking a toll on me. Strangely, I was looking forward to helping out my team without having to get injuries on or around my neck.

I had run down into the secret laboratory and gotten caught by the magical seal. I had done my best to make it look like my character was going in there to investigate the room and that he had no idea he would barely make it past the staircase. It needed to look like I had fallen into a trap.

As I expected, I wasn't killed. I was turned into a puppet. I existed in the dark recesses of a foreign mind. The experience was terrifying. I tried not to think about it, because the real test was coming up.

Step Three: Willpower.

There was a reason that I was happy to find out that I couldn't deliver Grace her little piece of information before I was possessed. As long as I still struggled to get that information to Grace, I would have buffed Grit. I wasn't sure how far I could exploit that, but so far, everything seemed to be working.

As Red Rock moved my body up the stairs, I realized that this passage led straight to the underground laboratory with the caged hosts. Cristobal and friends hadn't had to move me very far at all.

There was a large overstuffed chair in the corner away from all the magical equipment and industrial-sized vats filled with potions. In it, Red Rock's original host was slumped over like a puppet with its strings cut, wearing his mask. When Cristobal had force-fed me the mind control potion, Red Rock must have lost control of his original host body.

It was time to make a move.

I started fighting. I focused with every part of my being on resisting Red Rock's control. He tried to take a step forward, and I fought it. The first time it made no difference, but the second time, he tripped. I stumbled forward and smacked my face against the floor.

Still, I fought.

It felt like I was trying to peel my own skin off, but my heightened Grit pushed me through it.

Having high Grit was particularly useful in this storyline because of another trope in play: Chris's Willpower Is Magic trope. It guaranteed that all magic was resistible through sheer effort. I was counting on that meaning that possession would be too. With my temporarily high Grit, I stood a real chance.

I fought and pulled and screamed and banged my arms against the floor.

"What do you think you're doing?" Red Rock yelled to the best of his ability, but I was fighting him when he used my mouth too. "You're going to kill yourself!"

That was likely part of the motivation that kept other hosts from fighting back. By the time they were willing to destroy themselves to fight, they lacked the ability. That, and they were basic NPCs with at most one point of Grit. I didn't know how strong Red Rock was, but I could feel that my Grit stacked up well against his prowess.

"So what?" I yelled out to the best of *my* ability.

I jerked my neck forward, slamming my face against the ground again so hard that I felt a tooth come out. That jarred me for a moment, but luckily, it stunned him too.

I pulled as hard as I could to get control of my limbs. To my satisfaction, it was working.

But at a great cost.

As I pulled against him, I could feel parts of my body breaking under the pressure of the spell. Three ribs broke in succession. They were so loud I could hear them popping.

My left arm started folding backward, and then it snapped at my elbow joint, bending unnaturally. But I kept fighting because Red Rock was also suffering as I damaged my body.

Some of the host slaves in the cages stood and watched me struggle. A few even had enough control over their bodies to cheer.

I could feel myself winning. I could feel it with every broken bone, torn muscle, and ruptured organ.

With one last burst, I pulled against Red Rock's influence and attempted to crawl forward with my one good arm.

My right leg started to twist until my foot turned backward, and I heard a pop in my ankle.

Just a little further.

Only a little.

And all at once, I could feel myself regaining control.

I could barely breathe; it felt like one of my lungs had been pierced in the effort.

I did my best to stand. Despite my broken ankle, I was able to do so. High Grit really was useful. I knew the pain was there, but I could bear it somehow. It reminded me of the healing tropes that had been used on me during the Grotesque storyline. The injury was there, but like in a horror movie, I could power through it.

Moving made me tear up. But I had to go. With one glance back at Red Rock's limp body in the overstuffed chair, I began climbing the stairs out of the hidden laboratory.

Every step was excruciating. I just kept focusing on how it would be over soon. We were in the Finale, and all Grace had to do was reveal the truth.

Such a shame. I was really looking forward to watching Cristobal's plan play out.

After I managed to pull myself back into the aquarium room, where the secret staircase led, I made the effort to go back to the couch where I had hidden my Mr. Gray Amber mask. There were powerful sorcerers roaming the halls. One look at Mr. Evergreen, and I would get trapped in a painting or something.

I doubted my Grit was high enough to stop that.

I stuffed the Mr. Evergreen mask in the couch in its place.

Once again undercover, except for my extreme injuries, I began limping out into the hallway toward the door that led down to the cask room. I could only hope that my teammates would be on the periphery of that crowd like they had been before.

I wasn't let down.

The entrance had been clogged up with terrified partygoers. There was an uproar, and people were screaming and fearful. Cristobal and Mrs. Midnight were among them, assuring them that they would be safe, that they would capture Mr. Evergreen.

People started to notice that I was horribly injured, and I worried that that would cause problems with the plan. Luckily, most people were quite distracted. The tales of my horribly mangled body couldn't beat out people screaming about Mr. Evergreen being seen in the cask room.

My team, as expected, were on the outside of the crowd, and they spotted me as soon as I entered their eyeline.

They approached me quickly and took me to a side parlor where we wouldn't be seen. I had been off-screen for much of my escapades. Perhaps if I had been on-screen, Cristobal's guilt would have been revealed to the audience too soon. I wasn't sure how much of my fight against being controlled by the puppet serum had been on-screen, because I had been distracted.

As they approached me, I went on-screen.

"What happened to you?" Kimberly asked, her voice dripping with concern.

Chris reached forward and flipped my mask off just to be sure that I was who he thought I was and that I wasn't possessed. Without the mask, my teammates would be able to see whether I was infected or not.

"I've had a rough night," I said. Then I told them everything that had happened. Every detail. I didn't know which ones would be important.

Grace nodded as I went along. She clearly knew some of the facts that I had revealed.

"So Red Rock is out of commission now?" Grace asked.

"Yes," I said.

There was one last piece of information I had to give to Grace. It was the piece that had buffed me to the point of being able to break free from the spell.

"Mr. Midnight wanted to go out on his own and start his own society of some kind. He never did. Some people would have followed," I said. Then I told them how I had learned that.

Almost instantly after the words left my mouth, my Grit dropped back to my measly two points.

I started choking on my own blood.

Breathing was nearly impossible. It felt like I had an anvil on my chest. My arm hurt so bad that I wished it would just be cut off, and my leg might as well have not been there at all. Without all that extra Grit, these injuries were more than I could bear.

I passed out.

It had been hard to tell how injured I was with that massive Grit. I ended up dying anyway. Such a shame. At least this time it felt like falling asleep. Note to self: that was another really good reason to start equipping my Out like a Light trope—ending my suffering painlessly.

The next thing I knew, I was sitting in a movie theater, my eyes magically fixed on the screen, watching my team finish the story.

CHAPTER SIXTEEN

WHO'S PULLING THE STRINGS?

I was really hoping not to die again. At least I got to watch how it all played out.

Try as I might, I could not force my eyes over to see the audience members in the theater. I eventually gave up so that I could pay attention to the rest of the movie.

"We can just get in there and knock over all of the casks, right?" Antoine suggested, though I assumed he was just saying that in character.

Chris shook his head. "That would be like hitting a beehive with a baseball bat. Some of these creeps are actually safer locked away in those pods. We start busting them, who knows what kind of fight we'll have on our hands. I struggled enough against just one of them."

"We could get the serum from the dangerous ones," Kimberly suggested meekly. "We could make them swap bodies."

"Chris is right," Grace said. "A fight ends in us getting killed."

"So start suggesting a plan that won't get us killed, darling. I would really like to not get killed," Jack Goforth said. "Or possessed. I would really like to not get possessed. Dammit, how am I going to explain Riley to HR?"

They couldn't just knock over all of the casks, but not just because it would lead to a fight. Something Grace could not say on-screen was that she needed witnesses. Her Get the Truth Out trope required her to expose the truth of the mystery in order to beat the storyline. She wasn't going to be able to get the story printed in a newspaper or magazine as we had thought might be possible. She needed to reveal the mystery to the society itself. You can't have witnesses if you knock them out of their casks and turn them into blind cavefish.

I had an idea. I wondered if I would be able to communicate it through my Flashback Revelation trope.

As soon as I thought about it, a list of lines I had spoken on-screen in front of Grace appeared before me engraved on brass plates. At that moment, I realized firsthand how little I talked to my teammates on-screen. That was something I would have to change.

Luckily, as I lay dying, I *had* said something useful. I didn't know how to activate it, but Carousel seemed to understand what I wanted.

The screen cut back to me lying on a couch dying as Grace and the others gathered around to hear what had happened to me. I sure looked rough. No wonder I had died as soon as I was out of Grit.

"There's an aquarium room . . . with colorful fish," I struggled to say.

I had been talking about the secret passage to the laboratory. The flashback cut off there, presumably because the audience had already heard the rest of that dialogue.

That was all I had to say. I just hoped that Grace understood what I was trying to tell her.

As I watched her smile, it looked like she did.

"Here's what we do," she said.

I wasn't certain what happened after that, but the next scene showed Grace walking into a packed ballroom as society members looked to Cristobal for assurances about the now missing Mr. Evergreen.

She had gone with just Jack Goforth. He looked nervous. Grace didn't. She was ready for the show. It was interesting to see that the woman who spent so much time feeding people, bowling, and reading pulpy paperback novels could look so confident in a den of sorcerers.

"Everyone," Grace said, "I know who the killer is."

That was direct.

"I know who did it, why, and how. I can prove it."

Mr. Oakheart, one of the senior members below the Three, said, "Well, come out with it. Who did it?"

"The murderer," she said, "was none other than Mr. Red Rock!"

The crowd started to gasp at the revelation. Some couldn't believe the accusation.

"But he wasn't working at his own behest. He did it on someone else's orders," she said, looking directly at Cristobal and Mrs. Midnight.

Cristobal picked up on this immediately.

"What?" he said. "Why would I do such a thing?"

"Because Ms. Monarch was about to expose information about Mr. Midnight's supposed murder, and you could not let that happen."

"Are you accusing him of killing my husband?" Mrs. Midnight asked in a rage. "He loved my husband like his own flesh and blood."

"Yes, *Cristobal* was a great friend to Mr. Midnight, but you," she said, lifting a finger toward Cristobal, "were a terrible friend to *him*."

The party guests gasped again. Emotionally reacting to revelations was the only thing most of the society members got to do in this story, and they took the job seriously.

A look of rage overtook Cristobal's face and electricity started to spark from his fingers. Grace was in danger.

"Here's what happened," Grace said. As she did, whatever malicious intent might have been directed at her was superseded by her trope of the same name. Anytime Cristobal looked like he might attack her, the scene cut to a flashback. He could not kill her off-screen. She was safe as long as she explained the mystery.

"That's right," Grace said. "The man standing with us today is none other than Mr. Midnight!"

More gasps.

"Mr. and Mrs. Midnight always did live in Cristobal's shadow, didn't they?" Grace asked, directing her attention toward the party guests.

The screen cut away to flashbacks of Cristobal receiving adoring adulation while the Midnights went ignored in the background.

"You had considered leaving, but how could you? Your power relied on having a large following, and if you left, who would follow? No one, not if it meant leaving Cristobal. He was perfect in so many ways. They loved him, and he was powerful. Leaving wasn't an option."

The image changed. Now it showed Mr. and Mrs. Midnight arguing with each other inaudibly.

"That changed when you had an idea to use the Draught of New Life, the decanter vitae itself, against its creator. You brewed yourself into one of the casks downstairs and had your accomplices, Mrs. Midnight and Mr. Red Rock, help you. In fact, you're down there right now, aren't you? I don't know how they got Cristobal to drink your serum. Perhaps we will never know, but it is interesting that right before Mr. Midnight went missing, Mrs. Midnight had taken to drinking port wine, a much stouter drink than before. Perhaps it was stout enough to hide the taste of the mind-controlling serum?"

I hadn't heard about that part, but as Grace spoke, the scene she described came to life on the screen. Mrs. Midnight took Cristobal to bed and playfully force-fed him a thick red drink. Grace must have guessed right.

"It must be difficult, retaining control over such a powerful sorcerer," she continued. "That's why you have been so tired lately, right? It isn't because the Third is dead; it's because Cristobal, the real Cristobal, has been fighting you."

The image changed to show Cristobal/Mr. Midnight staring in the mirror as they fought for control.

"Cristobal couldn't ever really stop you. Doing so would destroy his precious body. Unlike us, he's very protective over his."

The camera cut back to the ballroom.

"But wait," Mr. Oakheart cried out. "You said Red Rock killed Ms. Monarch. That isn't possible. He was right here with us when she died. We saw him."

Some of the other members nodded their heads and voiced their agreement.

"I'm getting to that part," Grace said. "That was the real impressive feat. When Ms. Monarch told you she had information related to Mr. Midnight's death, you had to move to action. The truth is, she likely didn't know the implication of what she had seen. In fact, we may never know what it was, but if I were to offer a guess . . ." Grace paused for a moment to think. "She said that she spoke to Mr. Midnight before his death, but when was that, exactly? No one is clear on the date he actually died. Did she see something she shouldn't have? Maybe she saw Mr. Midnight after the point at which he was supposedly dead. Whatever the case, as a loyal member, she tried her best to get this information back to Cristobal himself."

Again, Grace was right on the money. A scene showed Ms. Monarch and Mr. Midnight talking to each other about something casually. A flash forward later showed her watching as Mr. Midnight helped someone carry a large metal cask into the aquarium room. When she went to get a closer look, both he and his helper were gone and the room was empty. They had closed the secret door. She looked confused.

"As soon as she talked to you at the party, you realized that she wasn't going to give up. Maybe you thought that she would start to doubt herself, but she never did. You had to kill her before she talked. But how could you do that with such short notice?"

Suddenly, the screen showed a panning shot of the cask room. In the shot, the magical seal was visible like blue electricity.

"The cask room is basically a fortress to anyone but Cristobal. No one could get in or out because of the seal. Magic couldn't get through the seal, even magic from a powerful sorcerer. None of the people in their casks could get out to commit the murder, even you, Mr. Midnight. Even if they could get out of their casks, they certainly couldn't get back in. But you got around it somehow. You killed her. It was a locked room mystery. I had no idea what to think of it at first."

Cut to Grace growing a sly smile. "But then I figured it out."

"You see," she explained, "the murderer was Mr. Red Rock as I claimed earlier. But how could that be possible? He was in the ballroom when Ms. Monarch's host showed her being murdered. He couldn't be in two places at once. Besides, wasn't a Mr. Evergreen the person she accused?

"The answer is that Mr. Red Rock was not in the ballroom at the time of the murder, but he was here for something that looked like one. The murder we saw wasn't real. It was a performance."

A flashback to the scene right before the murder took place. Cristobal was being led back to his bed at the side of the ballroom.

"You couldn't kill her, not with Cristobal's adoring fans watching your every move. But you did know a sorcerer's meditation that would allow you to take control of a body. Everyone knows that it was that very meditation that the decanter vitae was modeled to imitate. You and Cristobal worked on it together, as I am sure you remember."

The screen flashed back to the conversation Grace had with the former engineer who had explained how the Draught of New Life worked. I had been there for that conversation, but I wasn't in the shot.

"You couldn't control someone in the cask room—it was protected—but you could take over one of the puppets in the ballroom. So, you did. You lay there right in front of all of us and used your magic to steal control of Ms. Monarch's host body.

"No one knew that when the woman wearing the Ms. Monarch mask started screaming bloody murder that it was really you, having severed control from the real Ms. Monarch. You made her body act out being murdered in loud, excruciating detail."

The scene she described played out as she described.

"After you were done, you surrendered control of the host body, letting her go limp. Then, you declared she had been killed and sent your old friend Mr. Red Rock down into the cask room under the guise of checking on the victim. Of course, we would all consent to that. He had no problem getting in through the magic seal because we allowed it. Then, he ran to the cask containing the real Ms. Monarch and killed her with a knife, but that is where he made his most crucial mistake."

The scene changed to show Red Rock pulling the real body of Ms. Monarch out of her broken cask and viciously brandishing a knife at her.

"He attacked her with a knife. She had defensive wounds on her hands from where she had tried in vain to protect herself, and her throat was slit from ear to ear."

The scene showed it all in gory detail.

"I saw the wounds myself," Grace said.

Cristobal didn't respond. I could see on his face that he realized they had messed up.

"But that made no sense," Grace continued. "I watched Ms. Monarch get murdered, supposedly. She was stabbed in the chest repeatedly. I saw her reacting to it. We all did. How is it that Ms. Monarch's host reacted to being stabbed in the chest when she herself did not get stabbed there?"

"She's right," someone in the crowd of society members cried out. "Ms. Monarch's host looked like she was stabbed over and over!"

Now the crowd started to agree with Grace. They were very concerned.

"Your murder plan really was brilliant, Mr. Midnight, but Mr. Red Rock failed in the execution. He has always been a screwup. The real Cristobal knew that. But you kept him around because he was loyal to you, right, Mr. Midnight? It's strange. Many of Cristobal's lovers have noticed how cold he has become to them recently. It was all some of them could talk about."

In fact, Mrs. Cloudburst had mentioned something similar.

"This is a lie!" Cristobal/Mr. Midnight screamed. "Many of you saw Mr. Evergreen in the cask room. Tell the truth."

Many had seen someone in a Mr. Evergreen mask and verbally attested to it in a jumble of confusion. The crowd looked to Grace to combat that.

"That wasn't the killer you saw," Grace said. "That was one of the spare hosts possessed by Red Rock and dressed in the Mr. Evergreen mask—this Evergreen mask," she said, pulling the mask from her purse. She must have gone back and taken it from where I had stashed it. "Don't you think it strange that no one saw him pass through the seal? He couldn't. We hadn't consented."

The crowd was incensed by the revelation of the mask.

"But Mr. Red Rock screwed up again and lost control of his host. The man overpowered him and fought to the death to sever Red Rock's control. He even managed to crawl upstairs and tell me what happened to him. After all, willpower is often the strongest magic. If you need more proof, go look in the gentlemen's parlor. His body is still there, broken from the struggle."

Cristobal seethed with rage. He shot lightning from his fingertips into the air.

"None of this proves anything. This is just a story. I am Cristobal. You can't prove otherwise."

He started to move toward Grace.

"Grace," Jack Goforth said, reaching for her arm. "I'm noticing a fatal flaw in your plan here, babe."

He started to pull Grace away from Cristobal toward the exit, but before he could make any progress, Cristobal flew into the air, his hair blowing in the wind, and blocked the exit with a storm of neon blue electricity.

"You aren't going anywhere," Cristobal said.

"Come on, Chris, any minute now," Grace said under her breath.

Chris ran down a hallway with Antoine and Kimberly. They made a sharp turn into the aquarium room.

Cristobal lifted his hand out toward Grace. Lightning started crackling from his fingers.

"You aren't leaving until everyone knows that I am innocent. Tell them it was all a lie!" Cristobal screamed. "Mr. Midnight was my dearest friend. I loved the man. Of course, I could simply deny you all the power of the decanter vitae if you are not loyal."

He reached out a hand toward Mr. Oakheart, who had been a prominent voice among the society members. With great effort, he strained his hand and a thin, glowing thread appeared above Oakheart's head and was instantly broken. Mr. Oakheart's host dropped like a puppet with its strings cut.

He turned his hand to Grace and started to strain. "You do not deserve eternal life if you would use it to spite me, who gave it to you!"

If this continued, Mr. Midnight would realize that Grace was not a puppet and we might still be in trouble.

Chris climbed up to the top of the aquarium and brandished a large flask. He unscrewed the lid and turned it over. A greenish liquid poured out of the flask into the aquarium and started to dissipate into the water.

"You have a strong will," Cristobal said. "I wouldn't have exp—"

Suddenly, Cristobal leaned over, his arms falling as his body fell limp.

The scene flashed back to Grace explaining the plan.

"Go down into the cask room while we still have consent," she said. "Find the casks of as many powerful sorcerers as you can. Focus on those that are completely opaque. Mr. Midnight couldn't risk having his body seen. It would be one of the newer ones too."

"Then what?" Chris said.

"Give them a new host," Grace said.

Over a dozen society members fell limp just like Cristobal. Chris had not skimped.

The screen showed those colorful fish in the tank that Mrs. Cloudburst and I had looked at. Some of them did not swim rhythmically or gracefully. Some were downright panicking.

Chris had just turned those fish into puppets. Mr. Midnight probably didn't find his new host as suitable.

The needle on the Plot Cycle hit The End as the conclusion of the movie started to play out.

The truth had been exposed. Not just who had killed the victim or how, but the fact that Cristobal was not Cristobal. That was also a mystery that had needed to be exposed to the society.

The movie wasn't over yet; it had a short denouement. Our part was finished, though.

As members started crowding in toward Cristobal's body, he started to stand upright. At least, he tried. He was struggling to regain control of his limbs. Eventually, with enough help and encouragement from his flocks of adoring men and women, he found himself able to walk and embrace those around him.

Mrs. Midnight was nowhere to be seen. It was probably best she get as far away as possible.

"My people!" he cried out tearfully. They cheered for him.

They really did love that man.

"It's funny," one of the partygoers said in a hushed tone. "I always thought Ms. Emerald was a bit of a ditz."

There was no fight. There was no race out of the building. Grace had solved the mystery without getting our identities revealed. We got a happy ending—if you don't count my tragic death. The movie ended as Cristobal embraced Grace for having freed him. They chatted inaudibly as the camera faded to black.

As the credits started to roll, I woke up on a couch in the room I had died in. I could hear the party still going on on the other side of the mansion.

CHAPTER SEVENTEEN

PARTY FAVORS, PART ONE

As I awoke, I expected to hear Silas greeting me, but he didn't show up quite yet.

I reached up and felt that my Gray Amber mask was on. The tuxedo I had been wearing looked like new.

I got up off the couch and started wandering the halls of the sorcerers' mansion. I found my way back to the ballroom where my teammates were standing about, eating hors d'oeuvres.

That seemed particularly troubling, seeing as we needed to get out of that place before the sorcerers started attacking us. I didn't know how long it would take for the place to get dangerous again, but I knew that it would happen eventually.

I could barely contain my surprise when I saw that Grace was still having a conversation with a now-recovered Cristobal. As I walked closer to them, their attention turned toward me.

"Mr. Gray Amber," Cristobal cried out. "You missed all of the excitement." He was cheerful.

I looked over to Grace in hopes that she might explain.

"Cristobal has offered to allow us to stay at the mansion for a few days because our flights got canceled due to the storm. Isn't he kind?"

"The kindest," I said.

"I take care of my friends," Cristobal said. "You are all my friends. You may stay at the mansion while the other members and I take our leave. I do not know if I will ever come back to this place."

As a newbie, I had been engrained with a very strict "no fraternization with horrific killers" rule. Apparently, Grace had been taught a slightly altered version, where we could house-sit for them to weather a storm.

Cristobal was conversing with Grace about his experience as a mind slave to Mr. Midnight.

"There could be no better punishment for my sins," Cristobal said. "To be a slave in my own skin, unable to make amends, unable to forget. But fate is cruel. We are rarely punished alone . . ." He looked over at the crowds of NPCs, who suddenly looked very gaunt and tired.

After a little more talking, Cristobal wandered off with one of his many admirers.

"Is someone going to explain this?" I asked.

"We cleared the storyline," Chris said. "You know, they didn't always have lodges to go back to. Before, you cleared a storyline so that you would have a place to stay."

I was going to ask for a better explanation, but then I remembered . . .

The guest rooms in the Astralist's castle. The extra dorm rooms at Delta Epsilon Delta. The abandoned church from the Grotesque storyline. Even the underground lab from *The Subject of Inquiry*.

Dyer's Lodge wasn't the only convenient place to spend the night. They were all over. That was supposed to be part of the reward for clearing a storyline.

The modern set of players really had gotten lazy, hadn't they?

Soon, all of the NPCs had cleared out of the ballroom.

Silas the Showman arrived shortly after. I barely noticed. I was lost in thought about Anna and Camden.

Chris and Grace got their rewards first. Grace got a level and a trope as well as some money. Chris just got the money.

Antoine, Kimberly, and I each got two stat tickets from our ordeal. They had gotten a high star rating simply because they were so under-leveled for the storyline. They also did their tasks well with no major hiccups. I was higher level than them, so even though—in my humble opinion—I did more than them, I still got the same number of stars.

Antoine received two trope tickets.

Knight in Shining Armor
Type: Buff
Archetype: Any
Aspect: Any
Stat Used: Moxie

> Horror movies have little in common with the chivalric romances of old. One thing they do have in common is that the damsel has a valiant defender.
>
> When equipped, the player's Mettle and Grit will be buffed when defending their romantic interest. The extent of the buff will be based on how convincing their love is on-screen (Moxie).
>
> You may try to die for her, but really, you'll just die *before* her.

This would really work well with Kimberly's Looks Don't Last strategy.

> Everyone Loves a Winner
> Type: Rule
> Archetype: Athlete
> Aspect: Stud
> Stat Used: Moxie
>
> Whether you are Prince Charming or an unrepentant jackass, as an Athlete, everyone is your friend when you are winning.
>
> NPCs will be aware of a recent fictitious victory of some kind that the player's character has achieved. This news will win the player allies from those who admire them. This will give the player narrative footing to use these friends for their connections and information.
>
> Beware: when the mood shifts, so too will your influence.
>
> In movies, as in life, most people are just fair-weather fans.

This trope relied on Antoine taking advantage of the narrative leverage the trope afforded. I could see it being useful if he did.

Kimberly was awarded two tropes.

> Breaking the Veil of Silence
> Type: Insight
> Archetype: Female Major Archetype
> Aspect: Any
> Stat Used: Moxie
>
> Horrors don't always lie hidden. Sometimes they are an open secret. When someone who knows of the danger sees a potential victim, they are sometimes brave enough to lift the veil of silence and offer a brief warning.

In story: the player is likely to receive warnings about dangers from NPCs who know they are at risk. The warnings will be more explicit if the player is the next target on the enemy's priority list.

Out of story: the player will receive warnings from local NPCs of Omens where women are a primary target. They will also hint at what types of special rewards are available for the storyline, including hunting tags, pawn tickets, licenses, vouchers, travel tickets, Private Showings, rescue tickets, bounties, attestations of authenticity, Carousel tarot cards, writs, and more.

"Everyone knew something was going on. No one said anything!"

This one sounded extraordinarily useful. I didn't even know what some of the special rewards were. I had never even heard of them.

When in Rome
Type: Buff
Archetype: Any
Aspect: Any
Stat Used: Moxie

The Party phase is not meant to be a somber event filled with fact-finding and rigorous exploration. That can bore an audience to tears. In horror flicks, the fun before the killing starts is an essential ingredient.

When this trope is equipped, the player's Grit will be buffed until after First Blood if their portrayal matches the tone of the movie.

Only the Hysteric is supposed to act like they're about to die.

My best guess was that Kimberly had spent the Party afraid of her first death and it had affected her performance. As ghoulish as it may sound, her getting her first death in might actually help her get over her hang-up.

Well, as much as a person could get over their fear of death.

I also received two tropes.

Dead Man Walking
Type: Buff
Archetype: Any
Aspect: Any
Stat Used: N/A

> How many movies have a scene where the heroes stumble upon the destruction of the killer's rampage and find one dying survivor, whose final words are exposition used to prepare the main characters for what is to come?
>
> With this trope equipped, the player gains a huge buff in Grit upon receiving a fatal wound or condition, or otherwise has their death guaranteed. The buff will allow them to have a prolonged survival period so that they might warn those to come. This will not prevent their death, but it will put it off for a scene or two.
>
> Famous last words require an audience.

That really worked well with my strategy of encountering the bad guy and then informing the team about them. It also sounded like it was going to hurt. In many ways, low Grit was a blessing because it prevented a long, drawn-out death—not that I had gotten to benefit from that much so far. I would have to think about this trope.

> Coming to a Theater Near You
> Type: Insight
> Archetype: Film Buff
> Aspect: Any
> Stat Used: Savvy
>
> Did you know that movie trailers used to come *after* the movie? In Carousel, they still do!
>
> After completing a storyline, the player will be able to see movie trailers of other recent or ongoing films from around all of Carousel.
>
> If the player is on Deathwatch when their movie ends, they will be able to use applicable Deathwatch tropes in the trailer scenes.
>
> So, what are you going to watch next?

That was a powerful insight trope. It might be difficult to use in any practical way, but I could see how important it could be as a scouting trope.

As I read through my tropes, I dreaded the coming conversations. The real conversations about Anna and Camden. About the future.

Luckily, I had a very good excuse to avoid those conversations. I could watch the trailers for the other storylines. They might clue me into how the others were doing, assuming the trailers gave me any useful information.

I equipped the Coming to a Theater Near You trope and looked at the red wallpaper to watch the trailers. Like Director's Monitor, it allowed me to passively watch in my mind's eye. Unlike that trope, though, I had no idea what to expect.

The first trailer started to play.

* * *

Dark somber music filled my ears as the screen showed a large auditorium that I recognized as being part of the University of Carousel.

A narrator's voice boomed. "You thought the past was buried . . ."

A montage of black and white clips of people laughing and dancing during a party.

"The bone-chilling sequel to *Ten-Year Reunion.*"

A quick flash of a woman screaming.

A woman said in a panicked voice, "I told you he would be back; he will never let us forget what happened."

Next, I saw interspersed shots of people with scared expressions on their faces. I recognized some of them. They were players. I didn't know their names without having the red wallpaper available to read them, but I had seen them around camp.

The narrator continued. "He's back, and this time his vengeance is sharper."

I saw a shadowy figure in a rain slicker. His face was hidden. The glint of a sharpened crowbar in one hand and a tire iron in the other flashed in the moonlight. I saw more close-ups of frightened faces of people I recognized, intercut with scenes of them running through darkened streets. I could hear the sound of their heartbeats.

Back to a party scene filled with decorations, laughter, and dancing.

The narrator said, "Some secrets can never die."

As the dancing continued, the camera panned to the windows. The shadowy figure could be seen approaching the auditorium while carrying his weapons.

Suddenly, the music shifted. Something more twisted and ethereal started to play with a hint of sleigh bells, of all things.

The mysterious figure stood across the courtyard from the players. Dark snowflakes began to fall from the sky—the black snow. All of the characters, the players included, were confused by that, and they looked up at the cloud above in awe. As a snowflake landed on what I assumed was an NPC's skin, the camera cut to her eye as her blood vessels turned dark. Her eyes grew black quickly.

The killer, upon seeing the snow, displayed uncharacteristic fear. He quickly gathered his weapons in one hand and turned to rush for shelter in a nearby building. The area's snowfall continued to cover everything as the whole world became pillows of black.

"Some secrets . . . are colder than death."

The music got louder, and then a title appeared on the screen.

Eleven-Year Reunion: The Black Snow.

"Coming soon."

* * *

The black snow Apocalypse had taken over that storyline, turning it into some sort of disjointed sequel or reboot. I had no idea what fate awaited the players who had been caught in it.

Before I had time to process what I had just seen, the next trailer started to play.

The music shifted to a serene melody as images of lakes, rivers, and beaches appeared on the screen. Families laughed, kids played in the water, and couples lounged on the shore.

"Water, the essence of life . . ."

The scene shifted to a secluded pond nestled within the forest. The tranquility of the pond was accentuated by small waterfalls trickling from the surrounding rocks.

". . . and the harbinger of death . . ."

The camera zoomed out to show a handmade wooden fence surrounding the pond. Warning signs were prominently displayed, including signs that said "Private Property" and "No Trespassing." Nearby, a shrine of some sort could be seen adorned with candles and mysterious symbols.

A man's voice could be heard saying, "You know how much we paid for this vacation? We got the top package. If there's a private swimming hole, we deserve to swim in it. What are they going to do? Charge us extra?"

A group of tourists carrying hiking equipment walked through the forest, laughing and chatting with each other. They disregarded the warnings on the fence and climbed right over. One of them, with a mischievous grin, did a cannonball into the pristine water.

I recognized them. They were more players from the lodge. One of the stronger teams, if my memory was correct.

"Water has a memory of its own . . ."

Cut to a scene in a bathroom as one of the women in the hiking group was preparing for a shower. As she was getting ready, she looked over into the bathtub and saw that there was a long-haired figure behind the shower curtain. In a panic, she pulled the shower curtain open, only to reveal that no one was there.

The screen cut to black.

"Something is happening; we can't ignore this any longer," the woman said.

"We should have listened!"

The main characters gathered around an elder wearing spiritual regalia. He had a grave expression on his face. He spoke in a foreign tongue, his words displayed in subtitles.

"You must lift the curse before the next rainfall. If you fail to do this, you will be doomed."

In the next scene, dark clouds gathered overhead as the wind howled. The main characters, all of whom I recognized as players, looked up in horror.

"It's too early to rain already! We barely even started!" one of them said.

But of course, instead of rain, black snow started to fall from the clouds. Everyone stared at it in disbelief and horror.

The narrator continued. "Some secrets are buried deep underwater. Others under snow."

The screen faded back to black, and then the title emerged.

Head Below Water: The Black Snow.

"Coming soon."

CHAPTER EIGHTEEN

PARTY FAVORS, PART TWO

It looked like all of the storylines that had been running at the time the black snow Apocalypse was triggered were affected.

The next trailer started to play.

Intense eerie music started to build as the screen faded from black. A high-tech lab came into view with equipment scattered and alarms blaring.

A soldier armed to the gills, whom I recognized as Garrett, one of the players at the lodge, said, "You opened the door and you're surprised that they came through?"

"We followed protocol!" a scientist screamed back at him.

"We are the protocol," Garrett responded with a smirk. He was either a great actor or he really was enjoying himself.

A rapid montage began to show with flashing lights and horrifying images of grotesque and hellish creatures. Some were skeletal with meat hanging off their flesh and weapons fused to their bones. Others were imp-like demons quickly running around with burning fangs and claws clinging to every surface. Others were large blobs that appeared to explode with fire.

There was a fiery minotaur-like creature wielding an axe that had been somehow fused to the place where its hand should have been. Its axe was sharp and powerful, able to cut through an entire stone barricade in one slash.

A group of commandos, along with one scientist, all of whom I recognized as players, charged at the demonic creatures, machine guns firing all the way.

"If they didn't want to fight, they should have stayed in hell," Garrett said as he hurled a grenade into a mob of the red demons, resulting in them being splattered along the hallway.

I then saw an image of Garrett climbing up onto a gasoline tanker as a horde of various demons followed him and tried to get to him. He grabbed onto a rope that was dangling from a helicopter, which lifted him up. As it did, he dropped an incendiary device down onto the gasoline tanker.

Someone in the helicopter had a machine gun and was riddling both the tanker and the demons with holes. As the helicopter moved them away, the entire place exploded, sending demon parts every which way and killing most of the demons in the lot.

"Eat this!" someone said as they shoved a gun down a demon's gullet.

Some of the players had really taken to Carousel.

"We're going to have to touch down. A storm is approaching; it'll knock us out of the sky," the helicopter pilot screamed back at the players.

Garrett looked confused. "What are you talking about?"

He must have played this storyline before and didn't remember a storm ever approaching.

The familiar black cloud appeared in the sky, ominous and looming.

As the helicopter landed, everything turned silent for a brief moment. The team of soldiers watched in disbelief as the black snow started to fall in the distance. The remaining hellish creatures, apparently sensing some new kind of danger, began to run around in fear and started to burrow holes. However, the holes that they dug weren't in the earth. It appeared as if they were digging holes back into their hell dimension.

"What's going on?" one of the players asked.

Garrett didn't look sure. "If it's so bad they need to flee, then we better follow them," he said decisively.

The team approached a giant red insectoid demon, gnawing its way through reality, creating a fiery interdimensional rift on the side of a building. They filled it with bullets and then jumped through the hole it had just created.

As they did, the portal closed shut behind them.

The screen faded to black. Large fiery letters appeared.

"Parazoid Protocol."

Below them, frozen in ice, the words "The Black Snow" appeared.

Parazoid Protocol: The Black Snow.

The narrator returned. "Coming soon . . ."

I could only hope that they would survive. Some kind of bravery, jumping into hell itself to avoid the black snow.

Then one of the trailers I had been waiting for started to play.

* * *

Soft, uplifting music filled the air as I saw an aerial shot of Carousel looking picturesque. Families were playing in parks, children were laughing, and all of the houses were lined up neatly in rows. The footage almost made Carousel look normal. That ended quickly.

The narrator came on and said, "In a town where life was simple . . ."

That was a lie.

I saw a view of the chemical plant. With little warning, a massive explosion erupted, sending shockwaves throughout the town. Residents left their houses to look up and watch as a thick black cloud started to form and grow rapidly overhead.

"The old year came to a close, and a new world was born."

Quickly, the townspeople's curiosity turned into panic. People pointed up to the sky and started to shield their children. Black snowflakes began descending as all of the noises went eerily silent. Quiet chaos ensued.

The scene cut to the image of a woman smiling as she walked her dog near the chemical plant. They were among the first to be touched by the snowflakes. They didn't just get hit with one; they were soon covered. The transformation into an amalgam, a mutant freak, was rapid and shown through quick cuts.

This was the same creature that I had seen on the red wallpaper from the bus.

I saw a man hiding out in a shed. He was a large guy. I could see sweat and fear on his face as he nursed his injured knee. It was Reggie. The light inside the shed was dim with rays of sunshine poking through the rust holes in the metal exterior of the shed.

A creature that made the sound of a child crying was circling around the shed, blocking out the light that shone through. The screen went black. I held my breath as I waited for the worst. I didn't see anything, but I heard the sound of metal scraping.

The narrator continued. "This Christmas . . . the town of Carousel will unite in ways never imagined."

Something large was walking through the streets of Carousel. The camera never actually showed what it was, but it showed its shadow on the ground beneath. I could also hear the sound of a hundred people crying as it walked. Their haunting voices sounded in unison. They were one.

"Get ready for a holiday season like no other . . ."

The Black Snow.

"Coming this winter."

This Apocalypse was supposed to arrive in the winter . . . That made sense. But why had it shown up so early?

Was Reggie the only person who had been caught by the black snow outright? The others had been in other stories. Did that make a difference?

I didn't know if I wanted that to be true. While I had no desire to see players trapped in the black snow Apocalypse, the more players there were, the more likely it was that Reggie might survive.

Where were Anna and Camden? They had been with him. Why had I not seen them in the trailer? This new trope was giving me more questions than answers.

The next trailer started to play.

The deafening roar of a plane engine under duress filled the air. Inside, alarms blared, and the plane shook violently. A team of firefighters—the players who had loaded into the storyline, including Travis's team—were strapped down, hoping to survive.

The pilot turned his head to the passengers and screamed, "The storm damaged our engines. We're overweight. We can't stay in the sky much longer . . ."

After a few moments, he shouted, "Brace for impact!"

The screen started to shake as the sounds of metal screeching and trees breaking were heard. The scene of the plane crashing into the forest started to play. It sent up a cloud of dust and debris.

Players were crawling from the wreckage. They had to help each other because some were so injured that they had to limp or crawl. The smoke and the red-orange hues of the nearby fires painted them a grim backdrop.

They were starting out this storyline injured already. That spelled disaster.

The scene transitioned to a makeshift forest-firefighting encampment. A nurse ran over to help with the injured and give out orders as the players arrived.

After many of them had received some treatment, the nurse ran to them urgently and said, "We need to evacuate! The fires are coming this way!"

The camp quickly turned to chaos. As they started to evacuate, a thick wall of fire and smoke started to separate the group. Shouts and cries were muffled by the roaring flames.

Some unspecified time later, a lone firefighter, an NPC, soot-covered and exhausted, trudged through the charred remains of the forest. He stumbled upon a large metal plate emerging from the ground. It was covered in bizarre etchings. He crouched down to inspect it.

"What is this?" he asked. His voice sounded delirious.

As he touched one of the symbols on the metal plate, it began to tremble, and it started to lift. It was a door. The firefighter stumbled back, and from the dark void, a figure emerged.

This trailer didn't try to hide anything. The thing that came out of the dark hole was a robot. It was advanced and covered in alien markings. It appeared to be equipped with all sorts of weaponry, including a prehensile tail with a saw blade on it.

The screen cut to black at the moment the robot made contact with the NPC.

A few quick shots came by: firefighters screaming and running as the robot chased and attacked them, fires burning brighter in the distance.

One of the players, I couldn't tell which one, said, "Something was awakened."

Their voice was raspy and damaged from smoke. A quick shot of their face revealed that the voice I heard was Vernon's, Travis's brother. Not only had he been slightly injured in the plane crash, but he had also been burned by the fire and clearly had gotten smoke damage to his lungs.

Vernon was a tank. And getting injured that early into the storyline was not a good sign.

An aerial shot of the forest was shown. Most of it was burned down. Smoke still rose from the ashes.

A voice I recognized, Tori, cried out, "What does it want from us?"

The scene transitioned to a shot of the robot placing something into a yellow metal box. There was fogged-up glass on the side of the box. As the robot stacked it neatly on top of a row of boxes just like it, the camera zoomed in to show that they were filled with cryogenically frozen human body parts.

The narrator's voice came over, saying, "When nature's wrath meets an ancient terror, the fight isn't just against the flames."

The screen faded to black, and then a title emerged over it.

Preservation.

"Coming soon. Preserve your seats now."

I didn't want to make any predictions. I was afraid to follow my natural inclinations because, to me, they looked doomed. I could only hope that the trailer was more dire than the reality.

The final trailer started to play. As soon as it did, my heart broke.

Dark atmospheric music filled my head.

Shots of teenagers having fun at a roller rink. Everything looked happy. They were having a blast. The music, though, stayed dark and dreary.

The screen faded to black as I heard an explosion and then a sound that I couldn't place, which sounded almost like a building falling down but worse.

I saw a close-up shot of Anna. She looked worried as she spoke.

"You mean he's been traveling to places in time where people get killed?"

The room was dimly lit. I could barely see Camden shaking his head.

"No. He's using this book to target tragic events. His amulets can only move him to and from points in time where humans have suffered. The roller rink, the bridge collapse . . . He's even orchestrating his own mass casualty events now."

I saw a brief glimpse of a beat-up paperback book in Camden's hand. Its cover was splattered with blood, as were Camden's hand and clothes. The title of the book read, *The Town of Carousel: Horrific Events Through the Ages.*

Cut to frantic running through dirty alleyways and darkened streets as Anna and Camden tried to escape from a menacing figure in an overcoat. I could see the faint glimmer of some kind of amulet around the figure's neck.

Cut to a shocking scene that hit me right in the gut.

Camden was bound to a table. He was screaming in agony. His right arm was missing below the elbow. The mysterious figure from the alleyway stood over him. In one hand, he held the pendant that I had seen glowing earlier. And in the other, he held some sort of ice pick that he was using to inflict pain on Camden.

As he did, the pendant started to glow in sync with Camden's cries.

The camera panned over a table covered in newspaper clippings with black-and-white photos of various disasters—fires, floods, mass killings. All things from Carousel's grim history.

In the next scene, Camden was even more banged up, but it appeared he had somehow escaped from the unknown assailant.

"If we want to stand any chance, we have to get a step ahead of him! Do it!" Camden screamed.

There was a close-up shot of Anna holding a power drill. Her eyes were filled with tears and uncertainty.

"Do it!" Camden shouted in desperation.

Next, I could only see Anna's back as the drill whirred and Camden screamed. The amulet, or one that looked very similar to it, was around Anna's neck. As Camden screamed, it began to flicker and pulse, showing that their desperate plan was taking effect.

The screen faded to black. The title card appeared.

Post-Traumatic.

The narrator's voice said, "Some scars don't fade in time."

Post-Traumatic! That had been the title of the storyline that I had seen at the roller rink. After they had gotten off the helicopter, they must have run there to avoid the black snow.

I just hoped that it was enough to save them.

After the last trailer played, I fell to my knees. I was in shock.

As the others gathered around me to ask what had happened, I couldn't answer.

I felt helpless.

I didn't know what to do.

CHAPTER NINETEEN

BY THE FIRE

I saw them . . . ," I said.

It took the rest of the team a few seconds to realize what I was talking about. I was having trouble putting it into words.

"They're in a storyline that is stronger than this one!" I said. "They're alone . . ."

Grace started to protest, saying, "Reggie is wi—"

She stopped talking as she saw my new movie trailer trope on the red wallpaper.

"Where's Reggie?" she asked.

I looked at her and she knew from the way I couldn't speak that Reggie was stuck in the Apocalypse.

Grace grew faint.

"Let's get to the lounge over here," Chris said, gently grabbing Grace and guiding her across the hall to a room filled with opulent decorations as well as plenty of expensive furniture, including, appropriately enough, several fainting chairs.

Antoine and Kimberly encouraged me to follow, prying me up off the ground.

Grace sat quietly in her chair. I sat on a couch nearby.

They didn't force me to talk. The stress of having died again coupled with the sudden realization that my two oldest friends were doomed was difficult for me to process.

"I need a drink," I said.

Chris went back to the ballroom and procured us all something to sip on.

* * *

As time went by, the conversation started to open back up.

"What's it like out there?" Antoine asked.

"A lot of missing posters are about to be added to the wall," I said. "The people in the stories that were running . . . It's like the black snow took the movies over."

I explained how the trailers looked and how most of the running storylines had "The Black Snow" as their subtitle.

"So, we have at least two teams down?" Chris said, surprised. "Do you remember who was on them?"

Oh boy.

I tried my best to describe which players I had seen in which storyline. I then explained the dire situation that Anna and Camden were left in.

"They might make it," Kimberly said through tears. "You said they had a plan."

No one corrected her, but no one echoed her optimism either.

"Meg's team. Carl's run . . . ," Chris said.

"The team on the plane . . . ," I said.

Grace made eye contact with me at the mention of them.

"The plane crashed from the storm," I said. "They weren't a part of the black snow, but . . . they were in trouble."

This hit Grace again. The rest of her team was on that plane.

Time went on and we sat around not talking about anything important. Chris had taken to fortifying the room. He gathered up anything from around the mansion that could be used as a weapon as well as some food from the kitchen.

He said that it wasn't safe for us to be separated, that we would be sleeping in the lounge. There were plenty of couches to accommodate that.

Eventually, once he had accomplished his task, he and Antoine went out to the limousine to gather all of our clothes. They came back and reported that the limo had been abandoned. As far as they could tell, the NPCs and enemies were all gone.

"We don't know how long before they get back," Chris said. "We need to keep our masks on just in case. They should still work if the storyline starts back up, but hopefully, we'll be out of here before that happens. This one is tricky. Most of the time you have to kill all of the enemies before you can take over a place like this. It's not often you find yourself an ally to the bad guys when the story ends."

It really did seem such a shame that we had these very useful magical objects that could at least temporarily obscure our identities, and they were of no use anywhere in Carousel except for this one obscure story out in the hills.

I got up and started moving around. I picked an unclaimed area in the lounge and started moving a couch in that direction. Antoine helped me.

As night started to fall, Chris started a fire in the fireplace of the lounge. With it lit, all of the other lights could be turned off to transform the room into something that seemed at least slightly hospitable for sleep.

Sleeping in a place like that was a daunting proposition. Even if the NPCs and enemies were gone from the ballroom and the guest rooms, that surely didn't mean that the enemies and the casks downstairs had been hauled away. Knowing that there were dark sorcerers in walking distance was not pleasing. Then again, I had spent the night in a laboratory with a poltergeist. Eventually, I would get used to it.

Luckily, with my Out like a Light trope, actually getting to sleep would not be that difficult.

Kimberly found a record player and started playing classical music on it. I didn't recognize the music, but then again, it was Carousel. Everything seemed slightly off-brand.

Chris had asked Kimberly for one of her new tropes. He just wanted to examine it. It was the one called Breaking the Veil of Silence. He seemed confused by it.

Eventually, he was so perplexed that he was willing to talk to Grace about it, even though she had stayed silent since she had found out about her brother.

"What is a hunting tag or a writ or a tarot card?" Chris asked.

The trope description said that NPCs will ". . . hint at what types of special rewards are available for the storyline, including hunting tags, pawn tickets, licenses, vouchers, travel tickets, Private Showings, rescue tickets, bounties, attestations of authenticity, Carousel tarot cards, writs, and more." I had not recognized several of the special rewards. I thought I was just inexperienced.

Chris didn't know about most of them either.

Grace shrugged her shoulders.

"Guess their plan is ruined," Antoine said to Chris an hour or so later.

"Yeah, well . . . It probably wouldn't have worked anyway," Chris said.

I thought they were talking about the excursion trip to Snowblind. But then they kept talking.

"What plan?" Kimberly asked.

"Just something some of the players were planning," Chris said.

That piqued my interest. Was he talking about the Secret Lore runs?

"What were they planning?" I asked.

"You won't like it," Chris said.

Me specifically? What was he talking about?

"Won't like what?"

Chris started to laugh. "Some of the higher-level players were going to try something stupid. The excursion trip. We weren't going to bring Arthur. The plan was to leave a little early. I mean, I don't know why he wanted to come, but we didn't need him. Maybe we were going to try and make a break for the lights beyond the mountain between scenes of a storyline. Might have been too risky. Arthur always told us it was."

"Chris was going to bring me, Kimberly, and Anna," Antoine added. "He just told me, I swear."

"But I suppose Arthur told you why we're not supposed to do that, right?" Chris asked. "You're one of the people who know the secret, right? You know what happens to people who disappear, who, I assume, die without a missing poster, don't you?"

My eyes went wide. I heard breathing on my neck. I did know what would happen if you broke the rules. The axe murderer would kill you.

Chris started to laugh. "Don't worry about it. I know you won't tell us anything."

Had that been the thing that Chris and Antoine were talking about at the bowling alley? They knew that people who tried to sneak toward the mountain between the scenes of another storyline disappeared. Why would they do something so stupid?

"Carl was the one that was planning it," Chris said. "Crazy SOB. Guess he won't be now."

Carl was apparently one of the players who had been in a storyline when the black snow hit.

"Wait," Kimberly said, somehow more interested in my secret than Chris's. "So you do know something? Camden always said you had a secret you couldn't tell us."

I could hardly hear her over the sound of breathing in my ears.

"Please, can we not talk about this?" I begged. I considered using my sleeping trope to just fall asleep instantly. That would end the conversation. Luckily, Chris wasn't trying to cause trouble.

"I know, I know," Chris said. "Valerie always acted the same way when the subject came up."

No one talked for a while. All I could hear was the crackling of the fire as the sound of the axe murderer's breathing faded.

"How were you supposed to get Anna, Kimberly, and Antoine over there?" I asked. As far as I knew, they only had six tickets.

Chris laughed. "Guess it doesn't matter now. A few years ago, we found some missing pages from the atlas. They were in one of the campers' medical records. Just hidden where no one would look. That's where we learned some things about the excursion train. Arthur failed to mention them. Turned out, there are multiple ways to get tickets. Heck, Wallflowers don't even need tickets. The inspector just ignores them. Outsiders can stow away in the cargo hold. Eye Candy, like Kimberly here, can buy their own tickets, but just for them and a plus one. We've been planning this for a long time. Had a whole group about to go over there. Too late for that now. Most of them are dead with Carl, I figure."

Missing pages from the atlas? Camden had said there were tons of missing pages and altered entries. Why would they be hidden? What could Arthur and Adeline have been up to?

They were going to leave me too. I didn't want to think about this. I didn't want to be awake. Camden and Anna were gone, dead almost for certain. I wanted to go straight to sleep.

But then Grace started talking again.

"You know, it's a strange thing," Grace said. "Did I ever tell you the whole story of how my team got here?"

No one responded, but we looked in her direction from our various sleeping spots.

"You see, my then-fiancé, Jesse—you know Jesse—won an exclusive package to a couples retreat." She looked over at Chris. "You know the one up on Gallows Hill?"

Chris nodded.

"All we had to do to claim it was come to Carousel during the centennial celebration. They said they were going to feature us in a float that the hospitality coordinator oversaw. I didn't know any of that when I came. To me, this trip was all a surprise."

She stood and walked in front of the fireplace.

"Of course, when we got here, this was not the romantic getaway that Jesse had promised me. But that's enough said about that. A few years later, my brother, Reggie"—she struggled to say his name—"showed up with his friend Dirk and Dirk's girlfriend, Bella. You've met them. Who you never met was Reggie's fiancée, Trudy.

"They took a few years of leveling up to match our Plot Armor, but eventually, they joined Jesse and I, and we became a team. One day, we were doing the Laughter at Midnight storyline, and when we finished, we all reconvened to get our rewards, but Trudy never showed up. I asked Reggie what had happened to her because they both should have survived that storyline, and he said that he didn't know. She had gone missing. Disappeared, as it were.

"I'd heard that people would sometimes go missing with no explanation, but I didn't quite understand it. It never sat right with me no matter how much

Arthur and a select few others insisted that it was perfectly normal and not to press the issue. Suddenly, I saw that Reggie had joined in that small group of people who seemed to know some secret that the rest of us didn't.

"I'm a naturally curious person. I have been ever since I was a kid. Growing up, Reggie didn't have any secrets from me. I couldn't stand feeling like Reggie knew something and wasn't telling me. So, I ambushed him one day using all of my Detective tropes to try and get the truth out of him. Chief among them was this one," she said, brandishing her Human Lie Detector trope. "This is my most reliable trope. I promise, if you can tell when people are lying, you'll never want to give that ability up.

"So, I pressed him, and I asked what had happened to her. He avoided the topic. But I kept asking, and he literally ran from me. My brother Reggie, who never freaks out over anything, looked terrified just because I was asking him questions. I've seen him cut his own hand off to avoid a zombie infection. The look on his face from that was like he had a paper cut. But this broke him.

"I was using tropes to draw out answers and to force him to talk. You might have thought that I was driving needles under his fingernails from the way he acted. Eventually, I cornered him out on the docks on the lake. I almost asked him another question, but he stopped me. He said that if I kept asking him questions, he would jump out into the lake and swim out of the cove until the lake monster killed him.

"He was telling the truth," she said.

She drew closer to me.

"So, when you first came back with that old familiar news that Janet had disappeared, gone missing, I had my Human Lie Detector trope ready to go. I out-leveled you by so much that there was no way you could get anything past me. So, do you know what that trope told me when you said she went missing?"

I was terrified to answer. I could feel the Rulekeeper breathing down my neck like he was right behind me. I grabbed a pillow off of the couch and put it up to the back of my neck just in the hope that it might ease the sensation. It didn't.

Kimberly and Antoine watched on with shocked expressions because I was acting like a crazy person.

I couldn't answer her question. She kept talking anyway.

"No? Don't want to guess? I'll tell you anyway."

She paused for a moment.

I needed to go to sleep right at that moment with the power of my trope. I almost did, but then she answered her own question.

"It didn't tell me anything," she said. "Not a single damn thing. It didn't tell me if you were lying or telling the truth. It didn't even say the results were inconclusive. I've had this trope for years. I've used it in every circumstance where a human could tell a lie. I've been able to trust it in countless situations. And yet, whenever you people talk about the players that go missing, suddenly it and many of my other interrogation tropes stop working. Curious, wouldn't you say?"

She turned to Chris, Antoine, and Kimberly.

"It's almost as if Carousel doesn't want us to know what happened to the missing players. Our tropes simply won't let us discover it. Psychics have the same problem. Their tropes can be among the most insightful in the game, and yet they are completely blind to what happens to missing players. For years this blind spot was enough to keep the players at Dyer's Lodge from acting out. But even in the face of such risk, people get restless.

"I've heard the plans people have made to try to make a run for the mountain on the far side of the lake between scenes. Personally, I think they're stupid"—she looked at Chris when she said that—"but I understand the impulse."

"As do I," Chris echoed.

"Goodnight, you all," Grace said. "I need sleep."

I didn't wait for the breathing to go away again. I activated my trope and drifted off almost instantly.

CHAPTER TWENTY

DEAREST MR. GRAY AMBER

Why do they go through the trouble of making all of these nonsense histories for each and every storyline?" Grace asked as she flipped through a leather-bound book from the vast collection of the mansion's library.

"What's that one saying?" I asked, leafing through a tome related to the magic system for the storyline we had just finished.

"Carousel is the capital city of Hesteria, which appears to be a continent right in the spot where North America is supposed to be." She showed me the map she had been looking at, and, sure enough, Europe, Africa, Asia, and the other continents were there, but no North or South America. A different continent had taken its place, and Carousel was its capital.

"Hmm," Chris said. "Might explain why this storyline takes place outside the city. The Carousel we know has a bit of everything, but it isn't a metropolis."

"What do you mean by that?" I asked.

Chris started to laugh. "Haven't you heard the ways Carousel gets described in different storylines? Sometimes it's a big city, sometimes a little Podunk town in the middle of nowhere. Carousel is playing a role, just like us."

"Why would it need to do that?" Kimberly asked as she lay on a couch, reading a copy of *Eavesdropper Magazine*, the very gossip mag our characters had worked for. "Why not just write the stories to fit?"

"All we can do is ask questions," Chris said, "until Carousel decides to start giving some answers."

"This part is consistent," Grace said. She held out a page with a map of Carousel. "This map is from '81. The road we arrived on hadn't been built yet."

"The road to the mansion or . . . Wait. Do you mean the road to the parking lot? When did that show up?" I asked.

Grace nodded. "The parking lot and the entire road down to the corn maze didn't exist until 1989. I've been researching this for our hunt for Secret Lore. I figure the secrets might be old, so better see what Carousel has looked like over the years."

"Wait," Kimberly said. "Does that mean there were no players before 1989? No parking lot, no players."

Grace let out an exasperated laugh. "Well, you would think so, but the maps are not trustworthy for that sort of thing."

"Why?"

"The centennial," Chris said.

Grace nodded. "The centennial celebration occurs every time a new player arrives. How can it be the hundred-year anniversary of the town every year, sometimes multiple times a year? The history books and maps all change to reflect that. They're just props. So, we don't know if the parking lot really showed up in 1989, but that's what the maps have said since I got here."

That was smart—using old maps to track changes to Carousel over time.

"Wait," I asked. "Do new parts of Carousel keep showing up every year? I feel like I have heard some vets talking about something like that."

Chris nodded his head. "We think so. Records are spotty, and Carousel is hard to keep track of because the storylines all take place on different dates. Like in this one, it's 1992. Still, we all swear we see things change. Buildings appear on roads that were empty before, that sort of thing."

Before the conversation could go on, Antoine burst into the library holding a platter of food. We had been staying at the mansion for four days at that point. The food from the party was starting to get stale, so now we were having to cook our food from the vast stores in the pantry and walk-in cooler. Grace had been doing that for us, but Chris told Antoine it was his turn, to give her a break.

"Steaks and asparagus," Antoine said as he came into the room. "I know how to cook a steak. I made them all medium, give or take a few degrees. I wrapped the asparagus in bacon, but that burned."

"Thank you," Grace said, accepting her plate.

I agreed.

We ate in silence, all putting off the conversation that we didn't want to have.

We had to leave the mansion soon.

Chris said we couldn't risk staying for too much longer. I wanted to argue. To me, it seemed unlikely that we could trigger the storyline at the mansion again given the fact that the omen was in a limo back in Carousel.

They said that didn't guarantee anything. Apparently, there were multiple omens for some storylines that could bring you into different perspectives of the same story.

That made sense on some level. The version that we had entered made the storyline out to be a black comedy of sorts. A group of gossip columnists sneaking into a celebrity-filled party and finding out that it was filled with sorcerers who snatched bodies was surely not the only storyline such an elaborate set piece could be used for.

Still, the prospect of leaving was incredibly daunting.

"The room is right up here," I said as we wound up the secret staircase.

The black snow cloud had been so large that we were able to see it storming in the distance even from ground level, but as time went on it had started to shrink. In order to get a good look at it, we decided to climb the tower that Mrs. Cloudburst had shown me. We were hoping to find that the storm was over.

"So, she just took you up here all on her own?" Antoine asked.

"Well, I guess it was in the script. Or at least her version of it," I answered.

I led them to the room at the top of the tower and opened the door. I walked in and was soon greeted with a view of Carousel in the distance.

"Damn," I said.

The cloud had shrunk quite a bit, but it hadn't finished storming. I couldn't imagine what it would be like for the people caught in it. At that point, the monsters created by the black snow were only a secondary antagonist. The primary worry would be finding food and water. We had been very fortunate to be stuck in a well-stocked mansion.

"What happened while you were up here?" Kimberly asked.

"It was the strangest thing," I said. "She took me to the window and pointed at the black snow cloud and asked if it was going to move this way. She looked really worried. I suppose that means that she didn't have any information on it, which is very interesting to me."

Antoine and Kimberly looked at each other.

"And what happened after that?" Kimberly asked.

"She started getting us ready for the next scene," I said. "Ruffled her hair, kissed my collar. Had to make it look like we had hooked up. You know, I think the society members were swingers or something. I'm glad they didn't play up that angle too much. I was worried *Mr.* Cloudburst might show up."

"Oh," Antoine said. "Chris said NPCs usually won't try to get frisky, but enemies might if that's their MO. I figured she was technically an enemy . . ."

"You thought we hooked up?" I asked. I could imagine the way we looked would lead them to believe that. "Let's avoid storylines with those kinds of enemies, huh?"

Kimberly noticed something across the room. She walked over and grabbed it from on top of one of the pillows.

"I think this is for you," she said, handing me a letter addressed to Mr. Gray Amber. Yep, that was me, all right.

The letter had nothing but the name and a red stain on it, as if its sender had applied lipstick before kissing the envelope.

I stared at it for a moment.

"Are you going to open it?" Antoine asked.

"Give me a second. I need to think about it. Make sure it's not an Omen or something."

I tore the envelope open to find a letter written in fancy cursive.

Dearest Mr. Gray Amber,

I am leaving to go across the sea with Cristobal. You have every right to despise me, but I hope you will understand what is in my heart.

I was trapped in a prison before he came along. My body was frail and sickly. I had no idea that when I signed up for the society, I would eventually be trading one prison for another. That's what Cristobal's love is: captivation—I am truly his.

I regret the things I have done to people, but how can I change when I can never leave this cycle? When I look into his eyes during the moments I have with him, however fleeting, I cannot feel doubt, or shame, or guilt—only love. The secret we all know is that only change can save us, but it is difficult; I've tried to save myself in every way I know how. We all have in the society; we've screamed out to the gods, to Cristobal, "Please, please, save us." And he has done his best; he is the most powerful man in the world and very generous.

When I meet someone like you, I remember the pain, the torment given and taken, and I remember my desire to leave this all behind. Cristobal says that the pain is fleeting, that our lives together are forever, and I have to believe him. I no longer know if I deserve punishment for my sins, but the innocent and the deserving suffer together in this life, don't they?

I chose the name Cloudburst because I always felt like a storm of regret was chasing me, threatening to destroy my happiness. The storm came before I expected it, but it was all part of the greater plan, I think. And like the storm, the feelings between us will pass. What is next may be worse, but it's all part of that same plan.

I hope that you find a way to forget about me. You must succeed. All the good people like you must succeed in your fight against people like me. I am not a good person, though I wish I was, and you deserve better than this little detour with me. It's time we get back on our true paths; I hope you're ready.

Yours in passion,
Ms. Cloudburst

Antoine and Kimberly read the letter over my shoulders.

"You hooked up with a hundred-year-old lady, didn't you?" Antoine asked.

"No," I said.

"Is it normal for NPCs or . . . enemies, I guess, to leave love letters?" Kimberly asked.

"I don't know," I said. "This is my first."

"It isn't a love letter. It's a Dear John letter. She's leaving you to stay with the cult leader," Antoine said.

"Oh, I'm sorry, Riley," Kimberly said with a smile. "I thought you were a cute couple."

"It wasn't going to work out anyway," I said. I looked closer at the letter. "Should we show this to Grace and Chris?"

"We should show them everything," Antoine said. "And we've been talking. I think we should tell them about Dina's whole thing."

I was afraid he would say that. After the destruction of the black snow, our excuse for not telling the veterans about Dina's quest to save her son and the supposed communication from Carousel had become thinner and thinner.

"Look," I said, "we need to ask your brother about that Zoe chick. We've been putting it off too long because of the storm. If it is true that someone else in the past also had a quest like Dina's, that would legitimize it, and we need to know that before we go blabbing about everything."

Antoine shrugged his shoulders.

"If he really did have a friend who walked into an over-leveled storyline because she failed a quest, he's probably not going to be happy to find out that we've been secretly trying to figure out our own quest behind his back," Antoine said. "It may turn out that this whole thing was actually just Carousel messing with us. What are we going to do if it turns out that this was all a lie?"

I thought for a moment.

"If this is real, it might mean there is a way to win, to save Anna and Camden, even. I'm following the trail until we get to the end, whatever that might be."

I shouldn't have said their names. We had somehow gone a few minutes without agonizing over our imperiled friends.

"We should go have that talk," Antoine said.

He led us out of the room. I tucked the letter into my hoodie pocket. Cloudburst's script must have allowed her to leave any player who did that little side story with her a message. So strange. What was the point? Was it a quest item? Could I pawn it for some extra tickets?

Kimberly's recent trope revealed that there were mechanics no one knew about. It had me second-guessing everything.

I walked down the stairs quietly, pondering whether we should really tell Chris everything.

What could it really hurt?

CHAPTER TWENTY-ONE

GOFORTH AND PROSPER

We found Chris down in the same lounge where we had been sleeping. He was arranging various weapons that he had found around the mansion. Most of them were antiques. He had a jewel-encrusted sword and a morning star among them.

"You're really going to try and take those?" I asked.

I knew that you couldn't just take anything after clearing a storyline. You could take most things, but certain items, like weapons, had limitations that weren't quite clear.

"Oh, I'm going to try," Chris said.

The three of us stood in front of Chris. Kimberly and I looked at Antoine. Chris was his brother, so he should be the one to ask the questions.

"What do you guys need?" Chris asked, sensing that there was something we needed to talk about from our awkward body language.

Antoine didn't look like he wasn't sure what to say, but eventually, he came out with it. "Who was Zoe Paulson?"

Chris looked genuinely surprised at that question.

"Whoa," he said. And then he paused for a moment and looked into the distance. "Where did you hear that name?"

"We saw it in the *Carousel Atlas*," Antoine answered. "There was just one reference. We think Todd wrote it, so maybe you would know since you guys came here together."

Chris zoned out for a moment.

"Zoe Paulson. She's been gone for over seven years," Chris said. "Wait, how did you get a hold of the *Carousel Atlas*?"

At that question, Antoine looked back toward me.

"Some of the other players left it out one night, so we just took a look at it," I said.

"So, you just took a look at the book that you're not supposed to touch? What section was her name in?" he asked.

Before Antoine could answer, Chris walked out into the hall and yelled, "Grace! Come in here for a minute."

Grace took a bit to arrive. "What do you need, Chris?" she asked.

"Tell her what you told me," Chris said.

So Antoine did.

"I'm amazed you could find anything about her at all," Grace said. "Ashwood stole a lot of the entries from it before he . . . you know."

"Wait, you're saying that Winston Ashwood, the Psychic that tricked a bunch of people into getting killed, tore up the *Carousel Atlas*?" I asked. I had always assumed that Arthur had done it in order to censor it.

"Well, he's *one* of the people who messed with it," Chris said. "That book's been vandalized so many times that we keep it off-limits to anyone but a select few." He shot Grace an accusatory glance.

"What?" she asked. "It's my fault they stole it?"

"I wouldn't say we stole it," I said. "We returned it."

"None of this matters," Antoine said loudly. "We were just asking if you knew who Zoe Paulson was."

Chris looked like he didn't want to answer.

"Zoe Paulson was the person who invited me to Carousel," Chris said. "Me and Todd and Valerie—my whole team. Then, after less than a year here, she decides she can't take it, so she runs headfirst into a dangerous storyline and takes the easy way out. I guess we'll see her again if we ever beat this thing. Maybe. I have no idea."

"The entry in the book said that Zoe had some sort of quest. Do you know what that was talking about?" I asked.

Chris thought for a moment. "I don't know if you would call it a quest," he said. "She seemed to think that we would somehow find a cure for her sister. Her sister was sick, and she thought that we would find medicine or magic and take it back to her and save her life. That hope got dashed on the rocks pretty quick, obviously."

Antoine, Kimberly, and I looked at each other. That sounded very familiar.

"Why did that hope get dashed on the rocks?" Kimberly asked.

Chris threw up his hands. "You have to understand that she wasn't really making any sense, especially toward the end. She said that we picked the wrong type of Aspects. Is that what you wanted to know? I don't know what that means, but I remember her saying that a day or so before she left."

The wrong type of Aspects? What could that mean?

"You really shouldn't have taken that book without permission," Chris said. "If we lost that, I'm pretty sure Adeline would die of a heart attack. That thing has been around since before she got here."

"Sorry," I said. Kimberly and Antoine followed suit.

"There's something else we wanted to tell you about," Antoine said.

He was about to talk about Dina's quest to save her son. I still wasn't certain about that, but I wasn't going to be able to convince Antoine to keep secrets from his brother any longer.

"What?" Chris said.

Antoine looked back at me and Kimberly. "Something that we found out recently," he started. "We think that Carous—"

"Shh," Chris interjected. "There was someone outside the window just now."

I turned around to look out the window but was unable to see anything. For a moment we all stayed still, waiting, listening.

Then it came. A knock on the door.

"Weapons," Chris whispered to each of us.

We each moved to pick up a weapon from the collection of antiques that Chris had found around the mansion. I chose a large spear because I didn't want enemies getting anywhere near me, and those swords looked so sharp that I might cut my own fingers off.

Chris quietly crept out of the lounge and around the hallway so that he could face the front door. I could hear muffled yelling from the other side. I couldn't make out what they were saying.

"Is that . . . ?" Grace asked, wielding a small revolver.

The door was solid wood, so we couldn't see who was on the other side, but there were windows on either side of the door. I could see a figure pressing his face against the window, trying to see through the frosted glass into the building.

"Riley," Chris said, "is that an Omen?"

"No," I reported back. I was using my I Don't Like It Here . . . trope constantly to make sure that we weren't running into Omens around the mansion.

As we got closer, it became obvious who was on the other side of the door because they became visible on the red wallpaper once we could get a good look at them through the frosted glass.

It was Jack Goforth, our NPC companion from the storyline.

"What is *he* doing here?" Grace asked.

"I have no idea," Chris said. "Why would an NPC show up like this?"

Grace didn't seem to know.

"Do we let him in?" Chris asked.

"Still no Omens?" Grace asked, looking at me.

"Nope," I answered. "I would be able to tell by this point."

If he was an Omen, I would be able to see it. Even if the Omen he carried was very over-leveled, I'd still be able to tell that it was there, even if I couldn't read anything about it.

He knocked on the door again.

"So, this is what the It's Open trope is for," Grace said.

"Never thought I'd see a use for that," Chris said.

It's Open was a trope that allowed a player to unlock a door to a building or room they were already inside of, which someone else was trying to get into, simply by yelling, "It's open!" It did not work if the player was captured, or the door was visibly locked or barricaded.

I had seen the trope in movies before. It was a joke around Dyer's Lodge that it was a mostly useless trope.

"I'm just going to open it," Chris said. "It's an NPC. Be ready just in case."

Chris moved to the door. He cautiously unlocked it and opened it up.

As soon as there was a chance, Jack slid inside. He then turned to close the door behind him.

"You guys are still here?" Jack asked, breathing hard. "Are the cultists gone? Or are you . . . You're not puppets now, right?"

Grace and Chris looked at each other.

"They all left," Grace said. "We're just here to weather the storm. What are you doing back here?"

Jack fanned his face. It looked like he had been running.

"Came to find you," he said. He looked around and started walking into the ballroom where the liquor was kept for the party.

We followed.

"It's going to look like I'm drinking a mimosa," he said, retrieving a bottle of orange juice from a small refrigerator behind the bar and pouring it into a glass of champagne, "but let's pretend it's a beer or whiskey or something more macho."

"Where did you go?" Grace asked.

Jack drank the cocktail quickly before pouring himself another.

"I went . . . It doesn't matter where I went. I'm back, but not for long. We all need to go."

"Are the sorcerers coming back?" Grace asked.

"I would assume so," Jack said. "Messy situation that was, huh? If they had learned our secret," he said, looking back at me, Kimberly, and Antoine, "who knows what bad things could have happened? Secrets are funny that way."

We all looked at each other. It sounded like our friends in high places didn't want us to talk about Dina's quest.

"Yeah, it would have been terrible," Grace said, looking up at Chris to see if he knew what was going on. "So, you would have us leave?"

Jack nodded. "I would definitely have you leave. You have a house on Lake Dyer, right, Chris? Let's go there. We'll be safe there. Just a quick hike from here, huh?"

Chris took a moment to respond. "I have a house over there, sure, but you know how many . . . things are between us and it right now?"

"A few skirmishes, yeah, but I imagine most things near Carousel will be hiding because of the storm. If we stay close enough to town to avoid the wilderness and far enough away to avoid the storm, we should be fine."

"Just a second," Chris said. "Let's go back into the lounge for a moment, you guys, and get our stuff. Jack, you wait here."

Jack smiled. "You got it," he said.

We hurried back into the lounge where all of our stuff was.

"What the hell is going on?" Chris asked as soon as we were inside the room.

"I have no idea," Grace responded.

Antoine, Kimberly, and I looked at each other. We shrugged our shoulders and pretended that we had no idea why an NPC might be acting out of the ordinary.

"Are we supposed to stay in character?" Grace asked. "This is really unusual. Do you think it's because of the storm?"

"I have no idea. I've seen NPCs act weird once or twice, but this is something different. How can this not be part of an Omen?" Chris answered.

"Do you think . . . They say that the tutorial had NPCs who would guide you to storylines and help you find places to stay afterward. Do you think it's like that?" Grace asked.

"I don't know. I didn't do the tutorial," Chris said.

Most players had missed the tutorial when they arrived, including my friends and me. Players who had completed it reported that it was distressing and woefully uninformative. Because players were known to give up before finishing, the vets now intercepted new players and brought them to the corn maze.

"I mean, he's not an enemy, right?" Grace asked. "The level fifties can sometimes be bad guys but not outside of a storyline, surely."

I decided to jump in. "I didn't see any sign of him being an Omen. None of us have lived in storyline settings after beating them. Maybe this is always what happens: the NPCs stay in character and guide us once it's time to go."

"Maybe," Grace said. "I'm sure the old timers would have written about that in the atlas, but we'll never know since so many pages got ripped out."

I think she meant it as a joke, but no one laughed.

"We've already made some plans to get back to the lodge without running into anything too terrible. You have the maps?" Chris asked Grace.

"I do," she said.

"Get your bags and get ready," Chris said. "We need to move fast."

We each had a bag that contained everything we needed for the hike. Food, toiletries, and camping supplies, all gathered from around the mansion. Chris had also stuffed in some weapons and other loot just in case.

We grabbed them and went back out into the hall to meet Jack.

"Bug-out bags," Jack noted. "That has you written all over it, Chris. These were your idea, weren't they?"

Indeed, they were.

"I suppose you didn't make an extra?" Jack asked.

"Didn't know you were coming, Jack," Chris said.

"Neither did I, Chris. But I'm the well-known tabloid journalist, of course. That's who you want on a dangerous hike. I'm already prepared," he said with a smile, gesturing down at his tux.

We exited the mansion and headed west.

"You know, it's lucky my stepdad sent me to wilderness camps to toughen me up," Jack said. "I got dragged up and down these hills as a teen."

Jack's Plot Armor jumped up six points. Strange. I couldn't see his tropes or his stats, but I could see that.

"Well, that's convenient," I said.

Jack chuckled. "Indeed."

Goodbye mansion, hello camping.

CHAPTER TWENTY-TWO

A BRIDGE TOO FAR

My big fancy antique spear disappeared right out of my hands when we were about a mile west of the mansion. The pack that Chris had packed for me, a leather garment bag repurposed as a satchel, also got considerably lighter because other pieces of loot and weapons had disappeared from within it.

"It was worth a shot," Chris said at almost the exact same moment. Much of his loot had disappeared too.

All that remained were a few of the less ornate weapons, some books Grace had wanted, and the essential supplies, like food and water.

And the masks.

"Strange," Grace said. "The enchanted weapons disappear, but these masks stick around. I wonder how much they sell for."

I hadn't even been aware the spear was enchanted. That was a real loss.

"Not enough to be worth the hassle of getting them," Chris said.

Jack laughed. "You're just going to sell it?" he asked Grace.

"Not much else we can do with it," Grace answered.

Jack didn't really respond, but he stifled a hollow smile.

"Right?" Grace asked. "If we bring it into another storyline, it disappears. Can't use one storyline's magic in a different storyline, right?"

"Why are you asking me?" Jack asked dryly. "I'm just a gossip columnist. I have no idea what you're talking about."

As we walked, we would each try to elicit some kind of information out of Jack. He clearly knew things we didn't, but his comments were always more or less in character. Occasionally, he would send me a knowing glance or a sarcastic smirk.

"Who's in charge?" Chris asked.

"The people who buy our magazine," Jack said. "The customer is always right."

"But who brought us here?" Grace asked. "And why?"

They had apparently never had the opportunity to interrogate an NPC that would play along before. Grace was cycling through her Detective interrogation tropes but to no avail.

"That is a good question. The hiring decisions at the company have always been unorthodox. You should have been there when they hired me," he said. He thought for a moment. "It was a hostile takeover of the magazine I used to work at. A bloody mess. We printed a story that caught their attention. Guess they liked what they saw and just bought the whole brand, employees and all. To think, I had my resignation letter typed up and everything before it happened. They almost missed me. You know, you independent contractors are luckier than you think."

He chuckled.

Something about the way he spoke made an impression on all of us. We didn't ask more questions for a while. His little story took some time to digest.

"Chris," Antoine said. "Look at this."

He pointed down into a ravine to our left. I walked over and followed his gaze.

It was a snake as wide as a school bus and many times as long.

It was dead.

The serpent lay along the ravine, its mouth of fangs splayed open, as sometimes happens to snakes when killed. A powerful odor wafted up to the top of the ravine. Almost fishy, but wrong. Its belly was full and wiggling. A human arm, or close enough, reached out of a tear in its flesh as sounds emanated from within.

I couldn't tell if they were animalistic sounds or demonic, but I knew the sounds carried further than they logically should have. I could hear them as if they were right next to me.

"Omen?" Chris asked for the hundredth time.

"Nope," I said.

"What's happening down there?" Kimberly asked.

"Snake ate some goblins or something," I said. "Didn't chew his food."

"Let's get out of here," Chris said.

No one wanted to argue.

If there was a giant dead snake there, that meant there might be live monsters elsewhere. We were in real danger.

* * *

"If we keep going west, we're going to hit some Omens," Chris said.

"The banshee," I said. A forest blockaded the woods to the northwest of Camp Dyer with an Omen related to a banshee. I knew that much. We heard her out there sometimes, screaming bloody murder.

Chris nodded. "I don't think it's the banshee you have to worry about in that storyline. She is like an Omen within an Omen or something." He looked to Grace.

"Lara has been able to divine as much," Grace said. "The boundary Omens are the weirdest. They have different rules and harsher penalties. That's what makes them effective, I suppose."

"We need to start going south soon," Jack said. "But that means crossing a river—the White Cap River, I believe."

"There should be a bridge up ahead," Grace said. "It's on the map, though this one is quite old."

"I remember a bridge too," Jack said. He closed his eyes. "Legend . . . Yes, legend says the bridge is cursed."

"Cursed?" Grace asked. "You mean there is an Omen?"

"Of course there's an Omen on it," Chris said. "If there wasn't, I would be surprised. The question is, is the Omen active still? The storm took out so many of them for miles."

"I'll give it a gander," I said.

"We go south now until we hit the river, then follow it until we get to the bridge," Chris said.

And so, we did.

As we walked south, I started hearing the sound of running water up ahead. We managed to find the river. That's not all we found.

There was a large sewer pipe sticking out of the cliff on the other side. The concrete pipe was as wide as two grown men set end to end. The entire opening was covered in a large metal grate. Only a trickle managed to make its way out of the pipe and into the water, however, because the end was clogged.

Skeletons were stacked up against the grate. Human. Dog. Rat. Dozens of them. Remarkably, they stayed assembled despite being completely stripped of their flesh.

"What is that green slime?" Antoine asked.

I squinted to see what he was talking about. There was a green hue to the bodies.

"The Bloat," Grace said.

"Looks like it left the sewers and took to the river. The monsters all look like they're taking off," Chris said.

The Bloat must have been the name for whatever green goo creature lived in the sewer system under the city. Apparently, a lot of things lived down there in the sewers.

After a few moments to stare at the sewer grate, we turned and headed west.

"Stop," Chris said. "Something's up ahead."

Chris had been using his Gut Instinct trope to sense out danger. This was the first time it had activated with any real urgency.

We all listened intently to no avail.

"I need to go check it out," he added.

"No," I said. "I'll go. I can look for Omens, and I have a little trick for not getting killed."

My little trick was Oblivious Bystander.

I wasn't sure if it would work outside of a storyline like this, but I was betting it would. Even with no camera, other tropes seemed to work pretty well. The only tropes that appeared to be useless out of storylines were those that relied on the Plot Cycle as well as those that referenced other aspects inherent to storylines.

I was beginning to suspect that whether or not the Off Screen light was lit, we were always on camera. Not to mention the fact that Oblivious Bystander worked when *I* was Off Screen, when it shouldn't, because there was no audience watching.

More than that, letting Chris go was a mistake. If he left the group, the group lost 90 percent of its defenses.

It was just logical for me to go instead. I was more useful on my own. Always had been.

"You sure?" Chris asked.

I shrugged as I slipped on my sunglasses, headphones, and hood. If I thought about it too long, I would get more scared. Besides, in a way, I was safer on my own. Oblivious Bystander would not work well while I was in a group.

I trudged forward quietly, trying not to look too aware of my surroundings.

It didn't take too long for me to find out what the dangerous thing was.

I didn't have to walk too far to find the bridge. What I didn't expect to see was the figure that was standing on it.

There were no Omens to be afraid of, but that didn't mean there was no risk.

I heard voices, strange haunting voices that sounded oddly familiar, not because I had heard the speaker before, but because I had heard the strange nature of the sound. I was listening to voices from ghosts or spirits of some kind.

I found a grassy knoll to lie down on behind a tree. As I did, I stared up at the sky and put my hands above my head. I watched the bridge from the corner of my eye through a small gap in the trees.

I saw where the ghostly voices were coming from.

Three bodies floated through the air toward the bridge. Their spirits were partially extruded from them. I had seen that trick before. They did not appear to enjoy floating, as they struggled fruitlessly. As they bobbed along, they talked in oddly calm voices. It was quite discomforting to witness.

Two of them were babbling about a trespasser on their land and how they were going to kill him and sink their teeth into him. They were strange men dressed in shabby clothing. They spoke with strong country accents.

On the red wallpaper, they were called "Bog Brothers." Their Plot Armors were twenty-eight and thirty-one, respectively. They didn't have proper names. If I were to hazard a guess, I would say they were hillbilly cannibals or similar, but I couldn't be sure. I was too far away for Trope Master to activate.

They floated across the bridge and squabbled with each other stupidly.

The third floating body was called "The Samaritan." I recognized him. He was the shadowy enemy from the *Eleventh-Year Reunion* trailer I had seen earlier. His Plot Armor was thirty-seven. He had made it out of town without getting infected. Good for him.

"I waited ten long years to get my revenge," his partially disembodied spirit said. "I almost had it, but then I failed. They killed my son. They will pay. This year, I will take their lives like they took his that night in the rain."

"Yes, yes," a familiar voice said. "When I am finished, you will have your revenge. I guarantee it. As soon as I have mapped the astral plane, returning you to your revenge will be simple."

Simon Halle, the Astralist, stood on the bridge, effortlessly floating the men along as they struggled to free themselves.

But he was different. His Plot Armor was forty-six. That didn't make any sense at all. When we faced him, his Plot Armor had been around twelve.

I was suddenly nervous. I didn't remember him having telekinesis before. He also didn't have the ability to partially rip out your soul like he had done to his victims on the bridge.

It appeared that the Apocalypse had not ruined things for Dr. Halle. He had been collecting specimens for his experiments as they ran away from town.

Halle Castle would have been close by. It was on the northwest side of town. It made sense that it could have been outside of the storm's path, though the roads leading to it would certainly have been cut off.

That was a real problem. The Astralist was smart and fast. If he was hunting specimens, we would have a hard time passing by this way.

As soon as he had crossed the bridge and left the area, I stood up and made my way back to the others to report on what I had seen.

"That is interesting," Grace said. "He has a higher level when you bring a Beauty-Eye Candy or a Damsel into a storyline. Or a Researcher-Scholar. Or an Occultist-Psychic. Other than that, he has a low level. It's interesting that his higher level is the one he keeps outside a storyline."

"So, what do we do?" Kimberly asked. "We can't go near him again."

She had had a pretty rattling experience with him during his storyline.

"Do we just keep going west and hope to find another way across?" Antoine asked.

"Whatever we do," Chris said, "we can't stay here. Not if he's out hunting. We can't afford a fight, not without the ability to heal afterward."

Whatever the case, we needed to think of something fast because soon it would be dark. Camping in these woods would be suicide. We needed a plan.

IN TIME, PART TWO

Can he follow us?" I asked as we ran from the stampede.

Camden shook his head. I could tell he was in worse condition than he pretended.

"No, Anna," he said. "They can only—" He stopped and winced in pain. "There's some kind of limit. I don't understand it completely. He can only travel to historical disasters. But the magic can only open one portal to a particular disaster at once. Does that make sense? Unless he wants another version of himself to follow him. Then he has to kill a new victim. Whatever." He winced again. "Just, he shouldn't be able to follow us is all that matters. Not until the next recorded disaster."

Time traveling from disaster to disaster.

This disaster . . . the stampede.

The 1996 Carousel Summer Days Stampede took over forty lives. A carnival ride—a small, slow kiddie ride—had malfunctioned and threatened to derail a car from its spinning track. The ride operator managed to get it switched off, but the loud sound of metal bursting loose within the mechanism sounded much more dangerous than it was. The crowd panicked. Many thought a bomb had gone off.

The Town of Carousel: Horrific Events Through the Ages, the book the Generation Killer—as he was called on the red wallpaper—used to coordinate his time travel, stated that many of the victims had been trampled, but most had gotten tangled together in a narrow alleyway and succumbed to crowd crush. Everyone ran to exit the alleyway with such reckless haste that they jammed up against each other, their limbs getting caught around those next to them. Those in the front were killed as those in the back pushed forward, unable to see the carnage they were causing.

The image of it had been awful: bodies squeezed and tangled together until everyone involved was stuck so tight they couldn't breathe. I will never forget it.

The strange jewel the Generation Killer used had brought us right into the midst of the chaos. We were in Carousel in 1996.

"We have two days here," Camden said. "Then a houseboat sinks on Lake Dyer and he can come through to get us."

Two days until the next disaster.

"Did you say there are other versions of him?" I asked. In the excitement, I had almost missed that.

"Past, present, future," Camden said. "Several of them. The young ones are fast and strong but also kind of dumb. I managed to trick one and get away for a while before you showed up. The old ones are smarter but weaker and slower."

We ran until we found a corner between two buildings where we could stop running and hide. Camden plopped down on the ground and pulled out some medical supplies from his pocket. The Generation Killer had taken his arm but had also patched it up.

Camden must have seen me staring at his recently stitched stump.

"He didn't want me to die too quickly," he explained. "That magic pendant"—he pointed at the necklace I was wearing—"has to be jumpstarted through anguish. That's why his face and arms are covered in scars. He thought he would use me instead of himself for a while."

That was too terrible to think about.

Camden started trying to dress his wound. I quickly bent down to take over. I felt so useless, not knowing how to treat an amputation like this.

"These supplies are really old," I said. The style was not modern at all.

"They were all he had," Camden said. "He must have picked them up decades ago."

I dressed his wound as best I could. The stitches and cauterization that the Generation Killer had done were clumsy, but at least Camden would not bleed out.

Off Screen.

After I was done, I sat down on the ground across from Camden, and we just looked at each other for a moment. We had never gotten the chance to discuss what had happened to us since we started the storyline. The roller rink had collapsed into the earth soon after we arrived, and the story had not slowed down since then. Now, we were finally between scenes.

"Do you think Riley, Antoine, and Kimberly are okay?" I asked.

Camden didn't answer for a time, but then said, "They'll be fine. They have Chris and Grace."

"Are *we* going to be okay?"

Camden's eyes dropped.

"What do we do?" I asked. "How do we beat him? Where do we go?"

"Anna . . . ," Camden said.

"What?"

He looked at me with a soft expression. "We won't survive this."

I was afraid he would say that.

"No," I said. A lump rose up in my throat. "There has to be a way."

"There is a way," Camden said. "But we can't do it. Not just the two of us."

I couldn't accept that. It was my job to keep us positive when everything looked impossible.

"You just have to take some time to think it through," I said.

Camden shook his head. "I did. I was in that cell for over a week before you got there. I figured out how to beat him. You split him up. You grab as many of the amulets as you can and you take them to different times. He gets confused. I heard one of the older versions yelling at a teenage version about it. His memories get scrambled. There are ten versions. Used to be twelve, I think, once upon a time. Strand them in their own time periods and they can't time travel anymore. Then maybe kill them, I don't know. The time travel continuity in this story is nonsense. Riley would love it. I did my research. Paid the price for it too," he said, looking over at his missing arm.

"But there's only two of us . . . ," I said, dejected.

"There's only two," he repeated. "And we are horribly under-leveled."

This wasn't happening. We were really going to die. My family would never know what happened to me. I couldn't hold back the tears anymore.

"But I have an idea," he said.

I perked up at that. Did he have a plan to get us home?

"Just because we die doesn't mean we can't do something important. I think we can get back at Carousel and help the others. It's a long shot, but what else are we going to do?"

"Help the others from in here?" I asked. That didn't seem possible.

"If my idea works."

I thought for a moment. "Using time travel?"

He nodded.

"But you said you thought this was fake. That we aren't actually in the past," I said.

"Oh, it's fake," Camden said. "The question is, how good of a fake is it?"

After he explained his plan, I felt numb. We were going to die, that much seemed clear. The only thought that kept me from descending into a cycle of self-pity was that we might be able to help our friends.

But his plan . . . was difficult to go through with.

"We need anguish short of death to activate the pendant," Camden said. "We're traveling from the 1996 Stampede to the 2010 Red Hills Massacre. You got that?"

"I got it," I said.

He had explained it over and over. He made me read the entry for both events at least a dozen times. The traveler had to have a clear vision of where they wanted to go.

The Red Hills Massacre occurred just up the road from Camp Dyer. A group of college kids were found dead. Strangely, all of the deaths were ruled suicides. One student went missing completely and there were few witnesses.

That wasn't the hard part.

Activating the pendant was. Anguish short of death was more than I thought I could handle.

We had broken into a tool shed in a nice neighborhood. I held an electric drill in my hand.

On-screen.

"If we want to stand any chance, we have to get a step ahead of him! Do it!" Camden screamed.

I held the drill over him, but I couldn't bring myself to lower it. We had talked it over a hundred times. We just needed a shot of the drill breaking the skin. He thought he had enough Moxie to handle it from there, to play up his injury. But if that wasn't true . . . I would have to *really* hurt him.

I held the drill over him. I could barely see through the tears in my eyes.

"Do it!" Camden screamed again.

The drill cut into his arm, and he started to scream.

Not long after that, the pendant started to glow as I thought about the strange pictures I had seen depicting the victims of the Red Hills Massacre.

And then, suddenly, we were there. Carousel in 2010.

The drill traveled with us, taking the electric outlet and part of the wall of the shed with it.

I unplugged the drill and put it into a canvas bag I had slung over my shoulder.

We were in 2010. February 2010, or at least Carousel's version of it.

Camden chose it because there wasn't another disaster for three days afterward, giving us some time to enact his plan.

I thought back to our conversation in the alleyway when he had described the plan to me.

"A young version of him brought me to the year 2002 before we went to their hideout, where you rescued me. I managed to escape by pretending I was dead. He fell for it. I ran around Carousel for hours in 2002. There was nothing important to be done. I saw plenty of NPCs, but none of them wanted to interact with me. I kept hoping that Carousel would bring the story to me— that by escaping I could find a way to win. But I was off-screen the entire time. My entire escape was off-screen. It was like it had never happened. I could have screamed. Probably did.

"But as I walked around Carousel, I noticed something very strange. There was a restaurant near the center of town that had a bunch of cops and EMTs outside of it. They were just standing around going through their motions of pretending to be real. They were background characters. We see that a dozen times a day, but something about it felt oddly familiar to me. They were talking about some death that had occurred there.

"After the Generation Killer recaptured me, I sat in my cell and thought about it for hours until it dawned on me that the last time I had seen cops and paramedics acting that way was when I died in the Ranger Danger storyline. I woke up after it was over, and I pulled the sheet off of my face and looked around, and there were all these NPCs just going about their business, walking back and forth, talking about what had just happened. It was the exact same thing that was happening at the restaurant. That's when I figured it out." He paused for a moment.

"What?" I asked.

"What I was seeing had nothing to do with *this* storyline. I was seeing a scene from a different storyline altogether. I think Carousel recreated that day in 2002 down to every detail. I think players, actual players, had run a storyline at the restaurant that day in the original 2002. When Carousel needed to recreate 2002 for this time travel storyline, it just copied them, exactly as they were at that moment in the real timeline."

He was really throwing a lot out there. "So, what's your plan?"

"We go to 2010. Before the fall of that year."

"What happened in the fall of 2010?" I asked.

He smiled.

We ran from the horror of the Red Hills Massacre. We had been Off Screen from the time we left the crime scene. Camp Dyer was only a few miles away. We didn't know if we were being chased, but we ran anyway. Camden looked pale, but curiosity was driving him.

We ran straight to Dyer's Lodge.

"Please be there," Camden said. He said it several times. I guess it was our swan song, our Hail Mary. I hoped it was there too.

* * *

"You don't remember?" Camden asked.

I shook my head. "Vaguely."

"Rescue tropes disappeared in fall 2010. So, we go travel back to before that happened."

"Wait," I said. "You don't think we're going to find rescue tropes, do you?"

I was fairly certain that Carousel wouldn't make such an oversight.

He shook his head. "No."

As we got to Dyer's Lodge, we ran past the head camp counselor, who yelled something at us I couldn't hear. It didn't seem important.

We were inside the lodge in a flash. It looked different. Fewer couches. A lot of the knickknacks had disappeared along with many of the books.

"Look," Camden said, pointing to a chalkboard in the center of the common area. The board was covered in plans for a run to the mall. These players were high enough level to plan runs at the mall? We had been told it was way too dangerous.

"Oh my god!" I said.

Camden was right. Carousel recreated the time period down to the last detail, even including the things that players had left behind back then.

"If Carousel recreates past time periods exactly," Camden said, "down to the last detail, even going so far as having NPCs show up because some players had run a storyline on that same day, what if it recreates *everything*?"

"Everything?" I asked.

We rummaged through the lodge. There were no players there, but this was their hideout. Just like it was our hideout over ten years later. Players had been staying at Dyer's Lodge since before Adeline and Arthur were in charge.

"Found it!" Camden screamed out.

I ran toward the stairs and bounded up them.

He was sitting on a chair at the table where the high-level players always planned their runs. In front of him was the object of our desire: the *Carousel Atlas*.

"The player register. The register is still here," he said, overjoyed, having flipped to the very back. "It goes back to 1989."

Players had been in Carousel since 1989?

He sat and read through the book.

Something he read was quite sobering. "I think Riley might be onto something," he said.

There were all kinds of things in this past version of the atlas that ours didn't have. Entire sections. Ticket types I had never heard of were discussed in detail.

Camden pointed to a section of text.

"'We've discovered a new exploit for rescue tickets,'" Camden read aloud. "'Our "Insider" tells us to be cautious because he cannot keep Carousel distracted for too long, but the more we experiment, the more confident I am that we have found a way to increase our levels dramatically in the coming months. Testing continues. We must not tell the other players until we are sure it is safe.'"

"An exploit?" I asked. "Like cheating?"

"Not necessarily. I wonder if Adeline knows about it. I don't see where she's written anything in here. Arthur either."

"What if Carousel recreates Dyer's Lodge exactly as it was in 2010. What if it recreated the *Carousel Atlas* before it had so many of its pages torn out? Maybe a lot of information would still be there."

"Whoa," I said. Seeing the atlas before it had been defaced was huge. "But how does it help? How do we get it to our friends?"

"Oh, I have an idea," Camden said with a weak smirk.

He flipped to a part that discussed player Aspects. Then he flipped further to the Final Girl section, then the general section.

"This should work nicely," he said.

"Which Aspect do I need to pick?" I asked.

"Doesn't much matter," he said. "Pick whatever you like. Just follow the plan."

CHAPTER TWENTY-THREE

IN PLAIN SIGHT

Because of the Astralist skulking around, we had to take a much longer detour to get back in the direction we needed to go. Chris said that we couldn't risk going anywhere near him given the fact that the only way to beat him would be either using the chemicals in his lab or using his own machine against him. If we ran into him in the woods, neither of those things would be available.

We went as far west as we could until we hit the tree line where we finally found an Omen. It was the familiar Omen that stopped anyone from heading further around the lake. I had seen it before. We had to go south. Luckily, it only took us an hour or so to find a place where we could cross the river without touching the water.

Chris wasn't sure that the water itself was dangerous, but he wasn't going to risk it. He stood, poised with a rusty old weapon that had not been taken away after we left the mansion, ready for something to jump out of the water, but nothing did. His Gut Instinct trope was pretty good at predicting stuff like that, but he remained vigilant, as an enemy with a high enough level could still remain undetected.

By the time I saw the road that led to Camp Dyer, it was already dark. I could barely see the sign at the entrance. As we walked toward the lodge, the familiar chanting by the little campers caught my ears:

"Suzy Snyder, six foot five,

Haunts Camp Dyer, still alive . . ."

It almost felt comforting instead of terrifying. This place had not been touched by the black snow.

We made the last part of the trail on foot. I subconsciously walked faster during the last part, ready to be somewhere safe at last. When I got to the door and turned to look at the others, I noticed that Jack Goforth was nowhere to be found. Guess he wasn't needed anymore after he guided us around the woods.

When I opened the door and we walked in, I was greeted by dozens upon dozens of sullen faces. Most of the players at Dyer's Lodge had survived. But not all.

When we walked through the door, there was a spark of hope, but then, when it was only five of us, that was snuffed out.

Adeline came out to the common area from behind the bar in the kitchen and hugged Grace. They started whispering to each other. I was sure news of the fallen would reach everyone soon enough.

We were offered food, though all they had left were canned emergency supplies. I guess they had prepared to be holed up during an Apocalypse.

Dina was in the common room and tried to get my attention. I dodged her gaze. I was not ready to tell her about how her quest had been dashed against the rocks when we lost our Final Girl and Scholar. I'm sure she would be very disappointed to know that two of the people she was relying on to beat the game were gone.

I would talk to her in the morning. I just walked to my room and shut the door. I hated how quiet things were in there without Camden. Often, we would spend the nights before we went to sleep spitballing about how to get out of Carousel. We had theory after theory of what was going on and how it might be fixed. It was all dumb. What did we know?

I used my Out like a Light trope to go to sleep fast so that I didn't have to deal with the emerging emptiness inside of me.

The Apocalypse lasted for two more weeks. Then, one day, the radio in the kitchen just started playing its regular programming of unsettlingly positive hosts and music that sounded vaguely familiar but that I could never put my finger on.

The storm was never acknowledged by the hosts, even when they did the weather forecast.

A few days after we made it back, Garrett and his team—who had literally jumped into hell to escape the black snow—arrived. They were injured. They had come across some shadow people after clearing their storyline and suffered some cuts and broken bones as a result, along with wicked hand-shaped bruises. Fortunately, a Doctor Archetype was at the lodge to patch them up, but they were still on the mend for quite a while.

Eventually, we sent a scout out to take a look at town. When they reported back, they said everything was back to normal. No black snow. No mutants.

And just like that, life went back to normal at Dyer's Lodge. People were quiet like it was a funeral, but still, things slowly started to go back to the way they had been when we had arrived. I was reminded that the team that had arrived nearly a year before mine had been wiped out a matter of weeks before we got there, and if it weren't for their missing posters, I would never have known they were there. No one talked about them.

Camden and Anna were just gone. I got a few condolences but not much more. Death was a way of life at Camp Dyer. People were ready to get back to eating real food, so a run was planned to go to Eternal Savers Club for some bulk groceries.

People were talking about the excursion out west and their Secret Lore plans.

Lara used a Psychic trope to tell us the news of everyone who had died. The *Eleventh-Year Reunion* team and the *Head Below Water* team had been killed in the storm. Reggie had not made it either. Grace was a mess all over again because of it.

Travis's team and the remaining Bowlers had died as well but not in the *Preservation* storyline. They had completed that and died later. Lara was sparse on the details, but it seemed as though they somehow triggered a different storyline after completing their original one, or else the killer from a different storyline had found them in the woods. It wasn't clear to her.

She turned to me. I knew what she was going to say before she said it.

"Anna and Camden didn't make it," she said. "I'm sorry, Riley. I'm sure they tried their hardest."

I had been expecting the news but still wasn't ready to hear it. They were gone. Again, I retreated to sleep to escape my feelings.

Many players went to the missing poster wall to pay their respects. Kimberly and Antoine went with them. I didn't, because I couldn't do anything like that in public. I would go on my own later. The path there was safe enough to walk alone.

"Lara said they didn't suffer," Kimberly said as we sat on the back deck of the lodge after their trip to the wall.

"She was lying," I said. I knew they had suffered. I saw what had happened to Camden.

Kimberly started crying. She cried a lot. Antoine comforted her as best he could, but I could see everything was taking a toll on him too.

"I'm sorry," I said. I really sucked at being around people sometimes.

Dina was sitting on a chair nearby. "We can still save them," she said. "We just have to solv—"

"Yes, we're still going to help you," I interjected. "It's all you've wanted to talk about since we got back: whether we can still help you."

There was an awkward silence.

"It's not just me," Dina said. She got up out of her chair and went back inside.

I looked over at Kimberly and Antoine. "So, we just pretend they were never here? Don't you see that's what everyone here does? They just forget people."

"What do you want us to do?" Antoine asked.

The worst part of Carousel was that there was no one to be angry at. The bad guy had not shown his face. It was frustrating. There was no one to yell at.

"I don't know. I'm going back to sleep."

I stood up and walked back into the common room. The radio was still playing on the kitchen counter. No one had turned it off in the days since the storm abated.

I found a couch that was away from everyone else and lay down on it. Instead of sleeping, I spent a while just imagining scenarios where I could vent my anger. I wanted to scream at everyone.

"Riley?" someone behind me asked.

I turned over to see it was Grace. She was dressed like she was about to run a storyline. A handful of other players including Lara and Roxy were standing by the door near her.

"What's up?" I asked, trying to contain my emotions.

She pointed across the room at the chalkboards used to plan the Secret Lore runs. "I left those maps out on the table over there if you wanted to take a look," she said.

"Maps?" I asked.

"The maps of Carousel throughout the years. We talked about it at the mansion, remember?"

"Oh. Right. Thanks, I'll give them a look over," I said. "You're doing runs already?"

She nodded. "We have a good lead at the museum. We have to move forward. For Reggie and the others. We can't stop now."

"Right," I said. In my heart, I wasn't ready to start avenging my fallen friends yet. Grace, though, apparently was. "I'll see you when you get back."

She nodded. "Those maps are very interesting. Lots of fun details if you poke through them. You can see the entire town growing right before your eyes if you go through them in order."

I didn't respond.

Then she and her new team left.

Antoine and Kimberly stayed out on the deck with a group of other players. I didn't know where Dina was—probably off trying to convince herself that the black snow was somehow a good thing, that it had put her one step closer to reviving her son.

I was alone. I couldn't go back to my room, because then I would only be reminded that Camden was missing.

I decided to just lie back on the couch and use my sleeping trope to go to sleep. I listened to the soft, strange music playing over the radio in the kitchen area.

Just before I decided to doze off, the thought of the maps reentered my mind. I figured I might as well take a look.

I walked over to the table she had pointed me to and saw a pile of maps rolled up into scrolls and bound with rubber bands. They were labeled by year with a black permanent marker.

I grabbed the one that said "1989," the year Grace said the parking lot had arrived, and unrolled it. Then I grabbed "1988" to compare. Sure enough, the parking lot and the entire road leading to the farm with Benny's cornfield did not show up until that year.

Someone—maybe Grace, maybe not—had taken to circling each building the year it was added to the map. They had not finished, but I decided to follow along anyway by looking at all of the settings for stories I had completed.

The museum at Halle Castle appeared in 1999, along with the road that led up to it. That seemed way too late for its arrival. If memory served, that castle canonically was brought to America . . . I forgot when. I remembered being told this in the story. Luckily, I had a way to double-check.

I used my Director's Monitor trope to rewatch the Astralist storyline to the point where Judy, the museum caretaker NPC, had told us about the castle's history. There were a lot of strange cuts in that movie. Probably because my friends and I kept breaking character unintentionally.

"You know, this castle was actually brought over from Europe after the destruction of World War Two," Judy explained. "They brought it here piece by piece, the Halle family. They knew the importance of history."

That's what I thought. I flipped through the older maps. The castle was missing until 1999. The Astralist story took place in 1999, as a matter of fact.

I kept looking.

Camp Dyer showed up in 1997. In fact, Lake Dyer changed shape dramatically that year, becoming larger and changing the location of some key features, like several marinas and the dam.

If I were to hazard a guess, the storyline took place in 1997. Of course, the camp would have needed to be around long before that so that the abandoned cabin could have been . . . well, abandoned.

The Delta Epsilon Delta fraternity where the Ranger Danger storyline took place was called Sigma Alpha Epsilon until 2001. I remembered people dressing like it was the early 2000s. That checked out.

The church from the Grotesque storyline broke the pattern. It was always there, even though it had to have taken place in the last few decades. I assumed that the church set was used in several different storylines.

The Akers plot from the Fatal Folktales anthology was not important enough for a label, but the road that led out to the entrance only showed up in the mid-nineties. It was hard to tell exactly when because that area had very little in it and was not very detailed.

Patcher's Farm started in 1976 and turned into Patcher's Family Farm, the roadside attraction, seven years later.

There was no reference to the building from *Subject of Inquiry*, which made sense. It was a secret.

The mansion in the Carousel Hills wasn't labeled, but it did show up in 1992, the same year the storyline was set. That was wrong. The storyline stated that the mansion had been there for years by 1992.

The settings for each storyline showed up around the time the storyline took place, not when they should have arrived within the continuity of their stories. That meant that the oldest sites in Carousel would not necessarily be those that had been there for the longest according to their own lore.

That was assuming the dates were not rebooted by Carousel, which was a big assumption.

Eventually, my eyes wandered back to the parking lot where we had arrived. The nearest storyline was called *Permanent Vacancy*. The map didn't show the names of the storylines. I just remembered. We had been told that name when we arrived as Valerie had tried to explain the concept of Omens, or something like that. The terrified woman pleading to be freed as she tried to squeeze through the barbed-wire fence was seared into my memory.

On the map, that storyline took place at a hotel called "Olde Hill Bed and Breakfast: The Jewel of Carousel. (Condemned)." The bed-and-breakfast didn't exist until 1989, the same year it had been padlocked off and condemned, it would seem.

I wasn't sure if these maps were good for finding Secret Lore, but they still seemed important.

Something about that little bed-and-breakfast stood out to me as odd. I couldn't place my finger on what was so unusual about it.

But then I remembered what it was.

I could have laughed. The clues we had been given were finally starting to come together. I ran back to my room and grabbed my cell phone from where it stayed on the charger. There wasn't much use for it with no signal, but I still kept it charged out of habit.

I ran back to the table with the maps and clicked through my apps to find my messages.

I wanted to scream for joy. I had finally found something.

In the kitchen, the radio abruptly stopped playing the mellow music from before and started to play a tune I had never heard before, but still recognized.

"Under the neon glow, where the lucky ones go,
Bet your life on it, it's the Carousel Casino.
The stakes are high, but so is the fun,
Bet your life on it, the night's just begun!"

I stared at the radio aghast. That was the jingle that Winston Ashwood claimed meant there was treasure to be found—or, as I interpreted it, meant "jackpot."

I looked back at the map and then at my phone. I thought back to the tickets I had been awarded with coded messages on them.

Hidden in plain sight right in front of me was a Glitch in the Matrix, Accidentally Captured on Film.

CHAPTER TWENTY-FOUR

CLOSED FUR RENOVATIONS

Ever since I arrived, I could never really wrap my head around the idea that everything I was experiencing was real. I didn't deny that I was seeing what I saw or that I could feel what I felt. But in my head, I always divided things between the real world and Carousel. As I stared at the map, I started to realize how complicated that division might actually be.

No one who stayed here for very long thought that Carousel was actually a place located along some narrow forested street in the middle of the United States. It became very clear that whatever Carousel was, it was separate from a world that we had known.

But how separate? And exactly how was Carousel luring people from our world to its doorstep? At what point did our world end and Carousel begin?

I stepped away from my map. I needed to take a break.

I saw through the large glass window that there were people outside still, and I decided to go ask a series of questions that most of us here had asked at least a dozen times in some form or another.

"Where is Carousel?" I asked as I walked outside onto the deck where Antoine, Kimberly, and a collection of veterans were sitting.

These were not veterans that I spent a lot of time talking to. Truthfully, there were so many people at Dyer's Lodge that it was hard for me to keep track of them all. Even though I didn't know who they were, they did have some idea who I was.

"Depends on what you mean by that," Garrett said. He was still recovering from the wounds he had received on his way back to the lodge after escaping the black snow. "If you mean 'where did we enter it,' you should already know that. If you mean 'where does Carousel say it is,' that is harder to answer."

"I'm talking about within the lore of Carousel. Is there an actual location where it is located, or is it really different in every storyline?"

This elicited groans. I was asking questions that no one knew the answer to, but still, I needed to confirm my understanding one last time.

"Now you're getting into the weeds," another one of the veterans I did not know very well said. "It could be anywhere. I saw a map where it was in Massachusetts and another in southeast New Mexico with some aliens. It can't decide. If I remember right, this very camp is in New Jersey, or at least that's what the map in the administration office says."

"This place is built like the backlots of a movie studio," Garret said. "You need a desert? Go south. You need forest? Go west. Town square looks like it comes from some well-to-do town in Connecticut. Yet the town has a financial district with skyscrapers that you can't find unless you know the directions. Carousel is everywhere."

He echoed much the same sentiment that Chris had earlier. Carousel was just playing a role like we were. There was a setting here for everything. And if there wasn't, you could buy a train ticket or a plane ride to find a place that fit your fancy.

"I saw a trailer for a storyline with a Japanese shrine," I said. "And I know that *The Astralist* is set in a German castle."

"The Astralist's castle was brought to America, though," Antoine said. "The lady told us that first thing."

I shook my head. I had thought that too originally.

"No, she said it was brought 'here,'" I said. "I rewatched it. She never said it was brought to America. We just assumed."

"The more you know," Garrett said. He and the other veterans soon returned to their own conversation.

I looked over to Antoine and Kimberly. I needed to talk to them. They caught my gaze as I walked back inside.

"What's going on?" Antoine asked once we were in the common room away from the others.

"Do you know where Dina is? I found something."

"Found something?" Antoine asked.

"She was out by the docks," Kimberly said. "I'll go get her."

After a few minutes, the two of them returned ready to hear what it was I had discovered.

I had gone through all of the possibilities, but the one that rose to the top was simple.

"I have a theory," I said. "I think it's something we need to test. Why does Carousel have a German castle and an American university? Why does it have maps that put Carousel all over the globe and sometimes on different globes altogether? I mean, we've been talking about this forever."

And I did mean forever. Many people took this evidence to indicate that Carousel was some form of afterlife. Others assumed that it was some kind of Lovecraftian deity looking for entertainment, which had built this town as a torture chamber.

I paused for a moment to think.

"Do you remember that speech the red herring character, Evan, in the Ranger Danger storyline gave right before he accused me of being the killer? I've watched it a dozen times now. He said something about how people can be stopped from moving forward and their growth can be taken from them. I thought it was such an odd thing to talk about in the context of that story, that your dead friend won't ever grow out of being a jerk frat guy. I mean, Ruck was a jerk when the script said he was, but still, an odd thing to say. Now I don't think Evan was talking about Ruck. I think he was talking about himself, that *he* would never be able to move forward or grow. He was mourning for himself, but he had to stay in character."

I paced back and forth as I spoke.

"They've been talking to us this whole time," I said. I pulled Mrs. Cloudburst's letter out of my pocket. "But they all have to stay in character."

I opened the letter. "I noticed that if you only read every other line of the main body of this letter, it stops being a soppy love letter:

"'I was trapped in a prison before he came along. I had no idea that when I signed up for the society, I would eventually be trading one prison for another. I regret the things I have done to people, but how can I change when I can never leave this cycle?

"'The secret we all know is that only change can save us, but it is difficult; I've tried to save myself in every way I know how. Please, please, save us.

"'When I meet someone like you, I remember the pain, the torment given and taken, and I remember my desire to leave this all behind. I no longer know if I deserve punishment for my sins, but the innocent and the deserving suffer together in this life, don't they?

"'The storm came before I expected it, but it was all part of the greater plan, I think. What is next may be worse, but it's all part of that same plan. You must succeed, all the good people like you must succeed in your fight against people like me. It's time we get back on our true paths; I hope you're ready.'"

There were so many ways to read that letter. Some parts were clear, like her cry for help and her warning of things to come. Did she volunteer to play a role in Carousel and now regret it? Or was Mrs. Cloudburst a former player who was now stuck playing a minor villain? How would that work? Was the player the NPC being controlled or the hundred-year-old sorcerer in the cask downstairs?

Or was it possible that she wasn't playing a character at all?

"The demon at the bar talked like it was trapped here before it got its head blown off. Cristobal and Mrs. Cloudburst talked like they were here as punishment for their sins, but both said that they weren't the only ones. Cloudburst said that 'innocents' suffered with them."

"So, you think the NPCs are real people forced to play characters?" Kimberly asked. "We've talked about that before."

"No, not most of them," I said. "I think they're playing *themselves*. I think they are reenacting events that happened to them in their real lives back where they're really from. I think that somewhere in a parallel reality, there really was a society of rich folks that body-snatched people. I think Carousel brought them here—the sorcerers and the victims, brought here to relive the cycle over and over again. I've been thinking about that for a while, but it wasn't until I got this last piece of evidence that it all came together."

I showed them to the map on the desk and pointed at the bed-and-breakfast near where we had entered Carousel, where the bleeding woman had begged for our help.

"Olde Hill Bed and Breakfast: The Jewel of Carousel."

They stared at it for a moment.

"So?" Dina asked. "What does it mean?"

"When we were on our way to Carousel, we stopped to look at the map because we thought we had made a wrong turn. We didn't see any signs for Carousel, after all. Camden snapped a picture of a sign advertising a bed-and-breakfast—just some little hick hotel. We didn't think anything of it. The sign was really old. It had an arrow pointing down the road toward where the hotel would be. A lot of letters were missing, but someone wrote the words, 'closed fur renovations" on it. A typo that was kind of funny, I guess. That picture was the last message on the group chat. We lost signal after that."

I showed them the picture Camden had sent us. Even with all of the missing letters on the sign itself, we could tell what it said:

"Olde Hill Bed and Breakfast: The Jewel of the Ozarks."

"As in the Ozark Mountains," I said.

The Ozark Mountains. Carousel lured its victims in many ways, but there was one constant: we were all told to go to a town called Carousel. The directions we were given always led us to a small road in the center of the Ozark Mountains, in southern Missouri, in the middle of the United States. Every player had a similar story.

"Jewel of Carousel, Jewel of the Ozarks," I said. "I sifted through the possibilities, and there was only one that made sense to me. I think I know what's going on, or at least part of it," I said. "I think there was a real place called the Olde Hill Bed and Breakfast. A business that existed in the real world—*our* world. Their slogan was 'The Jewel of the Ozarks.' I think something terrible happened there in 1989, and because of that, Carousel absorbed it or something—the victims, the killers, the entire hotel. But when it got here, it was given a new version of the slogan that fit its new location. 'The Jewel of *Carousel*' instead of 'the Ozarks.' Everything that's brought here is rebranded as being part of Carousel."

I took three of the tickets I had received that had hidden messages on them.

"That's the Glitch in the Matrix from the tropes I was given after the Grotesque storyline. Our Friends in High Places want us to know about this hotel. A Glitch in the Matrix, Accidentally Captured on Film by Camden. Back to Where It All Started . . . I think our 'Friends' saw that he had taken that picture and designed the clues around it. I didn't realize it until I saw its slogan on the map here."

I really hoped I didn't sound like a crazed conspiracy theorist. I wasn't sure if I should tell them that the radio had been playing the commercial for the casino when I discovered the "Glitch." Would that make me sound more or less credible?

"Back to where it all started?" Kimberly asked.

"People from our world being brought to Carousel. The parking lot didn't exist until the hotel was brought here in 1989. I think that's how Carousel got access to us: through the storyline it took from our world."

Dina still wasn't sure. "So, you're going all in on Carousel being a completely different world from ours?"

Antoine had an answer for that. "If Carousel is an actual place in the United States, it would be less than forty miles from Branson, Missouri, based on the directions we were given. Before we got here, I didn't think it was a big deal. Now that I've gotten a look at it, it's way too big to stay hidden that close to a popular tourist town like Branson. Of course, Carousel could just stay hidden with magic, but I still don't think it fits. The only problem is, players have done that storyline before at the bed-and-breakfast. If it's so special, why didn't they find something?"

"I don't pretend to know," I said. "I just think this is where we are supposed to go. Maybe I'm completely wrong. Or maybe we find evidence that can help us escape."

There was a pause for a moment.

"What's the storyline there called again?" Antione asked.

"*Permanent Vacancy*," I answered. "And I think we can beat it."

CHAPTER TWENTY-FIVE

PLANNING A RUN

Antoine went to find Chris.

"Has he told his brother anything?" Dina asked Kimberly.

Kimberly shook her head. "He really doesn't like keeping secrets from Chris, but if there's a chance this can get us out, he's willing to. We just better hope this storyline is the right call."

I certainly hoped it was.

Eventually, Antoine returned with Chris. Chris was carrying the *Carousel Atlas*.

"I hear you all can't get enough of the action," he said. "I figure since you survived so much already, it's time you got a formal introduction to the atlas."

He held the enormous binder out for us to ogle.

"Antoine tells me you didn't look at any of the storyline spoilers when you stole it before," he said.

"Nope," I said. We had been warned about spoilers in general, after all.

Dina shot a glance at me. I hadn't caught her up on our previous conversation with Chris.

"It all starts with the map," he said as he set the binder on the table and opened it up to a page that contained a large map of Carousel. This one did not contain much information. It was more like a table of contents for the rest of the book. "You look at the section of Carousel where the storyline you're looking for is. You guys want this area over here to the east, so you go to page eighty-four."

He flipped to that page, and it had an enlarged map that only contained the area to the east of Carousel, where the parking lot and Benny's corn maze were. We had seen a similar mini map of the mall area when we had taken the atlas earlier.

"Then you find the individual storyline you're after, *Permanent Vacancy*, and you look for the numbers below it. The first number is the page where all the spoiler-free information is. The second number is the page with all the information we have, including spoilers. That stuff is good for when you're planning a run on a storyline you've already been through. Maybe if you're trying to get perfection or look for loot or, recently, find Secret Lore."

He flipped through to the spoiler-free page for the storyline and held the page out for us to see. There was more than I expected.

Title: Permanent Vacancy

Omen: A woman approaches the players from the other side of an iron fence and screams to be helped.

Location: Olde Hill Road, gated drive.

"Now, this top section can be one of the most useful sections on the entire page. It tells you which Archetype you should ask for scouting information for this specific storyline. Lucky for us, this type of information is not considered a spoiler as long as you obtain it from the player yourself. As you'll soon find out, scouting tropes can give you a lot," he said.

He pointed to a short list that read:

- Bounty Hunter

- Damsel

- Sheriff

"Unfortunately, we don't have any of those Archetypes here right now, but that's not the end of the world. If you think about it, just knowing that short list should tell you a lot about what you're about to be up against," he said with a subdued grin.

That was interesting. Bounty Hunters, Damsels, and Sheriffs had good information on this storyline. I hadn't even heard of the Sheriff Advanced Archetype before. The question was, why would these three have the best scouting information for *Permanent Vacancy*? I had my ideas.

"So, it means that—" Antoine started to say.

"Whoa," Chris said with a smile. "You're allowed to guess whatever you want and it won't be a spoiler, but if I ever confirm it, then it suddenly is."

He pointed down to the bottom section of the page.

"This information down here is gathered through special scouting tropes and is never considered to be a spoiler even if you did not consult the player who wrote it. Psychics, Adventurers, Antiquarians, and several others have a lot of tropes like this, though they aren't always useful. Film Buffs do too, now that I think about it," he said.

I read the entries at the bottom of the page. Chris gave us a rundown of what each one meant.

"'Psychic's Charmed Forecast: the Omen appears at seven twenty-three p.m., every day.' This tells you around when the Omen appears. It's pretty self-explanatory. It's not usually this specific, but this one has the actual time.

"'Athlete's I Have Practice Later: it'll be quick, an hour tops.' It's good to know how long a storyline is supposed to take. I'm just glad there was a way for Athletes to contribute because we get so few insight tropes.

"'Film Buff's Suitability Rating: adults only, graphic content.' That's exactly what it looks like. Sometimes there's more useful stuff with this trope. Interpret it how you will.

"'Antiquarian's Preliminary Appraisal: garbage—wouldn't even take it if it was free.' Not a lot of valuable loot. If the Antiquarian got a look at the storyline in the mansion we just ran, the rating would be through the roof.

"'Final Girl's Rise to the Occasion: it won't be easy, but we can take it! (Plot Armor around twenty-three).' This is one of several tropes that can estimate the level of a storyline. Just remember that this is not the most reliable part because storylines can become more difficult for a variety of reasons: the choices you make, the tropes you bring, Advanced Archetypes, et cetera. Remember to use buffs if you are a little under-leveled.

"'Doctor's Crime Scene Triage: two dead, two injured. (First and Second Blood require deaths).' This one is very useful. A Doctor Archetype can come across a completed storyline and determine how many necessary player deaths there are. It is really convenient to know if you need a First Blood sacrifice or not. We don't often get to know that."

He pushed the book back and turned to us.

"Now, don't go thinking that every storyline has this much information. Everybody's seen *Permanent Vacancy*, so it gets run more than some of the others. Part of the puzzle is trying to get as much information from what's available to you as possible. Now I have to tell you the story we all hear when we're first introduced to the *Carousel Atlas*," he said.

"Go for it," Antoine said.

"Adeline only came into possession of the atlas a year, maybe two before I got here. Before then, they had somebody who was in charge of guarding it to make sure that no one saw spoilers they weren't supposed to, as I understand it." From the look on his face, it wasn't clear that he believed that.

"Anyway, Adeline thought that it would be better if anyone was allowed to look at it. All those years of not letting people see it built up some resentment—whatever. So, she says go wild but whatever you do, don't spoil new stories for yourself. Of course, sometimes we do spoil stories if we're just trying to beat them, and we're not worried about getting experience. Of course, we run the risk of the story changing on us when we do that.

"Well, about a year after she starts that policy, maybe a little less than that, some Scholar decides that he's going to risk it. He's brand new to Carousel, but he hates the idea of going into a storyline unprepared. His thought was that if the performance was good enough, it would make up for the spoilers. That's not entirely ridiculous in theory, but a low-level player who's inexperienced wouldn't be able to cut it.

"So, the first story he tries it on—*The Astralist*, maybe; that one's been a common newbie storyline for a long time—he does it, and he can't really tell whether or not he's suffered because of the spoilers. So, he does it again and again. But slowly, it's apparent that his team is not leveling up as fast as they should and, of course, it's all because he's using spoilers, which cuts his loot down to a fraction of what it should have been.

"Eventually, the truth comes out, and now Adeline has to make a decision. She can't let him keep ruining things for his team, and it's too late for him because the damn kid has a trope that lets him memorize anything he looks at, and he chose to memorize the spoilers for most of the low-level storylines, so he's screwed. They decided to kick him off his original team so that his team could keep leveling up, but now they have to figure out what to do with him. The vets take him out on storylines just so he doesn't get in trouble." Chris shot a glance at me when he said that, obviously referencing the Janet incident.

"A year later and he hasn't leveled up much at all, hasn't gotten his Aspect, doesn't have a permanent team. The only solution was to team him up with people running more difficult stories because those were the ones he hadn't read. Sometimes they would alter stories with tropes to make them new to him. It was a huge ordeal and put him way behind. So that's the horror story. Now you know. Don't abuse the atlas."

It seemed so arbitrary, the difference between what was a spoiler and what wasn't. It was lucky that the consequence of having a storyline spoiled for you was so mild. The axe murderer didn't get up off his couch for just any old rule violation.

"What happened to the Scholar?" Kimberly asked.

"He wasn't here when I got here, so who knows," Chris answered. "Might be a missing poster of him near the diner. He might not even exist. Could be a story Adeline made up. Who knows."

He looked us over. "So, who are you bringing with you? Can't just go out with four players. It's not safe."

I had the same concerns. An Athlete, an Eye Candy, an Outsider, and a Film Buff is not a complete team. But anyone we brought would be let in on our secret.

We were missing two players—one of them our Final Girl. Our most important player.

"We hadn't figured out who to bring," Antoine said.

Chris breathed deeply. "You might consider inviting Bobby. He's around your level range, and I hear he's not a bad Wallflower. Bit chatty, but he has some good tropes, and I'm sure he's looking for something to do after his plans with Carl were interrupted."

Was Bobby one of the Wallflowers who would have been heading to Snowblind?

I was dreading that Chris would say to invite him. I wasn't sure if Bobby would want to do a run with me. It did make sense, though. Bobby had come to Carousel with us. If there was anyone that our "Friends" might be okay with being told the secret, it was him.

"It's a thought at least," Chris said. "You don't have to go right now, you know. We still have some time after an Apocalypse. There's no rush."

There was no way I was going to wait. Not with the chance to finally figure out what it was our Friends in High Places wanted.

Chris grabbed the atlas and took it back with him to wherever he had been when Antoine found him.

"Dina, how well do you know Bobby?" Antoine asked.

She shrugged. "No better than you. He's talked to me before. He likes to talk."

Antoine and I looked at each other.

"Maybe it's best if you go invite him on the storyline," he said.

Dina did not look thrilled, but she obliged.

There was a nervous energy between us. We were either about to finally move forward in the mystery, or we might just end up disappointed. Whatever the case, I was ready to know.

"What do you think we're going to find?" Kimberly asked. "And how are we going to find something that none of the others have found?"

I thought for a moment.

"We aren't going to do anything on our own," I said. "I know that sounds cynical, but I just get this feeling that someone is moving the pieces into place. I think we might get to find out what they've been planning. I can't help but notice how many invisible hands have worked to put us in this place. If this theory is correct, if we really are supposed to go on this storyline, how many variables had to be accounted for to get us to this point? And why?"

"You always talk like that," Antoine said. "We've sacrificed a lot. We're going to get through this. I don't care who has been messing with us. Eventually, something has to shake loose. We can't keep running in place forever."

That must have been the first time since the Straggler incident that Antoine had been optimistic about our situation, even if it was forced. I hoped he was right.

After all, we were about to find out.

CHAPTER TWENTY-SIX

THE WARNING

So, you're going out on a storyline already, huh?" Bobby asked after Dina had tracked him down.

Antoine nodded. "Something we've got to do."

"You lost two of your people. I'm sorry to hear that. The Final Girl was nice. She said some kind words to me after Janet . . . disappeared."

"Thanks. Anna and Camden will be missed," Antoine said.

"What do you need exactly?" Bobby asked. "A Wallflower is good for gathering information and some Finale tricks, or at least that's what I can do right now. Always around to lend a hand."

Antoine looked over at the rest of us. I shrugged. Frankly, I thought a warm body would be enough. We couldn't really ask too much. If fate—or the Friends in High Places—had not tied us together in some way, I wouldn't even agree to let him come. There was a real chance he could learn our secret, and he might not decide to keep it.

"We can use that," Antoine said.

Bobby nodded his head. He was an awkward guy. Sociable, sure, but not particularly charismatic. I couldn't really tell how old he was, just that he was older than us.

"I can come," Bobby said. "Do you need me to die? That's what I mostly did for Travis and the others."

"We should have that covered," Antoine said, though he didn't seem too keen to allow Kimberly to die. "We just need someone around to help out."

"I gotcha."

There wasn't much more discussion than that. We had a lot of walking to do if we were going to get across town in time to catch the Omen.

* * *

On our way across town, I made sure to give a wide berth to the town square. Part of my reasoning was that there were so many Omens concentrated in that area, and the other part was that I couldn't stand to walk past the walls of missing posters by the diner. That wound was too fresh.

Something that we had to invest in was a trope that would allow us to drive without getting bothered by Omens. I didn't know if such a thing existed, but if it did, I would snap it up at the first possible occasion. Our distance from town protected us and allowed us to sleep calmly at night, knowing that we were safe. It also made the trek into town a real hassle.

As usual, I led the pack, pointing out every Omen that we came across just to make sure that we didn't accidentally trigger one. Even if we were in no danger of coming in contact with a specific Omen, I still pointed it out because I could tell that it made Kimberly feel safer to have them called out.

As we walked along, I would point to things like a shadowy figure in the window of a home in a neighborhood we walked through or the group of hooded figures that crossed the road in front of us and tell them about what the Omen was and what we had to do to make sure that we didn't accidentally trigger it. In both cases, it was quite simple: don't shine a light in the window, don't look at the faces of the hooded figures. Easy stuff.

The further we went, the more I started to notice how few Omens we were coming across. The route we had chosen was designed to be mostly clear of Omens, but even then, we could walk ten minutes without seeing one. We were way too close to the center of town for that to make sense. It looked like we had gotten lucky. Or maybe our "Friends" were clearing a path for us.

Whatever the case, we marched onward.

At last, we could see the finish line, or at least the final lap. Olde Hill Road stood before us. To the left was Patcher's Family Farm. They still had their little agriculture-themed amusement park thing going on. I could hear people talking and laughing. I could see children running around happily. It was just as I remembered it from the day we walked through Benny's corn maze.

Though I would have loved to be able to stop there and buy a funnel cake, our business was further down the road. We walked right on by.

At least, we tried.

"Hey," a young woman's voice cried out. "Where are you all headed? You know we got a lot of fun things going on over here. All you have to do is buy some tickets."

We looked over to see a woman in a pair of beat-up denim overalls and a straw cowboy hat strolling toward us. The look on her face didn't match the words that she was saying. She looked worried.

"How about you come back this way? You don't want to wander in that direction once it gets dark. Just come on back, and I'll get you a free corn dog," the woman said.

Antoine, our de facto spokesperson with Anna gone, said, "We actually have business down that way. Thanks, though."

The woman was persistent; she walked even closer toward us. As she approached us, she paid special attention to Kimberly, grabbing her hand.

"Come on, don't go down there. Not this time of day; it's going to get dark soon."

She started to pull Kimberly back toward the farmhouse.

"We need to go this way," Dina said.

"What could be so important that you would have to go out there right now?"

"Our cars are out there," Antoine said, thinking quickly. It was true. Our cars had been there for weeks.

The woman looked truly upset. She looked over her shoulder. "Come back with me and I'll buy you a corn dog and we can talk," she said in a hushed voice.

Antoine shot a look at me, as if asking what I thought. I nodded.

We agreed to follow her. She took us back to Patcher's Family Farm and was true to her word. She bought us each a corn dog, though I'm pretty sure they were free for her.

On the red wallpaper, her name was "Eliza Patcher."

She wasn't an enemy. She wasn't an Omen.

As we assumed, she was Breaking the Veil of Silence.

Kimberly's new trope made it so that NPCs would go out of their way to inform her of any nearby Omens for storylines that specifically targeted women. *Permanent Vacancy* must have been such a storyline.

We knew the possibility existed. In the *Carousel Atlas*, the three Archetypes that had the most scouting information about that storyline were the Bounty Hunter, the Damsel, and the Sheriff. Those three combined gave very strong clues. We knew the likelihood that this story involved kidnapping not only because we had literally seen a woman escaping from the hotel on our first day in Carousel but also because the Damsel was an Advanced Archetype that specialized in being kidnapped.

The Bounty Hunter specialized in tracking down people, usually criminals.

The Sheriff was similar.

We had suspected that Kimberley's trope might activate on our way to the storyline. I never expected it to be that elaborate, however. In my head, I pictured a neighbor shouting, "Better not go that way," while trimming their hedges. Eliza, however, looked very concerned and was actively trying to convince us, and specifically Kimberly, out of walking in that direction.

We decided to listen to what she had to tell us. We had a little bit of time before we had to go trigger the Omen. It wasn't quite sunset yet.

"There are men down that way," Eliza said. "Strange men that have a funny manner about them. I don't think it's safe to go that direction for a young woman."

"Oh," Kimberly said. "What about them is strange?"

Eliza looked embarrassed. "They drove by. They were in a pickup truck. Two men were in the back. They said things to me that were vulgar. I know some of the other ladies around here have said the same thing. And I swear, at night sometimes, I hear screaming coming from down the road. I find myself checking the locks two or three times every night. Daddy says it isn't any of our business. He says that they're there to renovate the hotel, the bed-and-breakfast. I don't trust them. He says they'll be gone soon; best not to get involved. But I can't watch you go down that way without saying something."

She was on the verge of tears.

"Well, we're going to be careful, and I've got some guys with me, so they probably won't bother me," Kimberly said.

"You don't understand," Eliza said. "I don't think they would ca—"

"Eliza?" a man's voice called from outside. She had taken us inside the farmhouse and was talking to us as we sat in her living room.

I could hear the screen door at the entrance swing open.

"Eliza, we need your help outside with the carriage. Bucky is being very finicky aga—" The man stopped talking as he walked into the living room and saw us all there.

"Eliza, what is going on?" he asked. His name was Joshua Patcher.

"Daddy," she said cautiously, "these are some travelers I saw walking out east. I told them maybe they ought not to."

"What have you been running your mouth about, girl?" he yelled.

"We can't just let them go out there!" she said, trying to work up her courage.

"You should not be going around spreading rumors," Joshua said. "That's how you make a problem where there ain't one. If those men hear that you're saying this kind of stuff about them . . ." He shook his head. "That's the type of talk that you don't share with strangers."

"I was just thinking that maybe they could stay here for the night, and maybe you could drive them out to get their car in the morning," she said, still trying to convince him.

"You are going to bring trouble down on us. If these folks wanna go walking down a dark road in the middle of nowhere, that's their right. They just need to know that if the worst comes, nobody's gonna go rescue them."

He walked over to a closet and fetched something from within it.

It was a shotgun.

"Now, if you folks would like to stay and participate in the activities, by all means, go buy some tickets, but otherwise, you'd best be on your way. Now, I don't want anyone finding out that you heard what you heard, you understand. We aren't looking for trouble here."

He wasn't exactly aiming the shotgun at us, but it was clear what the threat was.

We all stood up to leave, but then Bobby asked, "Did they have any guns?"

"Excuse me?" the man asked.

Bobby thought for a moment. "Have you heard any gunshots coming from down that way?"

Joshua Patcher thought for a moment. "Sometimes, yeah. They must be shooting at rats or targets 'cause they go through hundreds of bullets a day out there. Been a week or so since I heard them, though. Boys like that gotta spend all their money on booze and bullets, and they got plenty of both."

More bad guys with guns.

In a movie, a main character can get shot half a dozen times before they die. I wondered how many times a Film Buff could get shot. I was betting it was only once.

"Thanks," Bobby said. "How many guys?"

"Four or five can't be sure. They don't exactly introduce themselves. One time they came down to the farm and started messing with the guests enjoying the amusements. Then their leader came and pulled them away. He was a fiery one. Guess he didn't want to draw attention. I'd say that they were hiding from the law, but I'm not here to accuse them of anything."

"Thanks again," Bobby said.

We turned and left the house.

It was interesting seeing how Bobby was able to ply that information from them. I took a look at his tropes on the red wallpaper. I saw the ability that let him do it.

<table>
<tr><td>

Background Noise

Type: Insight

Archetype: Wallflower

Aspect: Extra

Stat Used: Moxie

</td></tr>
<tr><td>

In the movies, background characters spend their time having muffled conversations at the edge of frame that will never be heard by the viewers of the film. They could be talking about anything.

</td></tr>
</table>

> With this trope equipped, the player will have a heightened chance of getting background information about a storyline from NPCs as long as the conversation takes place Off Screen. The information will only be related to things the NPC would plausibly know and be willing to say. The information cannot be repeated on-screen without finding a canon source for how the players learned it. Doing so may mutate the story to make the information false. While the information may be reliable, the NPC's explanation for how the information was obtained may still be fictitious. Beware.
>
> Background characters have to be talking about something. Why not something useful?

Kimberly's trope had made the Patchers a part of the story—even if they were only a temporary part to warn her of danger to come—allowing Bobby to come in and ask additional background questions with his trope. Normally, his ability likely wouldn't work on random NPCs who lived down the street from the setting of the storyline. Those tropes combined made a great scouting combo.

Of course, everything we learned was bad news.

As we walked away from the farm, Eliza raced behind us and said, "Good luck."

With every step down the dark road toward the Olde Hill Bed and Breakfast, I tried to hold my head high and act confidently.

But the truth was, I had never felt more uncertain.

CHAPTER TWENTY-SEVEN

PERMANENT VACANCY

Player Stats:

Player	Plot Armor	Mettle	Moxie	Hustle	Savvy	Grit
Riley	24/2	3	7	4	7	3
Antoine	21	5	4	5	1	6
Kimberly	19	3	6	4	1	5
Dina	19	2	3	4	3	7
Bobby	17	3	3	4	3	4

Players' Tropes:
Riley Lawrence is the Film Buff.

Trope Master grants me the ability to perceive enemy tropes, but at the cost of sacrificing half of my Plot Armor.

Cinema Seer buffs the Savvy and Grit of my allies when they hear me predict cinematic and impactful plot elements.

As an **Oblivious Bystander**, I remains untargeted by enemies if I convincingly act oblivious to their presence.

Escape Artist buffs my Hustle to help enact plausible escape plans.

Drawing on my upbringing, **Raised by Television** enhances relevant stats when I take larger-than-life or cinematic action inspired by TV or movies, though it often attracts a downturn in fortune soon afterward.

> **Director's Monitor** allows me to watch the rest of the storyline after my demise via Deathwatch.
>
> **Flashback Revelation** allows me to communicate with allies while on Deathwatch through flashbacks to my past dialogue.
>
> **Dead Man Walking** buffs my Grit after receiving an injury or condition that guarantees my death, stretching out my last moments.
>
> I did not equip **My Grandmother Had the Gift . . .** , **Coming to a Theater Near You, I Don't Like It Here . . .** , **Out like a Light**, **Location Scout**, or **Casting Director**.

Kimberly Madison is the Eye Candy.

> **Convenient Backstory** allows her to believably change her backstory to assist with the current task, buffing the relevant stat.
>
> **Social Awareness** allows her to see the Moxie stat of all enemies and NPCs.
>
> **Get a Room!** boosts the odds of important discoveries when exploring with a love interest during the Party.
>
> **A Hopeless Plea** forces the captor to explicitly deny her release when she asks to be released.
>
> **Pregnancy Reveal** buffs her Grit when she pretends that she is pregnant and buffs the father's Mettle if she dies.
>
> **When in Rome** buffs her Grit until Rebirth if her performance matches the tone of the movie.
>
> **Does Anyone Have a Scrunchie?** allows her to shift Moxie points into another stat by putting her hair up.
>
> She will be targeted for First Blood because **Looks Don't Last**, but the longer she survives, the weaker the enemies get.
>
> She did not equip **Carousel Academy Awards, Breaking the Veil of Silence**, or **That's What I Said!**

Antoine Stone is the Athlete.

> His **You Were Having a Nightmare . . .** trope allows him to repress or heal mental trauma. He is not strong enough to use its plot-resetting powers yet.
>
> **Gym Rat** buffs Mettle and Hustle by revealing athletic backstory.
>
> **It's Part of the Uniform** gives him higher Mettle when attacking with sports equipment.

Just Walk It Off heals the Hobbled status by walking.

Knight in Shining Armor buffs his Mettle and Grit when defending a love interest.

Time Out! allows him to go Off Screen during a fight, reducing enemy aggression.

Brandishing a weapon is **Like a Security Blanket**, buffing his Grit and soothing his and his allies' fear, whereas swinging a weapon will temporarily halt an enemy's attack because of **Swing Away**.

He did not equip **Everyone Loves a Winner**, **The Playbook**, **Reload After Cut**, or **Bad Luck Magnet**.

Dina Cano is the Outsider.

Guarded Personality resists all insight abilities.

An Outsider's Perspective alerts her to new, out-of-place, or unusual information.

Better Late than Never buffs Mettle and Hustle if she waits until the Finale to assist allies on-screen against the enemy.

A Haunted Past allows her to equip various tickets related to past trauma.

Encouragement from Beyond soothes her when stressed, scared, or in pain and may provide useful information.

Outside Looking In grants her the ability to discern ideal spots to linger and observe events without actively participating in the narrative.

They Fell Off allows her to quickly get out of handcuffs and similar restraints.

With **Pen Pal**, she can leave physical or mental messages in the story, which her allies can detect when in the location where she left them.

Bobby Gill is the Wallflower.

Background Noise
Type: Insight
Archetype: Wallflower
Aspect: Extra
Stat Used: Moxie

In the movies, background characters spend their time having muffled conversations at the edge of frame that will never be heard by the viewers of the film. They could be talking about anything.

With this trope equipped, the player will have a heightened chance of getting background information about a storyline from NPCs as long as the conversation takes place Off Screen. The information will only be related to things the NPC would plausibly know and be willing to say. The information cannot be repeated on-screen without finding a canon source for how the players learned it. Doing so may mutate the story to make the information false. While the information may be reliable, the NPC's explanation for how the information was obtained may still be fictitious. Beware.

Background characters have to be talking about something. Why not something useful?

The Good Samaritan
Type: Buff
Archetype: Wallflower
Aspect: Extra
Stat Used: Moxie

When a character has had a run-in with the antagonist and ends up injured, scared, and alone, sometimes it is the actions of unnamed strangers that make all the difference. They are the crowd that the character escapes into, the anonymous 911 caller who summons the police, or, as in this case, the passerby who engages with the killer, even if it causes their own demise.

With this trope equipped, the player gets a buff to their Mettle and Grit if they act to help a teammate in a dire situation. It only works if they have not interacted with the teammate on-screen by that point.

If everyone was this brave and self-sacrificing, there wouldn't be horror movies.

The "Wisdom" of Crowds
Type: Insight
Archetype: Wallflower
Aspect: Extra
Stat Used: Moxie

In a stressful situation, strangers can come together and . . . panic. In a survival scenario, groups of people are often less able to react effectively than individuals. They often dismiss harsh realities, rally against even reasonable ideas, and form tribes for arbitrary reasons.

When the player equips this trope, they will be able to collect opinions about the next course of action from a crowd of NPCs. Most of the ideas will be reactionary and unusable, but the crowd can still produce important information and even some solid plans. The player will have to sort them out.

Some decisions shouldn't be made by committee.

Last-Minute Casting
Type: Rule
Archetype: Wallflower
Aspect: Recast
Stat Used: N/A

The actor we hired to play one of the minor roles in the storyline is out with the flu. We just need someone to fill in. Any takers?

With this trope equipped, the player will instantly be assigned a moderately important NPC role. They will have no choice in the matter. They will receive limited access to the character script when playing the role but will have access to what they need. The role itself will give them a fresh vantage point on the story.

All you have to do is stand there and look scared. Got it?

From Humble Beginnings
Type: Rule/Buff
Archetype: Wallflower
Aspect: Underdog
Stat Used: Moxie

Everyone loves an underdog story. Unfortunately, the first step of climbing up out of the mud is being thrown in the mud in the first place.

With this trope equipped, the player's stats will receive a 30% debuff in the Party. However, their stats will raise 15% of their original amount in Rebirth, then again in the Finale, and then once more in the final battle.

If you can stick around long enough, you might just get the hang of this.

Craft Services Are the Real Heroes
Type: Perk
Archetype: Any
Aspect: Any
Stat Used: N/A

There can be no movie without food for the actors. Behind every production on the silver screen are the hard-working craft service professionals, who ensure there is always plenty of food to snack on.

With this trope equipped, food and beverages will be guaranteed to be found on the set of the story. If the story already has them, they will be of even better quality. This food will be available to players wherever it best makes sense in the narrative.

After all, you shouldn't run from a zombie on an empty stomach.

And That's Lunch
Type: Perk
Archetype: Wallflower
Aspect: Recast
Stat Used: N/A

After a long stretch of filming, sometimes you just need to take a break.

With this trope equipped, scene breaks will last longer, extending the time before players are required to return to the set. The player themselves will be able to see a countdown timer until it is time to return.

Just be sure you make it back on time or the Director will lose his cool.

He also had a trope called The Hidden Infection, which would delay the negative effects of an infection as long as the player kept knowledge of the infection secret. However, once uncovered, the player would feel the effects rapidly. It worked on all kinds of infections, from zombie bites to possession. Pretty cool.

"Don't see much use for this one," he said as he unequipped it.

I had to agree. Everything we knew about this storyline told us it was not supernatural.

The thing is, we couldn't use any of our scouting tropes until the Omen actually showed up, which was tricky because the Omen in this case was just the NPC running at us for help.

We waited in front of the wrought iron fence for the NPC to show up. I looked over at the sign on the gate down the road. I could see the name of the bed-and-breakfast, but its slogan was difficult to read because the bottom of the sign had been damaged.

I wondered if I was supposed to figure this out long ago. Could we have gotten to this part sooner?

"Even if this doesn't work out, we aren't going to let it stop us, right?" Antoine said.

No one said anything, so I said, "Right."

There were so many stories of players just giving up when their leads led them in circles. Most of those players didn't have a mysterious benefactor guiding their every move though, right?

"You don't have to be First Blood if you don't want to," Antoine said to Kimberly.

"No, I'll do it," she said. "I have to."

The tension was building as we waited for the NPC to make her way to us.

Eventually, we heard her in the distance. I heard a hound too.

She burst through the thick underbrush just as I remembered her. She was young and scared out of her mind.

Her pace was so frantic that she ran right into the gate, leaving a gash on her forehead.

On the red wallpaper, her name was "Samantha Cole, a Stranger in Need."

She was level fifty, and like all level fifty NPCs I had seen before her, she had tropes on the red wallpaper that I could not decipher.

Quickly, I equipped all of my scouting tropes that would work outside of storylines.

I Don't Like It Here . . . told me that we triggered the Omen by trying to open the gate. The difficulty was "This is scaring me," which meant it was tough but not impossible.

Location Scout told me there were thirteen rooms in the bed-and-breakfast. It had all the normal places a B and B would have, like a dining room, porch, kitchen. The only location that interested me was called "Graves."

I quickly relayed this to my friends.

Bobby's final trope was a Wallflower one called Cattle Call, which was a term used for the mass casting of extras in a movie. It was a scouting trope that let him know how many NPCs were in a storyline, though the insights it gave varied in utility. This time it gave pretty solid intel.

"There are only two NPCs in this storyline," he said. He looked bewildered.

He didn't need to take that trope into the storyline with him.

I didn't bother with Casting Director, because this story didn't appear that complicated from that perspective. I equipped everything I needed for a run.

It was time to go.

"There's a gate down that direction," I yelled to her. "Run!"

She looked in the direction I pointed and started to move that way. "They have another guy in the basement. My dad. Please help!" she screamed as she booked it toward the gate.

We followed her.

When we got to the gate . . . we were in trouble.

Antoine had brought a pair of bolt cutters so that we could get the gate open. They were in his back pocket . . . until they weren't.

The needle on the Plot Cycle was on Choice. Carousel had taken them away, and I knew why.

The gate had a trope. The last time I had seen something like this was the Astralist's machine, which warned of its indestructibility.

The gate, however, had a different trope.

TIME SUCK	This plot device cannot be used within the time frame you would like.

"Look for a rock. We're going to have to bust the lock," I said.

Dina grabbed the lock and started trying to pick it with what looked like a bobby pin. She wasn't having any luck.

"Hurry!" Samantha screamed. "They're coming!"

I looked around. We were meant to open the gate. It was just going to take a while.

"Got one!" Kimberly yelled.

I turned to look. She had found a large rock, probably the biggest rock Antoine could realistically lift.

"It's too big!" Samantha yelled.

"No," Antoine said, "I'm a weightlifter. Just give me a second."

His Mettle rose two points and his Hustle rose one. It had been a while since I had been around for him to activate Gym Rat. He hefted the large stone, carried it over to the lock, and struck it hard with the stone.

I was confident that this was going to work. But it didn't work fast enough.

He struck the lock one final time and it burst open. We were in.

The needle on the Plot Cycle switched to Party.

"No!" Samantha screamed as two men approached her from behind. I hadn't even seen them. They wore bandanas around their faces as masks, though I wasn't certain they were to hide their identities. The masks were covered in dirt.

One of them, a large one with a yellow bandana, grabbed Samantha and hauled her back in the direction they came.

The other one was thinner and looked very worried. He stared at us like a deer caught in the headlights. I could see him reaching for something in his pocket, but he was hesitant.

I could still hear the sounds of dogs in the distance, but I couldn't see any.

Before he could remove whatever it was from his pocket, a light hit his face. A car was coming from the direction of Carousel.

I turned to look. When I looked back at the masked assailant, he was gone.

I wasn't able to see either of them on the red wallpaper except for their titles, "Grave Robber."

I looked back at the headlights. Their yellow color was soon drowned out by red and blue.

"The cops?" Dina asked.

I wasn't expecting that.

The very old-model squad car approached the gate quickly. Soon, both doors opened, and out stepped two men.

One wore a sheriff's hat and uniform, though the uniform was dirty. On the red wallpaper, his name was "Sheriff Randall Halloway."

He held a gun out toward us. He was a man in his late thirties. He had a serious expression on his face. I had no doubt he would shoot us if given the opportunity.

The other man was wearing civilian clothing and a trucker hat. He brandished a gun. His name on the red wallpaper was "Deputy Bradley Speirs."

"Get on the ground!" the sheriff screamed. He sounded wickedly serious. "Get on the ground and put your hands in the air."

We had no choice but to comply.

"There's a woman in there!" Kimberly screamed. "She needs help."

"Shut your mouth!" Deputy Speirs yelled.

"If I see even one of you move, I will put a bullet in your brain!" Sheriff Holloway screamed.

He took a moment to assess the situation. I couldn't read his face.

"You said a woman was in there?" he asked.

"She was scared," Antoine pleaded cautiously. "She said she needed help."

"A woman . . . ," Sheriff Halloway repeated. "I see you breaking into property here with a rock, and you say you're trying to save a woman? What woman? You come into my town breaking shit, and then you lie to me."

Sheriff Halloway continued trying to think. He reached into the car and grabbed something.

"This is Sheriff Halloway, down on Olde Hill Road. We got four trespassers trying to break into the old bed-and-breakfast," he said.

I didn't hear the reply.

Four trespassers? There were five of us. I looked around.

Bobby was nowhere to be seen.

"Deputy Speirs," Sheriff Halloway said, "please restrain these lawbreakers."

He turned his attention to us.

"If you make me think you are going to harm my deputy—if you so much as give me an inkling—I'll be justified in shooting you. So don't you try me, you hear?"

I trembled at the thought. The scariest part of all of it was that the needle on the Plot Cycle was moving much faster than usual. This storyline was only supposed to take an hour. The Party phase couldn't last too long.

Deputy Speirs went around to each of us and grabbed us, twisting our hands behind our backs to put them in cuffs.

"Now, you don't have anything in your pockets that's gonna stick me, do you?" he asked Antoine as he put the cuffs on and patted him down. He turned to the sheriff. "He's got a baseball bat over there against the fence, you see? We caught ourselves some perpetrators."

Once all of us were handcuffed, lying face down in the dirt, the sheriff put his gun back in its holster. He and the deputy grabbed me and Antoine and hauled us into the back seat of the squad car.

They then walked over to Kimberly and Dina and grabbed them up off the ground.

"What do we do with these two?" Deputy Speirs asked with demented glee. "Hey, ladies, you lost?"

"We just hold onto them until Tank gets here," the sheriff said. "And don't hurt anybody. Your brother'll kill us both."

"I didn't do anything," Speirs said. He slammed Kimberly back against the hood of the car. She fell to the ground. "I'm just enforcing the law."

Deputy Speirs started laughing. Sheriff Halloway joined him.

"See, Randy," Deputy Speirs said. "I told you we should have been cops."

They continued to laugh together as the large man with the yellow bandana reappeared at the gate.

CHAPTER TWENTY-EIGHT

BLOOD RED SUNSET

Dina didn't waste any time escaping.

The larger man from before came back down to the squad car. He grabbed a hold of Kimberly and, after a quick instruction from the fake sheriff, pulled her along toward the property down a long driveway that wound haphazardly back away from the road.

I could hear Kimberly screaming, "Please don't hurt me! I'm pregnant. Please!"

She didn't have to act scared. She was scared. At least she managed to get her Pregnancy Reveal activated, though it only buffed her Grit by a single point. She had not really had time to set it up. I had a feeling that was going to be an issue with a lot of our tropes in this storyline. The Party phase was zooming by, and we were going to have trouble with that sort of thing.

The sheriff grabbed Dina and followed him.

The third guy gave me the absolute creeps. He was still called "Deputy Bradley Speirs" on the red wallpaper—whatever trope hid his identity was still blocking me. He looked thrilled as he ran up to Dina, ruffled her hair, and let out a hyena's laugh. He was younger, unshaven, unkempt.

Antoine and I were left in the back of the car as the three of them walked up to the property. Up close, it was clear that the vehicle we were in was not a modern police car—not even in 1989, when the story was set. It was old, rusty, and worn down. If we had seen it in daylight without the high beams in our eyes, our characters would have known those guys were not actual cops instantly.

Off Screen.

"I don't like this," Antoine said. I could see that he was testing the strength of his handcuffs against his pure strength, trying to squeeze his hand out of one of the cuffs. Of course, his efforts were in vain.

"I don't think you'll be able to do that off-screen," I said.

"I'm going to go for it when I get the chance," he said. "I did say I was a weightlifter, at least. Might help."

I shrugged. "It might if you pick your moment. Dina should be out of hers soon."

He nodded. "But what about Kimberly? Those guys . . . They looked dangerous. Did you see anything about their tropes?"

I shook my head. "The two with the masks were just called 'Grave Robbers.' I assume they have a trope to stop them from being scoped out from the road when they come to grab Samantha. The other two looked like NPCs still, but I'm guessing that will change."

Antoine nodded.

"We could try kicking out the window," I suggested, pointing to the window beside Antoine. There were bars blocking us from getting into the front seat. Unfortunately, as soon as I said it, I knew it wouldn't work. We were Captured on the red wallpaper. If my escape idea were plausible, I would have gotten a buff from my Escape Artist trope.

"Never mind," I said.

"Got to set you up for the TV buff, right?" Antoine asked.

I nodded. "We should try," I said. "I'm not sure we'll have time." Raised by Television required the audience to know I was a Film Buff so that I could do some movie hero stunt and get a boost for it. Like Kimberly's Pregnancy Reveal, I wasn't sure we would get the chance to set it up with how fast the plot was moving.

"And Bobby has already gone into his role somewhere," Antoine said. "Any idea when he'll show back up? Do we know for sure?"

"Finale at the worst. Finale for Dina too," I said.

He looked up ahead. I followed his gaze.

"Right on schedule," I said.

Two of the men, the larger guy and the sheriff, were running in our direction. They were absolutely booking it with a panic in their eyes.

The sheriff reached the car, and we were suddenly on-screen.

"Goddamn it," he said as he opened the driver's side door and got inside.

"What do I do?" the man with the yellow bandana asked. He had previously not had any important information on the red wallpaper other than "Grave Robber" but now had the name "Tank." Plot Armor: 18.

"Go find her!" the fake sheriff yelled. "Bring her to me!"

The sheriff reached to turn on the car, and I realized that he had left the keys in the ignition. That would explain why he was in such a hurry to get back to us—he didn't want Dina getting here first. Antoine and I couldn't have reached them.

Antoine and I screamed and yelled and threatened as we thought our characters would do in that situation.

He drove the car up the driveway. We curved around until the thick woods cleared and we could see a large worn-down plantation-style manor sitting upon a hill. The side paneling had once been white but was now gray from weathering. There were lights on in some of the rooms. Lumber had been piled up under tarps outside as if someone were planning to renovate.

It didn't look as decrepit as I was expecting from the sign in Camden's picture, but then, the sign was technically thirty years older than the building, which I believed had been brought to Carousel back in 1989.

Standing in front of the building was a man I had not yet seen. He was arguing with the fake deputy, pointing his finger out in the distance, clearly ordering the deputy off.

I could suddenly see both of them clearly on the red wallpaper. I looked at the sheriff driving us. I could see him in my mind too.

We pulled up in front of the house, and the sheriff opened his door.

"Got two of them right here, boss," the fake sheriff said like a kiss-ass. His name on the red wallpaper was still "Randall 'Randy' Halloway." Plot Amor: 19.

The man he had called Boss was named "Merritt Speirs." Plot Armor: 22. Off Screen.

I could see now that all of the enemies had three tropes in common.

DESPERATION	This villain is in a desperate situation. The worse their situation becomes, the more desperate and violent they will act. Debuffs Moxie and Savvy to buff Mettle and Hustle.
HOME-LAIR ADVANTAGE	The villain can travel freely and unnoticed due to their knowledge of the setting and its passages—both public and secret.
NOWHERE TO RUN	The setting for this story is isolated. There is no one to ask for help within the story and nowhere to go where the enemy will not find you.

That was a very concerning combination. Dina was supposed to find a way to get away and then stay off-screen until the Finale. That was the plan. The question was, would she be able to do it?

Each of the enemies had additional tropes that made them unique as well.

"The leader there and the crazy one are brothers," I whispered to Antoine, though he could probably guess that from their last names. "The leader has a trope called 'Avenger' that triggers with the death of a loved one."

"Ah. Kill the crazy one and the older brother gets more dangerous," Antoine said. "Don't kill the crazy one and you have to deal with the crazy one."

"That's it."

I told him about the tropes they all shared, but then we had to stop talking, as we were suddenly on-screen.

"Get out of the car," the sheriff yelled as he pulled open the door of the cop car.

The sheriff grabbed me by the hair and pulled me out. The man called Tank had returned and was holding onto Antoine. They forced us around the house until we came across a storm shelter about fifteen yards from the main building.

I could hear dogs howling from somewhere on the property as I had earlier. I still couldn't see them, though.

The leader, Merritt, opened the shelter, and we were forced down into it. Kimberly and the NPC, Samantha, were already inside.

We fell down into the hole, hard. I couldn't exactly catch myself with my hands handcuffed behind my back.

Then I stared up at Merritt. The sky above was the color of blood. It would be night soon.

"We got no aim to harm you," he said. "My crew and I, well, we just care about one thing: money. Ain't nothing else too important. We will not lay a finger on you as long as you do what you're told and you don't cause trouble. We'll be out of here in a few days' time, and then you can be on your way. As soon as our business here is finished, it'll be like this never happened. But you gotta do what we say, got it? You can trust us. We're good believers, after all."

None of us responded. He didn't wait for an answer.

The storm shelter door was closed. Everything went dark.

"Do you think Dina is okay?" Kimberly asked. "If they find her, she won't just let them take her alive."

We were still on-screen so we were limited on what we could talk about.

"She's probably halfway to Carousel by now," Antoine said reassuringly. "She'll have the real cops here soon; we'll be okay."

"Halfway to Carousel?" Samantha asked. "I hope she's not going in that direction. Won't find much."

"What?" Kimberly asked. "I thought Carousel was just down the road."

"Sure, it's there," Samantha said. "It's just there's no one there to help. Town's been pretty much abandoned for a decade now."

Oh. The Carousel of this story wasn't a Midwestern college town or a bustling metropolis. It was a ghost town. Carousel had its role to play too. After all, we had Nowhere to Run according to the enemies' trope. It might not matter. Dina was supposed to stick around and stay out of sight. We hadn't planned on her running back to Carousel. I hoped she didn't decide to.

"What is going on here?" Antoine asked.

Samantha was silent for a moment. The shelter was dark, so I couldn't quite see her, but then I heard her crying.

"Dad hired them as laborers to help fix up the old bed-and-breakfast. Of course, they were just trying to get in and start trouble. They have Dad locked in the basement. Think they can get even more money out of him. That's the only reason they haven't hurt me or the dogs, but that one . . . Gotta watch out for him. He's a violent man," Samantha said, looking at Kimberly. "I'm sorry for bringing you all here. I was just scared. And now you're here with us too. We're never going to leave."

"It's not your fault," Kimberly said gently. "You couldn't have known . . ."

I think Kimberly hugged her in the dark, or at least tried given the fact that her hands were bound behind her.

Whatever the case, Kimberly's Moxie jumped up three points. Samantha, the level fifty NPC, must have had a trope that activated because Kimberly comforted her.

"We need to get your hands out in front of you," Samantha said, suddenly affecting a much more calm and calculating demeanor. "I don't know how to break the locks, but if you can get your hands in front of you, we will have a better chance."

Samantha herself was not bound.

She walked us through, one at a time, stretching our arms down below our waists and sitting down, then trying to get our legs through the loop our arms made so that our arms could go all the way around in front of us.

Kimberly got hers done quickly. Antoine, who worried his larger muscles would get in the way, took a little longer. I wasn't really built for it. I only managed to get my hands in front of me because the others helped me force them. I had never played jump rope with my arms before. With that done, at least we stood a chance.

The needle on the Plot Cycle was ticking closer to First Blood. This story was moving faster than any I had been in. It was like we weren't even the main characters. We were just innocent bystanders who had been forcibly brought into Samantha's horrifying ordeal.

Not too long after we got our hands out in front of us, the door opened back up and the five figures we had seen were now standing before us. I finally got a good look at all of them on the red wallpaper.

Other than Desperation, Home-Lair Advantage, and Nowhere to Run, the kidnappers each had one or two unique tropes that defined their behavior. I tried to memorize everything so that I could predict what they would do.

BRADLEY SPEIRS	
Plot Armor: 22	
A crazed assailant with a hyena's laugh. He pretended to be a deputy to lure us into complying with him and his gang.	
Tropes	
DESPERATION	This villain is in a desperate situation. The worse their situation becomes, the more desperate and violent they will act. Debuffs Moxie and Savvy to buff Mettle and Hustle.
APPEAL TO AUTHORITY	This villain will first appear as an authority figure and will not be seen as an enemy until their true nature is discovered.
HOME-LAIR ADVANTAGE	The villain can travel freely and unnoticed due to their knowledge of the setting and its passages—both public and secret.
EVIL PLAYS FAVORITES	Evil hates everyone, but it hates some folks more than others. This villain is liable to target the object of their prejudice regardless of players' Plot Armor or tropes.
BLOOD JOY	This villain is energized by carnage. Witnessing or participating in murder, mutilation, or similar will buff an assortment of stats.
NOWHERE TO RUN	The setting for this story is isolated. There is no one to ask for help within the story and nowhere to go where the enemy will not find you.

This was the one to watch out for. Blood Joy was a nightmare that would make him stronger the more carnage he created. Evil Plays Favorites was a tricky one; we needed to figure out what his prejudices were to plan properly. Luckily, there was a good chance his prejudice was against women, seeing as we knew women were targeted specifically in this storyline.

TANK	
Plot Armor: 18	
A large man with a yellow bandana and a slow wit. He seems loyal to Merritt but is willing to help out any of his fellow villains. He was one of the assailants originally chasing Samantha.	
Tropes	
DESPERATION	This villain is in a desperate situation. The worse their situation becomes, the more desperate and violent they will act. Debuffs Moxie and Savvy to buff Mettle and Hustle.
FIGURE IN THE SHADOWS	This villain will be unidentifiable before they are properly introduced in the story.
HOME-LAIR ADVANTAGE	The villain can travel freely and unnoticed due to their knowledge of the setting and its passages—both public and secret.
NOWHERE TO RUN	The setting for this story is isolated. There is no one to ask for help within the story and nowhere to go where the enemy will not find you.
HOSTAGE TAKER	The villain will not outright kill the player in combat until the final battle. Instead, they will attempt to take the player hostage for some specific purpose.
JUST FOLLOWING ORDERS	This villain will do whatever their leader says regardless of their own morality.

This guy was strong but would kidnap you instead of just outright killing you. That was useful information.

MERRITT SPEIRS	
Plot Armor: 22	
The leader of the outfit. He is cunning and has some really ambitious ideas, if only he could keep control of his beloved brother.	
Tropes	
DESPERATION	This villain is in a desperate situation. The worse their situation becomes, the more desperate and violent they will act. Debuffs Moxie and Savvy to buff Mettle and Hustle.
HOME-LAIR ADVANTAGE	The villain can travel freely and unnoticed due to their knowledge of the setting and its passages—both public and secret.
NOWHERE TO RUN	The setting for this story is isolated. There is no one to ask for help within the story and nowhere to go where the enemy will not find you.
AVENGER	This villain will pursue with a fury those who harm their friends or loved ones. They will receive relevant buffs in doing so.

Avenger was a strong trope that would activate, presumably, when we killed his brother, Bradley. Combined with Desperation, he was going to be a formidable threat later in the storyline.

RANDALL "RANDY" HALLOWAY	
Plot Armor: 19	
Loyal but not particularly impassioned. Randy follows orders and is smart enough not to blow his own toes off. I'll watch out for him.	
Tropes	
DESPERATION	This villain is in a desperate situation. The worse their situation becomes, the more desperate and violent they will act. Debuffs Moxie and Savvy to buff Mettle and Hustle.
APPEAL TO AUTHORITY	This villain will first appear as an authority figure and will not be seen as an enemy until their true nature is discovered.

HOME-LAIR ADVANTAGE	The villain can travel freely and unnoticed due to their knowledge of the setting and its passages—both public and secret.
NOWHERE TO RUN	The setting for this story is isolated. There is no one to ask for help within the story and nowhere to go where the enemy will not find you.
CHATTY KATHY	This villain was cursed with the gift of gab. Perhaps you can make them pay for it.
JUST FOLLOWING ORDERS	This villain will do whatever their leader says regardless of their own morality.

You've got to love an enemy with a built-in weakness.

TIM	
Plot Armor: 18	
He is the youngest member of the group and the least comfortable with what they are up to. There still might be a chance to reach him.	
Tropes	
DESPERATION	This villain is in a desperate situation. The worse their situation becomes, the more desperate and violent they will act. Debuffs Moxie and Savvy to buff Mettle and Hustle.
FIGURE IN THE SHADOWS	This villain will be unidentifiable before they are properly introduced in the story.
HOME-LAIR ADVANTAGE	The villain can travel freely and unnoticed due to their knowledge of the setting and its passages—both public and secret.
LAST THREAD OF HUMANITY	This villain is not yet a complete monster, but with one tiny push, they may become one. Free of their burden of conscience, they will be uninhibited in their pursuit of murder. When activated, buffs Mettle and Hustle.
NOWHERE TO RUN	The setting for this story is isolated. There is no one to ask for help within the story and nowhere to go where the enemy will not find you.

This enemy was clearly meant to be turned into an ally of sorts given his Last Thread of Humanity trope. I wasn't sure if we would work that in or not. That sounded like a weakness for a longer storyline.

It was evident they had not found Dina, but our characters would not know that.

"Where is Dina?" I screamed.

"She'll be back soon, I'm sure. We'll find her. As a gesture of goodwill, I'm going to bring you inside. The basement has food, a place to sleep, and a restroom," Merritt said. "Now, don't test us. We will not hesitate to get violent if we are provoked."

The fake deputy, Bradley, leaned down into the shelter. If he noticed that we had our hands in front of us, he didn't say anything.

"One at a time," he said with a devilish smile.

Kimberly went up first.

Whatever was going to happen would happen soon. The needle on the Plot Cycle was practically on First Blood.

As Bradley lifted Kimberly up, he leaned down and whispered something in her ear. I couldn't hear what it was, but she took it as an opportunity. She headbutted him in the face. He maintained his grasp on her with one hand and backhanded her in the face with the other.

With that, the clock started. For every minute Kimberly survived, the weaker the enemies would become. This was not the ideal situation for that trope. They had firearms. I wasn't sure how long any of us could last.

As soon as he hit her, Antoine was up and out of the shelter. He bounded onto the fake sheriff, the only character other than the deputy who we had seen with a gun.

Antoine knocked him to the ground and kicked the gun from his hand.

Samantha was out of the shelter next, then me.

"You stupid girl!" Merritt yelled after Samantha as she ran away.

I jumped on the gun the fake sheriff had dropped and pointed it out in front of me. I pointed it at Merritt.

"Let us go!" I screamed.

Merritt looked at me with an annoyed expression. He looked at the fake sheriff, Randy.

Randy said, "It's not loaded. I did like you said."

They didn't put ammo in their guns? Why?

Merritt walked closer to me and moved to grab the gun.

I pulled the trigger out of instinct.

Nothing happened.

"You caught us," Merritt said. "It's best not to have a loaded gun around a prisoner. They might fight you and take it. Then what will you do?" He laughed loudly. "Besides, we're what you might call 'preserving ammunition' right now. I told you all we didn't mean you any harm. Didn't even load the guns. This can all work out in everyone's favor."

He grabbed a pistol of his own from within his waistband. He reached into his pocket to grab ammunition. He quickly loaded the gun.

"Now this one does have ammunition," he said as he cocked the gun. "So I advise you to listen up."

Tank had gotten hold of Antoine again and Bradley was still holding on to Kimberly.

They forced each of us to our knees.

"Now, I told you I was a believer, and I'm gonna show it right now by forgiving you. We're going to take you down to the basement. When you get there, tell the man downstairs how reasonable I was despite your indiscretions. That's all I ask."

He put the gun back in his waistband.

"Now," he said to his men, "get them down into the basement, and then find th—"

Bang.

A gun went off.

I turned to see Bradley, the fake deputy with the demented laugh. He was still aiming the gun down at Kimberly, who lay strewn out on the ground.

Antoine broke free from Tank and lunged at Bradley, but it was too late.

She was dead.

Antoine got several good hits on the deputy's face and gut. The man cried out in pain at each blow but also laughed a sickly laugh after each one. There was only so much Antoine could do in handcuffs.

Before Antoine could exact further vengeance on the deputy, Tank grabbed him and kneeled down on him. He was pinned.

"What did you do that for?" Merritt screamed at his brother. He came and grabbed him. It looked like he would strangle him. "Don't you understand what you just did?"

"She broke my nose. We was gonna kill 'em later anyway. You said so," the deputy protested.

"We needed the guy downstairs to trust that we wouldn't hurt him or his daughter while he makes the withdrawal, that we are men of our word. Reasonable. You went and ruined that. You idiot! If he thinks we're psycho killers, he's just gonna go to the police." Merritt cursed loudly. "You can't control it for ten minutes?"

So, they planned to extort the owner of the bed-and-breakfast. They needed him to think they would let him go afterward, and Merritt wanted us to be some sort of proof that they were not violent.

"Merritt, I didn't think about it like that," Bradley said as Merritt laid into him with a punch of his own. "Merritt, I'm sorry."

Merritt turned to the man who had dressed as a sheriff. "I told you to watch him! Who gave him bullets, anyway?"

"He must have swiped them himself," the fake sheriff protested. "Honest. I didn't give him any. It was like you said. We didn't want loaded guns around the hostages."

Antoine reached out for Kimberly's fallen body while Merritt screamed in frustration.

"It's just one thing after another. This was a simple shakedown. Threaten the guy's daughter and get money. How do you manage to screw that up?" Merritt screamed.

"I'm sorry, Merritt. I didn't think about it like that. She did break my nose, though; I wasn't lying about that."

"I don't give a damn about your broken nose!" Merritt screamed. "Now we've got a mess on our hands."

Kimberly had only survived for a couple of minutes or so at most while Merritt had done his dramatic speech. Enough to drop them down a single point. Maybe the trope rounded up.

As Antoine and I struggled to free ourselves, an increasingly disheveled Merritt paced back and forth, his hand on his waistband right next to his gun.

CHAPTER TWENTY-NINE

THE DAMSEL IN DISTRESS

Merritt paced back and forth, growing more distressed with each step. He muttered under his breath, cursing his brother, mostly. His hand never left his waistband where he kept his gun.

In the distance, I heard hounds howling and barking. I had heard them when we first arrived but had yet to see them. If memory served, I had heard them on my first day in Carousel too when we had passed Samantha.

The noises got closer.

Soon, Merritt's attention turned to the large hound that appeared from around the other side of the bed-and-breakfast and jumped upon him, grasping his wrist in its jaws.

There were more hounds, at least six, most of which were larger breeds.

Bradley, the psychotic one, was aiming his gun at the dogs, warding them off with loud shots, even hitting one of them. Then he ran out of bullets.

One dog sank its teeth into Tank's thigh, another into his forearm.

He let go of Antoine.

Antoine seized the opportunity. He started to pull at his restraints with all of his might. We were on-screen, so if he was going to go *Incredible Hulk* and break out of his cuffs, that would be the time to do it. He had already said he was a weightlifter, after all.

He pulled.

At first, it didn't look like anything was happening.

I had to shuffle around as the dogs attacked the men, letting loose haunting howls as they did so. I didn't get a good view for a moment as I broke free from the man who was holding onto me. One of the dogs snapped at me but was clearly more interested in the other men. When I looked back, I saw that Antoine was making progress.

He wasn't breaking the cuffs. He was succeeding in pulling his left hand out of its cuff, though the process tore his skin, practically degloving his hand.

He pulled with his greatest effort, and then he had done it. His hand was free—mangled, but free.

With his hands free, one dripping with blood, he grabbed Merritt, who had finally gotten the opportunity to grab his gun. Antoine pushed him with all of his might. Merritt fell backward down into the storm shelter they had just let us out of.

"Don't you touch him!" Bradley Speirs screamed.

He couldn't do much. One of the dogs had taken to his ankle and opened a gash in it.

"Run!" a voice from up near the house cried out. It was Samantha, the NPC. She waved us to come toward her.

Antoine was preoccupied, in shock over Kimberly's body. I grabbed him and pulled him away.

"We have to go!" I screamed.

We didn't have long until the men would recover from the surprise attack of the dogs.

Antoine put his shoulder into Tank and knocked him on his backside.

After breaking his gaze away from Kimberly and punching the fake sheriff in the face, he finally got with the program, and we ran back toward Samantha.

Antoine was hurling insults at the men the whole way, clearly distressed over what they had done to Kimberly.

Samantha whistled loudly. The dogs immediately took notice and stopped attacking. Some ran into the distance, perhaps back to whatever pen they had been let out of. Two of them ran toward Samantha. One lay on the ground, unmoving.

"Come on!" she screamed to Antoine and me. "We have to get inside and trap them out here."

Sounded like a plan.

She waved us around to the nearest entrance to the house and we followed. It was up a few steps, and then we were inside. She slammed the door behind us. The two dogs that had followed us immediately sought Samantha's attention. The dogs must have missed her.

"Dad brought them up here for the renovation. They haven't got to see me in a while," she explained as she locked the door. "Help me move this." She pointed to a large upright piano that was up against the wall.

Antoine jumped in to help. They moved the piano over in front of the door.

"They already boarded up most of the windows and doors on the first level to try to keep me from escaping," she explained. "We need to get my dad from the basement."

She led us away from the back entrance toward what looked like the kitchen area. It was kind of hard to tell with the renovations that were going on.

"Samantha!" I heard Bobby screaming—from somewhere in the house.

"Dad!" she screamed back as she ran for the basement door.

She opened it to reveal Bobby. His Wallflower trope had recast him as the only other non-enemy NPC in the story: Samantha's father.

They hugged.

Antoine looked numb as he cared for his injured hand, but he still engaged in hurried conversation for the camera as he, Bobby, and Samantha talked.

I, however, was distracted.

I saw a piece of furniture in the corner of the room that I had seen in many hotels before. It was one of those brochure holders that were always in the lobbies advertising nearby resorts and attractions.

Something about it caught my eye.

I walked over to it and started shuffling through the brochures for plays, musicals, one-man shows, an amusement park, and more. Most of them had one thing in common.

As I shuffled through them, we went Off Screen.

"What are you doing over there?" Antoine asked.

I pulled out one brochure after another, glancing at them before moving to the next. Even with my handcuffed hands, my fingers moved nimbly, even if they did shake.

"Silver Dollar City," I said, holding up one brochure. That was a real amusement park in our world. "Branson, Missouri." As I ran through the brochures, I read one after another, "Branson. Branson. Near Branson."

Antoine quickly walked over to the brochure stand and looked through them himself.

"So it's true," he said. "This story is from our world."

"Wait, what?" Bobby asked.

"You're from our world too, aren't you?" I asked Samantha.

She didn't answer, but a strange look moved over her face. It appeared an awful lot like she was ashamed.

A thought occurred to me. I ran into the kitchen and opened the refrigerator.

I started to laugh and grabbed a few dark red cans from the shelf and brought them back to the others. I couldn't explain the explosions of joy that overcame me at seeing something so simple, something from home.

I handed one to Antoine and another to Bobby.

I opened mine and took a swig.

It was Dr. Pepper.

I wasn't even much of a soda drinker, and yet, seeing it there thrilled me.

Antoine wasn't as excited as me. He had just finished wrapping his injured hand in a cloth he had found, but he still opened his and took a drink.

"Those fake Carousel brands everywhere," I said. "They aren't fake. They're just from different worlds!"

This storyline was from our world, so it had our brands. I was right. I could have cried to finally be moving forward and gaining some understanding.

"You're from our world," I repeated to Samantha. "What happened? Why are we here?"

She was slow to answer. "I'm sorry for bringing you all here. I was just scared. And now you're here with us too. We're never going to leave."

She had told us that same line when we had been on-screen a few minutes earlier.

"That's one of her lines," Bobby said. "I'm not sure if they really understand Carousel. I've tried talking to NPCs about . . . my wife. They don't seem to know what I'm talking about."

We hadn't brought Bobby up to speed yet.

"Can you explain?" I asked Samantha again. "This storyline is from our world. What are we supposed to learn here? Is there a way out?"

Samantha waited for a moment and then said, "We should go upstairs. There is only one stairway. We can more easily defend ourselves from up there."

That made sense, but I was getting the dreadful feeling that she was ducking my question.

Then she said, "Dad hired these men to do work on the house. They did for a while, but then . . . Well, you can probably guess that things devolved."

"I have lots of information on that," Bobby said helpfully. "My Recast Aspect is pretty limited, but that kind of stuff I can see in the script."

We followed Samantha up the stairs. Once we got to the landing, she turned to me.

She looked me right in the eye.

"They said that if I went along with their plans, I would live. If I gave them what they wanted," she said.

"Yeah," Bobby added. "They want me to go to the bank to withdraw a bunch of money, and then they'll let us go. That's what they say at least."

"Just a second, Bobby," Antoine said.

I kept eye contact with Samantha.

"They told you to go along with their plans and you would live?" I asked.

She nodded.

"They wanted me . . . to be their perfect hostage. I was scared. I didn't want to die . . . It's my fault you're here. I was afraid."

Antoine and I made eye contact.

"Someone offered to let you live if you did what they said?" Antoine asked. "And that's why we're here?"

"They were looking . . . for a perfect hostage," she said tearfully. "I'm so sorry."

"The man on the top floor?" I asked. "Is that the person who made you the offer? He watches us through violet lights. He looks for dark stories?"

That was what the demon at the bar had said to Dina about the person who could help her save her son.

Samantha continued to cry. She didn't say yes or no, but I felt I was not far off track.

"A plan," she said. "A plan to save us. I've had all the time in the world . . . I will do whatever it takes to help you. It's my fault you're here."

"A plan?" I asked. "The plan from our friends in high places?"

"There's a way to survive," she said in agreement. She had to use her lines to communicate. She didn't seem as good at it as Jack Goforth had been.

"What is happening here? It's almost like . . . You said that this storyline was from our world, that she was," Bobby said. "Does that mean NPCs are real?"

I nodded.

"I knew it!" he said. "Travis always said I was being too sentimental." An idea struck him. "Do you know what happened to my wife?" he asked Samantha. "She disappeared. Her name was Janet Gill. Do you have any information about her at all?"

Samantha gave him a look of sympathy.

"Mom?" she asked. Bobby was playing her father. She had to stay in character. Calling Janet her mother might let her do that. "I don't know where she is," Samantha said. "But I have to believe that we will see her again."

That answer energized Bobby.

"But how?" Bobby asked. He had started to tear up. "It's my fault that she came. She didn't want to. He told me she would be safe."

Wait.

"Who told you she would be safe?" I asked.

Bobby wiped the tears from his eyes. "Dropstone Don. The man on the forum who invited me to the horror convention. His real name was Donny. Well . . . not really, I guess. We talked about it. He said that his wife didn't like scary things either, that she was . . . frail. Like Janet." He struggled to hold back his tears. "He said she wouldn't have to do any of the scary events, that there were events for people who were afraid. He said she could hang out with his wife . . ."

He got quiet.

I couldn't imagine the guilt he must feel. Samantha could, though. She was crying at his story.

"I'm sorry," she said.

"What's the plan?" I asked.

She took a moment to compose herself.

"They're strange men, all of them, but that one is stranger than the rest. His interests are dark. When they found the cemetery on the property, they started digging, grave robbing, desecrating. Merritt didn't like it, but it occupied his brother, and that was a small miracle. Bradley took to it quickly. The others, they wanted jewelry and trinkets. Stuff they could pawn. Bradley, the sick fuck, he just liked to mess with the bodies. To use them for target practice. To defile them, to use their bones to make . . . art. He made an ashtray out of a woman's skull . . ."

She stared into the distance.

"Wait a second," Bobby said once he regained composure. "These are her lines, but . . . they aren't right."

"What do you mean?" I asked.

"I can't see a whole lot, but there are different scripts for different versions of the same storyline. She's saying lines from a different script. I can't really get a good look at it."

A different script?

"Like when a trope changes a script?" Antoine asked. "Or a Detective turning a storyline into a mystery?"

Bobby nodded.

"I hear them at night," she whispered. "Dad tells me it's all in my head, but I hear them crying out, begging, warning. I think tonight's the night."

"Honey," Bobby said, "this is just a scary moment, and your mind is running away with it. Don't lose your head. We're going to be okay if we just do what these men want."

It sounded like he was reading off his lines from his version of the script.

"Except," he added, "this should be happening on-screen."

"So that's the plan?" I asked. "To switch to a different version of the script?"

I thought we were going to get to see the real version of events for the storyline, but apparently not.

"How do we do that?" Antoine asked.

Without an Advanced Archetype or tropes, we were left with pure improvisation to make the change, and that hardly felt within my grasp. I was just now learning how to manipulate a story that way.

Samantha reached into her pocket with two fingers and pulled out a ticket. A player ticket. It was purple, which meant it changed the rules of the story. She held it out so that we could see.

<table>
<tr><td>

The Captor Is Captured
Type: Rule
Archetype: Damsel
Aspect: Any
Stat Used: Moxie

</td></tr>
<tr><td>

Sometimes, the only way for things to get better for the protagonist is if they get way worse first. Horror Films often have antagonists who are thwarted with the help of other, deadlier antagonists.

Bigger Bad: this trope will pull in a Bigger Bad from potential antagonists suggested in the storyline.

The Bigger Bad must be set up before the midpoint of Rebirth. The Bigger Bad may target any character that fits the narrative, including players, unless acted upon by another trope, but they will always clash with the initial antagonist.

With this trope equipped, the player will be able to draw in an additional antagonist—a Bigger Bad—as long as there is a narrative foundation for them to do so and they help push the story in that direction. Can only be activated while the player is Captured or when capture is imminent. The Bigger Bad will attempt to, at least metaphorically, capture the enemy. If inapplicable, they will simply kill them.

Beware: this trope can summon enemies beyond the player's level. There is no rule that prevents the Bigger Bad from attacking the player or their allies.

Survive the Night, Kill the Enemy, and Give It What It Wants are now Win Conditions if narratively compatible.

Caution to the player: they say the devil you know is better than the one you don't.

</td></tr>
</table>

She was a Damsel, an Advanced Archetype that specialized in being kidnapped. *A perfect hostage.*

"I knew you level fifties had player tropes," I said. I had seen Jack Goforth use Convenient Backstory. I was sure of it.

She tucked the ticket back in her pocket after we had gotten the chance to read it. So that was how we would do it: activating her player trope.

We didn't have long. The midpoint would start in around fifteen minutes.

And even if we succeeded, we would be awakening a Bigger Bad.
But why did we need to do it at all?
There was no time for questions.
It was time to raise the dead.

CHAPTER THIRTY

THE BIGGER BAD

I took a moment to think. I didn't have much more than that.

We needed to set the stage for Samantha's trope to activate. How did we set up a shift that large? We weren't just trying to invite in another group of criminals; we were trying to change the genre completely, shifting toward a supernatural storyline.

"I have a plan," I said. "Samantha, you said the men told you to go along with their plan and you and your dad would be okay. When we're on-screen again, can you explain to the audience that you were going to do what the men demanded of you, that you weren't going to run away, and the only reason you did was because of the ominous premonitions related to the things you hear at night?"

She nodded.

Samantha had alluded to supernatural voices crying in the night, which were a part of a different version of the script. We had to lean into that. It seemed pretty clear where this was going. The men were grave robbers. That was something we knew and might have even been established to the audience already before our characters entered the story. After all, they were all covered in dirt from their digging. Carousel would have to explain that to the audience, surely.

"Then start to really lay the warnings on thick—be emotional and scared. You're trying to warn us of the things to come. But we aren't listening. Antoine and I will be having a discussion . . . No . . . an argument. We'll be arguing, really laying into each other while you're trying to get our attention."

I thought for a moment.

"Bobby, you help her. Use any lines your character might have that are relevant and try to help her move things along," I said. "Help make it look like her warnings are falling on deaf ears."

Was that enough?

"Two characters are distracted arguing while danger brews in the background. That's a start, but it isn't enough, because we have the goons outside. Add in a woman frantically trying to warn them of a bigger threat and that should get the job done. Dramatic irony. The audience will know about the Bigger Bad approaching, but we will be none the wiser. So, Antoine, Bobby, and me, we just ignore it for as long as possible. Really let the tension build."

I nodded to myself, trying to double-check my plan in my head.

"We ignore it and that makes it more likely to happen?" Antoine said, testing his understanding.

"A great director once said that if a hidden bomb blows up, the audience will be surprised, but they will have spent the entire scene until that moment not feeling anything. If you show them the bomb beforehand, though, and let them know that any minute the characters will meet an untimely end, that is how you create suspense." I looked at Samantha. "That's how we activate your trope," I said. "The Bigger Bad is our bomb. The longer we ignore Samantha trying to warn us about it, the more the audience sits on the edge of their seats. Carousel won't be able to resist letting it explode."

It wouldn't be enough on its own, but with her trope, it should work.

We went over our plan a few more times. It would have to work. We didn't have much time.

As soon as we were on-screen again, I could hear one of the men yelling outside. It was the crazed one, the one who had pretended to be a deputy. Bradley Speirs. The corpse defiler. We were up on the second-floor landing, so I couldn't hear what he was saying, but he sounded more like he was having fun than anything else. It was disturbing.

"I was going to do what they said," Samantha said through tears. "They said to just go along with it. They wouldn't hurt me. They wouldn't hurt you." She looked at Bobby.

"I know, honey," Bobby said. "I was scared too. It's okay. This isn't your fault."

"No," Samantha said. "I was afraid of them, but I ran . . ." She got quiet. She looked into the distance. "I ran from the voices. I can hear them, crying in the dark of the night. They're coming. I was afraid of them."

Bobby looked perplexed.

"Don't worry about that, sweetheart," he said. "You're just scared. That's all."

Bobby would be a passable actor if only he didn't pause to read the script every time he spoke.

Samantha pulled away from him. "No, Dad, you have to believe me. They told me to run. I can hear them when I am trying to sleep. I think tonight's the night."

Bobby and Samantha continued talking on the subject. Antoine and I had to ignore them.

"I could jump down and run for help," I suggested.

"You're not some action hero!" Antoine yelled. "You'll break your leg. We just need to build up a fortress here."

"And then what?" I asked. "They wait us out? They kill us in the morning instead? What's the plan?"

Antoine crossed the room and got in my face. "No," he said. "I'm going to wait for them to turn their backs, and then I'm going to make them pay." His words caught in his throat. "For Kimberly."

I didn't want to say anything. I knew that Antoine was expressing real pain, but I needed to continue the ruse. That was the plan. I had to escalate the tension.

"That's going to get us killed for sure!" I yelled back. "You're not the only one who cared about Kimberly. We can't stick around just so that you can get revenge!"

"We aren't going to run out into the night and let them hunt us down!" Antoine screamed. "Our only chance is to stay here and face them head on."

"Guys," Samantha said. "We really shouldn't be arguing right now. I can feel them in the distance. We have to get ready. They're coming."

We ignored her.

Nothing makes the boogeyman come out like ignoring the person who warned you about him. The whole time we had been talking, the Off Screen indicator had been turning off for a few moments at a time. Hopefully, they were cutting to show the audience the trouble to come.

I just hoped it would be enough. We were almost out of time. Her trope couldn't be activated after the midpoint revelation.

"Of course," I said. "I'm not going to stay here and get shot to hell so that you can prove how much of a man you are. Do whatever you want, but don't pretend that it's about Kimberly."

Antoine pulled back his fist and punched me.

I couldn't tell if he was taking it easy on me. It hurt.

"Everything is about Kimberly!" Antoine screamed with a tear.

I leaned forward and buried my shoulder into him, driving him back against the wall.

"Bullshit!" I screamed. "We're never getting out of here. Not unless we run. I'm not going to die in this rotted-out hell house!"

"Please stop!" Samantha cried out.

Bobby tried to comfort her. "Everything's going to be all right, honey," he said nervously.

"I can hear them!" she said. "They're angry. Listen to me!"

Still, we ignored her. It wasn't enough yet.

"I don't even know why I agreed to come here with you guys," I said. "You don't even like me!"

"Wasn't my idea to invite you!" Antoine said as he pushed me back.

"Listen to me!" Samantha screamed. "We are going to die here if we don't do something!"

She was trembling. I couldn't tell if she was just a good actress or if her fear was real.

I finally decided to look at her, to pay attention to what she had been saying. I couldn't ignore her forever. That wouldn't be realistic. I turned to her. She stood with her back to a window on the landing, which faced the fields behind the house.

I could see, creeping in from the distance, a thick white fog. The dogs started howling in the distance.

The fog moved with a purpose, like a living thing crawling across the field or a blanket being pulled over the land by an unseen hand. I pretended I didn't see it.

"We need to block the stairwell now. We aren't leaving. Not until morning. We need to get ready," she said. "Otherwise, none of us will be—"

A loud crash echoed through the house as a window downstairs broke.

"You sons of bitches!" Bradley, the unhinged grave mutilator, screamed. "I'm going to cut you into pieces!"

"We need to block the stairs," Antoine said.

This was a welcome distraction. We needed to give the Bigger Bad room to make an appearance. Our characters couldn't suddenly believe Samantha. We would need proof, and that would take a bit to show up. Focusing on the grave-robbing goons was just the opportunity we needed. They should distract our characters long enough.

"Bookshelf," I said decisively.

Antoine stared down in the direction of the noise and then followed me over to grab a large wooden bookshelf that mostly housed phone books and those old encyclopedias with a different book for each letter.

The unit was large and heavy. Bobby pulled away from Samantha to come help us.

The three of us managed to drag it across the floor and tip it sideways across the staircase, creating the first of many layers between us and the men below.

Next, we stacked a side table and a cabinet. I wasn't sure how much time we had before the fighting started. When it did, we would be in trouble. They had guns.

Moving furniture is notoriously noisy, and we quickly drew the attention of the men.

"You can hide up there all you want," Merritt said. "We don't need to get to you as long as you can't leave. You've trapped yourselves."

"And we're gonna burn this place to the ground with you in it!" Bradley added. Not exactly the tone his brother was going for.

That was one worry. I really hoped arson wasn't in the script.

"Oh hell," the fake sheriff, Randy, said below as he slowly stepped up the stairs. "My friend wants you to be calm is all. He still can't give up on all that money you were going to give us for letting you live. Guess I'm a little less trusting."

He continued to walk up the stairs slowly.

As he walked, I could hear something hard scraping along the wall as he went. I wasn't sure what it was until he got to the top of the stairs and I saw Antoine's baseball bat swing high and come crashing down onto the backing of the bookshelf.

I couldn't see him behind the stack of furniture, just the bat when he swung it over his head.

The shelving unit held firm. The baseball bat was no match for it. That, or the sheriff hadn't invested enough points in Mettle.

"Come out now or come out a week from now. It doesn't matter," he said.

He smashed the bat against the shelves again, as if to scare us.

"Move aside, Randy," Bradley said.

I heard the gun cocking sound that you often hear in movies.

"Get back!" I yelled only moments before Bradley fired his gun up at the furniture.

The bullet hit the bookshelf with a splintering sound, but I couldn't see any damage from my vantage point across the landing.

"What are you doing, you idiot!" Randy screamed. "I'm right here!"

"I didn't hit you," Bradley said.

"Could have gotten hit by shrapnel or a ricochet!" Randy yelled.

Bradley fired the gun again.

That bullet had just as little of an effect.

"You bastard!" Randy screamed as he stomped down the stairs.

For a moment, there was silence.

Off Screen.

"How long is this going to take?" Antoine asked.

"If it worked, then it won't be long," Bobby said. "Midpoint of Rebirth is right now."

He was right.

I cautiously looked outside toward the field. The fog had gotten even closer to the house. Whatever it carried, it would be here soon.

"Looks like we succeeded," Antoine said, following my gaze.

"Yay us," I said with an extra dose of sarcasm. "Now we've got to survive this too."

I watched as something in the distance stirred. It was too far away to see clearly, but there were solid shapes emerging from the fog in the distance.

"They're coming," Samantha said.

"I hope you and our friends upstairs know what you're doing," I said. "'Cause it sure looks like you just made this whole thing a lot harder."

"I'll do whatever it takes to save you," she said. A tear fell from her eye.

I pursed my lips. I wasn't ready to believe anything, but I was desperate enough to go along with whatever plan might have a chance of giving us some answers, of getting Anna and Camden back, of getting us out of here.

I could hear pounding on the door below. Then Tank started hollering. Within a minute or so, I heard them let him in. He must have been too big to fit through whatever broken window they had used to enter.

"Something's out there," he said. He sounded scared to death. "Get the guns."

"What are you yapping about, big 'un?" Randy asked with a laugh.

Tank didn't answer at first.

I could hear someone slamming cabinets and rifling through drawers downstairs.

The men sounded amused.

Those of us upstairs were only on-screen for a flash here and there as we reacted to the sounds we heard downstairs. Other than that, we just hunkered down on the floor, dreading what was to come.

Then we heard them.

An orchestra, an absolute orchestra of moaning, groaning, growling, crying, and screaming started to play outside. The sounds grew closer.

The men downstairs went silent all of a sudden.

"What the—?" one of them—I couldn't tell which—said aloud.

"Holy hell!" Randy screamed. "What the hell is that?"

The moaning got louder as the men started to panic. They started hurling expletives in a jumbled mess. I couldn't make out much of what they were say-ing, because they had gotten quiet again.

"Board up the windows," Merritt commanded.

I could hear wood being moved around from the construction beneath. Then desperate hammering.

"What the heck is going on?" Bradley exclaimed. Suddenly, he didn't seem to be enjoying himself. "Are those . . . Are those people or . . ."

There was silence for a few minutes. My heart beat so loudly I could hear it and nothing else.

Except for the orchestra of lethargic guttural noises outside.

I thought I knew what was out there, but I was afraid to look. Even knowing they would arrive, I wasn't ready.

Whatever reward we got from this had better be worth it.

I could hear a woman crying outside. Her voice sounded . . . fresher . . . than the rest. I couldn't force myself to look.

I shot a glance at Antoine. We must have had the same thought. He mouthed, "Dina?" at me.

I shook my head. It didn't sound like her.

We didn't have too long to focus on it because a crash sounded from down below as a window was busted out.

"Randy!" Merritt screamed. "Randy, just hold my hand!"

The whole time I could hear the fake sheriff screaming and glass breaking.

"Help!" he screamed. "It's got me! Grab me! Please!"

I could hear scuffling down below.

He screamed in pain, he screamed from fear, and then, suddenly, his screams got quiet.

"No! Why did you let go?" Merritt yelled. "You just let go!"

I heard a jingle of metal.

"I got his keys," Bradley said. "His cruiser is right out there. We can make a break for it."

"You let him go . . . ," Merritt said again in disbelief at what his brother had done. I heard the pain in his voice.

Eventually, curiosity won out, and I crawled over to the window to see the Bigger Bad.

What I saw was a horde of rotten corpses standing upright. Many were missing limbs, even heads. Most of them were dressed in the suits and dresses they had been buried in, though those were now tattered and stained. This wasn't unexpected, but still, I was terrified.

There were hundreds of them.

They didn't exist separately on the red wallpaper. They were a unit, all of them as one.

"The Avenging Dead." Plot Armor: 52.

In the distance, I could hear Randy screaming as the Avenging Dead dragged him further away in the direction of the cemetery.

I cowered down as their cries filled my heart with fear.

CHAPTER THIRTY-ONE

DEAD MAN'S FALL

I stared at the horrifying creatures before me. For a while, I was too terrified to even think about looking at their tropes on the red wallpaper. When I did, I was in for a shock. Usually, when I looked at the tropes of a high-level enemy, there were some that I couldn't see. Trope Master was a Savvy-based ability, after all. Most strong enemies have enough Savvy to block that trope to some extent.

With the Avenging Dead, that wasn't the case at all. I could see every single trope they had, which meant one thing: they had little to no Savvy.

They *were* zombies after all. Even spiritual avenging zombies didn't need Savvy or Moxie or Hustle. That meant that the horde's entire fifty-two points of Plot Armor was devoted to some combination of Grit and Mettle. That was terrifying.

As I scanned through the tropes, I found that their lack of Savvy, Moxie, and Hustle was countered by abilities that circumvented those weaknesses. Something I had learned from the vets was that as the recommended Plot Armor in storylines scaled, the difficulty in completing them scaled faster.

At level twenty, fighting a level twenty enemy was difficult but not impossible. At level fifty, fighting a level fifty enemy was a nightmare. Thinking back on it, I was lucky that the Grotesques had had a readily accessible weakness.

This situation could illustrate that phenomenon. Enemies who could completely circumvent stat differences with a single trope were in a league of their own. When an enemy suddenly no longer has to worry about a stat, it can devote those points to another stat.

THE AVENGING DEAD	
Plot Armor: 52	

Tropes	
FUNGIBLE ENEMY	This enemy is composed of countless largely interchangeable units whose numbers will not diminish until the scene is concluded. There always seems to be more to come.
DEATH FINDS A WAY	This enemy will have a heightened chance of finding the victims it seeks, regardless of how likely that scenario may be on paper. Determined by a comparison of effective Plot Armor.
INESCAPABLE DEATH SEQUENCE	Once this killer has initiated its kill sequence, the victim is doomed unless counteracted by a trope or a saving throw. Even though, logically, the victim should be able to escape or fight back, they will fail.
HIVE MIND	This creature's mind is linked to that of similar creatures.
SOFT MAGIC IS CONFUSING	The enemy's lore is vague and broad and offers little insight into the specifics of how the enemy operates.
MINDFULLY MINDLESS	Despite having little to no intelligence, this enemy will somehow manage to thwart the well-laid plans of very intelligent adversaries. Buffs Savvy-saving throws.
FATE DOESN'T RUN	This enemy will not run after its victim, yet it is never far behind in a chase scene. Buffs Hustle-saving throws.
JOIN US	This enemy has some means of increasing its numbers through conversion.
THE UNSEEN HAND	This enemy is guided by a greater force. This guidance may be a part of the lore or the meta.
CONFESS!	The presence of this enemy will compel those nearby to ponder their morality, grievances, and outlook on death.

YOUR BLOOD RUNS COLD	Seeing this enemy will cause great mental distress. Debuffs Moxie and Savvy.
STRENGTH IN NUMBERS	The enemy is at its strongest in groups. Singling its members out will weaken them substantially.
TERRITORIAL	This killer will punish those who harm its domain.
WHISPERS IN THE DARK	This creature can sense a player or NPC's vulnerabilities and manipulate them via impulsive thoughts, perceived as whispers.
CLOAKED IN ATMOSPHERE	When this enemy enters a scene, it will change lighting and sound design and possibly have other noticeable effects.
CONVENIENT SPIRITUALITY	Does this enemy have powers beyond its physical body? It must, even if it doesn't often show them.
KEEP YOU ON YOUR TOES	This enemy has a heightened chance of finding and subduing victims who are not paying attention.

I explained their tropes to everyone as quickly as I could. Then we made our plan. Soon, it was time to execute it.

On-screen.

Immediately, the wandering spirits outside started back in with their zombie moans. It was overwhelming. The sound of their cries set my mind in a frenzy.

"What the hell is going on?" I screamed.

"I told you!" Samantha said. "Those men defiled the graves at the cemetery in the forest across the field, and now the dead are here to take their revenge."

She was being comforted by the two dogs she had let into the house when we came in. The dogs were clearly disturbed and would occasionally let out a haunting howl, as if communicating with the other dogs outside.

"Defiled the graves . . . Grave robbing?" I asked. "The men were covered in dirt. Is that what you're talking about?"

She nodded.

Bobby decided to chime in. "After they sold all of my tools and valuables that I had at the hotel, they started looking for another source of quick cash. Even threatened to sell my dogs. One of them came up with the idea of stealing jewelry right out of the graves at the cemetery. I don't know exactly where it started, but it keeps most of them out of the house, so their leader lets them do it."

"But they didn't stop there," Samantha said through tears. "That one, Bradley, has done far worse. He brutalized the corpses. Defiled them. The spirits couldn't rest after what he did to them. They cried out, begging for help."

"Wait," I said in my best panicky, terrified voice. "If they *are* after the grave robbers, then maybe they won't bother us. They're avenging spirits, right? We didn't do anything to them. Nothing to avenge."

Cinema Seer was set up.

Antoine looked skeptical. "*You* can try that. One of those things gets near me and I'm not going to just stand there."

Downstairs, the dead continued to try to break into the house. Their attempts were met with gratuitous gunfire.

The men must have realized that was fruitless because I soon heard the sound of them pounding their way up the stairs.

"Let us up!" Merritt screamed. "Please! We won't hurt you."

They started pounding on the stack of furniture we had piled up. Unlike before, they were making progress. I imagined they had the bigger fellow, Tank, doing a lot of the heavy lifting.

"We can't let them in here," I said.

The four of us put all of our strength into pushing back against the furniture, hoping to prevent the men from pushing their way past.

But Tank was strong and desperate.

He shoved against us with all his might and managed to push the bookshelf and all of the other furniture back toward us enough to make an opening.

Even though it was only open for a moment, it was enough time for Bradley to slip through.

"Get back!" he yelled, holding out his gun. "Let them through. Now."

He wasn't messing around like he had been earlier that night. He was angry and scared. For the first time, I thought I saw his true face.

What could we do? It wasn't Second Blood yet. If he shot one of us, we would die for nothing.

We backed away and let Tank push the shelving back so that Merritt and Tim, the other grave robber, who had not made much of an impression so far, through. In the original version of the story, I think players were supposed to try to convince Tim to help them. He was quiet but clearly uncomfortable with the things his group was doing. In this version of events, that didn't seem as important yet.

After everyone had slid through, Tank himself tried to squeeze in, but as he did, a look of terror came over his face and he fell to the ground. He was kicking at something on the staircase. He tried to crawl forward.

Behind him, the moans of the dead were louder. Strangely, I could barely hear their footsteps.

"Help him!" Merritt screamed. "And don't you let go!"

The men grabbed onto Tank's arms and pulled against the zombies on the other side.

They wouldn't succeed. They couldn't. The Avenging Dead had the Inescapable Death Sequence trope that made it impossible to escape them once they had started your death sequence, even if it seemed you should be able to. Tank's death sequence was underway. They had him in their grasp.

I could see Antoine contemplating attacking our captors while they were distracted.

It wasn't a bad idea. He could easily shove them forward so that they were all within reach of the zombie horde. It was possible that the zombies could take each and every one of them out right at that moment. I could understand his urge.

But there were risks in attacking them here.

Right then, the story was about the tables being turned on a group of evil men. If those men died before the Finale, then the story would have to be about something else. Carousel would make sure of that. Either it would ensure that Antoine's attack failed, or it would raise the stakes for the Finale. We didn't want that. We had heard stories of players trying to defeat the enemy prematurely. Carousel would always get creative.

We could, of course, pick them off one at a time, but we still had to wait for the moment to be right.

Soon, it became clear that Tank was a lost cause as his screams of fear turned into screams of pain. We could hear his bones breaking as the dead pulled at his legs and tore his flesh. The zombies eventually succeeded, and Tank was dragged back down the stairs behind the bookshelf.

With him out of the way, we rushed to push the shelf back, closing off the staircase.

The dead still cried out behind the bookshelf, but they didn't have the pure explosive power that Tank had, so the bookshelf held firm. That could change at any moment.

"Don't you dare stop pushing on that shelf," Merritt said.

"What the hell is going on?" Bradley screamed. He paced around the landing, waving his gun around.

"You know what's happening!" young Tim screamed. He was crying and shaking from fear. "They don't like what we did to them. That we dug 'em up. Hung 'em. Shot 'em. Now they're gonna drag us to hell."

Bradley was enraged. "They aren't going to do shit to me!" he screamed. "I am not dying here. You got that?"

He pointed his gun at Tim, but only for a moment. Then, in frustration, he tore off to some other part of the second story as Tank's screams faded into the distance.

For a while, that was how time passed. The dead were making all kinds of ruckus, but they were not able to make it past the barricade. I knew that they eventually would. Their tropes made it clear that they would be able to get to their targets even if it didn't make sense. Soon, we would need to find a way to push the story forward, or else the story would go forward on its own in a way that was unpredictable and not to our advantage.

"You know, it's funny," Merritt said. "You guys wasted all our bullets using their bodies as target practice and now they're up and walking around, trying to kill us, and we don't have any ammo."

No one laughed but him. The cracks were beginning to show in his authoritative demeanor.

We were in and out of being on-screen. My best explanation was that Dina was out doing something worth watching, but I wasn't sure what.

Finally, we went on-screen for good.

With the speed that the storyline was moving, it was almost Second Blood and the final battle wouldn't be far behind it.

Bradley came back to the landing waving his gun around.

He then trained it on me.

"Come here," he commanded.

I had been helping hold the bookshelf against the stair opening. I was hesitant to stop.

"Don't you dare move away from that bookshelf," Merritt said, pulling his own gun on me. "What do you need him for?"

Bradley pointed back in the direction he had come from.

"There's a ledge out there," he said. "He's gonna take the keys to the cruiser and bring it around so that we can drop down on it and get out of here."

"How is he supposed to get down to the cruiser? If the fall doesn't kill him, the dead will," Merritt said.

Bradley shook his head.

"We gotta try something. There's a part of the house over there with no windows or doors on the first floor. There are barely any of those things over there to worry about. We drop him down. He gets the car and brings it around next to the house for us to climb down on. Then we drive away. I already threw a mattress out on the ground for him to land on. And if it doesn't work, who cares?"

Their Desperation trope made them more dangerous as their situation got worse. It also lowered their Savvy. Not unlike real life. I was picked for this little project because of my low effective Plot Armor, no doubt.

"I'm not jumping off the roof," I said. Carousel was having fun with me. I had just suggested the same thing as filler for my fake argument with Antoine. "You know how far down that is?"

"You're going to do whatever I say!" Bradley screamed. He grabbed hold of my hair and put the gun against the side of my head. He was strong. Too strong for me to do anything about.

He pulled me away from the bookshelf and dragged me down the hallway toward a room on the other side of the bed-and-breakfast.

He shoved me through the door, and I saw that he had already broken out one of the windows to make extra room for the mattress he had thrown down on the ground.

There was a small ledge outside the window.

"Get out there," he said. He thrust the keys into my hand.

"I can't do this," I said.

He practically shoved me out the window. I crawled out on the small section of roofing on my hands and knees.

"Jump," he said.

I refused. If I was going to die, it would be on my terms.

"Get down there right now or I'll push you off!" he screamed.

I moved to the edge of the roof, as far away from him as I could.

He had to lean all of the way out the window to get to me, but even then, only the tips of his fingers could reach.

"I'm not going. You'll have to shoot me," I said.

I looked down at the ground and saw the mattress. I could barely see it through the fog. He had thrown it about ten feet from the house. I would have to jump to get to it.

While it was true that there were fewer dead around this part of the house, there were still plenty nearby. Jumping was a death sentence.

"Get off the roof this minute, you pussy!" he screamed.

He pointed the gun at me but never pulled the trigger. We both knew why. The idiot had wasted his bullets already on the zombies. If he had ammo, he would have shot me by now. I had to pretend my character hadn't thought of that yet.

He tucked the gun in his waistband and leaned out further onto the roof. In the background, Merritt watched cautiously.

Bradley leaned out to me. I was barely able to avoid his grasp.

Eventually, he gave up. His desperation grew too great. He climbed up out of the window and moved closer to me.

"Get over there!" he screamed.

A little closer.

The funny part was that his plan might have worked. Who knows. I didn't want it to. I had plans of my own.

As he got closer, my heart beat so fast I worried it might explode. It was now or never. Second Blood was upon us.

He reached out to try and push me, to urge me to jump out onto the mattress. His left hand reached toward me. The other held onto the window frame.

I tossed the keys up at his right side. His instincts were sharp. He reached out to grab them with his right hand. He caught them right out of the air. Without those keys, his plan would fail. His escape would be ruined.

As he let go of the window frame, I grabbed his left hand and pulled with all my might. I may not have that much Mettle, but I did have some weight to throw around. I grabbed onto him and pushed off the ledge with my legs. I wanted to push him off and climb back inside. That is what my character would try to do. That was a pipe dream, though. There was no way I could avoid falling.

In an ordinary matchup, he would beat me ten times out of ten. But this wasn't a physical matchup. This was a battle of wits, and he was out of bullets.

He was unable to grab hold of anything to save himself.

We fell off the roof together. We didn't get anywhere near the mattress. I hit the ground first. There was something hard there, under the fog—a cement block retaining wall, if I was to guess.

Something broke inside me. I couldn't say what, but as I lay in shock trying to evaluate my pain, I realized that there was very little. I had broken my back, perhaps. I couldn't move my legs very well. My arms still worked, though moving them was difficult.

My Grit jumped up ten points. My Dead Man Walking trope had triggered. It was ironic: I couldn't walk at all. Still, the moment of my death was now stretched out. I was bleeding from the back of my head, and I could taste blood in my mouth.

It was enough for Second Blood to trigger. It was possible the camera would never look at me again. I might as well be dead.

"Get back!" I heard Bradley yelling.

Through the pain, I managed to turn my head to see him. He was barely injured. The dead surrounded him, though. For a moment, he even tried to point his gun at them, as if they could be intimidated.

He tried backing away from them, but then something ran up to him and latched onto his arm with its teeth.

It was a dog, but not an ordinary one. This dog had crossed to the other side. It was the one that Bradley himself had killed. I could see its deadly wound. It's strange that zombie animals seem to move at normal speed but human zombies are usually slow. Maybe it's because we walk upright.

That's when I saw her.

She was stumbling forward from the horde.

Kimberly.

She had risen from the dead.

Her skin was pale and her clothes bloody. She shuffled forward, a large hole in the back of her head. One hand was on her stomach, as if out of habit.

On the red wallpaper, she was Dead and Infected, though this wasn't a typical zombie infection.

She approached Bradley and grabbed him as he turned to look at her.

"No!" he screamed. He cursed at her and threatened her with acts of violence and depravity, but none of that mattered now.

She grabbed him, and soon others did too.

They started dragging him back toward the cemetery.

For a moment, I thought I saw Kimberly look at me, as if she was still there, still in control, but that moment passed, and she continued to drag Bradley away while his brother screamed from upstairs.

It would have been better for the story if Antoine had killed Bradley out of revenge. I just couldn't pass up the opportunity.

I lay there and wondered how long I would be kept alive, dead in all ways but my last ounce of consciousness. I stared up at the nearby zombies and waited to see if they would take me as they had Bradley. They didn't seem to care that I existed at all.

Either way, I would be joining them soon.

Whatever the case, the Finale was here, and it would soon be over. I just hoped Antoine and Bobby could figure it out.

CHAPTER THIRTY-TWO

BACK TO WHERE IT ALL STARTED, PART ONE

I was dying.

Dead Man Walking as a trope was starting to look like a real bust. I lay there on the ground barely able to move. My statuses were flaring constantly, including the one labeled "Dead."

And yet I did not die. My sudden boost of Grit prevented me from blacking out. My adrenaline was still pumping, so I did everything I could to try to get back to the action, even though it was hopeless.

My legs weren't doing what I was telling them to do. My arms, though, were at least operational. It hurt to move them, but I had to try.

I pushed and I crawled for what felt like an eternity, but I maybe moved five yards. Just far enough to see the other side of the bed-and-breakfast. Useless.

As I watched the zombies surrounding the house, something caught my eye. Lying on the ground next to the busted window, where the sheriff had presumably been dragged away, was Antoine's baseball bat.

I couldn't do anything with it, but I still tried to crawl toward it.

I failed. I just didn't have it in me.

Something was happening inside of the house that I couldn't see. An argument or a fight. I heard a loud crack, and then, less than a minute later, Tim, the quiet, young grave robber, was being dragged out of the house kicking and screaming. He was terrified out of his mind.

And then, to my surprise, even though I had literally predicted it on-screen with Cinema Seer, the dead started to walk away.

They had claimed their last guilty soul.

I couldn't believe what I was seeing. My mind was so belabored that I could barely hear when Dina finally made her appearance.

"Riley?" she asked quietly. "What happened here? This was supposed to be a straight up home invasion or something, I thought."

I couldn't speak. I turned to look at her, hoping that I might be able to summon some information for her that would help us. The Finale wasn't over. We still had a fight. I could hear something going on in the house. There was one last enemy to be defeated.

With my last bit of strength, I pointed over toward Antoine's baseball bat. That would have to be my contribution. Dina seemed to understand. She quickly walked over, grabbed the bat, and then took a deep breath before walking around to the other side of the bed-and-breakfast.

The entire encounter was off-screen. To the audience, I was likely dead.

Soon after that, I died for real.

I woke in a theater watching the remainder of the story.

Merritt stormed out of the bed-and-breakfast like he was going to chase after the zombie horde. He looked angry in a way I had not yet seen him. All of his tropes were designed to maximize how dangerous he was the more desperate he was. They also made him stronger if his brother was killed. He was probably a real threat in that moment.

He screamed back in the house, "Why didn't they take me? They took my brother; why didn't they take me?"

Samantha walked out of the house with a limp. She had been struck in the face. After a moment it became clear that she had probably been hit with the same hammer that Merritt had in his hand.

"You didn't hurt them," Samantha said. "They only wanted to get revenge on those who disturbed their peace."

Merritt didn't take that well. Unfortunately, he was beyond reason.

"You did this!" he screamed. "You . . . invited them, didn't you?"

"No, I swear!" Samantha cried out.

Merritt grabbed her and lifted the hammer over his head. Before he could bring the hammer down on Samantha, something struck him. He jumped out of the way, reeling in pain from the hit.

Standing behind him, holding Antoine's baseball bat, was Dina.

Merritt didn't hesitate to attack her. She swung at him, but he was stronger and completely unafraid of being hit. He managed to strike her in the arm with the hammer. She had high Grit, so it looked like she would recover. Then he tackled her. He pinned her against the ground with one hand and raised the hammer. He struck her three times, though I couldn't actually see the blows.

In an instant, one of the dogs that had been in the house ran outside and latched on to Merritt, but he easily threw the dog aside. It was enough of a distraction for Dina to take the baseball bat and hit Merritt in the face with it.

It wasn't a hard swing, and she didn't have much leverage, but it was enough to get him to fall off of her so that she could get up. She then went for another blow to his back. She was causing damage, but not enough.

Just as he was about to attack her again, he was struck by a flying coffee table. An entire coffee table.

The camera cut to Antoine standing in the doorway. It looked like he had been badly beaten. Still, he limped out the door, and with each step, he seemed to get stronger and bolder.

Merritt lay on the ground, trying to scramble to his feet.

Antoine stopped next to Dina and held out his hand. Dina handed over the baseball bat.

He laid into Merritt, screaming and raging. He struck him over and over and over.

Eventually, the muted thumps of the baseball bat gave way to crunchy, wet sounds as the baseball bat destroyed Merritt's skull.

After that, the camera panned around to the results of the carnage.

It showed undead Kimberly lumbering to the graveyard and finding a hole that had been dug. She lowered herself down into the hole, giving one look back toward the bed-and-breakfast.

It showed Bobby lying on the floor of the upstairs landing. He was dead. I couldn't see his head, but from the amount of blood, it looked like that hammer had been involved. Merritt must have killed him while I was lying around useless.

I woke up quickly. I was lying on the ground fifteen feet or so from where I had died. Zombie Riley had been trying to crawl to the cemetery. All healed up, I stood and ran around the bed-and-breakfast to find Antoine and Dina standing almost in the same place as they had been in the movie.

They had been healed, as had Samantha. It only took another minute for Bobby to make his way down.

"Kimberly's in a grave at the cemetery," I said.

Antoine looked in that direction and soon we were all walking there, the five of us. With every step, I started to wonder what the point of all this was.

Why had we been summoned to this place? Wasn't this supposed to be the special storyline that would somehow reveal everything to us? It wasn't so long ago that we had been contemplating whether or not we would get rescue tropes as a reward for this storyline, but once we got here, everything that I had predicted had been thrown asunder.

This storyline wasn't easy, but Samantha's intervention had probably made things better, not worse. Those zombies definitely helped us take out the bad guys.

That wasn't supposed to be what happened. This was supposed to be an overwhelming challenge, and we were supposed to rise to the occasion and prove ourselves. Wasn't that how this part of the story was supposed to go?

Where was all the information about how we had ended up in Carousel? This was the storyline from our world; it was supposed to tell us things that we didn't know, but aside from getting my theories confirmed, we hadn't learned anything new. I started to fear in my heart that this whole quest was just a trick. That this was part of the hellish torture that Carousel had prepared for us. That it gave us hope just to take it away.

The cemetery was old, and it didn't look like anyone had been buried there in over a decade. It was clear to see the destruction the grave robbers had caused in the cemetery. Corpses were littered about. Many had been strung up in trees and used as target practice. Those in the trees were still animate. Those who had returned to the earth appeared to be dead once again.

The ones hanging from the trees would growl and try to shake down from where they were trapped. It was a disturbing sight to see.

We quickly found the hole that Kimberly had lowered herself down into. She was standing next to it, brushing graveyard dirt off of herself. She wasn't ready to talk when we arrived. I couldn't blame her. That was her first death, and though it had been instant, I knew that dying took a toll regardless.

Predictably, once we were all gathered together after the storyline, Silas the Mechanical Showman made his appearance.

"Congratulations, you won a ticket!" he said in that tired old tone.

If we were going to get answers, this might be the time.

We walked closer, and as Antoine was about to press the red button, Silas disappeared.

He reappeared thirty yards away eastward.

We looked at each other in confusion. Then we walked toward him. Before we could get close enough to push his button, he disappeared again and reappeared thirty yards further away in that same direction. And so we followed, our paths lit by the moon and Silas's yellow lights.

As we went, I noticed there was something very strange about this cemetery. At first, it appeared to be a regular lot with a hundred or so graves out in the backwoods, like I had been expecting. But the further we walked, the further the cemetery went.

Soon we had left the cemetery proper, and yet we still saw graves in the forest. We even saw bodies strung up in the trees the same as we had around the cemetery. They moved and growled, but they didn't seem too harmful.

And it just kept going like that for hundreds of yards.

We walked for ten minutes. Twenty minutes. Half an hour.

More graves and more bodies strung up in trees.

"Is this a glitch?" Antoine asked.

I wasn't sure.

"Maybe," I said. "Might just be how Carousel manages to get an unlimited amount of zombies. In zombie movies, there are always tons of them, and they seem to come out of nowhere. Maybe this is just how Carousel pulls off that trick."

I wasn't sure, though. If it was a glitch, what would it mean?

"I'm so sorry," Samantha said.

I turned to look at her. My heart raced just from the possible implications of what she had said. What was she sorry about?

"I told you I would do anything to save you," she said. She was crying. She looked terrified. "This was the only way."

"What are you talking about?" Antoine asked.

But before she could answer I realized that something was different. I heard something in the distance and right behind me at the same time. Breathing.

It was the axe murderer. I could hear him back in the direction we had come from. That was the gift of having been in his presence before. I could detect him.

"Go," she said. "Go!"

"Let's move," I said. I needed to be careful because one wrong word and I would be cut in half.

I ushered the others to move quickly.

"What's going on?" Dina asked.

I didn't have time to think about an answer. "We need to follow Silas," I said.

Maybe it was something in the tone of my voice, but they stopped questioning me—for that moment, at least.

Samantha stayed behind. She turned and started walking, then running back in the direction we had come from.

Ten minutes later, the sound of the breathing had faded. I could only guess what had happened.

How many rules had she broken to help us?

CHAPTER THIRTY-THREE

BACK TO WHERE IT ALL STARTED, PART TWO

Silas continued his game, and we continued to follow him.

We walked for a long time. In the end, it was over an hour. It didn't seem like we were getting anywhere. I just saw the same types of graves and the occasional body hanging from a tree that had been used as target practice.

A growing feeling of unease overtook me the further we moved into the unending forest of graves.

Something special was happening. I should have been excited. Silas was bringing us somewhere for a reason. All I could think about was what false assumptions I had made along the way and how we were about to pay for them.

Eventually, Silas stopped.

We all looked at each other. Antoine was not in the mood to wait around. He was the first to hit the button.

At least half a dozen tickets came out of Silas's dispenser. Ticket types I had never seen before. I wasn't interested in most of them just yet. There was one ticket type I was looking for. A marigold yellow trope ticket.

Antoine shuffled through his rewards looking for it.

And there it was:

A Race Against Time
Type: Rescue
Archetype: Athlete
Aspect: Sport
Stat Used: Hustle

Monsters and serial killers make formidable foes, but one enemy takes more victims than all of them put together. Time. When everything is at stake, will you make it across the finish line?

Rescue: when a player enters a compatible storyline with this trope, while possessing any missing posters of deceased players who died in that same storyline, the storyline will be changed into a Rescue. Succeeding in the Rescue will revive the dead players. This ticket will indicate on the red wallpaper if a nearby storyline is applicable.

With this trope equipped and activated successfully, the storyline will shift into a scenario where the players are forced to race against an established time limit to accomplish a discrete task to save downed players. Downed players will not be able to assist in their rescue, barring a trope that allows them to. The race will, as it sounds, be a feat of Hustle but may incorporate other tests as well.

Applicable stories will typically be those with high-Savvy enemies, who can design the race, or high-Hustle enemies, who can race against the player.

Countdown: the player will be able to see the timer related to this trope.

Takeover: this trope will cancel out any story alterations except those inherent to the Archetype or Advanced Archetype associated with this ticket.

Beat the Clock is the only Win Condition. No others may be added to the Rescue.

Lived to Tell the Tale: any players who survive a storyline altered by this trope will not die, regardless of whether the storyline is failed. Those who die will need to be rescued.

I sure hope you didn't slack on cardio.

My heart skipped a beat. A genuine rescue trope. Most players I had met had never even seen one. I was still skeptical. I had been fearing this very thing.

"This is good, though, right?" Kimberly said, desperately. She must have seen the look on my face. "We can save everyone now."

Dina and Bobby sounded overjoyed in the background.

I didn't trust good things that I didn't earn. I was more interested in finding out *why* we were just now getting rescue tropes. Why take them away just to give them back like this? Why bring us into this weird, never-ending wooded graveyard?

I went and hit Silas's red button. We all did, one after another.

Antoine got one stat ticket, two tropes—including his A Race Against Time rescue ticket—and three tickets we had never heard of before.

No one had ever mentioned some of these ticket types. I was dumbfounded.

The first was called a "luggage tag," which I immediately understood.

"It's an item inventory," I said. I was so taken aback by the realization that we had been playing without our inventories this whole time. Why would we just now be receiving something this essential?

Small Luggage Tag
Weight Limit: 10 Pounds
Transferable: No
Sign this ticket and place it inside the carrying implement of your choice, be it a backpack, purse, or similar item. This luggage will become your inventory on the red wallpaper. Any objects that could feasibly be placed in the luggage will be able to fit, in any amount up to the combined Weight Limit of all Luggage Tags. Contents will appear on the red wallpaper. The luggage will never get heavier. Items placed in the luggage will only be retrievable in storylines if they make sense in the narrative.

When an additional tag is required, you will be alerted on the red wallpaper. Every time the luggage is damaged in a story, the Luggage Tag has a chance of needing to be replaced.

I thought back to the overstuffed bag that Arthur carried into storylines, which contained all of his monster-hunting equipment. To think, with luggage tags he could have carried everything in a small duffel or even a satchel. Did Arthur just not know they existed?

His next ticket was a criminal bounty.

Criminal Bounty
Name: The Star-Crossed Killers
Plot Armor: 20–40
Wanted for Torture, Mayhem, Murder, Witchcraft.
Reward: 10 Dollars Dead, 100 Dollars per killer Alive.
Last Known Location: east of Carousel, across the Hanging Bridge.
Details: the killers' spree has left several dead and many others wounded. Bringing them to justice remains a high priority for the Carousel Police Department.

Antoine explained that he could see a wanted poster for these Star-Crossed Killers on the red wallpaper, though the faces were blank.

His final ticket was something called a "keepsake."

> Congratulations, you have earned a Keepsake. Please select an applicable Trophy item to keep in your possession from what remains of the killers you defeated. This Keepsake may not be used for its usual purpose in a storyline, but it can be spent for a one-time use of one of the following rewards:
> A boost to a saving throw for [Mettle]
> or
> Use of the trope [Desperation: as the situation gets more desperate, move stats from Moxie and Savvy to Mettle and Hustle]
> or
> Assistance in the following situation: N/A

I wasn't sure what an applicable Trophy was, but that ticket sounded great. Again, no one back at Dyer's Lodge had mentioned this type of ticket before.

His trope reward, other than the rescue ticket, was:

> Coyote in a Trap
> Type: Action
> Archetype: Any
> Aspect: Any
> Stat Used: Grit
>
> In a life-or-death situation, a survivor must choose anything that isn't death—even horrific injury.
> With this trope equipped, the player will have a greatly increased chance of escaping when Captured or of winning a Chase Scene if they injure themselves in order to accomplish the feat. They will be able to survive longer than usual with their injury. The success of escape depends on the narrative, enemy tropes, the player's Grit, and whether the injury is sufficient to aid in escape.
> They say a coyote will gnaw its own leg off to escape a trap. What are you willing to do?

It was easy to tell what feat landed him with this reward. Personally, I liked my Escape Artist more. It was only a buff, but I was getting really tired of hurting myself.

For killing Merritt, Antoine got a killer collectible card.

Merritt Speirs
Criminal

In the dim shadows lurked Merritt Speirs, a strategist with plans ever so intricate. Yet the wild whims of his brother Bradley threatened to unravel it all. As the weight of desperation grew heavier, Merritt's once composed demeanor began its chilling transformation. From shrewd mastermind to monstrous malevolence, he stands as a testament to the perils of brotherly love unchecked.

Kimberly didn't get a stat ticket. She got one trope and two other tickets. One of the other tickets was a luggage tag like the one Antoine got. The other one was something she was thrilled to see.

Carousel Rewards Program
Reward: The Red Mist trope
To gain the reward, the player must: die for First Blood [5] times

The ticket had a hole punched in it already, inside a little square. She needed four more hole punches to get the reward. The Red Mist was a trope that guaranteed an instant death. Roxy had that trope. It was the envy of everyone who saw it.

Surely someone would have mentioned these.

Kimberly was lucky. She died once and got The Red Mist, with a few extra steps. I imagined it was because her death had been instant, but still, I was jealous.

Kimberly also got a marigold yellow ticket.

The Woman in Mourning
Type: Rescue
Archetype: Eye Candy
Aspect: Beauty
Stat Used: Moxie

Killers are not just guilty of harming their primary victims. They are also guilty of a cascade of pain that washes over everyone who knew and loved the victim.

Our scene begins with a funeral.

Rescue: when a player enters a compatible storyline with this trope, while possessing any missing posters of deceased players who died in that same storyline, the storyline will be changed into a Rescue. Succeeding in the Rescue will revive the dead players. This ticket will indicate on the red wallpaper if a nearby storyline is applicable.

With this trope equipped and activated successfully, the storyline will pick up a week after the events of the downed players' deaths. A funeral will be held. It will be raining outside. Everyone will be asking why this tragedy occurred. Little do they know, the tragedy has just begun.

The killer is at the funeral and only the player suspects them.

The player will accrue benefits for establishing a strong emotional connection to the deceased.

The story will play out as a thriller, as the Woman in Mourning tries to prove the killer is to blame and get them arrested, or even kill them if narratively applicable. Situations will arise to bring higher stakes and tension.

Applicable stories will typically be those with high-Savvy or high-Moxie human or human-passing enemies. Most supernatural plots will be excluded depending on the capabilities of the enemy to adapt to the new role.

Known Killer: the player will know who the killer is immediately, regardless of their tropes. They do not need a strong explanation for their knowledge in the narrative. If the enemy has a disguise trope, the player will have a more difficult time proving the killer's identity to anyone else.

Takeover: this trope will cancel out any story alterations except those inherent to the Archetype or Advanced Archetype associated with this ticket.

Bring Them to Justice is the only Win Condition. No others may be added to the Rescue.

Rescue Variant: a Rescue trope of the same name exists for the Craven-Hysteric and the Seer-Psychic. The tropes are compatible and offer a bonus when used together.

Odds are, no one will believe you until it is too late.

I was starting to see how rescues worked. They were very specific as to what storylines they were compatible with.

Dina didn't get any stat tickets. She got a rescue ticket and a luggage tag.

You Don't Know Me, But . . .
Type: Rescue
Archetype: Outsider
Aspect: Stranger
Stat Used: Moxie

When a tragedy occurs, many wonder what they could have done differently. Others wish they could have sent a warning somehow.

Now, you can.

Rescue: when a player enters a compatible storyline with this trope, while possessing any missing posters of deceased players who died in that same storyline, the storyline will be changed into a Rescue. Succeeding in the Rescue will revive the dead players. This ticket will indicate on the red wallpaper if a nearby storyline is applicable.

With this trope equipped and activated successfully, the storyline will play out the way it would have originally if there were no players involved. All player roles will be played by NPCs. Those NPCs representing downed players will be shown on the red wallpaper. The story will, of course, end in the worst possible way. Unless you can stop it.

Stay in the shadows, stay out of the limelight. Give the NPCs warnings or advice. Help them out of view of the audience. Players in the Rescue can use buffs and other tropes to aid from the sidelines, but they must be compatible with staying in the background. Players will not be the main characters. All incompatible player tropes will be unequipped at the start of the Rescue. Some tropes will work differently but still be usable.

Applicable stories will typically be those with a versatile main cast. Be warned: this Rescue will activate in storylines that it does not synergize well with. Further, some enemies with meta-knowledge will be able to interfere with the players.

Takeover: this trope will cancel out any story alterations except those inherent to the Archetype or Advanced Archetype associated with this ticket.

Save the Innocents is the only Win Condition. No others may be added to the Rescue.

Lived to Tell the Tale: any players who survive a storyline altered by this trope will not die, regardless of whether the storyline is failed. Those who die will need to be rescued.

You can tell them how to survive. Better hope they listen.

That sounded like a nightmare to use. Maybe Dina and Bobby would be able to work together on a rescue like the one described, but it would be a while before they would have the tropes needed to make it work. This rescue basically turned the whole team into Wallflowers or Outsiders.

Bobby got a stat ticket, a luggage tag, and a trope. He didn't get a rescue ticket.

My Only Role Is Exposition
Type: Insight/Rule
Archetype: Wallflower
Aspect: Recast
Stat Used: Moxie

Nuanced characters and subtle storytelling are for snobs. We need the information right away so that we can get to the slashing.

With this trope equipped, the player will be given more interesting and useful information during the Party and Rebirth. While important plot points may not be revealed, the player will have some insight into where to obtain such information. The nature of the information they obtain will depend on the role they are cast in. They will only have access to the information while on-screen. When the player is delivering exposition, allies who are not nearby will go Off Screen.

Beware: the player will lose access to the extra information if the audience gets bored during the exposition, so try to be engaging.

Don't be afraid to take notes.

I wasn't sure if this was meant to be an ironic reward or not. Seemed useful.

Lastly, I received two tropes, the same keepsake Antoine had, a killer collectible, and a luggage tag. No stat tickets for me.

I got a trope for pointing out where Antoine's baseball bat was. Sometimes the feats that earned tropes astounded me.

The Insert Shot
Type: Insight/Action/Buff
Archetype: Film Buff
Aspect: Filmmaker
Stat Used: Savvy, Moxie

An insert shot is when the camera shows a close-up of an object or detail in a scene. The filmmaker chooses it to convey importance.

During the Party, the player will have increased odds of finding important objects for the story, be it a weapon, MacGuffin, or similar. They will be able to mark it on the red wallpaper, alerting fellow players to its presence and causing the camera to get several key insert shots of the object to help build its importance to the audience.

The object will have an increased usefulness in the Finale, whether that means granting higher Mettle for a weapon, higher Savvy for a book, or similar.

If the object was relevant to the player's death, this trope can be used after the Party while on Deathwatch.

Try this trope in conjunction with Chekov's Stagehand.

An object's power grows with the audience's anticipation.

Like my friends, I received a rescue trope.

The Wrong Reel
Type: Rescue
Archetype: Film Buff
Aspect: Filmmaker
Stat Used: Savvy

Not everyone has an uncle in the industry who can get their dream projects funded. Some people have to work freelance just to make ends meet while trying to make their filmmaking dreams come true.

That's what you did. You became a freelance editor, piecing together wedding videos and the occasional indie film. That is, until you got a few film reels that no one was ever supposed to see.

Rescue: when a player enters a compatible storyline with this trope, while possessing any missing posters of deceased players who died in that same storyline, the storyline will be changed into a Rescue. Succeeding in the Rescue will revive the dead players. This ticket will indicate on the red wallpaper if a nearby storyline is applicable.

With this trope equipped and activated successfully, the player will begin by viewing raw footage of the failed storyline as if it were filmed by the killer or victims themselves. Horrified by what they see, they begin to call the police. The phone line is dead. That's only the beginning of their problems. They were never supposed to see that footage, and now the killer knows they have it. The killer will besiege the player as they and their "roommates" hope to survive until help comes in the morning.

Applicable stories will typically be those with high-Savvy enemies who either filmed the carnage of the previous run or were otherwise capable of learning that the player possesses the footage. Some supernatural entities will also be applicable.

Additional Requirements: a Base where the player will be besieged. A room where the player will watch the footage. When they have this trope equipped and the missing posters in their inventory, the footage and equipment to edit it will be delivered to the player's door by post.

> Countdown: the player will be able to see the timer related to this trope.
>
> Takeover: this trope will cancel out any story alterations except those inherent to the Archetype or Advanced Archetype associated with this ticket.
>
> Survive the Night is the only Win Condition. No others may be added to the Rescue.
>
> Better pay attention to the film. You won't get many chances to watch it again.

So, there it was. My own rescue ticket. Would this be the one we used to save Camden and Anna? Only time would tell.

I was surprised to find that I had been given the credit for Bradley's death. Often when a death got too attenuated, the player wouldn't count as having killed them. There were obviously some rules I had not been told about.

> Bradley Speirs
> Psychopath Slasher
>
> In the inky depths of malevolence, Bradley Speirs thrives. A creature of impulsive cruelties, dark curiosities, and feigned stupidity, he is a storm that even his brother Merritt struggles to contain. Time and again, he derails Merritt's meticulous machinations, leaving chaos in his wake. Yet, beneath the surface, a sinister delight bubbles; Bradley revels in the bloody aftermath. For where his brother sees strategy, Bradley only craves the thrill of the spatter.

So, the good news was that we got rescue tropes.

What was the bad news?

CHAPTER THIRTY-FOUR

BACK TO WHERE IT ALL STARTED, PART THREE

As we stared at our new rescue tropes, Silas flashed his lights. He disappeared and reappeared five feet away. Except he wasn't facing us. The back of his machine was to us. And there was something on it.

A cloth bag with something large and rectangular was duct-taped to the back of Silas's box. Taped to that was an envelope with three names on it: Riley, Antoine, and Kimberly.

"What?" Antoine asked.

I shared the sentiment.

The others had stopped freaking out over the rescue tickets. We approached the object carefully. I grabbed the envelope and ripped the cloth bag open. Inside the bag was the last thing I could have expected: the *Carousel Atlas*.

Antoine flipped through the book. I focused on the letter in the envelope.

"Guys," I said. I didn't get their attention at first. "Guys," I said louder.

They all looked at me.

I held out the letter.

"It's from Anna," I said, almost not believing it myself.

They were speechless. I was speechless.

After my brain started working again, I straightened out the letter and started to read it aloud.

Dear Riley, Kimberly, and Antoine,

If you're reading this, that means Silas agreed to Camden's plan. Camden is a genius by the way. This was all his idea.

I'm sure you know this by now, but the helicopter ride we were meant to take to our storyline was doomed. We ended up running to the roller rink Riley pointed out near the airport. Reggie used a trope to sacrifice himself so that we could get there in time to beat the black snow. I hope he survived. I wish I could tell Grace how much of a hero he was.

The storyline was called Post-Traumatic. *It involved time travel. Camden tells me I cannot say too much because we don't want to spoil the story. Suffice it to say, he realized Carousel didn't use real time travel to make the story work. It just recreated the past. He figured that a version of the* Carousel Atlas *existed in the past, so we went to pick one up. It was amazing.*

As much as I would like to say that we are going to try our best and conquer this storyline just the two of us, I know that isn't realistic. When Camden passes, I will officially be the Last One Alive and Silas will show up to give me my Aspect. I will attach the atlas to the back of Silas so other players don't see it. It contains information that they should never see.

I had written up pages and pages to send. I wanted to talk about the times we shared before Carousel. I wanted to talk about the feelings I have for each of you, and I wanted to tell you how much I love you all.

I didn't include those, because Camden showed me the Atlas Holder's Journal. In those writings, I found hope—horror, too, but above all else, hope.

You don't need me to send you a letter telling you how I feel, because I want you to come and save me so I can tell you in person.

I will choose the Girl Next Door Aspect. I think it fits my personality the best. Look it up in the atlas so you will know what to expect when you come to save us.

With love,

Anna

P.S. Camden says hello. He is in his own world right now, marking up the atlas so that you can find the important information quickly. He isn't feeling very well either.

The Atlas Holder's Journal? I didn't remember the version we had read even having that section. Antoine quickly turned to the page Camden had helpfully listed as "Start Here."

Camden had gone through and marked every single entry that he wanted us to read. He had likely searched them out with his Eureka! trope.

We opened the book right there on the forest floor and started to read the entries that Camden had put a star next to. Silas moved his flashlight to help us see it. What a gent. The journal started in 2001, which didn't make much sense at first, but I kept reading. There were entire sections that had been blacked out to the point where they couldn't be deciphered.

December 4, 2001

Mark's team wiped this morning. It was the Alienist. The goddamn Alienist. Easiest storyline to avoid in the whole town, and somehow, he ended up getting mixed up in it. His team isn't the only one. Patrick tells me that the strong group of friendlies we ran into in May got postered last week. Shame. Even if they didn't want to share resources, it was nice knowing that they were out there trying to figure out the Throughline.

—CW

December 12, 2001

Everything is getting harder. When I got here back in '98, the tutorial was difficult and confusing, but we still managed to get through it. Now, newbies routinely fail it or even go missing before it's over. If they succeed, the trouble isn't over. They get pushed out the door toward stories on the Throughline that are way out of their league. That didn't happen to us back then. We've been talking about finding a way to prevent players from entering the tutorial at all. It's all just hot air. No one wants to piss off Carousel, even to save lives.

The last group of newbies failed completely. Took my best brawlers across town to try to greet them. Thought we could guide them, train them. Show them the kindness we never got. Guess it didn't matter.

Got to thinking about Tommy again for a long time. Wonder if he still plays baseball. He would be 15 now. He's growing up. Bet he goes by Tom or Thomas now. I hope I can see him again one day.

—CW

February 24, 2002

Picked up a Film Buff today. Came to Carousel all by herself, can you believe it? A Film Buff Archetype. We went through the tutorial with her so she didn't get swallowed by Froggy. What a silly idea. I can't even imagine how a class like that could be useful in a story. Her main trope cuts her effective PA in half. Sounds like another Lamb class to me.

She's smart as a whip, though. We'll get some use out of her. Amelia. Amelia the Film Buff. She's a firecracker, all right.

—CW

March 15, 2002

Amelia got her Aspect last week. Fanatic. That's her, all right. A fanatic for all things. Movies. Walks in the park. Carousel's strange music. Food. God, does she love food. She dragged me out to the Italian place on Gore Street a few nights ago. She has the place all scoped out already. Didn't run into a single Omen. She's fearless and maybe even smarter than Carousel itself.

I laughed until my cheeks hurt. It's been a long time. Thought I forgot how.
—CW

June 7, 2002

I feel numb all over. I told Amelia I loved her today. I know it's early, but we could die tomorrow. Heck, it's Carousel. We could die at any moment.

She told me that she loved me too, but she wanted me to know something.

She had a secret. She wasn't trapped in Carousel like me. She wasn't tricked. She came here on purpose. She has these letters that are from someone calling themselves our "Insider," who wants to help her find her parents . . . Her parents, who disappeared last year when their boat vanished in the Caribbean.

For such a smart woman, how can she believe letters like this? Clearly, this is some demented trick from Carousel. She says she doesn't think so. She says to trust her. And I do, but it's difficult. I said we were in a horror movie. Nothing good will ever happen to us.

She grabbed my hands and said, "We can change the story together. Don't you see that? ███████████████████████████████████ ███████ *"*

This is not a place for happy thoughts and fairy dust.

She wants my help, but I can't even think about that right now. I'm sick to my stomach.

I need to go think.
—CW

June 15, 2002

NPC acted weird yesterday. Level fifty, one of the Paragons. The Beauty Paragon, I believe. She said that Amelia and I were meant to be. She could tell by looking at us. Just came up to me while we were at the market getting groceries. Told me to trust my heart. Got all heavy-handed with it. Almost out of character.

I'm afraid. Afraid to die. Afraid to fail and never see my son again. Afraid to trust someone and have it all be a cruel trick.

Amelia says not to worry.

How can she be so optimistic? We spent the day at a baseball game. Had to leave before the flying saucer got there, of course, but for a few hours it was like we were just a normal couple. When you're in love with someone, it feels like the world loves you too. Even Carousel somehow gave us a break. We strolled along the Riverwalk. It was a nice sabbatical from my normal existence, where I am afraid all the time.

I had never even seen the Riverwalk. It doesn't even make sense to be there, geographically. The river shouldn't even exist in that spot. It turns out it is only there if you walk toward downtown from the baseball field. I wonder how big this place would be if you unfolded it. If you laid it out from end to end.

I told Amelia I would do anything for her. Even her quest. I won't trust the Insider, but I will trust her.

—CW

July 30, 2002

Amelia has a theory about the Throughline. She says it's like a video game. She thinks we have been forced into someone else's game—their "save file," she called it. I liken it to picking up a book halfway through. It's hard to understand what's happening if you don't know what came before. ▮▮▮ ▮▮▮▮▮▮
▮▮▮▮▮▮▮▮▮▮▮▮▮▮▮▮▮▮▮▮▮▮▮▮▮▮▮.

We don't know the beginning of the story at all. The Throughline has always been super confusing. I thought that was because this is a horror story. Amelia says it wasn't supposed to be like this. It's like Carousel thinks we know what all of the players that came before have accomplished, that we are sharing information.

Honestly, we should have been sharing info. It's hard when half the people here will attack you for going near their base and the other half are actively trying to find your base so they can steal your stuff.

She has been talking to the Insider. Silas appears to be in on it, though I can't tell if he is a real person or just the world's most infuriating telephone. She also sees clues everywhere. She gets information from NPCs at every turn.

She says the Insider is trying to figure out something they are calling "Project Rewind."

The idea is to "rewind" the Throughline back to the beginning so that we can understand what the hell we are supposed to be doing. I've been working at completing the Throughline for years. It doesn't matter how strong we get. If you don't know where you've been, you can't know where you're going.

I only vaguely know much of anything. The strong group who wiped last year seemed to have some idea. Of course, that does us no good. We aren't strong enough to rescue them. What were they doing messing around near the Highwayman, anyway?

We let Cordelia in on our little secret. It's nice to have a Final Girl in the know. She can really be an asset. ███████████████████████████ ███████████████████.

—CW

November 15, 2002

I went through and censored any mention of the plot of the Throughline. Entire years of information are now gone from this journal. The last two holders of the atlas have been all but wiped from its pages. Amelia says that she and the Insider think the Throughline can be spoiled like an ordinary story, but they aren't sure. I think they aren't telling me something. That might be one reason for our inability to move forward in the story. I can't say for sure. The information we had wasn't exactly that helpful. The original Atlas Holder got here back in '92. We even had some oral histories from people who got here in '89, though not too much. They're all gone now. The last vestiges of them have been hidden away for the "Highrollers" to find.

Apparently, that's an inside joke between Amelia and the Insider. The Highrollers are an elite group of players that we are supposed to be setting up to beat the Throughline and save us all. Highrollers is a better name than what they were called before: the Party of Promise. That was a little too dorky. Amelia is keeping things about Project Rewind hush-hush for now, even from me.

I would get upset, but she seems so thrilled to be making progress that I can't help but be a little optimistic too. She talks to Silas like she is talking to an employee. You'd think she was the one in charge by the way the Insider listens to her. The Paragons greet her like they are all friends. Everyone loves her. She's brighter than the sun in this place.

—CW

April 20, 2003

Brought a new group of players into the fold. They beat the tutorial by themselves. They will be an asset to our group.

I asked Amelia if they were the Highrollers. She avoided the question. Guess not.

Something happened with the Throughline today. The mayor seems ticked off at us for not completing the last storyline he pointed us to. Says we'll have to wait for next year now. I have moved from confusion to frustration to apathy on this matter. We don't have access to the Omen for the story he wants us to go on. Where are we supposed to find it? I think it is a portable Omen. Did some other team pick it up and then get postered?

What's the point of leveling up if we can't even get to the next story in the main plot?

The Throughline is getting more dangerous. Amelia says that players on other teams are over-leveling and causing the Throughline itself to get more difficult as it compensates. She says we need to make an envoy to the other groups around Carousel to warn them against over-leveling, but I told her it was hopeless. Whatever trust existed a decade ago is long spent.

—CW

April 30, 2003

So, Amelia just let me in on the current plan. I am terrified of what might happen.

The Insider thinks they can distract Carousel indefinitely. I have no idea how they would do that. They aim to take the Throughline offline so that it doesn't keep interfering with us. We won't even be able to see it on the red wall. The Insider says that to do that, they will have to prevent Silas from distributing many different ticket types, as those tend to have unpredictable results, which could jeopardize Project Rewind.

I am hesitant to go along with this. They said they were getting rid of basic things like licenses and luggage tags. I can't imagine that will be a good thing. I said that they could accidentally cause a second cataclysm. They didn't respond. It's like they want that to happen.

—CW

June 4, 2003

I took a look at the missing poster wall today. Several dozen players just got put up there, including groups of players we had been feuding with. I asked Amelia if she knew anything about that and she got quiet. That means yes.

Those players were dangerous to us, but they were still people. How did the Insider even do it?

—CW

March 17, 2004

Not much has happened related to Project Rewind in the last year. I am writing today because the Insider finally figured it out. Carousel is sleeping, almost. The Throughline is not on the red wall anymore, and the NPCs have quieted down. As I was warned, Silas has stopped handing out all manner of tickets now other than tropes, stat tickets, and the killer collectibles.

The tutorial is in shambles. You could hardly call it a tutorial now.

I am starting to wonder what else the Insider did to change Carousel before we met.

Amelia tells me not to worry. That isn't quite doing it for me anymore.

I got to level 80 last week. Finally managed to get the Witch Doctor AA. Now I can play a fun kind of Doctor, Amelia says. Now I can justify all those points I put in Moxie. Still no exit in sight. Amelia is catching up fast. We ate at a fancy French restaurant to celebrate. Didn't even mind when the Soul Eaters showed up and we had to kill them. That's romance in Carousel for you.

—CW

October 1, 2004

How could I not see it?

The clues were there the whole time. Amelia has been hinting at the problem with the Throughline this whole time and I have been willfully ignorant of the solution. She just came out and said it. I can't avoid it now.

This is wrong. It's against everything I stand for. I can't argue with the logic, but if this is the cost of Project Rewind, I don't know if I can help her.

I don't have it in me. I can't.

I am sick with the thought that my sweet, amazing Amelia could even go along with something like that, let alone pioneer it.

They have solidified their plan. They say it will take a decade or more to get operational. Project Rewind has started. How can I look at the faces of the players in our group, knowing what we have to do to them?

Amelia says to trust her, that she knows what it sounds like, but it is the only way. She talked to Samantha Cole about it. Even though the Paragons can't exactly break character, it's clear that Samantha is willing to make the sacrifice. She blames herself for getting all the players trapped here. Can't argue with that logic, but still, she is willing to fall on her sword.

I guess I'll have to do the same eventually.

–CW

December 11, 2006

Found a new base of operations. It seems too good to be true. A lodge with enough rooms for over a hundred players. All we have to do is avoid entering a locked cabin. Apocalypses don't even reach all the way out here. What a steal.

Been training our replacements. Soon, every player who lived in Carousel before the second cataclysm will have to take the quick way out. Adeline, William, and Arthur will be fine leaders once we're gone. They don't know anything they aren't supposed to. The Throughline was so messed up by the time they arrived that they never saw more than a few stray plotlines of it. They should be fine.

Arthur is trying to become a Monster Hunter. If there is anyone who can do it, it is him. He reminds me of Tommy.

Of course, we will need someone to carry forward Project Rewind in our absence. The Insider has chosen Winston, or whatever Ethan is calling himself nowadays. Even talks to him through the radio, more or less. I used my Psychiatrist tropes on him to make sure he was trustworthy. I think he is. He has the exact kind of cold, detached personality to be able to do what needs to be done. Plus, there is little danger of him making friends with the other players and not being able to go through with it. He's . . . a character.

When it's time to go, Winston will be the next Atlas Holder. I hope he has what it takes. Otherwise, our sacrifice will be in vain.

I have come to terms with it. Amelia says that we will need to be preserved to help beat the Throughline when the time comes. She talks about it like we are just going to sleep, to be awoken again one day in the future. She uses the words destiny and fate a lot. Carousel has not broken her.

It'll be like we're sleeping, she says over and over. She acts like I am afraid of death. I have died more times than I can remember. This is something different.

–CW

March 4, 2008

Winston has been doing his part. We are the only group in Carousel now. Once we figured out how to intercept players before the tutorial, our numbers really started to take off.

Amelia and I went to all of our favorite places today. We watched baseball, went to the Riverwalk, and ate at the Italian place again.

We are going to leave together. Cordelia went a month ago. She chose the monster plant to the north. It sedates its victims with a hallucinogenic poison. Not a bad way to go out. We're the only ones left who truly remember the Throughline. Our very presence threatens to reawaken Carousel. Hopefully, our sacrifice will be enough to fix things and Project Rewind will never need to be executed.

But I know that's just an empty hope. I've always said that Carousel isn't a place for happy thoughts and fairy dust.

I am leaving the atlas in the hands of Winston now. He knows what to do.

I am not afraid anymore. I will simply be going on a long walk with my best friend. I know that there is a real chance we won't ever be rescued, but I have to believe in the Highrollers. We've put in so much work to give them the best chance possible of succeeding.

I hope they don't waste it.

Amelia is the love of my life, and I would love another fifty years with her, but if the past six are all we get, I still count myself the luckiest man in Carousel.

—CW & AW

July 2009

Preparations are being made to commence Project Rewind. Everything is moving as scheduled.

The Insider has a lead on an exploit for rescue tropes that will allow players to accelerate their levels. If the exploit turns out to be a punishable offense, then our plan will move forward as written. If not, at least we will have a way to conquer the most powerful storylines. We will be able to rescue Amelia and the others and move forward with a different plan.

I believe the plan will work, however. As long as it doesn't wake Carousel too early, we should be okay.

—Winston Ashwood, Esq.

October 2009

The exploit failed. There is good news, however.

We've discovered a new exploit for rescue tickets. Our Insider tells us to be cautious because he cannot keep Carousel distracted for too long, but the more we experiment, the more confident I am that we have found a way to increase our levels dramatically in the coming months. Testing continues. We must not tell the other players until we are sure it is safe.

And if it isn't safe, we certainly mustn't tell them.

The Monster Hunter continues to be a thorn in my side. I can see his jealousy. Curtis never let him see the atlas, and then he left it to me. I can feel a power play coming.

—Winston Ashwood, Esq.

January 2010

I was right to sense a power struggle. I need to consider giving them the atlas before they just take it. I will need to rid it of any knowledge that might clue them into Project Rewind. I am certain they will not like their role in it.

Something Amelia was not able to tell Curtis was that even though the Throughline was not on the red wall anymore, many players have accidentally stumbled upon knowledge related to it, even without meaning to. After they gain enough information, they are brought into the Throughline, even without their knowing it. Curtis did not have the constitution to deal with the implications of that.

All players with a connection to the Throughline must be taken off the board. Including myself.

Soon, I will be censoring the atlas once again as all of the holders have done before me. I will leave entries about rescue tropes and anything that does not give too much information about the Throughline or the Party of Promise for now. I will hide the pages for the proper eyes to find. If only I could think of a place to store them where only the Party of Promise would see them. These pages would be a boon to anyone trying to complete the Throughline, I imagine.

Personally, I never liked the "Highrollers" moniker. It is all too casual.

I have been doing my duties according to Project Rewind for some years now. I have fortified my mind to prepare for the next stage. I have intentionally distanced myself from the players at the lodge. Doing so makes my destiny more palatable, but also makes them not trust me.

I sincerely hope the worst does not happen. Silas gave me a trope to help me conceal my mission from even the most prying investigators. I can only hope it succeeds.
—Winston Ashwood, Esq.

I was speechless. Truly speechless. Whatever Project Rewind was, I needed to learn more about it. Luckily, Camden had the page marked for me. I turned to it. It was a single page. Its steps were written simply and without any more detail than needed.

Project Rewind
- *Take the Throughline off the red wallpaper and keep Carousel sedated until Project Rewind has concluded.*
- *Find a punishable exploit for rescue tropes. This will trigger an immediate recall.*
- *After that, Silas will simply stop distributing rescue tropes. Without the ability to rescue postered players, the third cataclysm will arrive.*
- *The remaining players will be sent to fail various storylines at all levels. An equal distribution for the missing poster wall is optimal.*

- *The Insider will select a team, henceforth known as the Highrollers because they're getting all the comps. This team will consist of at least one invitee, one guide, and one Secret Keeper. A single player can be all three, though that is not recommended.*
- *The Highrollers will be trained to understand how storylines work. They will be given knowledge of Secret Lore and will be made aware of the Insider.*
- *They will be directed toward a storyline with an out-of-bounds zone, preferably* Permanent Vacancy. *This must be done within the first few months of their arrival because otherwise the Highrollers risk being inadvertently brought into the Throughline, causing Project Rewind to fail.*
- *Once there, the Insider will trigger all manner of mobile Omens to ensure the pacification of all remaining players.*
- *Once the Highrollers are out-of-bounds and all other players have been postered, Project Rewind will come to fruition.*
- *The Insider will reinstate the Throughline, which will reset back to the beginning.*
- *The Highrollers will exit the out-of-bounds area. They will have every advantage our years of toil have set up for them.*
- *They will have the knowledge needed to win.*
- *They will have an invitee, a guide, and a Secret Keeper.*
- *They will have access to all ticket types, including rescue tropes.*
- *They will have a well-stocked wall of missing posters that they can use to accelerate their levels as they advance along the Throughline.*
- *With the Throughline reinstated, the Insider will go into hiding in an effort to escape the wrath of Carousel.*
- *The Highrollers will carry with them all of the hopes, dreams, and good-will of those who came before them.*

I wish them luck,
Amelia

Everything was a setup. Everything. I knew we were being guided around, but I could never imagine this.

My mind was ready to explode. Suddenly, so much made sense. How the players at the lodge had gone so long without progressing. How they had not even known what the main plot was.

It was kept from them!

The others had a similar reaction. Even Dina was shaken, and she had been ready to watch the world burn since she got here.

"Did it say that all the other players would be postered?" Antoine asked.

"Oh my god," I said.

I pulled out my Coming to a Theater Near You trope. I equipped it and was soon watching trailers in my mind's eye.

CHAPTER THIRTY-FIVE

BACK TO WHERE IT ALL STARTED, PART FOUR

The first trailer opened in black and white as the camera showed a large building with stone columns and a giant banner hung across its face that read:

Carousel Museum of Natural History
Join Us for a Limited-Time Exhibit:
Unraveling the Secrets of the Sands!

Guests arrived wearing tuxes and dresses. Among them, intercut in flashes, were Roxy, Grace, and Lara, as well as the other players they had brought with them, distributed throughout several different flashes of the crowd. They were all dressed for the event, but I could tell they were distressed.

Inside a large showroom, a woman stood in front of a podium and said, "Welcome to the first in a series of exhibits that the Carousel Museum of Natural History will be hosting about ancient cultures from around the world. This year's exhibit will be an exciting opportunity. We have in our collection the contents of the tomb of the lost pharaoh, Setemkara!"

The crowd clapped and cheered. A red curtain in the center of the room was raised to reveal an ornate sarcophagus.

The camera cut to a man in a fedora whispering to Grace with a smile, "Who did they have to bribe to get a hold of that?"

"It's supposed to be donated from a collector," Grace replied.

The woman at the podium continued. "We stand here tonight on the very anniversary of King Setemkara's discovery fifty years ago. We are proud to be the first host of these artifacts in a public exhibit in their entire history. We hope to send the message that history truly belongs to everyone."

The party went on and people drank and celebrated the exhibit. Suddenly, the lights went out. The entire room went completely dark. There was a loud sound of stone scraping against stone.

When the lights came back on, the sarcophagus was open. There was nothing inside.

Cut to a scene where Grace explained, "King Setemkara was paranoid that someone would exhume his body and use it in a ritual to condemn him in the afterlife. These scrolls indicate that he had a trap built. It doesn't explain what the trap was, only that it would ensure anyone who disturbed his rest would be punished. But it's clear it wasn't a simple booby trap."

"Then what did it do?" Roxy asked.

"Ladies," Lara said, shining a flashlight down a dark hallway with an exit sign hanging from the ceiling. At the end of the hallway, there was no exit, only a passage made of stone. Hieroglyphics adorned the walls. "This isn't just the museum anymore. We're inside his tomb."

Cut to scenes of well-dressed people running from something down a museum hallway that transitioned into another ancient corridor. Someone stepped on a stone that they shouldn't have, and the door behind them closed. Sand started to pour down from the ceiling.

"We have to find our way out of the tomb!" Roxy screamed. "We can't kill it. We have to run."

She was afraid. Roxy had been a good actress, but I thought her fear looked real.

"The museum has changed," the man in the fedora said in a panic. "He's filled it with traps of all kinds. A labyrinth with no way out."

The familiar narrator's voice came on over the loudspeaker. "Maybe history doesn't belong to everyone."

There was a flash of a figure standing in a doorway. They were only visible as a silhouette, but it was clear that the figure was wrapped in bandages from head to toe. An ornamental crown could be seen on its head.

The screen cut to black. The words "Whispers of Sand" appeared on the screen but were soon blown away by the wind.

The narrator came back to say, "Coming soon."

Grace, Roxy, and Lara were doomed if Project Rewind was set up correctly.

The second trailer opened with hundreds of people pushing shopping carts through the aisles of a large warehouse. I recognized it immediately as Eternal Savers Club. That was the store where we got all of our food.

"Look, I'm going to need you to come in next Monday. I know it's a holiday, and I know I said that you could take it off, but we really need you. And you do know that evaluations are just around the corner, and this would look really good for you," a man wearing a red shirt and a tie said to one of the employees, who was wearing an Eternal Savers Club vest with a small circle that had the letters "ESC" on it.

The employee he was talking to looked completely dead in the face. No emotion at all. He stood up from the chair he was sitting in and walked over to a desk with a bunch of security monitors on it as well as a microphone.

He reached down, picked up the microphone, and said, "We have a code crimson in the manager's office. A code crimson."

The man, apparently the manager, said, "What are you talking about? There's no crimson on the chart."

Moments later, several more employees showed up. Their faces were emotionless.

"What are you doing?" the manager asked. Then the screen cut away and there was a loud scream.

The screen cut to one of the players I recognized but whose name I didn't recall. "Look, kids," she said. "This move is going to be good for us. I finally get the promotion I've been working to get for years."

"At a grocery store," a young man said. He was another player.

"Eternal Savers Club is more than just a grocery store. You should know that I just got both of you jobs there," the woman said.

The young man was sitting next to a young woman and exclaimed, "What?"

This story definitely had horror-comedy vibes to it.

Cut to a scene of the young man, presumably the son in the family, mopping up a floor inside Eternal Savers Club. Underneath one of the shelving units, he found a wallet. He pulled out an employee ID card that showed the wallet had belonged to the slain manager.

"What did they say happened to the old manager?" the son asked his mother somewhere off-screen.

"He retired. That's what it says in the system," the woman said.

The young man mumbled to himself in a different scene, "He was only forty-five. How could he have retired?"

Cut to another scene inside Eternal Savers Club. While the young man was restocking the shelves during the night, he saw a group of cloaked figures walking to the storeroom. He followed them, but when he got there, they were nowhere to be found.

There was then a montage of characters running. The brother and sister characters were in a cage next to what looked like some sort of demonic altar.

The player portraying the sister was panicking and said, "This isn't supposed to be here!"

The one playing her brother said quickly, "Well, yeah, devil worship para-phernalia is supposed to be on aisle six."

The trailer moved on to show a few action scenes that were hard to discern, followed by a scene of a cloaked figure wielding a knife. He moved the knife downward, and there was a demonic laugh.

A demonic voice said, "More. I need to consume more."

A bit heavy-handed with the symbolism.

"What's happening?" the mother character asked in a panic to some other players in a scene. They all looked genuinely confused. Maybe it was just because I had never seen this particular storyline before, but it seemed like they were genuinely perplexed by something. It was possible that that was just a neces-sary scene, but still, there was something off about it to me. "Ritual sacrifice. Demons. I didn't read anything about that in the . . . manual."

The way she said "manual" sounded unnatural and forced, like she was not actually talking about the employee manual. It struck me that she must have been talking about the *Carousel Atlas*.

Or it was all just a joke because the movie was some sort of black comedy.

The screen cut to black.

The Eternal Savers Club.

The narrator's voice came back. "Coming to a theater near you!"

I didn't know much about the *Eternal Savers Club* storyline, but the players looked like they had been surprised by something.

The next trailer started and instantly my blood ran cold.

I recognized the image in front of me.

I was looking at Camp Dyer. The familiar children NPCs were playing kids' games out in a field next to the lodge.

"Is it true what they say about this place?" one of the campers asked a shell-shocked Valerie. "That a girl died here?"

Valerie paused for a moment but then tried to regain her composure.

"Yes," she said. "But that was a long time ago. And it was a terrible accident. You have nothing to worry about."

There were more scenes intercut of the campers and the lake.

"We came here to do what we have to do," a male NPC said. I recognized him. He was a camp counselor who slept in one of the cabins to watch the chil-dren. "There's no going back. We don't have any time."

I couldn't see who he was talking to.

I could hear the campers singing their little rhyme:

"Suzy Snyder, six foot five,
Haunts Camp Dyer, still alive."

That rhyme faded quickly as a little girl was seen walking away from the abandoned cabin. She walked up to Arthur as he lay back in a reclining beach chair in the shade.

"Mr. Arthur," the little girl said, "I found this in that cabin over there. Am I allowed to have it?"

She reached out and dropped a large plastic locket into Arthur's lap. The locket opened. It started to play a song that sounded like a nineties teen idol was singing, but the locket was low on batteries, so the song came out all deep and stretched out.

"Girl, I can't say no to summer with you,
And I think that you are feeling it too."

Arthur's eyes got large, and he screamed, "What the hell is this? Why?"

Cut to a scene of players being chased by an unseen figure. There were so many players. More than I had ever heard of in a story all at once. More than I thought was possible.

The music from the locket continued:

"As the seasons change, one thing will always be true,
That I'll never say no to summer, to summer with you."

The camera cut to a large pale hand shoving a piece of rebar down on an unseen target. Then I saw Chris's face of surprise, the apparent victim.

The last frame before the title card was of an imposing figure walking out of the water. They were difficult to see, but it was clear that they had long hair and a jacket so large it was too big even on their hulking frame. Their legs and feet were bare. Something was weird about their face, but I couldn't tell what, because it was in shadow.

The title card appeared.

Say No to Summer.

"Coming soon."

"What's going on?" Kimberly asked.

I looked at Antoine and then at Kimberly.

"Camp Dyer," I said. "The storyline at Camp Dyer was triggered. It got everyone."

"No," Antoine said. He realized the implication immediately. "How strong is that storyline? Do you know?"

"I have no idea," I said. "Grace's team and the team that went on a grocery run were also in storylines that looked strong."

I took time to explain all of the trailers I had just seen. We stood there in the middle of the strange woods, silently contemplating the meaning of all of this.

Project Rewind required that they all be wiped out. Every single one of them.

We were alone.

We were all jarred as a voice started to cackle right next to us. Silas started delivering a rhyme. It reminded me of the one we heard when we first got to Carousel, with some notable differences.

"Welcome to Carousel, the town where movies come to life.
Will you rise to the occasion or fall to the knife?
The film's about to start, and you're in the front row!
The audience is watching you, so give them a show."

"You had better be willing to do what it takes,
Because even as I'm speaking, Carousel wakes."

ABOUT THE AUTHOR

Rob M. Lastrel is the author of the Game at Carousel series, originally released on Royal Road. Fascinated by the eerie and unknown, he writes weird, otherworldly escapism. When he isn't writing, he spends his time hiking and hopes to one day visit every national park in the United States.

Podium

www.ingramcontent.com/pod-product-compliance
Lightning Source LLC
Chambersburg PA
CBHW031253120726
47906CB00003B/727